SAVIOUR

THE SIREN SAGA
BOOK 3

JADE THORN

ISBN: 978-0-6455818-7-4

Cover design by: Natasha Williams of DAZED Designs
https://www.dazed-designs.com/

Edited by: CB Editing Service
https://www.facebook.com/CBlackEdits/

Please note that due to its content this book is not meant for readers under the age of 18. Readers should also be aware there are dubious consent scenes in this book.

ACKNOWLEDGMENTS

In the writing process there are always people who help you along. In the publishing process, there are even more! There are some people who I need to thank for helping me.

First and foremost, thank you to my husband for supporting me in my creative madness. For listening to me mutter into long cold cups of tea, for taking the kids to the park to allow me writing time, and for supporting me as I create.

To my editor, Charlotte Black - just wow. Your work is top calibre, speedy and you put up with my crazy. THANK YOU. Your encouragement uplifts me and keeps me focused and your attention to detail is phenomenal. In you I have found not only an amazing editor but a friend for life.

To my street team, my ARC team and my Beta readers - these women help share the word, keep me going and allow me time to keep on writing so I can share more of the strange worlds in my head. You watch over my shoulder as I write and your positivity helps keep my "darkness" at bay. Thank you for everything.

To Maria and Sandi who have kept me on the straight and narrow, kept track of things like eye colour and details that constantly escape me, and reminded me to make inner conversations italic, lol. Thank you for being my memory.

To 'Tash Will' - cover designer extraordinaire, you lady, took my request for a "non-traditional academy" cover and raised it to the next level. You are kind, talented and so giving. You are more than my designer, you're an inspiration and a dear friend.

Finally, Andrea Miles Rhoads - you took me in as an orphaned indie, and have organised all my teams and stopped me from forgetting posts and takeovers lol. Your insight and graphics have been incredibly helpful, and your friendship is greatly appreciated. Thank you.

Happy reading, everyone, and thank you to this great team who helped me get here and who keep me going,

Jade Thorn
xoxo

PROLOGUE

SHAY

I'm standing in a clearing in front of a house, although 'house' is kind of an insulting word. The place is fucking massive. A central log cabin that's bigger than most suburban homes, but the two stone wings make the place palatial. Who the fuck lives here? The sense of pride in my chest is disorienting. I don't know this place at all.

Gravel crunches under my feet as my body moves forward without my permission. I climb the steps and the door opens before I get to it. There's nobody there, but from somewhere deeper in the house, I can hear a woman screaming.

The place smells like blood and antiseptic, although I can faintly smell food nearby, and there's the clatter of plates coming from my right. My guess is there's a kitchen there, but it's not where I want to go. I shouldn't be able to scent all these things, my sense of smell isn't that acute. My confusion grows.

I drift past gleaming furniture, blankets strewn across the backs of lounges and the ground scattered with cots. There are a lot of people living in this room, although not a single one of them is visible in this moment. What's going on? In a place this size, surely they have enough bedrooms?

To my left, stairs ascend to an open hallway, the doors visible from the ground floor. Behind one of them, the woman is screaming, pleading for something to stop. Whatever it is, I don't want to know any more about it. She sounds terrified, and all I want to do is get out of here as soon as I can.

Who are these people who can calmly prepare a meal while a woman is being tortured upstairs?

"Any news?" asks a deep voice, and I let out a squeak, spinning around.

A woman is wringing her hands in a tea-towel, facing a behemoth of a man. For all his size, his voice is quiet and his movements are slow and gentle.

"Fleur says it's a difficult birth. One of the pups is stuck. She was never created to carry a child, never mind four."

Is that what the screams are? Not someone being tortured, but a woman in labour? Well, it certainly puts a different light on things, and definitely explains why people are cooking loudly in the kitchen. There's nothing worse than listening to labour pains when there's nothing you can do for the woman. It's best to keep busy with practical things, leaving the birth to those who know what they're doing. Which also explains where all the inhabitants have gone. Those not involved would do best to stay away.

My heart lifts a little, until the next piercing cry rings out.
"SHAYLA! I NEED SHAYLA!"

Time stills. What did she just say?

I blink and find myself at the top of the stairs, another blink and I'm at a door which automatically opens for me.

There are no words for what I see on the other side. This can't be true, it can't be real. This is impossible. I must *be dreaming.*

Catriona lies in a bed, pale and sweating, a clear bulge in her abdomen tensing as it contracts, and another long scream is dragged from her throat. There are men everywhere, or at least it seems to be so. How can so many of them be present for the birth?

A tiny woman kneels on the foot of the bed, her hands between Catriona's thighs doing something I don't even want to think about.

"Stop pushing, Catriona, I need you to pant through these contractions until I can get the baby turned around," she commands.

The midwife then.

Even from across the room I can feel Catriona's energy ebbing. Our link pings in alarm, just as it has so many times in the last few months. Each time breaking my heart a little more. It's good to see her, to know she's still alive, even as I'm sure that I'm about to witness her death.

Is this real? Is it happening? Is this why I've been brought here, to witness her death?

"You need to make her take energy from you," growls the midwife. "Even my wolf can tell she's flagging."

Another giant of a man at the back begins to push forward, but the others won't let him near her. Instead, one of the men kneeling beside her, his face broadcasting his worry, stands and leans over her.

"Sweetie, please," he says hoarsely, as if he's been screaming along with her. "Take from my wolf, you know we'd die for you."

That knocks me backwards. A wolf willing to die for one of us? That can't be true. Was he the one who knocked her up?

"Not killing you," she murmurs weakly, stroking his face as she pants between contractions. "The pack needs you too much. They need all of you."

"We need you more," says another male, wiping her sweaty face with a cloth, and putting an ice chip in her mouth. "Catriona, you have to take from us, any of us, just do it. You're going to die. Hell, if that won't persuade you, the pups are going to die."

Ah, there it is, the clincher. Of course they're not worried about her, it's the fucking hybrids they've managed to breed on her. When I find out which one of them did it, I'm going to rip his cock off and shove it up his ass. Then I'm going to take his balls and shove them down his throat. He can fucking spit roast himself.

"I can't risk you, any of you. You've no idea how important you all are —" her voice drifts away, as though a breeze has wafted it from her. There's a tugging sensation behind my navel, and I look down expecting to find a hook or a rope around me.

There's nothing there, but the pulling sensation persists. I'm dragged backwards out the door, which closes in my face, even as yelling and howling begins on the other side. Their grief is palpable, a physical force that knocks into me, sending me flying down the stairs and out the door, pushing me out. Pushing me away.

By the time I stop, I have no idea where I am. The tugging sensation is gone, as is the pushing force.

~

I realise I'm somewhere completely different again. I must be dreaming, but hell, what a nightmare to have had.

Catriona isn't dead. I know that. I've experienced the death of my mother, my sisters and daughters. Not even sleeping draughts can keep me unconscious for that. If she had died, I'd be awake and not here. Wherever *here* is.

Whatever is going on, this feels more real than the scene where I saw Catriona giving birth. It kind of makes sense. There's no way that could happen. I feel kinda silly for thinking I was somehow witnessing it. Of course she's not giving birth.

With a wry chuckle at my own dark fancy, I examine the garden where I've ended up. There're white stone benches, neatly tended garden beds, and a sense of peace I've never encountered before. When I complete turning on the spot, I'm facing two beautiful women.

Now, I don't usually roll that way. Sirens need cocks to survive, although I don't mind other bed partners as long as my needs are fulfilled by at least one person. But the two women in front of me have an ethereal beauty that takes my breath away. A part of me wishes they could sate my hunger, because I think at the very least the brunette would make for a very good companion in bed.

The blonde, there's something off-putting about her. I get a sense of wrongness, although I'm not sure if it's her per se, or the idea of bedding her that has my senses rearing backwards with a firm fucking 'no'.

Well, I can't say I've had that reaction with one of your daughters before, sister, says the brunette on the left.

I sense the words in my head rather than hear them, but somehow I know who said them. Am I still dreaming?

The blonde frowns at her, then turns her gaze back to me.

Daughter, do you know who I am? the woman asks.

No, but I know you're not my fucking mother, I think with a snort, but I know they can't hear me. Instead of trying to talk, I shake my head.

The brunette purses her lips, but her eyes twinkle merrily and her shoulders shake. Finally, she can hold it in no more, and she bursts forth with peals of laughter.

I can't help but stare at her in wonder. Although I still don't hear the sound, the feeling of it spreads through my soul, easing tension I didn't even know was there. I experience the woman's mirth like it's my own. My heart feels lighter and it's impossible to keep the smile from spreading across my face.

Oh this one should have been mine, the brunette says.

Shayla, I'm Zaya, goddess of the Sirens, the blonde says.

What the ever-loving fuck?

I pinch myself and it hurts. I can feel the tickle of grass under my bare feet, the swish of the dress I'm wearing against my skin.

6

Wait. I'm wearing a fucking dress?

Sure enough, as my gaze moves down my body, I'm wearing a simple white shift that reaches my ankles, my bare feet barely poking out from underneath. It's similar to the gowns the two women are wearing.

Damn, not a slit or a miniskirt in sight. It's positively frigid.

Oh, I can assure you, they're anything but frigid, a warm, male voice says.

I look up in surprise to see a man standing between the two women. They each turn and give him a kiss, and it's not a friendly peck on the cheek. There's a full exchange of oral fluids, and as a siren, I can feel the bonds between them all.

He sips from their lips like he's drugged, his chest heaving and eyelids lowered. Eventually the blonde one, Zaya herself apparently, raises her head and catches a glimpse of me. She blushes — the goddess of the sirens actually fucking blushes — and clears her throat.

The other two pull apart, the brunette grinning unrepentantly and the man sighing in regret.

Forgive us, daughter. This is all very new to us, we haven't indulged ourselves like this in millennia, she says.

I'm a fucking siren, far be it for me to judge. More power to them. Literally, in Zaya's case.

The brunette snickers again. *I really do like this one, Zaya. Are you sure I can't have her too?*

What a fucking weirdo. Doesn't she get how sirens work? Play is nice, but we need cocks. Full stop. This is getting ordinary very fast, either I need to wake up, or I need to work out how to move on from here.

Be at peace, daughter, says the man. *Come, I have a gift for you.*

A gift? Is that what he's calling it? Sure. If I can fuck a weird dude in my sleep and get some energy, it'll save me hunting in the morning while I look for a new safehouse. There was something off about the man staring at me the night before. All this running has made me tired and hungry. If he's picked up what I am, I'm in serious danger.

As I go to step forward, the skirt swings strangely against my legs. Glancing down, I'm surprised to discover that the previously full-length skirt is now a ring of strips of fabric, each step forward makes them part, my dark skin contrasting beautifully with the pure white cloth. It reveals a lot of my legs, yet at the same time, it's also discretely covering everything I don't want to show by being knotted intricately for a few inches. The overall effect is stunning.

I'm glad you approve, you will come to understand that we do care very much about you and Catriona, even if it may seem like we don't, he says, putting his hands on my shoulders.

Whoa, when did he get so close?

The world spins for a moment, and a great weight seems to descend upon me. My knees give out, but the strong hands on my shoulders shift to my waist, holding me up.

I blink once and find myself seated on a bench, the two women bracketing me as the man kneels before me. It's disconcerting to find these time slips happening. Am I falling asleep? Blacking out?

You are in the godly realm, Daughter, says the brunette. *I'm Mara, goddess of the wolf shifters, and this is V'dar, god of the dragon shifters and all the other fae.*

The godly realm? Did I die?

Oh goodness no, Daughter. You are merely with us in a vision, although your mortal mind is struggling a little with the magic. Catriona did too the first time she came here.

Catriona was here?

Sister, we are running out of time, Zaya says.

I hope to see you again another time, Shayla, your mind is refreshingly blunt. I must leave you now, but I give you this gift. Use it to run, your instincts are right, you have been found by a wolf shifter and he is not one you want to catch you.

She kisses my temple and then simply fades away. My skin tingles where her lips touched me, and I feel renewed, full of energy, as though I'd fucked all night and slept all day. In short, I feel magnificent.

I'm sorry, daughter, that this must now be rushed, but perhaps it is better this way, Zaya says. *Catriona needs you. She doesn't realise it, yet it changes nothing. She will explain more when you find her, but tell her I said your presence is but one more step. It rules out so many other catastrophes. She will explain it all to you.*

Where? Where *am I supposed to find her?*

You already know where she is. She hasn't left the wolves she visited that night. Ironically, if you are to be safe anywhere, Shayla, it will be there. Do not fear those wolves, nor the dragons. Not the ones living on Triune lands.

I'm not going to a shifter pack, I insist. I've seen what happens to a siren with a pack of shifters too many times.

I know your fear, daughter. Do you think I would send you into danger?

I gape at her, she really had the balls to ask that?

I do not understand, Daughter? When have I ever sent you into trouble?

Not just me, I scream in my head. *All of us! We prayed, we begged, we pleaded for you to save us, and yet still we died by the hundreds. The best thing you did to us was to take away our fertility when we asked for it, but it only made them more desperate. Where were you when we needed you? Where were you when we were raped, butchered and murdered? How can you call yourself our goddess when you left us in that shithole? No, I don't believe you for a second when you say it's safe.*

Zaya's eyes flash angrily, golden light filling them before they return to the darker bronze they had been to start with.

You speak of things you do not understand, things you do not know. There is more to the universe than the earthly realm, and the war we have been fighting is on many planes. I did everything I could to save my daughters, it's why you're not extinct. It's why there are some of you left. I can't just snap my fingers and make things happen, there are other forces in the universe far more powerful than I am. All you need to understand is that I did everything I could and I saved as many of you as I was able.

Like it or not, you and Catriona have been chosen to act as the will of the gods in this war. You are both our earthly representatives, along with my handmaiden, Fleur. Catriona is my vessel. You, however, are my warrior. Go now, and do your duty to your people. If you do not undertake this task, not only will I be unable to save you from the wolf that is stalking you even as you sleep, but I will be unable to save the rest of our kind. We will be lost, and the entire planet will be enslaved.

With a final huff, Zaya disappears.

V'dar is the only one left, kneeling in front of me. He gives me a rueful smile.

She chose you because you are passionate, because you are a warrior at heart. She did not expect you to challenge her. Do not change, little siren. It will do her good, even if it pisses her off.

He stood and held out a hand, helping me to rise.

Besides, he says with a wink. *She's a lot more fun in bed when she's all riled up.*

On that note, he too leaves.

I stand there, watching as the garden around me fades away, leaving me in a misty blankness. It's unnerving, especially when it turns darker.

T he flickering of a streetlight nearby announces my return to reality. I'm surprised to find myself dressed in leather, my backpack on my back, and a gleaming new motorcycle in front of me, the helmet in my hands. Stale urine assaults my senses, and whispered rustlings makes me think of rats. That is, until I hear voices.

"What do you mean she's not here? She was fucking here less than five minutes ago, tossing and turning in her sleep. She's a fucking siren, not a witch, she can't just disappear, find her, find her now."

And that's my cue to leave. Quickly I put the helmet on, not questioning how I got there; deep in my heart I already know. The bike starts with a simple button, and I pop the clutch, flying along the alleyway. Howls behind me letting me know they've discovered my escape.

It's too late for them, I'm too fast. I've already lost them, and I speed across the city, more clarity in my path than there has been for some time.

I have a mission, a purpose, and I *will not* fail Catriona.

JUDE

"Hold on Alpha Quentin, they're going to come soon," I tell him but Quentin is silent and my chest hurts.

The heavy body in my arms is starting to go cold, but I can't let go. Not for an instant. He means too much to me to let him lie in the dirt. This man — he's everything. He's been saving me for my entire life, and now he's dying, because he saved me one last time.

The agony in my leg is now a dull throb compared to the pain in my chest, but still I hold Quentin to me tightly. I'm vaguely aware of the pack bond buzzing in the back of my head, but I don't answer. No, I have to focus, stay awake, just in case I'm wrong. Just in case the other wolves come back.

The new alpha, she can heal, right? She can't replace stuff, but she can repair it. She's been healing him for weeks, she knows his body inside out. Of course she can fix him.

I relax a little. Yeah, the alpha will fix him. Then I can tell him how fucking sorry I am, and how much he means to me. I can let him know my secret, something even my father doesn't know. Something my mother hid very carefully. Something that has guided my every effort. Especially tonight. So, Quentin can't be dead, because he needs to know.

I'm his son.

I can hear people coming. I grip Quentin to me tighter, there's no way they're going to take him. He's mine, my saviour, my *real* dad. They can't have him. The alpha is going to fix him, and then I'm going to tell him. I always promised Mum that I wouldn't — somehow I knew in my bones from a very young age. She made me promise not to tell anyone. She said it would hurt a great many people if the truth got out. Well, my father — the one who raised me — died in one of Sinclair's attacks, so now it's okay.

Mum is also being courted by someone else already. I know we're short on females, but it's not even been three months!

The only person my secret could hurt was my father, and he's gone. I don't think she was worried so much about hurting people as she was about being hurt. She had a mate bond, and she broke it and I was the result.

Losing your mate is a horrific thing. Most wolves go mad and are put down. Not Quentin. No.

He may have been a bit more horny than usual, but he upheld his station and he never showed his grief in public. He was a strong wolf, an amazing wolf, and I'm going to be just like him.

Is; he *is*.

He *is* a strong wolf. He's going to be even more amazing when the alpha fixes him.

The voices of the people are getting louder, more excited. Someone kneels down beside me and tries to make me let him go, but I won't.

No. No. No.

He's *my* father. *Mine.*

I won't let him go. I wasn't raised in the lodge like his other sons, but he never treated me as anything less and he never treated them as anything more. He made me want to try harder, to be worthy of him, because I knew one day I'd tell him, and he'd realise that somewhere in his heart, he'd always known.

I rock Quentin as I talk to him. I remind him about all the times he looked after me as I was growing up. How he helped clean me up when I fell into that marsh and I stank so bad my mother wouldn't let me in the house. Or the time when I couldn't reach the last apple in the tree and he hoisted me up on his shoulders until I could get it. And then we sat together against the trunk and ate it between us.

I stroke his hair as I remind him about the time I saw Josie Adams flirting and kissing with one of the other boys and how it damn near destroyed my heart. And he found me in the orchard, crying my eyes out. How he held me and rocked me just like this until I felt better.

So, that's what I'm gonna do. Yeah. I'm gonna hold him and rock him and look after him until the alpha can come and make him better.

"Fucking hell," mutters a voice beside me and I look up to see the new alpha, Marcus, squatting beside me.

"Alpha, you have to get Alpha Catriona. Quentin is hurt real bad. We gotta make him better," I plead and his eyes look so sad that if I didn't have my arms full of my Dad, I'd give him a hug. "Please, Alpha. I've gotta tell him, he didn't know, I gotta tell him."

"He knows how much you care about him, son. He loved all his wolves. He would have done anything for them. But you have to let him go, now. These men are going to take him and lay him out, and we need to get you back to Alpha Catriona so we can fix that leg of yours before it starts to set," he tells me.

No, no, no.

He doesn't understand. It's hard to hear him because my wolf is howling so loud inside me. I wish he'd stop.

"Quentin isn't dead," I tell the Alpha. "He's just resting because he's so tired. He's hurt. We just need to make him better. I need to tell him something, it's so important. Mama said I could never tell anyone, but it was only so we didn't hurt my father. But he died, so now it's okay. I need to tell him, I need to tell Quentin my secret."

Alpha Marcus is shaking his head. Why won't he understand? Does he think I'm trying to wheedle my way into my dad's affections, to get him to take his oath back and make me his heir? Because I don't want that. I just want my real dad. I've always wanted him, and now? Now it's finally okay to have him. To let him know.

"Let me talk to him," says another man, and he crouches down beside us. "Hey man, I'm Matt. What's your name?"

"Jude," I tell him. "Please, you gotta convince Alpha Marcus to take Quentin back to Alpha Catriona. She's gotta make him better, so I can tell him my secret."

"Okay, Jude, here's what needs to happen. We can't carry you both at the same time. We need you to let him go so we can get him back to the bunker. That's where Alpha Catriona is. Time is of the essence, we need to move quickly, so you need to let him go. See, we've got a blanket here as a stretcher. We're going to carry him back to her, and we've got more guys here who are waiting to carry you. We really need to get your leg set before the bone starts joining up again, okay? Otherwise, we're going to have to break it, and I bet that hurt a fuck-ton the first time, yeah?" He grins at me. "I'm willing to bet you wanna avoid that."

"Yes, sir," I say, and relax my hold. Straight away the other men come and take him from me, carefully gathering up his guts that hang in loops all over the ground. We rolled around a bit when we killed that fucker.

"What's the secret that you need to tell him?" Marcus asks. "If it's important, then as your alpha I should know."

I think about it for a moment. It's true, he should know, if only so he doesn't get worried that I want the pack. That's the last thing I need.

"You have to promise you won't tell anyone else, because really, he ought to be the first person who knows, and you the second. But I don't want to worry you, so I figure I can tell you now, and you act surprised, later, okay?"

"Sure, I can do that," he agrees.

"My mum, she cheated on her mate. It was just after Quentin lost Maria, his last mate. He swore he wasn't taking on another female, but Mum said he always found relief in a woman's arms after losing a mate. I mean, girls are nice to hug, right?" I smile at him and he nods. "But with my mum, well, it was more than a hug, and then I came along."

The smile vanishes from Alpha Marcus' face.

"No, no, no! You don't understand. I don't want it, the pack, it's yours. I'd never challenge you for it. All I've ever wanted was my dad. I've known since I was little, but my mum said I couldn't tell anyone. So, I've been waiting until it was okay. And my father, he got killed, so it can't hurt him anymore. So, we need to fix Quentin, so I can tell him. I'm his son, his last son. He'll be happy. He was always nice to me, and now we can spend time together, because you're looking after the pack now, so he has time to rest and do fun stuff with me. And I can make him proud. I can be the son he's always wanted."

Alpha Marcus just grabs me in a hug and holds me close.

"I'll tell him. Now, we're going to move you onto this blanket, it's going to hurt like a fucker, but then we'll take you to Alpha Catriona, alright? She's gonna fix your leg up real good, and we'll find your mother."

Aw man, mum's going to lose her shit. "She's gonna fuss, Alpha. Can we just—can you just tell her I'm okay, and I'll see her in the morning?"

Men come around us and tilt me a bit, sliding something under me, then they tilt me the other way, and it moves my leg. I almost chew my tongue off trying to hold back the scream.

"Hey, hey, you're doing great, Jude. We got you. Your mother is going to be so damn proud of you."

I can barely hear him over my panting, but he's holding my hand as we walk back. It's kind of nice, it's something Quentin would have done, only he'd drop it when we were in sight of everyone else.

"How old are you, Jude?" Marcus asks as we head back.

"Eighteen," I tell him proudly. He can't deny me the right to be here.

Marcus huffs. Is he annoyed?

"When did you turn eighteen, Jude?" he asks, and I know that he's seen right through me. He's a good alpha like that.

"Last week, sir," I tell him, chagrined.

It still counts. It might only be a week ago, but it still counts. I took out a vampire all by myself, and then helped Alpha Quentin take out the one that attacked us.

"Of course it counts, Jude. We're all really proud of you. You're an adult now, you're going to have to look after your mum. Do you have any siblings?"

How did he know what I was thinking? Is he a mind reader? That would be so cool, like an X-Man or something.

"Nah, just me. And Mum will be fine. She's already being courted again. Abe will look after her."

"I'll have a chat with her before she sees you. I promise, no embarrassing mum things, okay?"

Man, he's good. He knows exactly what I'm worried about. I might have taken out a vampire, but the sucker broke my leg, so everyone is going to think I'm weak. I'm an adult now, a real wolf, I can help protect them all.

We lurch to a stop and Alpha Marcus is kneeling beside me.

"Jude," he says, his tone deadly serious. "Nobody thinks you're weak. Even our toughest fighters have trouble taking out a vampire alone, and they're never uninjured. You not only did that, but helped Quentin take out another one, even when you were hurt. You are every bit a real wolf, and you definitely count as an adult. I just wish you'd had your childhood for a bit longer."

He's doing it again. He's reading my mind. Is he a god?

Marcus' face gets sadder, I didn't even know it was possible.

"Jude, you're in shock. I'm not reading your mind, you're saying all of this aloud. We can all hear you. It's okay. We're going to get you fixed, and then everything will be a bit clearer."

Matt is standing on the other side of me. He's one of the betas, I recognise him now. I've heard good things about him too. About all of the Triune Wolves. Alpha Quentin said they're good stock. I'm going to be just like them when I'm older. Good fighters, good protectors, good leaders. Alpha Quentin can give me all the hints.

Matt's smile looks a little forced when he looks at me. "Tell me what happened, Jude. How did you end up with a broken leg?"

Oh, well, that story is easy.

"We were sent down to the southwest corner. One of the trucks was crossing the field next to us. We were going to follow it to see where they were trying to cross the border, but they saw us and stopped. The doors opened and they just came out in a flood."

"How did they cross the wards, do you know?" Matt asks.

"Not exactly. There was a woman with them in the front of the truck. She opened the door, shouted some stuff at us, and then her hands went blue, like blue fire. Except it was more like lightning. Then it struck towards us, but it hit like a bubble of something. Wherever it hit the bubble, a hole appeared, but not for long, so the vampires rushed through before it closed. She had to keep making them, but it meant they came at us a bit slower rather than all at once, which helped."

"A witch," Marcus says grimly.

"I don't know, Sir, just a lady with magic is all I can tell you. We fought the vampires, one of them broke my leg as we wrestled, but I tore out his throat. I couldn't get up to fight anymore, but the others ran off, and my unit needed to follow them. I told them to hide me between the porta-potties because they stank so much nobody would smell me."

Matt chuckles. "That was actually a really good idea. I doubt any of us would have thought of that under fire."

Ah, well, I'd done it before. "We were playing hide and seek with the little ones, helping them to learn to track. They were supposed to be focussing on what they could see as well, but they kept using their noses. So, I hid out here to make them work for it, they had to follow my footprints. When I needed to hide my scent again, it just made sense to try it, especially when we were already so close."

"You've been helping out with the kids?" Marcus asks, curious.

"Yeah, I'm not old enough to help with the building, and I'm no good with the elders. I dunno how to talk to them. I'm not very good at cooking, but the kids like me, and they're fun. So, I help out there. I'm not skilled enough to apply to be an enforcer, so I'm just doing anything and everything I can while we settle. Then, when everything is safe again, I can start learning how to fight properly."

Matt grips my shoulder. "Jude, you took out a vampire at eighteen. I think you already have a pretty good idea of how to fight. We'll just refine your skills a bit. You're going to make a great enforcer."

Hope lit me up. Really? They'd let me do that?

I don't get to ask. We're nearly back at the bunker, and people are rushing up to Alpha Marcus and Matt, asking them questions and leading them away.

Matt takes five steps before he stops and comes back to me.

"Jude, I need you to know that what you've done today is amazing. You're a hero to this pack. You're my hero. I want to be like you when I grow up."

I just stare at him. He's nuts. He's the beta. One step away from leading. All the boys want to be Marcus or Matt.

To the men carrying me, Matt says, "This man is one of our bravest warriors and a rising star. Treat him with the respect he deserves."

"Yes, Beta," the men chorus.

My heart swells with pride. Damn. Alpha Quentin is going to be so proud of me.

That's when I see her.

Alpha Catriona.

We're not even inside yet, and she's come out here to see me. I know that because she's telling me. That's not what has my jaw dropping.

She's glowing. Like a fucking star is inside her. All this light is coming out of her. She's shining in the darkness.

Then she touches my head, and some of that light goes into me. Someone shoves cloth in my mouth, I know what it's for. I've been watching her heal. I bite down on it hard to stop myself from screaming. It feels like a hot poker is moving around inside my leg, but as quickly as it starts, it's gone. Behind Alpha Catriona, a man sinks to his knees. Others rush forward and help him to walk away.

I've seen that before too. He used his energy to help her heal me.

"Tell him I said thank you, please?"

She smiles down at me and strokes hair from my sweaty forehead. "I'll do that, Jude," she promises.

She looks like an angel.

"How's Alpha Quentin? Is he awake?"

Her face is sad. Did I say something wrong?

"He's not awake, Jude. You need to rest. We all need to rest."

Her hand curls around her belly, and I can see the bump there clearly moving. She's tired. That's why she looks sad. She's so tired.

"He told me how good you've been to him," I tell her, trying to lift her spirits. "He thinks he's a drain on the pack, on your healing. He thinks it's better if he dies. I know you love him like I do, like a dad. I know you like helping him. We'll make him understand that when he wakes up."

Catriona's light dims. Her face falls. Tears well in her eyes.

Something is wrong.

Protect her.

I must protect her.

"Protect the alpha!" I shout at the men around me. "She's going to collapse. Fucking drop me and catch the alpha."

My voice sounds different, I can hear it, feel it, but I don't have time to examine it. All four of the wolves immediately dump me and move to catch her as she falls.

A melodic voice rings in my head. *You are called to be her guardian. Protect her with all that you have. The fate of the world rests on her shoulders.*

My wolf shudders and submits, bowing low inside me to the voice. I didn't need his recommendation. The sense of purpose that overcomes me fills my every pore.

Yes, I will protect her, for I *am* her guardian.

1

Marcus

The aftermath of the attack is even worse than previous ones. For starters, with more wolves, we have more injured, and less who are well enough to act as Catriona's batteries. Healing is slow, most wolves are patched up and left to heal on their own. The dragons, thankfully, don't need healing, so several of them agree to act as her batteries to save those wolves who are at risk.

It's not just the physical injuries we have to worry about. Morale is at an all-time low. We might have defeated Sinclair, an initial source of great joy, until we had to tell them he was no longer the alpha, and the serpent that strikes at us has a new head.

Alistair.

My half brother.

For all the pups he sired over the years, trying to build himself a powerbase by insisting he had breeding rights with any and all females in the pack, my father only ever managed to sire two sons. It's a fact that I know rankles him, especially when I didn't follow in his footsteps.

Alistair was the perfect son, a real chip off the old fucktard, so he didn't need a spare heir. It doesn't stop him wanting one. It's why he never really let me go. Oh, he indulged me when I left and started up Triune with my friends, but Sinclair never took us seriously. Part of the problem was we didn't take ourselves seriously either. My father knew he could come and ground me under his boot at any given time, so there was no urgency to it.

We never really had a reason to fight him.

Not until Catriona.

She's really taken us to the next level, whether she realises it or not. It's like in her, we've found our purpose, our very reason for living. I fucking hate how it happened, that I took the choice from her, embodied her worst nightmare. I hate how everything is being stripped from her.

She was a human, then a siren, now she has a wolf and a fucking dragon.

Yeah, that's still pushing my wolf's buttons. He hates that he's no longer the only powerful male in her sights. Not that he ever was, the turd, the original men of the Triune Pack are no weaklings. There was a reason our families didn't come after us and haul us home — no matter how old we were.

Now, here I am in my own worst nightmare.

Politics.

I fucking hate them, but with both Quentin and Lisa gone, I'm it. The lone alpha for over three hundred wolves and a token alpha over the dragons. I can't see how this is following the old ways anymore. Packs were never meant to get this big. With good reason. It places too big of a strain on the alpha.

If a pack grows too large, gains too much power, then there's an imbalance. We're no longer a pack, we're a threat to all the others. Checks and balances are important. The mental well-being of the alpha holds the pack size in check.

I don't know how my father got around that. Or even if he did. If he's been absorbing smaller packs but not adding them to our main compound to hide it, and it drove him mad, it would explain a fucking lot. Not that I forgive him, because he went way over the line. But it would make his megalomania more understandable. It would also explain how they gained influence over him.

My father is power hungry, but to side with the vampires is sheer lunacy.

Alpha? a voice calls over the pack link.

Yes, who is this?

This is Ken, I'm on the gate. I got a bunch of women here, they say they're seeking refuge. But they ain't shifters. They've got kids and babies and just about everything they own in these cars. What do I do?

Fuck. I have no idea.

Just hold tight, I'll be down there soon.

I jog over to the bunker, most of the council should be there now that we're not tied up in Catriona's bed so much. Not that I'm complaining. I miss fucking like rabbits, but right now we've got people to feed and house and there's just no time.

Inside the bunker it's chaos. We've housed as many of the Pasadena wolves in here as we can. Three more family cottages went up yesterday, but they've already been temporarily reassigned as dormitories rather than family abodes. The first snow fell yesterday, and although it didn't last long enough to hit the ground, it didn't change the fact that it was fucking cold.

It takes me a moment to spot who I'm looking for. Men are sitting on their cots, three abreast, with the unused cots folded out of the way, trying to allow people to move through. It's still our dining hall, but rather than having all the tables set up, we've only got five. Thankfully, the appliances are now up and running thanks to the influx of trades that came with the Pasadena Pack.

"Alpha, do you have a moment to take my vow?" a wolf asks, stepping into my path.

Immediately, ten wolves around him stand up, ready to make theirs as well. On the one hand, I don't have the time. On the other hand, I really need them to do it. I'm torn. I look up at Matt who nods. He's no idea about the thing at the gate, but if it's not that, then it's something else just as urgent.

"Yeah, that would be wonderful, thank you," I tell him.

Matt saunters over. "So, the Alpha is not going to be able to call you by name, due to the circumstances, although I know he really wants to." He coughs into his hand. "Hhhf control freak, hhfff."

The waiting wolves snicker.

"So, we're going to do this as a group, because he's got fifty things he needs done two days ago, and a couple hundred wolves to get through. I know it's not personal, and we don't want it like that either, but it's the hand we've been dealt. To do this, you're going to give your oath to him like usual, but Alpha Marcus is going to address you as 'my wolves', because you better believe that his wolf is claiming every single one of your asses. You're wanted here, you're needed, and you have a home here."

That's why Matt's my right hand. Every single wolf in front of him stands taller, prouder, stronger. He's got them eating out of his hand. I get the big picture stuff. He gets the details nailed. I can negotiate the politics like a pro, but Matt has the human interest thing down pat. People respect me because I lead them. They respect Matt because they like him.

"Do you all know the words? Because I'm betting it's been a while since you've done this. I nearly swallowed my tongue trying to remember."

The men laugh, and the last of their anxiety is gone. The scent of it is wiped away by the trust and camaraderie that Matt is engendering.

I owe you for this, I tell him.

All part of the service, man, he replies.

He can say that all he wants, we both know it for the lie it is.

The men line up, ready and waiting. I give them a nod, and they begin in unison. The buzzing at the back of my head telling me they're using part of their old pack link. How it's intact, I don't know, but I suspect it's because Lisa gave her oath to me. At the very end, she did the right thing by them. I won't take that from them, no matter what I think of her.

"Marcus, I give my oath to you. To fight where you fight, to follow where you lead, to go where you direct, and to do as you command. I acknowledge you as my alpha, and I give my life in service to you and your pack."

"My wolves, I receive your oath with joy. I swear to lead you in truth, honour and justice. I will heed your advice, and protect you as my own blood."

Immediately I feel a tiny weight taken from me as their oaths settle into place. Given the number of wolves remaining, it's not a huge difference, but when you're running on fumes, every ounce counts.

The men are all slapping each other on the back, Matt and the other council members moving in to do the same. It's the man standing at the back and watching it all that I want, so, after a dignified nodding of my head, I make my way over.

"Alpha Dean," I greet him.

"Alpha Marcus," he replies with a slight twist of his lips.

I'm not sure if it's a smile or not, but I'm taking it as one.

"I was wondering if you'd like to take a little stroll down to the gate with me. We could look at the perimeter together and see what else can be done to strengthen it."

Dean gives me an odd look, but because we're not in a pack together, I can't speak to him mentally. I roll my eyes at him and jerk my head to the side in a 'come along' gesture.

I don't know whether the penny drops, or whether he's just humouring me, but Dean gives a half bow and gestures for me to lead the way out.

2

Marcus

There are as many ears listening to us as there are eyes watching us, so we'll have to wait until we're halfway down the drive before I can clue him in.

It's not just wolves watching us either. As we head outside, I can see two massive dragons up on the Pasadena lands, doing work with the building crews there. Despite the unexpected merging of the pack, we're still going to be housing people up there. Wolves need space, and I don't want to cut into our forested area any more than we have. The land over there is cleared, it makes sense to use it. We can sort the legals out later, although I'm certain that something will come along to bite me on the ass.

"Your people work well together, despite such uncertain times," Dean comments idly as we walk.

We're still within easy hearing distance of anyone moving around, so I keep a tight lid on my real purpose for drawing him out.

"It's because we have a common enemy. This is a safe haven for all who come here, it's in their best interests to put aside any differences and work for the common good. I'm sure they'll return to their usual argumentative selves once the threat is over."

Dean snorts and nods. He gets it. There might not be many of his people left, but their personalities are as large as their beasts. His own mother is a prime example.

"How's your mother settling in?"

This time, the dragon alpha growls. "She's holding court amongst your seniors. They seem to be silly enough to listen to her. I'll try to keep a lid on it as much as I can. Tamara is acting as her aide, but in reality she's reporting to me. I'm pretty sure my mother knows, but I don't give a crap. Knowing that your mate is V'dar's chosen vessel, however, has turned her scheming in a new direction."

Dean winces as he looks at me out of the corner of his eye. I can tell he's wondering if I know. Of course I fucking know. I snicker, putting him at ease.

"She can tout the size and length of your cock until she's blue in the face. You're not the one V'dar chose for Catriona, who's having trouble enough accepting she's to be bound to yet another male without her consent."

To say the dragon alpha moves fast is an understatement. I'm pinned against the trunk of a tree before I realise Dean has moved against me. Fuck, that's fast.

"Ethan is my beta, and the most honourable fucking dragon I've ever met. You will not disparage him again."

"I didn't—" a clawed hand wraps around my throat.

"He will not bond her without her consent. I don't know what you wolves do, but dragons don't do that."

With no air coming in, all I can do is nod. Dean lets me go instantly.

"Please, forgive my poor choice of wording. It wasn't what I meant."

Dean rumbles a growl but says nothing.

"Catriona—" I husk, pausing to clear my throat and try again. "Catriona didn't choose us for herself. The goddesses interfered and put compulsions on us all. They made us fated mates. Just as they've done to Ethan. He doesn't get a choice in this either. The two of them have to make the most of a contrived situation. We need her to choose to bond him, or we're all fucked. She knows it, and it's killing me, because she's trying to fall in love with a stranger in the middle of a war. It's being forced upon her."

"She has a choice," Dean says coldly.

Now it's my turn to growl at the dragon. "Yeah, open your legs and heart or the entire planet is enslaved. Some fucking choice."

Dean's mouth opens to argue, but I've had enough.

"Look, Alpha. That's not why I called you here," I tell him, as I grab his arm and we walk down the drive, picking up the pace. "I got a message. There are women at the gate, asking for refuge. They've got kids and young ones with them. I've no experience with magic users, my guard says they don't smell like shifters, so I'm guessing witches. Have you dealt with them before?"

The dragon alpha rounds on me. "Kill them, now. The witches have sided with your father."

"He's dead, it's Alistair now, and it's not as simple as that. Catriona spoke to the gods, Yna is staying out of the conflict, allowing her people to choose as they see fit. Aidal is doing the same. We may get groups of witches or mages coming to help us."

"That is your call, Alpha," the dragon says.

"It needs to be an informed one. I've never dealt with a witch, I wouldn't know one if she bit me. I want to know if it's possible to identify them. Can you detect their magic or something? Can you tell if they're lying?"

Dean looks at me for a moment before nodding. "I can scent a witch, you will understand once you have. They have a fragrance that is as distinct as that of a vampire."

"They stink?" I ask, unhappy. If they're the real deal, I'll let them in, but we don't need a bad smell on top of everything else. Wolf noses are far too sensitive.

He waggles his head at me. "No, not stink. Vampires stink. Witches, it's spicy, sweet, a little too sweet for me, if you get my understanding. Fae smell like trees and grass and loam. Mages smell like fire and ashes and hot spices like chilli and curry or turmeric. Witches are more like fruit and spun sugar, cinnamon and cloves. You'll know it when you smell it. They're as distinct as the vampires are."

"Vampires smell like unwashed ass and rotten fruit," I tell him.

Dean roars with laughter. "Unwashed ass, I'll remember that one. I gather you've had the misfortune?"

I snicker. "Yeah, in the early days here, we had human tradesmen working on plumbing and electrical. Let's just say this plumber's crack was even more ghastly in reality than it was in appearance."

The dragon winces.

Our brisk pace has us within hearing range of those at the gate now, so we let the conversation drop. The more time I spend with the alpha, the more I like him. I can see us working together beyond this crisis. Providing we all survive it.

Hell, we have to survive it.

Ken is on the other side of the gate, standing patiently in front of the latch, while a rather robust woman is in his face and giving him an earful. While she threatens him repeatedly, she makes no actual move to attack him, which tells me that it's all bluster to let off steam, and to test him.

As I walk forward, Dean falls a step behind me, clearly signifying that I'm in the lead. The breeze shifts, and I can now understand what he was talking about. The aroma coming from the women is incredibly sweet, not overwhelmingly so, but enough to be quite distinctive. They are indeed witches.

Whether they're on our side or not is another matter. I wouldn't put it past my brother to be more subtle about his attacks. Brute force has failed several times now, although if he keeps coming at us with those kinds of numbers, we won't be able to maintain our strength. We're already close to breaking point as it is, even with the new influx of wolves.

"Are you the alpha?" her strident voice calls, as she looks past me at Dean.

"That would be me, Alpha Marcus," I correct her.

Her gaze swivels to mine, and she gives me a brief once over before looking at Dean again behind me.

"But he's bigger," she protests.

Several wolves snicker, but we all ignore them.

"He's also a dragon," I inform her, and her posture immediately changes from a take-charge attitude to a defensive one.

"It wasn't us," she says, backing towards her car, her confidence completely wiped away. "It was half our coven, but it wasn't us. We refused, which is why we're now being hunted as traitors."

I have no idea what the fuck she's talking about, but Dean obviously does, because he shoves me aside and storms forward, growling.

The woman squeaks and runs back towards her car, but Dean is too fast. He's on her, holding her arms as he gives her a thorough shake.

"Promise me, swear to me on a blood oath and I'll say no more," he growls in her face.

In one of the cars behind her, a child starts crying, and soon several more join in. Regardless of what the adults may or may not have done, the children are innocent. For their sake, and their sake alone, I dare to intervene.

"Dean, the children," I remind him.

Shifters are highly protective of their young, and that extends to the young of all species. As quickly as it spiked, Dean's anger abates, but it doesn't disappear.

"Your oath in blood," he reminds her, letting her go.

The woman produces a knife and slices her thumb, looking to Dean for direction. He cups his hands and a flame appears in them, it flickers purple on occasion, telling me it's not just magic produced, but a spell in and of itself.

"By the power of Yna, by the binding of three, I give my oath and my truth to thee," she says.

She drips her blood into the bowl created by Dean's hands, and then looks him in the eye.

"Neither I, nor any of the witches here with us, had anything to do with the attack on your clan. We refused and were cast out. Then we were attacked by vampires, our former coven doing nothing to aid us. We are on the run, and have come to beg asylum with you."

The flame rises in Dean's hands, burning blue then white before disappearing. Dropping them to his sides, he gives her a half bow before returning to me.

"She tells the truth," he informs me, then moves to stand at my back again.

It's not lost on the woman that the dragon defers to me. Good. She shouldn't underestimate me. If she's going to come at me, then she better make it her best fucking shot.

"We're running out of room, but you're welcome to what space we have," I tell her. "How many do you have?"

"Fourteen adults and eight children plus three babes still suckling."

I nod. We can work with that. It might be more reassuring for Catriona to have babies around her. I know she's worried about how to handle the pups.

"Are any of you able to work wards?" Dean asks them.

Fuck. It hadn't even crossed my mind. Please, I beg the goddess. Please, let one of them be able to do something.

"All of us can to some degree or another. We will help with the wards on your boundaries, it is the least we can do in thanks."

One more layer of security, it's as flimsy as all the rest of them, but the combined effect is greater than the sum of the individual parts, or so Dean told me the last time we worked on the wards.

"Open the gates, get the road cleared," I order the wolves, then direct my attention back to the woman. "Do you have any injured? We have a healer of sorts."

The woman looks at me, surprised. "No, we're capable of healing ourselves. I would like to meet your healer. I was not aware of any witches in your pack."

I chuckle even as I step out of the way. "Catriona is my mate, the alpha female, and she's no witch."

"Then what is she?" the woman presses.

"Something we don't have a name for, but she's pretty fucking amazing nonetheless."

She smiles at me for the first time. "You love her," she states.

"Love seems like such an insignificant word for what I feel, but it is the best explanation for now."

Dean snorts behind me, it sounds suspiciously like he muttered pussy-whipped. I'm ignoring it, or else I'll end up doing something that'll scare the kids all over again.

"I'm Eva," the woman says, hesitantly holding a hand out to me.

I don't wait, I take it, giving it a firm shake before releasing her. She never has to be afraid of me, not unless she betrays us.

"Marcus Triune." I'm not using my birth name, I reject it. My pack is a good enough name for me now.

She gives me another smile and heads back to her car, the small convoy quickly passing me and heading up the secret drive toward the lodge.

Fleur, fourteen adult females, eight kids and three babes. They're witches seeking refuge and are about to arrive at the lodge. Can you find them somewhere to sleep?

Of course I fucking can, they're just not going to like it, but one word of bitching and I'll put them in their place, comes Fleur's tart reply.

Fuck, I hope she doesn't start a war there.

"Get my mother to help with the babes," Dean advises as we walk back up to the lodge. "She'll melt. You'll never see her softer than when she's holding an infant, and it could keep her out of the way and out of trouble. She'll be too busy cooing to cause trouble for anyone else."

"Aren't you going a bit heavy on the stereotype there?"

Dean snorts at me. "No, Marcus. If anything, I'm downplaying it. We haven't had young for a very long time. She's clucky, but unable to breed herself. She'll do anything for those kids, including giving her life, even though they're not dragons."

Fleur, snag Ramona. Dean says she's charmed by babies. Give one to her to pacify her and stick her in a corner out of the way.

You did not just go there, Alpha, Fleur sends in a warning tone. *That kind of shit went out the window a long time ago. Women are more than baby-making machines.*

I'm only paraphrasing what Dean told me. They haven't had young for a very long time, and Ramona is pining for them.

There's no further reply, so I have to assume it's all sorted.

"Fleur's on it," I tell Dean.

"And my mother?"

"She's handling Ramona too."

"Thank fuck for that," Dean says. "I like your mate, but I've no intention of making a move on her, and it's driving my mother crazy. Ergo, she's driving me crazy."

I chuckle. Of course the snooty bitch wants Catriona for her son. Tough luck though, she's not getting her. Catriona is already well and truly spoken for. She's mine.

I'll share her with the others, but she's *mine*.

3

CATRIONA

The pups are wriggling again, they really are getting feisty. I put my hand on my distended abdomen, it feels like it's growing every minute, my skin feels tight, that stretchy uncomfortable feeling like I've had sunburn and done nothing to soothe the skin. Every time the pups move, it stretches even further, making it itch.

"Here," says Fleur, thrusting a jar at me. "Get one of your mates to rub that on your belly. You need to look after your skin better than that, or it won't recover."

She's talking to me, saying something else, but all I'm focussed on is the massive hickey on her neck. Way to go Craig!

After he swept her off her feet in the council room, the pair of them disappeared for two days. She emerged only to give me my green goop, Craig hovering over her the entire time. As soon as I'd drunk it, he hauled her over his shoulder again and took off with her. It's been the funniest thing to witness, the usually cantankerous Accoucheur swung around like a ragdoll by an incredibly horny and possessive mate.

Put it this way, I've learned to drink that green shit a lot faster.

"I'll help," says Joe, popping up from nowhere.

Frankly, it's not hard for anyone to sneak up on me in the lodge. Between the three packs of wolves, the dragons, and now the witches, we're stretched way beyond capacity. Thankfully the cabins and dorms are going up much faster with the help of our new friends.

One of the witches suggested using the dragons to thaw the earth, as well as digging the trenches, and then heating the concrete so it dried quicker. The dragons obliged us all with the first two, but using their flames to heat the concrete meant setting the wooden formwork around it on fire. So, the witches took over using a heating spell to keep the whole thing warm enough for it to cure like it would in warmer weather.

This is fantastic, but also a drain on the witches' magic.

There has to be a better way, but none of us can think of it. We're all running on empty trying to get as much done as possible. The Pasadena wolves have moved things forward tremendously with the numbers of tradespeople they had in their ranks. Which is helping raise morale a little.

"I can help the alpha," Jude pipes up from beside me. "I'm her guardian, whatever she needs I can help her with."

That's another problem I have to deal with. Jude has taken Quentin's death hard.

Unfortunately, he's transferred his desperate need for approval from his father to me instead. The goddess calling him to be my guardian has only made it worse. He's appointed himself as my personal assistant, which means I'm allowed to do even less than before to help, and he's now running interference with people wanting to see me.

Everyone has been indulging him, because most of them saw the mess he was in mentally when he was brought back to the bunker, but I know that's not going to last forever, especially with the tensions rising in the cramped space.

Joe's face takes on a sly twist, and I know he's going to cause trouble before he even opens his mouth.

"You want to rub moisturiser into the alpha's breasts? I thought you were called to be her guardian, not her mate. Should we tell Ethan he's got competition?"

Jude blanches then blushes furiously.

"I thought it was for her belly, it's growing so fast and she's always scratching it. I just wanted to help."

He's speaking so fast his words run into one another, and now I want to kick Joe in the shins for making the poor kid so uncomfortable.

Really, Joe? He's only just turned eighteen, give the kid a break, I growl at him.

Joe's gaze snaps to mine, the mirth there gone.

Yeah, I'm going to go there, because he can't sit on the fence. He's either man enough to take on this role, and therefore adult enough to realise he can't keep wallowing in his grief like a kid, or he's a kid who needs to be given a task to keep him from being underfoot until he can get his shit sorted out. We're in the middle of a war here, Catriona, and you're the alpha female of the pack. You're also vulnerable and a huge target because of the pups. Either he's your guardian and steps up to the role, or he steps aside until he's ready to take it on.

He's been trying hard, he's so helpful and he's been through a tonne of shit, I argue.

One, he's your guardian, not your secretary. He needs to fucking guard you, not run around like an errand boy. He should be silent, in the background and watching everything with suspicion. Two, yeah, he's been through a tonne of shit. So. Have. You. So has everyone here. We can't afford to give him special treatment.

I know Joe's right, but at the same time, I just want to protect him. He's so lost and alone. I know what that feels like.

Look, Joe offers, *I'll explain it to Fleur, get her to talk to him. She can do that whole motherly thing while still whipping his ass into shape. The kid isn't making progress, because we're not guiding him, we're not helping him, we've just left him to it and he's fucking lost. This is what pack does, Catriona, we keep each other going when things get tough. Don't sweat it, we'll sort him out.*

I sigh. I hate doing this. "He's right, Jude, sorry. I have supernumerary teats now on my belly in preparation for the pups. They're pretty hard to avoid. Joe can help me. If you can guard the door to stop anyone wandering in, that would be best."

Given a duty, Jude nods eagerly and waits for them to move.

It's obvious though, as soon as the door is closed behind us, that Joe has more than just helping my skin on his mind as he runs his hands over my belly and grinds his erection against my ass.

"Pretty sure that thing can't give me the kind of cream I need, and your dry hands aren't going to do much either," I tell him with a giggle.

Joe huffs behind me, pushing me towards the bed, but when I get there, he stops me before I get on, pushing on my shoulders until I'm bent over the edge. My belly swings in front of me a little, my breasts resting just on the edge while the dugs hang lower making them look even larger.

He slides his fingers into the waistband and removes my loose maternity pants and underwear in one movement, cold air rushing in on my sex and making the dampness there even colder. One finger sweeps through my folds, spreading the moisture all the way up to my clit, circling it and then coming back down again.

Oh goddess that feels so good.

Now that I don't need to start my day with a feed, I often wake to find myself alone in bed, our sexcapades have drastically reduced. The whole pack knows I'm free from my orgy needs and they're demanding the attention of my men a lot more.

Going from a diet of practically non-stop sex to almost complete abstinence has been a shock to my system.

Joe replaces his finger with his tongue, licking up and down my folds and fucking my hole, while his finger drifts in lazy circles around my clit. His other hand moves between my legs and then reaches up to play with my nipples, dugs, and breasts alike. It's torture, but it's fucking amazing.

45

I can't believe how much he's enjoying it too. There's not even a hint of anticipation from him, although I know his cock has to be weeping, he's so aroused. It seems he just wants to pleasure me.

Between his tongue, his fingers and his arousal, Joe quickly has me peaking.

"I need you baby, I can't come otherwise. The goddess may have fixed my energy needs, but that bit hasn't changed."

Joe just laughs against my folds, rubbing harder and faster. My core clenches hard, but I can't come, not without him inside me, and I don't dare feed my pleasure to him. If he comes while he's kneeling behind me, I'll have to wait for him to peak again.

"Joe," I whimper.

He stops. He fucking stops, and not just to change position.

He blows cool air onto my slick folds, cooling things down and allowing me to come down with it. "I could do this all day, alpha. Keep you on the edge, listen to you whimper and groan. I'll make you beg for me, alpha. Beg for my cock to fill you, to make you come and clench hard around me."

Oh goddess. His dirty mouth!

I never knew Joe had it in him, then again, I never get to have time with them one on one. I'm realising now that's something I need to address. Especially now that I have the freedom to do so. I wanted the ability to fuck when I wanted, rather than non-stop for survival. Now I needed to make the most of it, not only for myself, but for my mates.

There is one thing I'm fairly sure of, however. Joe doesn't want *me* to beg.

"I've wanted to do this to you since the first night, alpha," he tells me quietly, interspersing every other word with a long, slow lick.

"Really, Joe?" I tease him breathlessly. "Because I seem to remember a wolf lying on his back on the bathroom floor, and he looked pretty desperate to please me. It was one of the sexiest things I've ever seen."

Joe stills. I know I've got him.

"Joe?" I purr, putting a little croon in it, and he moans at the sense of command, even before I've said anything.

"You're not allowed to touch your cock until I say, Joe."

"Yes, alpha," he pants, and there's no mistaking the thrill that floods him. He's really turned on by me being in control.

It's a shame Marcus isn't here, because I know he'd fucking love watching this, although he wouldn't be able to hold himself back from participating.

"Stand up," I tell him, but there's no control in it. If he wants to follow my commands in the bedroom, then it's going to be of his own free will.

"Yes, alpha."

When he moves, I'm free to get up myself. As much as I was enjoying what he was doing, my back is beginning to ache from the position. It takes me only moments to rearrange the pillows so that I'm supported while still sitting at the edge of the bed. I know it's bad for the pups for me to lie directly on my back, but supported like this I should be okay.

"Kneel, Joe."

He drops so fast I fear for his kneecaps when they thud against the floor, but he's a shifter, so if he's chipped them, they'll be healed before he comes. Hell, if I make him wait, he could probably heal a broken leg. That thought makes me snicker and his gaze snaps to mine.

"I was just thinking your knees would be healed before we finish," I tell him, and if anything, his eyes burn even hotter. He licks his lips, lowering his eyes to stare at where he's so desperate to touch me.

"Lick it once," I tell him, and I can't tell if the surge in lust is from me or him as he does so, all I know is that it feels amazing.

As if my earlier thoughts summoned him, I feel Marcus approaching. I can already feel lust burning through the bond. I thought I'd shielded myself pretty carefully, but it seems there's no escaping him when I'm having sex.

The door opens but it's not Marcus who walks in, it's Ethan, and his gaze is immediately fixed on where Joe's tongue is giving me the longest, slowest lick.

He jostles forward when Marcus pushes him in from behind, closing the door, but he's shocked when he turns around and sees what I'm doing.

"I was having private time with my mate," I chide Marcus.

Neither of the men move, and it's starting to piss me off. I grab the sheet and pull it over Joe's head, covering myself from the waist down. He finally finishes that long, slow pass and hovers just above me, neither moving the sheet nor his head away from where he wants to be.

His patience, his level of fucking control is turning me on in a big way, and I realise I'm releasing pheromones when I see the pair of them inhale deeply, their pupils blowing wide.

"Marcus," I snap, and he jumps.

"He's your fated mate, Catriona, I'm not going to throw him out."

Something stirs inside me, and it's not the pups. It's not my wolf either. My dragon uncoils and sits up, her anger fuelling my own.

"It's not your permission he needs," I growl, my dragon augmenting my voice.

Marcus rolls his eyes, he fucking rolls his eyes at me! Something snaps inside.

"Or would you take that choice from me too, Marcus? Are you going to hold me down while he rapes me? Or just jerk off as you watch?"

Ethan growls, loud and long, a burning gaze fixed on Marcus that's no longer lustful. "You raped her?" he asks, dangerously quiet.

"Never," Marcus insists, holding up his hands.

"Only my mind and soul," I correct him, and Ethan spins to look at me, horrified. Marcus, however, looks stricken. "He claimed me during sex without asking. He forced Matt to claim me during sex when I said he wasn't allowed."

One second Ethan looks at me in horror, the next, Marcus is held by his throat against the wall, while Ethan's claws rip through his shirt.

"Say the word, mate, and I will rip him to shreds," he offers. Marcus doesn't resist.

So, he does realise.

I leave him hanging there, letting him think I'm considering it. Ethan's dragon is fuming, I can sense it somehow, and my own dragon is responding, the two of them spiralling together.

It's then that Joe intervenes, lowering his head and suckling my clit while a finger starts thrusting inside me. It's so unexpected, so amazing, that it completely derails my thought process. My hips buck and I let out a long, low moan, distracting Ethan, whose gaze zeroes in on the moving sheet at my waist.

"Let him go, Ethan," I tell him, but it takes a few seconds for the thought to process. Marcus' knees buckle when he's finally released, and he slides down the wall to the floor.

"I haven't chosen you yet, Ethan," I tell him sternly.

His gaze flicks to mine, then back to what Joe is doing, even though it's hidden by a fold of the sheet. The bastard hasn't stopped, and I'm starting to climb that peak again.

"I know," he rumbles. "I can wait, I will wait, but when I claim you, it will not be like this. Your wolves will not be welcome, my dragon won't tolerate them. You will be mine that night, and all of that night, and I will ensure your entire body knows it."

Fuck.

Why does that alpha bullshit turn me on?

My core clenches, and I know he can smell it. He smirks at me before he leaves.

"All night, little mate," he reiterates, then closes the door behind him.

4

CATRIONA

"Y ou're still mad. I thought you'd forgiven me," Marcus says quietly from the floor.

Fuck.

"Marcus, I'm not going to lie to you. I will always be a little mad at you for that. I've forgiven you, but I haven't forgotten it, and part of me is always going to be disappointed that it's how we started our relationship — me wanting to kill myself to escape the fate of my mother. The same fate you lined me up for."

The sheet slips back and Joe sits up, staring at me. "You wanted to die?"

I grimace. He's seen my nightmares, and he still doesn't get it?

"Joe," Marcus asks hoarsely. "How bad was her nightmare? Because that's what she thought was going to happen to her. That's what she thought we were going to do."

I sit up a bit more now that Joe has moved back. "Correction, that is what *will* happen to me if your brother gets a hold of me. He will use me exactly as every siren has been used during the wars, although with a dragon and a wolf inside me, it will be much harder to kill me. I'll last a lot longer now."

"Over my dead body," snarls Marcus.

"Yes, and that's hardly a comfort," I snap back.

"He will not get you," Marcus growls, prowling over the bed towards me. "You are mine, ours, and nobody else's. I will tear apart the planet to protect you. I will defy the goddess herself."

"Yes, alpha," Joe purrs, kneeling at my feet, but his adoring gaze isn't on me, it's on Marcus.

Something clicks into place then.

It's not just me that Joe lusts after, it's his alpha, too. There's a buzz at the base of my skull, but before I can find out what it's about, Marcus' mouth crashes into mine. A beat later, Joe consumes my folds, licking and sucking at a frantic pace, while his fingers piston inside me. With the lust I'm getting from both of them through the bond, it's only moments before I'm edging, held at the perpetual brink of an orgasm while I wait for one of them to fuck me.

I rip my mouth from Marcus, gasping in a breath and begging. "Please, please, I need this, I need you."

Joe stands, shucks his pants and sheathes himself inside me, making me groan. Marcus tugs my top and bra off, then undresses himself, but rather than offering his cock to my mouth, he steps behind Joe. What's he going to do? The angle is wrong for double penetration.

Above me, Joe freezes and then *moans*. It's a loud, deep and primal sound. So dirty, my heart skips a beat.

I was wrong.

For Joe, the angle is perfect for double penetration. Just as Joe impales me, Marcus is buried deep inside him. Both men still and pant as they adjust.

Marcus moves backwards, but Joe is still frozen, his eyes rolled back in bliss as he hangs there between us. I pinch his nipple, but although his eyes open in shock, he still doesn't move. Impatient, Marcus grabs his hips and draws him backwards, making him withdraw from my slick channel.

I assume the move is backwards onto Marcus' cock, but then Marcus slams forward, a second later, Joe shunts into me with the force of the man behind him.

Marcus might be sheathed in Joe, but he is most certainly fucking the pair of us.

Goddess.

If I could come of my own free will, this thought alone would be enough to take me over the edge.

Joe comes to life again, pushing back against Marcus, then slamming forward into me, before returning to his alpha. He shuttles back and forth, pleasing the two of us, and by his moans, he's getting a lot out of it too.

"Alphas," he says, on a high-pitched moan. I've never heard a sound like that from him before. If he were sixteen and female, I'd say he was fangirling, but despite being high, it's much more carnal.

"Yes, Joe," Marcus responds. "Your alphas are here, and we're both fucking you. Hard and deep, just as you like it."

Joe positively writhes, squirming against my dugs as Marcus holds him pinned there, small thrusts pumping against him as Marcus brings them both closer and closer to the brink.

"Give me your hands, Joe," Marcus orders, and Joe immediately folds them behind his back.

Marcus grabs them both in one hand and leans back, fucking Joe harder as he stands up, holding Joe in place against me. It strikes me then, this isn't the first time they've done this. In fact, while Marcus claiming Matt while fucking me was a surprise to them both, this isn't a new thing to Marcus. He's been fucking Joe for quite a while.

The pair of them are comfortable with each other, Joe knew exactly what Marcus wanted when he asked for it. Looking at the bonds between the two of them, it makes a lot more sense.

Marcus is the dom, and Joe is his sub. This is not a new dynamic for them. Both of these men want me, but they want each other too.

"So. Fucking. Hot," I whisper, as Joe begins to peak. I take his pleasure and feed it to Marcus along with my own. He likes to pride himself on his ability to hold out, but I'm too impatient to feel them come inside me. Joe already had me waiting before Marcus arrived.

"You don't mind?" Joe whispers against my shoulder, as Marcus pounds into him now, using Joe's outstretched arms like reins on a horse.

I grab his head and turn it, bringing his lips to mine. "I fucking love it," I tell him honestly, then fuse our mouths together.

Joe thrusts his tongue in my mouth, the action mimicking what his cock is doing inside me, all at the pace set by Marcus in his ass. He's there, at the cusp, but I keep stealing his pleasure and feeding it to Marcus who is trying not to come, so Joe is being edged between us, while Marcus fights it.

Enough.

For once, he doesn't get to control this. "Marcus," I croon at him, and his eyes glaze. His wolf surges to the fore, but it seems more happy to see me than worried. Even just saying his name like that turns him on, exactly like Joe. It's an interesting thing to note, and something I'm going to have to explore another time. Right now, I want to bring us all over the edge.

"Come like a freight train and share your pleasure with your mates."

"MIIIIINE!" roars Marcus, and his teeth sink into Joe's shoulder.

Before I can even begin to feed any pleasure to Joe, his balls draw up and his release begins, the pain sending him over the edge.

"My love," he moans, and then his teeth are in the crook of my neck, holding me still as his hips stutter above mine.

It's delightful and orgasmic, but I don't care right at that moment. I can feel the bonds between us strengthen and the energy from them both flows into me. I haven't experienced that before, but I'm guessing the goddess has made some tweaks to the power flow. That's good to know, because I plan to get Joe pinned between me and one of our lovers a lot more often.

5

MATT

I would have thought that getting the buildings up faster would have improved morale, but it's only made things more tense. Everyone is indoors, which is awesome, but cabin fever is beginning to strike. With up to twenty people per family cottage — ideally designed for six at the most, there is little room and less privacy.

Most of them don't have electricity or plumbing, leaving their occupants to tramp across the frozen ground to the bunker or one of the dorms to use the facilities to clean up. Which means a lot of wolves are desperate to move out of their confined quarters and into something more spacious.

Right now, I have five males with mates telling me why their family should be the first to get one of the cottages, while the witches and dragons watch on in the background, their expressions surly and rebellious. It doesn't escape me that the wolves haven't even considered them.

"Enough," I growl, the wolf in my voice catching their attention.

The men clamp their jaws shut. While I've never thought about leading an entire pack, I'm a strong enough wolf to produce alpha tones when I want. Right now it's not what I want to do, but I will if necessary.

"I'm a fair man, I'm going to give you all a choice," I tell them.

The witches and dragons frown at what they perceive as species favouritism.

"You can have a contained space for your family, or you can remain in your current quarters as you are."

The five men exchange glances, wondering what the catch is, but at the end of the day, they're too selfish to even think about it.

"It's a no-brainer. We'll take the private space," says one.

I look at them all. "You agree?"

"Yes, Beta," they chorus.

I clap my hands together, pleased. This will teach them a lesson.

"Excellent. Well, the witches and dragons you see behind you are living in vehicles in the barn. They're getting the next lot of buildings. You get your choice of the vehicles they leave behind. I'm sure if you talk nicely to them, they'll tell you how best to navigate the icy ground when your four-year-old needs to go to the toilet at three a.m. Oh wait, none of you have young children. Never mind. I'm sure they'll tell you the best place to hang your washing inside, because there's not enough dryers for us all. Or how to make friends with a species that seems to think you're not worth the time of day because you came as a refugee. Never mind the fact that those same people arrived as refugees as well."

The smile that I give them is menacing enough to make them step backwards.

"Maybe if you ask them nicely enough, they'll tell you how to deal with a bunch of entitled fucktards who seem to think the world revolves around their sorry asses and that everything should be delivered to them on a silver platter, because they're so much more deserving than anyone else, including the young, the elderly, and the injured."

Several of the witches have clapped hands over their mouths to hide their smiles. The dragons aren't so discreet. They're grinning openly at the discomfort of the males in front of them.

Now, if these wolves had young, or elderly, if they were more than two couples per family, I'd consider it. After all, it's easier to get along in a confined space if it's family rather than strangers. But these are all groups of four, wanting buildings that can hold so many more. They're lucky I don't set them a penance.

The wolves stare at me slack-jawed, unbelieving. How could I not give them what they want?

Very fucking easily.

"Get the fuck out of my sight before I find the most unpleasant of tasks and assign you and your fucking healthy adult families to it for the next six months."

Four of them bow their heads, unhappy but unable to act on it. The fifth one, however, is stupid enough to challenge me.

He barely starts to growl before I've shifted. I knock him on his ass and put my teeth to his throat. He's one that hasn't given oath to Marcus and Catriona yet, I can smell it on him. He belongs to Lisa's spoiled pack. It's no fucking wonder they loved her, she indulged their every whim.

Marcus, I call him on the pack link. *Get your mangy ass down to the bunker. I need you to take an oath or banish this fucker before I kill him.*

There's quite a pause before he answers. *Kinda busy, give me five minutes.*

Stop fucking our mate and get down here. Besides, she's going to take longer than five minutes.

The guy stinks, and holding him in my jaws is going to make me puke. I know it's hard to get in a shower, but this guy is rank. I don't think he's bathed since he arrived from the funk on him.

I'm not fucking her. I'm fucking Joe, he's fucking her.

Damn, that sounds like quite a sight. It's not my thing, despite what happened when I claimed Catriona, but I don't mind watching it. I know Marcus and Joe have been fulfilling each other's needs for quite some time, but including Catriona? That's hot.

Then they don't need you. I'm going to rip his throat out just for his smell alone. I need you here.

MIIIINE.

Ok, I'm guessing he doesn't need five minutes either. Well, maybe three to get dressed.

"Beta, we can smell him from over here. I can't imagine how he tastes, but judging by the amount of saliva pouring out of your mouth, it can't be good," one of the dragons says with a deep, Scottish brogue.

I can't see him from this angle, but I'm pretty sure it's Connor. He's right. Drool pools on the idiot's neck and runs down to the floor. I'm quite sure it's the closest thing he's come to a bath in weeks. I wonder if it's as off-putting to the vampires as it is to me. He may have something there with an offensive weapon, although I don't know that I'd encourage anyone to try it. We're all snapping at each other as it is.

"If you will permit, Beta, I can hold him there with my magic. I can even make him think it's you, if that's an issue."

It's obvious he's trying to help without standing on my toes, which I appreciate. I let the fucker go, but put a paw on his chest to stop him from rising, then I shift back, my paw becoming my hand holding him in place. As soon as it has fingers, they're wrapped around his neck, replacing my teeth. In my human form, it's the next best thing.

"Thank you, Connor, I would appreciate you holding him. The glamour isn't necessary, although the offer is quite tempting. I'd love to make the fucker piss himself."

The idiot has the gall to let his wolf rise to the surface in anger, his eyes turning golden and glaring at me. I've had enough.

"On second thoughts," I say, as I stand. "This foreigner is showing insufficient respect to pack leadership. I challenge you."

The man is on his feet in an instant, his fellow protestors crying out in shock, telling him to back down.

"You think I'm soft because I'm gay?" he snarls.

I just laugh at him. "My alpha is fucking one of my co-mates right now. That's why we're waiting. I don't have an issue with gay. I think you're soft because you've been spoiled by your old alpha. Look what that's got you."

If he were in his wolf form, his hackles would be rising, his ears pinned back and his teeth snarling. As it is, he bares his teeth at me in a rictus.

"What the fuck is going on here?" Marcus demands as he approaches, the aroma of sex and our mate lingering around him.

"It's a challenge, out of your hands, Alpha, you took too long getting here."

"You call me soft, but you call in your alpha for backup?" the man sneers.

"I'm calling you entitled, soft, and spoiled, and I called my alpha to take your fucking vow, not because I needed him to settle my fights. I'm his beta because I choose not to challenge him. He's a fine alpha, and I'll follow him to hell itself. As for you? I'm about to send your sorry ass there if you can't fix your attitude."

"Fuck," Marcus mutters. "Who the hell brought this asshole to my pack?"

Although I can feel his anger through our bond, it's not at me, it's at this idiot in front of me. Connor has stepped back, allowing us the space to sort this out.

"I'm sorry, Matt, but we need all the fighting wolves we can get, and we can't spare the energy to heal him."

No! He's not going to take this from me, but before I can protest, Marcus clarifies things.

"I don't know your name, and right now, I don't care. You've riled my beta, a man who is calm and in control when all hell breaks loose. It takes a special kind of lowlife to achieve that. Even so, I'm giving you a choice. Take the knee and give your vow right now, or go outside to a death match. Because when you lose, I'm not having you run off and join the enemy like your cowardly ass would, and if you win, I'm not wasting the fucking energy to heal you after you were given an alternative — not that you have a hope of winning."

The man snorts. "So, give my oath or die? What fucking kind of choice is that?"

"The same one we're all facing, idiot," snaps one of the witches. "Stand loyally behind this man, or die. It's the same choice we all faced, and we're fucking here behind him. If you're not with him, then you're the same as the enemy."

Pasadena wolves now surround us, word having spread, but not a single one of them protests.

"I hold your provisional oath through Lisa. She gave it to me with her dying breath. She brought you here to me to keep you safe. If you can't accept that, then get out of my fucking way, I've got a war to win."

It's too much to hope the idiot can see past his own hubris.

"Where's your challenge circle?" he asks, foolishly.

Well, *fuck*. We don't have one.

"Connor, would you and your dragon accompany me to the challenge circle?" Marcus asks.

What are you planning? We don't have a fucking challenge circle.

Should have thought of that before you fucking challenged him, Marcus retorts.

I snort. Yeah, I fucking should have.

"Choose your second," I snap at the wolf, before he can turn and trundle off behind them. Whatever Marcus is up to, he's going to have to do it fast. There's loud crunching outside, then the sound of great leathery wings groaning as a dragon takes off.

Where the fuck are you going?

To clear some grass in front of the mill. We can use the wood chips to sop up the blood, and the funeral pyres are handy for disposing of his body.

Well damn. Sometimes Marcus is a little *too much* like his father for comfort, although I'd never tell him that.

I look around, but none of my co-mates are here. The best man for this job is Sam.

"Lucas," the idiot calls out.

Two wolves step forward. One smells as bad as the idiot in front of me, the other looks at me coolly. I'm betting the latter is Lucas.

"Tyler, what the fuck have you done?" the smelly one whisper-shouts.

"Name your second," Lucas tells me. He smells of Triune, but not of Catriona's bond. So, he's given his oath to Marcus but not her.

It's enough. He will do the honourable thing by the pack if his companion loses.

"Sam," I call, both physically and over our bond.

Yeah?

I need you to come to the bunker, then we're going to the mill. I'm about to kill an idiot in a challenge.

What the fuck, dude? Marcus is going to rip you a new one. We need all the fighting wolves we can get.

Marcus and one of the dragons are clearing the land for the challenge. We don't need this fucking wolf, trust me on that. He wants a cabin for him and his pals, and fuck the witches and dragons who are sleeping in vans. An entire cabin. For four of them. At least the other fucktards had the common sense to back down when I threw it back in their faces.

Aw fuck. Do we need to warn Catriona?

Nah, the fucktard hasn't made his oath to either of them. There's something off about him.

Okay, I'm almost there.

"Where is your second?" Lucas asks me.

The door opens and Sam walks in.

"Right there," I point at him.

Lucas nods and goes over to confer with Sam. Meanwhile, the two stinky wolves are conferring.

"I don't need a private space," the newer wolf whines. "Tyler, all I need is you, and if you die for this, it will kill me."

Aw fuck. There's more to this than it seems, but I can't back down now and neither can Marcus.

"I promised to love and protect you, to cherish you above all else. I would die for you, Cain."

I approach the pair of them, and they fall silent, watching me warily.

"You've never had another alpha other than Lisa, have you?" I ask them.

Cain looks down at his feet when he answers. "I was part of pack Lunares before Sinclair took us over. His enforcers caught me with my lover and they took offence—"

He shudders and draws nearer to Tyler for protection.

"He has PTSD," Tyler says quietly. "He can't handle the communal showers. They raped the pair of them and killed his lover. He escaped that night and eventually made it to Pasadena. The irony was they were going there anyway, it was their farewell party when Sinclair hit."

Cain whimpers and buries his face in Tyler's neck.

It makes a lot more sense. The stink, his aggression because he needed to protect his mate. The other couple they invited to come with them were probably the only other wolves they trusted.

Fuck.

Matt

They've been fucking stupid in the way they handled all of this. If they'd told us, we would have done everything we could to help them. But to assume we wouldn't understand or didn't care, it's brought this whole fucking mess to a head.

Marcus, we need to change the outcome, I send to him. Then I quickly outline what was going on.

Leave it with me, I need to think about this.

"You should have come to me about this, to any of us. We can't give you a separate cabin, but we could have arranged for the pair of you to use the bathrooms at the lodge. We could have arranged for you to share a cabin with people you trust. We're all under duress here, but we're pack. We pull together, especially when shit gets bad. Now we're stuck in a position where you have to be punished, and I honestly don't know whether I can pull things back and save your life or not, because believe me, I'm stronger than you."

Cain begins to weep silently, clinging to Tyler who runs a soothing hand up and down his back while he looks at me.

"We're gay. It's frowned on a lot. We haven't exactly had a great track run in packs. Lisa left us to it, we had a lot of freedom there, we finally felt safe from persecution."

"Yeah, but you weren't safe from anything else," I counter.

Tyler nods. "We didn't know that. Now we come here, and everything is chaos, and people keep arriving that we don't know. We're supposed to take your word that Lisa gave her bond willingly to Marcus, but how do we know that for sure? How do we know he didn't take her out, offer to save her if she gave an oath, and then killed her anyway?"

My wolf surges to the surface. He's had enough of this asshole, but I can see where he's coming from. These wolves have been persecuted for a long time. They don't know who to trust anymore.

"All I can say is, we didn't force her to come here. She could have taken the pack anywhere. But when she was in trouble, she came to Marcus, the fucking son of her enemy. She wouldn't have done that if she didn't trust him on some level. Lisa loved you all deeply, that much is clear, however she was not a good alpha for the pack, and now you're all paying for it. I can't promise that Marcus will hold your hand, although I've seen him do that for men and women alike. He won't sugar-coat things, or pretend everything is fine when it's all going to shit."

Other wolves are pressing forward to listen to me.

"What I can promise is that he'll fight for you until his dying breath. He'll do everything he fucking can to keep you safe, and he'll take as many factors into account as he can. Marcus isn't infallible, goddess knows I've seen him come out with some clangers, but he's honourable. We follow the old ways in Triune, and the goddess herself has seen fit to bless us with a litter. A fucking litter. I know you all don't believe it, but my mate is about to have four pups, and she wasn't born a wolf."

There are gasps around me. Things have been so chaotic we haven't really had time to get to know them yet, nor they us.

"Catriona was born human, and became a siren towards the end of the Siren wars. I can tell you everything you were likely taught as a pup about sirens is inaccurate. I've seen the ancient pack records of what we used to do to these women. How we tortured them for our own gain, and it makes me sick to the stomach."

"How can she bear pups if she's not a wolf?" a voice asks from the back.

"Because she's the chosen vessel of three gods," Fleur's tart voice responds. "Inhale, take in my scent. You all know who I am, what I do."

There are more gasps and exclamations as people recognise the Accoucheur, now looking hundreds of years younger.

"I too have been blessed by Mara, and she has given me back my youth, and a strong wolf mate who is fated to me. You know me, you trust me, so hear what I say," she pauses, looking around the wolves gathered. "You will not find a more honourable wolf than Marcus Montgomery. You will also never find another woman like Catriona. Born human, made Siren, given a wolf and a dragon

69

form. She has been blessed by Zaya, Mara, and V'dar and is their chosen vessel."

Catriona steps into the circle then, and she glows. Not just the flushed beauty of pregnancy, she actually fucking glows. She's always stunned me, but right now she looks fucking divine.

Several wolves drop to their knees, but Catriona quickly rushes to them and begs them to stand.

"I am not a goddess. I am merely blessed by one. These blessings I am able to share with those whom I see as fit. You have all come here in terror, fleeing for your lives, many having lost loved ones. We grieve your loss with you. These are not empty words, one of my own mates was killed, and my heart will forever have a hole in it where he belongs."

There are murmurs of agreement from around the room. Fated or not, many know what it's like to lose a mate. Especially the males, as females become rarer and rarer and childbirth becomes more dangerous for them, the number of grieving males grows.

"Triune is a pack that has the blessing of the gods. If you are here, consider yourselves lucky. We may be at the frontline of the war, but while you're here, you will have all the freedoms we can provide. We only ask one thing of you — your loyalty. Help us to build a better pack, a stronger pack, a safer pack. For what we are together, is greater than the sum of our individual parts."

A hushed silence falls over the wolves gathered, even the witches and dragons are enraptured.

"I wish to give my oath to the alphas," a voice calls out.

"Aye, me too," calls another.

"And me, and my mate, and we'll vouch for our son who is underage."

Voices clamour, each one speaking over the last, all of them pledging their support. The irony isn't lost on me. In the space of half an hour, we've gone from a hysterical wolf to the Pasadena Pack pledging their loyalty, because it looks like every fucking one of them has gathered here now.

"She's pregnant," calls Fleur over the noise. "And a new wolf. You cannot all give your oaths at once, however, we can do it in groups, and you can all give proxy oaths to the council members. You're a wonderful bunch, but you're a bit fucking much all in one go."

Chuckles overtake those clamouring for acceptance.

"Before we do that, we must see through the challenge," Marcus calls, having returned.

The mood turns sombre again. Having just won the hearts of these wolves, are we about to lose them because I was impatient?

"After hearing evidence from a third party, I am willing to reduce the sentence of the challenge from the death penalty, to a life oath. This would mean the loser would give an oath of obeisance, to the pack, not just to the alphas. He would be unable to leave the pack, unless it was destroyed. Do you accept the changes, Tyler?"

Cain looks at Marcus like the sun shines out of his ass. "Say yes, you idiot," he urges his mate.

"It means you would be bound here too," Tyler warns him. "If you didn't like it, we would have to try to break our bond."

"If Tyler loses, I will also give this oath," Cain declares confidently, then looks at Catriona. "I would give it to her, though, not to any pack, but to the woman who has been blessed by the gods."

Catriona looks at him, stunned. Then gathers herself like the queen she is. "While I appreciate your fervour, I cannot accept these conditions. I may be blessed, but I am still mortal and my survival is not guaranteed. My kind are not made to bear children, and I'm about to give birth to four of them. For the good of the pack, I must insist you give your oaths to the pack, rather than to me."

Damn, she's good. She's nailed the issue right on the head. Of course, it would have been awkward as fuck for one of us to say that, but she took the bull by the horns and put it out there.

Cain sighs and nods. "Then I would like to give my personal oath to you right now," he counters.

"She will take the oaths of ten wolves," Fleur announces. "Your old betas will organise you all. The other council members can take up to thirty oaths each. Triune already has a siren and a dragon. We accept oaths from all species here. So, witches and dragons are also free to make binding promises, or their leaders may do so on behalf of their peoples. We are more than just a pack. We are a nation. We are the descendants of the dragons, those who preceded even the fae. Let no-one be turned away who genuinely seeks solace and asylum."

I go to grab her to shut her up, but then I see her face. Her eyes have rolled back in her head, and she glows like Catriona does, although not as brightly. It's not Fleur talking to us, it's Mara.

I drop to my knees as soon as I realise, wolves around me are doing the same, although I can hear some asking why we're doing it now when Catriona said not to.

Silence falls when they see Catriona kneeling too, then not a single person is left standing. Even the witches and dragons pay homage.

"The Triune Pack has my blessing," Mara says through Fleur, her voice resonant. "Especially the alpha pair and their co-mates. We have put our faith and our power in Catriona, to deliver not only you, but all who exist on this plane. We ask you to do the same, and trust in them."

Fleur turns to Catriona and holds out her hands. "Daughter, your time grows short. I have summoned your sister to come to your aid. Send only those you trust to greet her, for I would have no harm come to her. She is also V'dar's chosen vessel."

"My sister?" Catriona asks, confused, but the glow on Fleur fades.

Craig is there to catch her before her knees can do more than twitch. He holds her limp form in his arms, his face buried in her neck and breathing deeply. We all relax when he does, knowing she'll be okay.

"Put me down, you great lump. What are you thinking of?" Fleur snaps.

Yep, she's going to be just fine.

Catriona, however, is pale.

"What's wrong?" I ask her, catching her hands which are cold and clammy.

"The goddess is sending one of my sisters here."

I look at her, confused. "That's bad, because—"

"She's a siren, Matt. The only sisters I have are sirens. My human family is long dead. She also said this woman was V'dar's vessel, which means she also has a dragon. Just how well do you think we're going to be able to protect a new female dragon once the males here find out?"

Fuck, she has a point. "Connor?" I call out to him, and he strides over to us.

"We have a problem, and I've no idea how to go about this. It's a dragon thing, so I'm asking you, beta to beta. How do we protect an unmated female dragon about to arrive, from being overwhelmed and harassed by the single male dragons?"

Connor's teeth lengthen and scales appear on his skin. "Explain, and be very concise about this, Matt. If you think our dragons are dishonourable enough to rape or claim a female without her permission, then we're going to have a problem."

"Connor, she's also a siren. She's been given a dragon form by V'dar, just like Catriona. Even you reacted to her pheromones, and she was already mated to a bunch of wolves. Now imagine a stressed and hungry siren, remember what they smell like? And she's also a dragon. How well do you think your males are going to cope with that?"

"Fuck," Connor growls. "None of us are going to cope with that well. When will she arrive?"

"We don't know. Soon, from what the goddess said, but that could be today or tomorrow, or three days' time. I don't know. Who knows what "soon" translates as for someone as old as a deity."

Connor grins at me. "I'm five thousand years old, Matt. Give or take. It still means any of the definitions you gave to me. Ask me again in another five thousand."

"Matt, we need to get this challenge done," Marcus calls loudly.

Right, yes, the challenge. Why does it always seem that fifty things happen at once?

"Ok, can you go down to the gate and keep an eye out for her until I can sort something out with Dean and Marcus?"

"And miss your challenge? Not a fucking chance. I will, however, go down there as soon as it's decided. I don't need to watch the vows. You won't take long, will you?"

"Not now that I know I don't need to kill him. I'll make him submit in under a minute."

"Cocky, aren't you?" Connor chuckles.

"No, I'm an alpha who never took up the mantle. Tyler isn't even strong enough to be an enforcer. He doesn't stand a chance."

Connor looks me over, reassessing. "Alpha, huh?"

"I prefer the beta role. I like to facilitate things, negotiate, and manipulate where necessary. I leave the politics to Marcus. He hates it, but he was groomed from a young age. It's like mother's milk to him. His instinct is invaluable."

"He's that good?"

I chuckle. "Don't ever try to negotiate against him. You'll walk away with less than you started with if you piss him off. He knows exactly how to word things so you think you've got the better end of the bargain."

"But I won't," Connor voices the unspoken threat.

"Not fucking remotely."

He grins. "Duly noted, I'll warn Dean too."

"You do that if you think it will help." My answering smile is pure evil.

"Matt!" Marcus snaps.

Right, the fucking challenge. Time to cross the next thing off my to-do list. I'm sure by the time I'm done, five more things will be added. It's just how things are right now.

They say there's no rest for the wicked. I think I'll find time tonight to earn the penance I'm paying. I'm going to find my mate and do very wicked things to her, until she forgets how many mates she has.

7

CATRIONA

I f Marcus thinks he can talk me out of witnessing this, he can fucking think again. I'm a healer. My mate is going into battle. Of course I'm going to be here. I don't care what the witches say they can do to help.

Surprisingly, he doesn't even try. Clever man.

He does, however, set me up with two guards, which I can tell pisses off Jude — at least until he's included.

"Alex, I need you to go to the front gate. There may or may not be one of Catriona's sisters arriving to help her."

Alex nods and heads off at a jog, not wasting time.

Alex, I call him on the link. I'm not sure Marcus has thought to warn him any further than what he's said aloud.

Yes, Mate?

Do you understand what she is and why we need you to be there?

She's your sister.

Alex, she's a siren. She's also a dragon. I daresay, she'll also be pissed she has to come here, she'll be feeling vulnerable, emotional, and tired. What happens to a siren when she's low on energy?

Fuck.

Yes, we need to do that. Now, she's a tired siren, who has a dragon. Unmated. Can you see why she might need a little backup?

Yeah, okay, I got her back. Thanks for the heads up.

I thought you might need it, Marcus is juggling too many balls right now.

Really? I thought he was just fondling Joe's?

I can feel his snicker through the link.

Ass.

No, he fucked that, it was Joe's balls he was playing with.

I'm going to strangle him. *Alex?*

Yes, Mate?

Shut up.

I can feel his amusement — again.

Love you too, Catriona. Then his presence is gone from my mind.

He loves me? And he had to tell me right now? Men!

"Toby, Scott, you're to be with her at all times. She's so close to term, I don't want to risk her or the pups. The stress isn't good, but I think it'll be worse if she isn't on hand to heal him."

"Yes, Alpha," they respond.

It's funny to hear them call him that, but the pack is no longer the laid-back group of friends it once was. For the greater good, they all need to stick to their roles in public.

"Jude, you too. You're her guardian, make sure you've got her back. Micah?"

"Yes, Alpha?"

"Coordinate with Jude. Toby and Scott are for her health and well-being. You're her guardians. The chaos during a challenge is the perfect time for a strike if there are any more traitors here."

"Gotcha," Micah replies, heading over to Jude and lowering his head to confer with the younger shifter.

It warms my heart to see Micah taking the other guardian under his wing like this. It makes sense for them to work together. There was so much going on, it hadn't occurred to me to introduce them.

"Joe, I need you to coordinate with the enforcers, Craig is tied up with Fleur, so you're going to have to stand in his stead. Grab Stan, hell, get Travis on this too. I want you all sorting out crowd control. Just because it's not to the death, doesn't mean that people aren't going to get their panties in a twist about it."

"On it, Alpha," Joe says, heading over to the wolves in question.

Then he turns to me. "Come on, Alpha, let's get this farce over with." Marcus links an arm through mine, pulling me with him out of the bunker and onto the road.

"Want a piggyback?" Toby asks playfully.

As much as I want to take him up on it, I'm pretty sure it isn't the right time. Alpha dignity and all that rubbish.

"Knock it off, Toby," Marcus growls.

"No, you dial it back a notch. Your mate is pregnant and stressed. I don't care how stupid I have to look, I'm going to make her laugh a little."

I give him a huge smile and he returns it tenfold.

"Come here, sweetness, at least let me hold your hand and swing it like we're childhood sweethearts. Matt's going to be fine, he'll be all over this guy's ass and then we'll have to walk all the way back up."

"I can give her a lift," pipes up a voice behind them.

Turning to see who it is, my ankle twists on a loose rock, the world spinning as I begin to fall. Thankfully Scott catches one arm, and Marcus the other.

"Ow," I mutter, wincing when I try to put my weight on it. With my accelerated healing it shouldn't take long to heal up, but it's time we don't really have.

"She's pregnant, I'm not risking her on a dragon without a fucking saddle. *I* nearly fell off, and I was expecting it to be bumpy," Marcus snarls, trying to pull me along again.

The ass. I pull back, refusing to be budged until I know my foot can take the weight. Marcus tugs again, but this time Toby steps in and frees my arm from him, standing between us both. Marcus growls, his canines elongating.

"I'm here for her wellbeing, asshole. She just hurt her foot, she can't fucking walk."

Marcus looks at me, surprised. "I thought you just tripped?"

"No," I say reluctantly. "I twisted it. Give it a few minutes and it should heal up."

"But then you'll be tired again, here, take from me," he offers his hand.

"Och hen, you should take from me, given I was the cause," Connor offers. "Besides, I'm a bigger battery than they are." He smirks at the wolves who growl.

"Where's Ethan?" I ask him, and the dragon's face tightens. Did I imagine that?

"I sent him to the gate to greet your sister. I thought it appropriate given he's your mate, or might be, and she's important to you and is a dragon herself. If anyone can keep her safe and keep his hands off her, it's Ethan."

"Oh!" I exclaim, delighted. "Connor, that's so thoughtful, thank you. I forgot he wouldn't be affected."

Connor snickers. "Oh, he'll still be affected, but his dragon won't let him act on it, even if his human side is overcome. Our beasts are more loyal than our human form if there's a fated mate involved, however, if it's just a normal mate bond, our humans are more loyal than our beasts."

"Well, that's not confusing," Marcus murmurs.

"Right?" Connor says with a grin. "Come on, lass. Let me be the hero for once and give you a wee boost."

He holds out his hand to me and I take it, gently drawing from his strength. His dragon opens an eye and examines me, purring loudly in approval. The other eye opens, and he begins to preen for me, stretching his wings and his muscles, showing how well he's formed.

My own dragon stirs inside and watches, but gives no further reaction. Connor's takes it as encouragement, because he begins to hum.

It's a little too intense for me, so I quickly take what I need, forcing it down to heal my ankle, using up much more than I would healing the same injury on someone else. Then, as soon as it's done, I take a little bit more and release him.

When my eyes open and I look at Connor to thank him, the slitted eyes of his dragon look back, admiring me openly.

"Thank you, Connor and dragon. I feel much better."

"The pleasure was truly ours," the dragon rumbles through Connor's mouth. "We would be happy to fill you up at any time."

Something tells me he's no longer talking about his strength. His dragon is flirting with me, but mine has curled up and gone back to sleep, uninterested.

My mates came to the same conclusion, stepping between them and cutting off Connor's access.

"Nine is just as good a number as eight, Catriona. Isaac isn't the only one who's attracted," Connor calls.

Wait, Isaac? Still?

"Now you're exaggerating," Toby replies, a fixed smile on his face. "After what you just said, I know for a fact Isaac can't be interested."

"Oh? I think you misunderstand, Toby. Dragons won't cheat if they have a fated mate. But if they don't, they don't have any issue joining the harem of a female who already has a fated mate."

Three wolves growl loudly, while Micah and Jude look on worriedly. It isn't a threat to me, so it isn't like they can do anything about him.

"Dragon females have harems?" Jude asks, and the others stare at him, except Connor who just smiles.

"More males than females. It wasn't always the way, but yes, usually our females take on several mates. So, Catriona is a perfect dragon mate in that regard."

It's time to nip this in the bud. "Connor, I have seven wolves here, and now Ethan to consider. My dance card is pretty full already."

He grins unapologetically and shrugs. "The more the merrier."

I roll my eyes. "Come on, we need to go, I've held us up long enough as it is."

I wonder if they're making me take the longer route so I'll be late and miss it all. It wouldn't surprise me although I would think Marcus would want to be there for it.

"They can't start without us," Marcus says, almost answering my thoughts. "I might not be able to adjudicate, but I am required to start and call the battle. It's then up to the seconds to declare any protests if they don't agree with my judgement."

"So, they're all waiting on us?" I shriek, moving faster. "Why are we taking the long way?"

"Because everyone cutting through the middle of the pack lands is doing it in their wolf forms. Awkward for you because you can't shift. The ground is uneven, and I don't want them barrelling you over. The younger ones, especially, will be excited. We don't have many challenges anymore. We're not as uptight as we used to be."

"Come on," Toby urges. "Nobody is going to see us, they're already there. Let me give you a ride, I can run holding you, and it will get us there sooner."

I don't even hesitate. I'm on his back before Marcus can open his mouth in protest. We really do need to get a move along.

Toby takes off at a good pace, and the others are forced to jog to keep up with him. Even Connor keeps up with us. I expect him to walk sedately, but when I turn to watch him over my shoulder, his eyes are fixed firmly on my ass.

He's going to be trouble, I know it.

Just before we reach the bend in the road leading to the mill, Toby halts and gently lets me down. All my nipples are sensitive from rubbing against his back, and I'm already aroused. He groans and pulls me in for a fierce kiss before letting me go.

"Fuck, come on. I'm going to be hard the entire time now, especially when you smell like that."

"He's not the only one," Connor mutters, and my wolves growl at him again.

"Still not getting in," growls Marcus.

"Still not your call, pup," Connor replies.

Can they really not focus on the task at hand? "Enough," I snap. "We'll deal with this later, right now, I'm here for Matt. Let's get this sorted, then I'm going to go and lie down. If I wasn't pregnant, I'd have a glass of wine, but I think some quiet time is just what I need."

While riding on Toby's back might have teased my nipples, it's also put my back out. The pups are getting heavy, and even though I'm not showing anywhere near as much as I expect with four babies, they're still pulling my back out of alignment. Right now, it means I'm in enough pain that my movements have become stiff.

"What's wrong?" Scott asks. Of course he notices before the rest of them, he's always looking out for my well-being.

"Sciatica," I growl. "Fleur warned me about this. My joints are loosened by the hormones to allow my hips to spread for birthing. The babies are an unnatural weight pulling me forward, so my whole back is out, especially the lower parts. I'm sorry, Toby, but that piggyback with you running really didn't help it. Give it a minute or two and it should settle."

They all watch as I hobble forward. I feel like a freaking grandmother, a far cry from the wild thing who first arrived here. Although as harrowing as my time has been, I wouldn't change much of it — except I'd spend more time with Felix.

"Go ahead, Marcus. They'll look after me. We need to get this done as soon as possible, so we can move onto the next fifty things."

He gives me a small smile and a brief kiss. "Stay with them," he commands and I roll my eyes.

Didn't I just say they'd look after me? Hard to do if I leave them behind. Grouchy alpha-hole.

The look he gives me promises retribution for the eyeroll, and my outlook picks up a little, almost distracting me from the pain in my back and legs.

I am right of course, the more I walk, the more the pain settles until it's almost gone. Scott takes my elbow as we leave the road and walk across the grass to where all the wolves are gathered. There's a gap to one side, so I make straight for it. I figure there's got to be an advantage to being alpha and pregnant to boot. Nobody is going to stop me from pushing my way to the front.

Scott and Toby walk either side of me, and the other three trail us. We make quite the procession through the crowd as we approach the ring. As Marcus said earlier, the clearing is filled with sawdust which has been sprayed with water, presumably from the tanker we have. It forms a compacted surface, good for fighting and falling on, and even better for absorbing blood.

Matt and Sam stand on one side of the circle. I'm no good at distance, but it looks broad enough for two men to lie down head to toe across it. So, that would make it about twelve feet in diameter. More than enough room for the pair of them to circle each other.

On the opposite side to my men, are Tyler and Lucas, Cain hovering worriedly behind them. I grab Jude's arm and pull him close to me.

"Go ask Cain to join us, he shouldn't be alone while this is happening," I tell him.

He surprises me with his frown. "No, Alpha. I'm to stay here and protect you. Send one of the others."

Well, shit. Of course he'll say that, more fool me. I shift my weight on my feet again as my back twinges. Leaning to the side to talk to him has set it all off again, just when I thought it had settled. I try leaning to the other side, but it makes no difference, a dull ache settles in and stays. Excellent, just what I need while I stand here with everyone else, not a chair in sight, and the prospect of walking all the way back in front of me. There's no way I'm going to let Toby piggyback me again.

I've been so busy worrying about myself, I've missed half of what Marcus has said, but both men are now in the centre either side of him with their shirts off. Tyler holds no interest for me, but Matt looks amazing. He smirks when he catches me staring at him, flexing his pecs, much to the enjoyment of the witches beside me who murmur their approval.

I half expect my wolf or dragon to rise up to the challenge, but they're nowhere to be seen.

"He's one of mine," I tell the witches.

"One of?" questions one of them. "Just how many do you have?"

"Seven wolves and possibly a dragon," I tell them.

"Damn, that's a lot of cock," she says, just as there's a lull in the noise of the crowd. Her voice carries, before several people chuckle, the conversation level rising again as they all discuss that like a bunch of old hens.

"Two dragons," Connor corrects me.

"Possibly one," I say firmly.

"Then that's fucking unlucky for Ethan," Connor growls, slipping an arm around my waist and pulling me to his side.

It's all I can do not to hiss in pain as the movement makes my sciatica ping. I grab his ear and pull it firmly down to my mouth so he can hear me over all of the calls of support for one fighter or the other, but also so nobody else hears. There's only one fight scheduled here, and I'd like to keep it at that.

"You're hurting my back, Connor, please let me go before I can't walk again." I let his ear go.

Before I can dodge it, he turns, brushing his lips lightly across mine. "My apologies, Alpha," he says gently, helping me stand upright again.

Marcus is watching us from across the ring, and the look in his eyes promises retribution for Connor. If he's heard what I've just said to Connor, it'll be the dragon's death, regardless of the difference in the size of their shifted beasts.

"Stand ready," Marcus calls to the wolves.

Both of them quickly shuck their pants, shifting on the spot before anyone gets flashed too much flesh. Not that it bothers the shifters, but the witches might be another thing altogether.

Judging by the quick spate of catcalls, however, I think they're just fine. It's not lost on me there are no men with them, and plenty available wolves.

"Fight!" Marcus calls, and the two wolves leap at each other.

8

CATRIONA

It's almost over before it even starts. Matt's wolf is bigger than Tyler's, although not by a lot. While they might be evenly matched in size, it's quickly obvious Matt's skill level is much higher.

Within seconds he rolls Tyler on his back, jaw clamping around his throat.

The crowd falls silent in surprise. There's no prolonged battle, no risk of injury, they clash and it's immediately over. Only, it's not over. Why is it not over? Marcus hasn't made the call.

Just as I look up at him in confusion, he lifts his eyes from his phone and calls the match in Matt's favour.

Lucas walks into the ring. "He concedes the challenge," he says clearly, and Tyler whimpers, although he doesn't try to get up.

Matt is still holding him tightly in place, now adding a paw to Tyler's chest. Before anyone can protest further, Matt shifts, and now it's his hand holding Tyler down, in a parody of what happened inside the bunker.

"Shift," Matt orders him.

Tyler whimpers again, but does so, lying there, waiting.

"You will give your oath to the pack now," Matt commands, and Tyler nods, Cain coming to kneel beside him in the wood shavings.

"I give my life's blood oath to the Triune Pack. I will fight for them, live for them, and die for them. I go where they call me, and I serve with honour. I acknowledge them as my pack for the rest of my life and give my heart and soul in service to its members. I acknowledge Marcus and Catriona as the current alphas and I swear my oath to them and their successors, whoever they may be."

Quickly, Cain copies him.

It's all fascinating, but I almost miss Marcus' reply when the twinge in my back gets a lot stronger. I'm going to need to sit down. It's embarrassing to say the least.

"Tyler, Cain, we receive your life oaths with joy. I swear to lead you in truth, honour and justice. I will heed your advice, and protect you as my own blood. The pack grows in strength from your service and we are honoured by your loyalty. Rise now, as life members of the pack."

Matt releases Tyler, who sits up and beams at us all, as though a great weight has been taken from his shoulders.

Cain is weeping, and pulls his mate's face in for a long kiss that has the wolves whooping and catcalling.

My focus, however, is not on the celebrations in front of me. Once again, my mind is turned in on myself, but this time for a different reason. A steady trickle of fluid runs down my leg, and the pain in my back is magnified tenfold, now wrapping around the front and squeezing hard.

It's not sciatica at all.

It's a contraction.

"My waters have broken," I say in a grunt as I double over.

The witches beside me respond instantly, gathering around and holding me so I don't fall, while Jude and Micah try to fend them off, fearing an attack.

"What the fuck is wrong with her?" yells Marcus, as he pushes through them all, pulling me from their grasp and pushing me behind him. "What the fuck are you trying to do to her?"

Unfortunately, he is removing my support right before another contraction hits, and my knees buckle, sending me to the ground.

"Trying to stop that, you asshole, she's in labour," snaps one of the witches.

"She's not fucking in labour, she's—" Marcus finally turns to me, dropping to the ground in front of me, right in the puddle of fluid my body seems keen on creating.

"Catriona, baby, what's wrong?"

I grab his hands when he holds them out to me and grip tightly, squeezing with all my might. Words are beyond me, so I just hold on as wave after wave of pain hits.

When it finally releases me, I pant, looking up at him dazedly. I didn't think it's supposed to happen this fast, but what do I know? My only experience with birthing is with humans. Maybe wolves do it faster?

"Fleur, I need Fleur," I groan, as another wave hits. Oh, these are close together, too close together.

"Catriona, are the babies coming?" Matt asks from beside me.

When did he get here? I let go of one of Marcus' hands and grab onto Matt's. Tears pour down my face as I try to ride it out without screaming. This really fucking hurts.

"Sweetie?" Matt asks again, and I realise I forgot to answer him.

I can't. Breathing is beyond me, never mind speech.

I nod.

"Fuck!" Marcus yells, but there's buzzing at the back of my head. I know someone just called Fleur.

"Out of the way, musclehead. Someone get a car and bring it as close as you can, she's not walking back to the lodge like this, the contractions are too close together," one of the witches says, putting a hand on my forehead, then stroking my face.

"You in there, sweetie?" she asks, looking at my eyes.

I pant and nod, hating that I can't even speak for the pain.

"Ok, tell me when this one ends, and we're going to time it until the next one, okay?"

I nod again.

"Let's get her on her feet, walking will help relax her pelvis, and we need to get her to the road."

There are hands all over my body, helping me stand whether I want to or not. And I don't want to. It *hurts*.

"I know it hurts, Catriona, but you need to get up, we need to get you moving."

"Get out of the fucking way," snarls a voice, and then Connor scoops me into his arms, hurrying me over to the road.

The bouncing is killing me, and I beg him to slow down.

"Connor, please, it hurts," I plead.

"I know, honey, I'm going as fast as I can."

"No, that's what hurts," I grunt as the next wave hits and I realise I forgot to tell the witch. "Oooh!" I moan, unable to help it, they're getting stronger.

"Is that the next one, love?" the witch asks, looking at her watch.

"Mmmm," I respond, nodding, biting on my lip to stop from screaming out.

"She's nodding," Connor translates for me, as my men push people back.

The wolves all try to congregate around me to either see or congratulate me. Fuck, I'm still in labour, it's too early for that shit, what are they trying to do? Jinx me?

"Gah," I moan, when the contraction finally stops.

"Ok, I'm taking that as the end," the witch says, and I nod.

There's a roar of a car engine tearing down the road, but the next wave hits before I get to see it.

"Ooooh," I cry out, unable to hold it back any longer.

I can feel fluid practically streaming from me now, poor Connor is going to be soaked. My mates have given up trying to convince him to let me go. I hear the door being opened, but I'm in too much pain to pay much attention, until Connor passes me to someone on the back seat.

I look up into Marcus' chocolate-brown eyes, staring at me in concern. The witch hops in the back with us on the other side. "Gun it," she says, and the driver does so, speeding us up the lane to the pack lodge.

The motion makes me dizzy and I close my eyes, my head flopping against Marcus' shoulder when the contraction ends. I pant into his shoulder as he strokes me with his hands.

"Catriona, stay awake, honey, we need to monitor these contractions."

When the next one hits, I sink my teeth into Marcus' shoulder. He grunts, but says nothing else, his soothing strokes getting faster with his agitation.

"Attagirl," the witch croons to me, watching. "You show this fucker a hint of your pain. Let him try to push these little ones out and see if he can do it with half the grace you're managing."

Her hands are stripping my feet of my boots and socks, and as soon as they're free, she's rubbing my legs. I know she wants my pants off, but it's too cramped in the back of the car, and I don't want to flash everyone when we get out either.

When the contraction eases, I don't let go of Marcus' shoulder, I just stop clenching my jaw.

"I got you sweetheart," he tells me, not protesting at all.

The car screeches to a halt, the door flung open beside me, but another contraction hits, and this one is different. It almost feels like I'm going to shit my pants, I want to push something out, anything to stop this pain. I can't take much more of it.

This time, there's no stopping my scream, even as my jaw clamps onto Marcus' flesh. My right arm is crushed between the two of us, and I'm gripping his shirt, my left is stretched across his body, fingers clawed in the fabric on his right shoulder. But it's not enough. The gripping sensation takes hold, my wolf rises to the surface, as does my dragon, but rather than fighting, they're both there, helping and supporting me.

My left hand lets go, scrabbling for better purchase, something more satisfying to grip, as Marcus slides us across the seat and tries to get out. There are hands behind me, tugging me away from him, but I'm not letting go, it feels too good to bite him.

My fingers wrap in his hair just as the contraction peaks, and I yank on it, making him grunt again. It's not enough, not right, and I release him, my fingers clawing at his neck, searching for something. What, I don't know, but his skin isn't what I want.

His cock?

Maybe, but my fear is I'll rip it off with the next contraction and I know he kind of needs it. Still, the thought of damaging the very thing that got me into this situation is gratifying.

"Let her go," growls a voice.

"I am, fucktard, she's gripping me. That's her teeth in my fucking shoulder. I'm not removing them, if she needs to bite me, she needs to bite me."

Fuck.

I'm such a bitch, but it *does* feel good.

The hands stop plucking at me, but I don't care anymore. The overwhelming clenching hits again.

Marcus wriggles us out of the car and then leaps up the stairs two at a time. The front door is wide open, wolves lining the route to the stairwell and watching as Marcus barrels up it.

"Where the fuck is Fleur?" he's yelling at the top of his lungs as he reaches the first landing. Marcus practically leaps across it, storming up the remaining stairs to our bedroom.

Several women wait inside with piles of small cloths, of various textures, tiny outfits and all sorts of sundries newborns might need. Not one of them, however, is Fleur.

I let go of Marcus long enough to shout at them. "I need Fleur, I need to push."

Towels are laid thickly across the bed and in contrast to what we usually do there, Marcus lays me down, his hands pulling at my clothing, even as I cry out and try to latch onto him again, but he's down by my ankles and I can't reach.

A strangled cry escapes me, building in intensity as the contraction peaks, my teeth snapping at the air.

"What the fuck is she doing?" a male asks.

I can't tell who it is, my whole world consists only of the pain in my body.

"She's trying to bite my shoulder again. For fuck's sake, someone give her their flesh to chew," commands Marcus.

Instantly there's a presence beside me, a shoulder placed within easy reach. I twist, pouncing on him as I sink my teeth in, and it's only then that I taste Joe. Of course he would offer. My submissive wolf would do anything for me.

I send a surge of affection to him down the bond in thanks. His wolf rumbles an approximation of a purr as he kisses my forehead.

"Whatever you need, sweetheart," he says quietly.

There's no chance to respond, the urge is hitting again. They're now flowing so quickly together that there's no break from one to the next. My dragon sends me another surge of energy, helping me to cope with the overwhelming pain. My abdomen is like a rock and my vagina feels like someone shoved a knife in there.

Someone kneels on the bed, cold hands parting my thighs and exposing me to everyone there.

Get them out of here. I want Fleur and my mates. Everyone else goes, I send to my mates, angrily.

"Sweetie, Fleur is still out cold. You're going to have to keep one of them," Joe tells me.

Not the one that just flashed my goods to everyone else, I grumble to them, and Marcus chuckles. *The door is open, asshole, anyone walking past can get an eyeful.*

"Out!" roars Marcus no longer laughing. "Who's the senior midwife here? You stay, the rest of you, get out. This isn't a circus."

"We need to be here for the pups," one of them protests, standing her ground.

Get the fuck out of my room, the pups aren't here. We'll pass them out to you when they are. I do not need fifteen women in my room while I labour, I send across the pack link with a hint of alpha voice.

The women jump and quickly leave, Marcus restraining the one he's chosen to stay, although she fights him until he makes it a command.

It's eighteen, actually, Toby tells me, and I snarl at him.

I'm chewing on Toby next, I tell them all, but it's a moot point. The contractions are so fast, I can't bear to let go of Joe.

Pain, it's all I can think of. This is hurting far too much, something is wrong.

Goddess, I call to her in my heart. *Mara, Zaya, V'dar — I need you. Please. I need Fleur, something is wrong with the pups.*

"Catriona, I want you to start pushing with the next contraction," the woman says, kneeling between my legs. "I can see the first baby."

This can't be right, it's too early, I'm not due for another three weeks. I'm not ready, and I don't think the pups are either. We can't get them medical treatment, what if something goes wrong? My anxiety begins to skyrocket as the pain continues to increase. I thought it was supposed to plateau, but the pain is just getting sharper.

I don't know whether it's my prayer, or just very fortunate timing, but only moments later I can hear her.

"Put me down you great big oaf. I am not entering that room ass first."

She doesn't have to worry about it now, that image is firmly fixed in my head whether she does it or not. I whimper out a laugh, even as I adjust my teeth and bite Joe harder.

"What the fuck are you doing to your mate?" Fleur snaps as she walks into the room.

Whatever the fuck my wolf tells me to do, I growl at her in the link.

Fleur tries to nudge the other woman out of the way, but she's crouched between my thighs, her hands held out like she's going to catch a football.

"Keep pushing, alpha," the woman coos to me, giving Fleur a dirty look. "The head is crowning."

Fleur takes one look and turns to Craig. "Get her the fuck out of here, that's not the head, that's the ass. The baby is breech and she's going to kill the pair of them if she keeps this shit up."

Craig reaches forward, picks the woman up by the scruff of her neck and the seat of her pants and lifts her bodily out of the way, depositing her on her knees outside the door someone has opened for him.

"Come back in here, and I'll rip your head off myself," Craig growls.

The woman stammers weak objections.

"Catriona, you need to stop pushing," Fleur tells me. "I want you to pant through the next contraction while I try to turn the baby around. No wonder it was hurting honey, I'm sorry. You chew on poor Joe there until we can get this sorted.

Joe kisses my temple sweetly. "Anything for my mate," he says gently. "If it scars, you know I'm going to fucking brag about it forever."

Of course he is. Oh Joe! I should have known — he's deviously sexy, even when he's submitting.

Fleur's hands are cold as she passes them between my legs and slides one inside me. It hurts even more on top of the contractions and the increasing pressure inside my pelvis. Each contraction takes a little more out of me, and my wolf slumps, unable to give me more. My dragon isn't much better. They've been sustaining me throughout the whole thing, even though I know this labour is much faster than normal.

Well, at least what I think normal is.

Fleur's shoulder drops and it feels like she's stabbing me inside. For the first time, I don't want to bite down. I do what comes naturally and throw my head back and scream as it feels like she rips my innards in two.

The door crashes open with a thud, and a familiar figure stands there, bracketed by wild-eyed wolves and Connor who stares at her in anger.

"Just what in the ever-loving-fuck do you think you're doing to my sister?" Shay asks.

It's the final straw, the one thing I hoped for and feared the most.

Shay is here.

Alone.

Unmated.

In a house full of shifters.

They're never going to let her leave.

Everything turns white, then grey, and then a blessed blackness steals me away.

9

SCOTT

I wipe the sweaty hair from Catriona's forehead with a cloth, popping another small ice chip in the side of her mouth where it's still clamped onto Joe's shoulder. Her lips are dry and cracked, she's beginning to dehydrate which isn't good for her or the pups. I might not be the genetic father of these babies, but they're as much mine as they are my co-mates'.

Then a tiny woman comes barrelling into the room, takes stock of the situation, and sweeps over to me, shoving me out of the way.

"Are you one of her mates?" she asks on a fierce note. "Is this what you call looking after her? Feeding her ice chips when she's this dehydrated? For fuck's sake. Do you have a brain in there at all, or are you just thinking with your cock like the rest of them?"

It takes a moment for the penny to drop. I mean, I know they aren't from the same human mother, but still, I was kind of expecting them to look a bit alike. Knowing they would be different and seeing are two completely different things.

She's Catriona's sister. Catriona's *siren* sister.

They're like chalk and cheese.

Catriona's brown hair is dark with sweat and water from the washcloth I've been using to keep her cool and a little refreshed. Her normally alabaster skin looks even more pallid, and her green eyes are huge in her sunken face. This labour, despite its brevity, is taking a lot out of her.

The sister, because she hasn't given us a name yet, also has brown hair, although hers is darker. That's where their similarities end. Angry brown eyes regard me sternly beneath bangs of tight ringlets over skin the colour of sandalwood.

Despite their physical differences though, two things are absolutely clear.

Catriona's sister smells amazing, although nothing could entice me from Catriona, I can understand how the sirens of old were so hard to resist. I thought it was just my fated mate luring me in, but there's something about the scent of a siren that has my wolf lifting his snout, before he realises it's not *his* siren.

She also smells like a dragon. Now I've been around them enough, I know what to scent for. It's not a dragon on her, it's *her* dragon. So she's got something going on like Catriona, although I can't smell a wolf in her at all.

"Not the sharpest tool in the shed there, are you, sweetie?" she asks in a saccharine voice, when I delay for far too long.

"She can't die," I tell the woman. "I don't know what to do, but we can't let her die. She's my mate. I can't let her die."

The furious woman's face softens.

"She's not going to die, we're not going to let her. But, we do need to get some energy into her. There's a way for her to take some from you, is that right?"

"You can't do that?" I ask her.

"No, sweetie. It's not how sirens work. We fuck guys until they come inside us, and we get the energy from their release," she explains patiently.

I snort a laugh. "No, I mean, I knew that. We've done that. It's just the gods gave her a wolf and a dragon, and they help with her energy too. I thought your dragon might help you, or that you've also been gifted with the ability to do it."

The woman's face turns furious again as she turns and glares at Connor by the door. "He's not my fucking dragon, I don't care what he says."

When I look at Connor, my hackles rise. It's not the man looking back at me, it's the dragon. Although he's in his human form, the pupils of his eyes are vertical slits, and a smattering of red scales form a half-mask on his face, making him look like he's at a costume party.

Connor is barely holding his shit together, and if he loses it, then my mate could be hurt.

Before I can think better of it, a growl rips from my throat and my wolf rushes to the surface.

"Get your fucking dragon under control, or get out of here, I won't have you harming my mate," I snap at him.

"And I'm not leaving my fucking mate alone with a bunch of wolves who won't take no for an answer," he snarls back.

Ouch. I wasn't here for that bit, but I've heard the story by now from a shame-faced Matt. He sat us all down and explained what had happened. Then he told us what the goddesses had said before we had the chance to rip his head off and go after Marcus.

I know they were compelled, that they didn't have a say in the matter, but it doesn't make it any easier to hear they claimed her without her consent. It might not have been rape, but it was a denial of her will when it came to who she ended up bonded to. I'm glad she nailed them in the balls and stabbed them with glass. If I'd been there, I'd have ripped their fucking heads off.

It also doesn't make it forgivable.

"Shut the fuck up, the pair of you. I'm trying to turn the baby around, and I need to concentrate," Fleur snaps. "Craig, if they start shit up, you can toss them out too."

Her gaze fastens on the stranger. "You, young miss, had better get your head together. Get over your prejudices, your fears, and your desires. Right now, you're here to serve her, are you not?"

The woman nods.

"Then help her. Sort out some power for her, I'm busy, and she's fading."

The tiny woman stiffens, looking desperately at Catriona, before casting her eyes across the group.

"You," she demands, pointing at Ethan. "Come and give your mate your power."

Ethan looks like a deer in the headlights as we all growl at him. On the one hand, it's got to be his greatest desire, on the other, his worst fear.

"I'm not her mate," he says in a broken voice.

"Then what the fuck are you doing in here? Get out, this isn't some cheap peep show," she snarls.

"He's her potential mate," Marcus says, stepping forward. "V'dar has asked Catriona to consider taking him as her mate. They're fated."

"Ah, here he is. The fucking alpha that got her tangled in this mess in the first place, and now you're advocating yet another mate for her. Well done all round there."

Catriona is plucking feebly at her arm as the woman continues to snap and growl at all of us, and I've had enough.

"Get the fuck out," I tell her.

The woman rounds on me with fury in her eyes, but it's nothing compared to what's going on inside me.

"I don't give a fuck who you are to her, you don't get to waltz in here like a fucking tornado when she's in this much pain, and cause her even more by attacking us. Either pull your head out of your ass, or get the fuck out of this room until she's well enough to deal with your shit."

Her jaw snaps shut.

"I haven't slept in three days," she says quietly. "The goddess showed me a vision, different to this, where I watched her die. You were all standing around like this, doing nothing."

Liquid brown eyes look up sorrowfully at me.

"I have exactly two sisters left. She's one of them. I've had over a hundred. And I had thirty daughters. It's just the three of us left. Do you know what it's like to lose someone you're bonded to?"

I nod, and her eyes widen. "Our brother, Felix, one of Catriona's mates. He was killed by a vampire in an attack by the Montgomery Pack. I know."

"I've lost over a hundred and thirty, I'm not adding her to the list."

I nod again. "Neither are we. Tell us what to do."

"I'm Shayla," she says, hesitantly holding out a hand to me.

"Scott. I'm not going to inundate you with names, I meant what I said, tell us what to do."

"Sippy cup, straw, something, keep those fluids up to her. If you have any healers, get them in here to deal with the pain. We don't do well with drugs. And big guy," she says, turning back to Ethan. "I don't give a fuck if you're mated or not, if you care, come donate."

Ethan steps forward and kneels beside her. Catriona shakes her head, but Shayla gets up in her face.

"You're not fucking leaving me. Whatever is going on with him, we can sort later, right now, you need to survive this birth, you need to save your baby."

"Babies," I tell her, when nobody else does. "There are four of them."

Shayla gapes at me, then rolls her eyes. "Of course there are fucking four of them, because you can't do it like anyone else, can you, Kat? You have to show us all up and save the world while you're at it."

Catriona grunts weekly, her jaw still locked on Joe's shoulder. It has to hurt, but he looks like he's in fucking heaven. Lucky bastard. I'd give anything to be doing something practical like that for her.

I head over to the door, opening it to the waiting women outside. "See if any of the witch healers can come and help, it's not going well and she's fading. We may need a roster of people willing to donate strength to her, and we need something to get her to drink from. Sippy cup, travel mug, straw. Preferably something that we can't spill easily."

One of the women nods and dashes downstairs. The others stand there primly, holding onto the wraps and cloths that they had ready, their disapproval clear on their faces.

I shrug. "If the accoucheur herself is fine with this, what reason do you have to gripe?"

I turn back to Fleur, because she's been entirely too quiet through this, it doesn't inspire me with confidence. When I walk around the bed to see her face, her eyes are closed and her face is ashen while she frowns in concentration.

Sidling up to Craig, I nudge him with my elbow and jerk my head in Fleur's direction, raising an eyebrow in question.

"It took a lot out of her. She's still not recovered," he says quietly. "She'd only just come to when someone came in calling for her. I had to hold a mug for her to drink water, feed her a sandwich piecemeal and help her to the bathroom before we came. I'm worried about my mate."

I slap a hand on his shoulder in camaraderie, we both fucking are.

Within minutes, there's a quiet tap at the door, all while Catriona is still trying to hold back her screams as Fleur manipulates the babies. I open it to see the woman who ran off. She shoves a travel mug in my hands. I can smell it's not water and look at her questioningly.

"Electrolyte drink," she tells me. "Better than water, if she's losing amniotic fluid, she'll need the salts. One of the healers is coming, they've gone to fetch her. I've got some crackers and cheese here if she'll eat them. Jude and Micah are organising a roster. Most of the dragons insist on being first."

"That's fantastic, thank you. Put the first two people on the roster on alert, and tell everyone else to stand down. As we call one in, put the next one on alert, so we've always got two primed to go, and the others aren't sitting nervously waiting."

"Yes, sir," she tells me, stepping back, before hesitating.

I wait.

"We're behind you all, you know that, right? She may not be my mate, but my fate is as tied to hers as yours is. We're all here, hoping, waiting, praying. The pack is here, sir. For you, and for her."

My heart swells, my eyes watering.

This.

This is what a pack should be.

Not the vying for females, or power or political bickering. This sense of camaraderie, coming together and supporting each other. An extended family. It's all a pack was ever meant to be. A source of love, support, and encouragement. A haven. Triune is slowly becoming the kind of pack every wolf dreams of, and we're doing it together.

10

CATRIONA

E than stares at me helplessly, his dragon peering through his eyes, worried and humbled by what is happening to my body.

Silently, he holds out his hand, and I can see him waiting for the rejection. I don't hesitate to accept it, immediately drawing on him.

In an instant, I regret it.

I thought I'd hit the plateau, that place where the pain is just so overwhelming the brain switches off from it. But it seems I was just slowly passing out instead. With every second, as I pull more energy into me, my awareness expands. I can feel the pups squirming, Fleur's hand in my channel, stretching me way beyond my comfort zone.

And pain.

All the pain I felt earlier comes rushing back, acutely increasing my discomfort as my body wrenches itself apart trying to get these babies out.

I can feel it in my lower back, where it feels like I'm lying on a bruise, have a muscle cramp, and need to poop all at the same time. Shayla sits beside me, stroking my hand and feeding me chips of ice until Scott comes over with a travel mug and holds it to my mouth, gently prising my jaw from Joe's skin.

It's as though the ice chips never happened. I can feel the moisture entering through my membranes before I even swallow it. The skin on my face feels less tight, my throat less raw, and I can hear it burbling happily down my gullet when I swallow. It tastes tangy and bitter with a hint of sugar.

"Electrolytes," Scott tells me when he sees my surprise.

Damn, apparently I needed that.

"More," I whisper hoarsely when the straw makes a disgusting slurping noise, indicating the thing is empty.

"Not yet, missy," Fleur tells me. "I don't want to be fighting a full bladder while I'm turning these babies, and I will not be impressed if you piss all over me."

She gives me a wink to make me realise she's kidding. I'm quite sure some of the fluid that's been pouring out of me has been urine, and she's just too nice to bring it to my attention. Fleur has been doing this for a very long time. She knows exactly what a delivering mother needs. Even an odd-ball case like my own.

"Ok, change of plan," Fleur announces. "I've got the bumwards one out of the way, and one of the buggers facing the right way around is coming out first. He's already crowing sweetie, so when I say push, you give it your fucking best, alright?"

Ethan flops to the side, making me realise I was still drawing on him. Feeling frightened, I let him go and he falls backward on the floor with a goofy grin on his face.

"Someone see to that," Fleur commands, tapping my thigh to get my attention. "Got enough juice to do a few pushes, Alpha?"

I have no idea, but I nod anyway. My body clenches and Fleur tells me to push. So, I push.

I've got Shay's hand on one side, and Joe's on the other. There's no shoulder for me to chew this time, but I no longer want it. I want to push this baby out. The third time I bear down, there's a shout from the far end of the bed where my mates have gathered to watch, except for Ethan who's sitting against the wall, watching me bemusedly.

The door to the room opens, and two women come in. One moves beside Joe and places a cool hand on my head before she begins to chant. Quickly, the pain is numbed, although I can still feel the tension in my uterus. I can also feel Fleur as she reaches inside me again to line up another baby.

Off to the side, the other woman has my baby on a bench, rubbing his limbs as he screams lustily, declaring his dissatisfaction with the whole process. She professionally checks him over, then wraps him up and hands him over to Matt who stares down at the small bundle in wonder.

"I have a son," he whispers, and my eyes prickle. I can feel his awe through the bond, and the love he has for his son is overwhelming.

I look up at the woman who has given me enough relief to be able to enjoy this part, even as my body clenches down hard again. "Thank you," I whisper.

She nods. "I'll be back in an hour if you need more. It will wear off. I won't go far, just downstairs to the living area," she tells us all.

My men beam at her, thanking her as she passes.

"Look what you did, Catriona," Joe says, kissing my cheek. "You made a miracle pup, you clever thing you."

I giggle at him, which was probably the point, as his brown eyes twinkle back at me.

"You had a baby," Shay says, looking at me in awe. "A little tiny you. The first male siren to be born!"

Well. I hadn't thought of it like that.

I grunt as my body contracts again, stealing the air from my lungs even though it doesn't hurt. Damn, I'd hoped that getting rid of the pain would deal with that, but it's just a muscular reaction after all.

"Ok, Catriona, push, sweetie, we've got the second one," Fleur tells me.

I give it everything I have, but it's not enough. Even I can tell the baby didn't move. Fleur gives me an assessing gaze and then looks around the room.

"Toby, Alex, give her some juice, your girl is flat again."

Matt looks at me in concern, but I just give him a smile, looking at our baby and grinning wider. I don't need to ask them how they know who the Dad is, even I can tell that he smells a bit like Matt from all the way over here.

Toby shoves his hand into mine, and Alex pulls Joe off the bed and takes his place, stroking my cheek before he kisses it, holding his lips there while I draw from them both at the same time.

"Push, Catriona," Fleur tells me again.

It's hard to do that while still drawing from two mates at once, so I stop pulling from Toby, although I still hold his hand tightly.

On my other side, Shay has a cloth and is patting it on my brow, quietly telling me how amazing I am, and encouraging me to keep going.

It's only then that I realise I'm groaning loudly as I push. I feel Alex wobble a little and release him, quickly drawing from Toby.

Joe, I send, unable to stop groaning to speak. *Catch Alex.*

Joe moves quickly, grabbing his packmate and guiding him over to lean against the wall.

There's a loud squawk, and my second son exits my body to a chorus of pleased adult male cries. I don't even need to scent him, the shock of thick, black hair pronouncing him Sam's. He soon accepts his son with trembling hands, smiling down at him and stroking his cheek. The tiny face turns to Sam's finger, latching on and sucking hungrily.

"Well, you'll have no problem feeding that one," the woman who examined him announces. She passes a large bucket to Fleur, who sets it aside, rubbing my belly.

"Let's see if we can't get this backwards boy out, he's in front of the last one," Fleur tells me and I nod, flinching when she puts her hand back inside me. I felt that. The spell must be wearing off a little.

Fleur pats my leg, nodding, letting me know she noticed. Her brow furrows as she concentrates, then she leans back and smiles.

"Much easier now we've got some room to play," she tells me.

My body clenches, but she doesn't have to tell me what to do. I bear down, pushing my son out. I can see Fleur more clearly now that the marquee that was my belly has deflated some. She's pale, paler than I'd like. If I had more energy, I'd give it to her, but as it is, I don't know if I can get this baby out.

I pant between contractions, now that the blockage has been removed, the pressure is so much less, I can actually labour properly. My wolf and dragon lie limply inside me, they've already given me their all.

I squeeze Toby's hand tightly and he nods, he's ready. I draw down on him again until I can tell he's getting wobbly too, but Joe is already there, helping him before I can even tell him what's happening. He smiles at me then goes to the door, bringing one of the dragon males in with him.

It's Isaac.

"It's the least I can do," he tells me when I glare up at him. "Please, at least let me offer this as reparations. Every single female wolf here has chewed me out. Most of the male ones too, to be honest. I'd like a second chance."

I nod and take his hand, pulling hard and fast, drawing as much as I can from him in one huge gulp, before releasing him. I'll take his energy, but I don't want to hold onto him any longer than necessary.

"Fucking hell," he whispers, as he gets unsteadily to his feet.

Joe shepherds him to the door, mumbles something to the people outside and escorts another dragon in. He eyes Shay with interest until she growls at him, then he just grins and averts his gaze, but it's obvious he's still noting everything she does.

I'm distracted by the mini-tableau long enough for my third son to slide from my body. I was pushing without even realising it, although by my sudden need for air, apparently I was holding my breath.

Fleur scowls at the screaming baby. "Kind of fitting that the baby holding everything up, the one that wanted to come out ass first, is the alpha's son," she says tartly.

"An asshole from an asshole, huh?" Shay quips, and I giggle.

Every male in the room, including the three dragons, turns to look at me, while the wolves all give Marcus a hard time. He doesn't care, tears are pouring down his face as he watches his son get cleaned up, weighed, measured, and bundled into a diaper and a warm wrap before being passed to him.

"Two alpha sons," Fleur tells me, nodding approvingly.

"What?" I ask her, as I rest. I still have one more son to go, and then the afterbirth.

"Matt's son is also an alpha, you can smell it on the pair of them. They'll either bond closer than the rest, or fight like cats and dogs."

Well, there's something else to worry about. Awesome!

I look at the end of the bed to realise that there are no more expectant fathers. This last baby is Felix's. My heart aches that he's not here for this, that I won't get to see the wonder on his face as his son takes his first breath.

Fleur rubs my belly hard, making the uterus contract a little more each time, forcing the baby down to the birth canal. I grab onto the dragon who has been watching me this whole time, his back to the business end of things as he sits on the edge of the bed.

"An honour to serve, alpha," he says quietly. I nod, and begin drawing from him. Unlike Isaac, I take it a little slower, and stop a little sooner. I release him, and jerk my head for him to go. Hopefully that's the last donor I'll need to take from, I don't want to leave the pack and their allies weak.

"Ready, Catriona?" Fleur asks me. When I nod, she gives my thigh a tap. "Good, on the next contraction then. Let's meet this last little man."

Shay wipes the hair back from my face again, while Joe holds onto my other hand. The two of them have been wonderful for this stage of the labour, and I'm ready for this to be over. I want to hold one of my sons, and I can see that the other three won't be coming near me any time soon, my men fussing and crooning over all of them.

Sam has his pinkie finger firmly ensconced in his son's mouth. The baby sucking and slurping away at it and making increasingly disgruntled noises. Looks like I might get to hold one after all, he's going to need to be fed, and soon.

My body tenses. "Here we go," mutters Fleur, already looking down.

"Well," she says after a pause. "This one isn't going to be as fast. He's got a fucking huge head. I'm guessing he's the largest of the litter."

I look up at her, alarmed.

"Don't stress, alpha, you've been through a lot already and delivered three fine sons. This one's just going to take a little longer is all."

The urge to bear down strikes and I start pushing, but even I can feel that nothing is happening.

"Get her some juice, and get some volunteers. She's going to need a bit of help with this one."

Scott brings me the cup with more electrolytes, and another dragon appears by my bed. I don't know his name, and he blushes furiously as he sits there, also facing the head of the bed and not where Fleur has discreetly draped a sheet over my nether regions.

I suck down energy like water into sand. It filters in and disappears to goddess knows where in my body. The spell is wearing off and I can feel the pain begin to build again, but we're nearly done. The afterbirth is supposed to be a lot easier than the baby, so I shouldn't need too much, right? When I've taken as much as he can safely give, I release his hand and he wobbles from the room, only to be replaced by another dragon, and after him, a third.

By the time the third one is done, I'm ready, and in a lot more pain than I'd anticipated, but I'm bearing down again and Fleur is counting me through the contractions. Making me push for ten seconds at a time, even when my body just wants to do it continuously and not pause.

"Stop it," she snaps, giving my thigh a whack when I fail to take a break.

"I can't, the pressure is too high, he's stuck," I whine.

Fleur runs her finger around my opening, sighing. "He really fucking is. I'm going to have to try and guide him back inside and see what's going on. I don't like the feel of this, his positioning is off."

My body bucks and rebels when it feels the baby going back inside at Fleur's gentle insistence. It's more her pushing from the outside than anything else, and it hurts like hell, as well as making me nauseous.

The baby doesn't want to wait, surging back down the birthing channel as soon as she pauses. Fleur looks up at me and sighs.

"I'm going to need to make a small tear. I want you to pant, not push, until I say so, alright?" She turns to Craig behind her. "Bring back the witch, will you, love? She's going to need a little pain relief with this."

11

CATRIONA

Fleur unrolls a packet of tools that I didn't notice earlier, goodness knows where she had them stored. She sets out a needle laced with thread in a shallow bowl, a pair of curved scissors and some bandages that she soaks in a solution that makes my nose twitch before I sneeze.

She looks up at me, alarmed. "If you need to do that, get it out of your system now, before I do the episiotomy, otherwise this baby is going to shoot out of you like a fucking cannonball and you're going to tear like there's no tomorrow. If the alcohol annoys your nose, don't breathe through it."

She puts a small scalpel into the dish with the needle and thread, and my stomach lurches, but my muscles contract before I can do more than moan.

"Pant, Catriona," Fleur tells me.

It's fucking hard work, not pushing when all of your instincts are telling you to.

The witch rushes in, straight to my head where she makes contact and chants again. Immediately my body relaxes, the strain easing from my muscles, except those clenching and trying to expel the baby.

Fleur looks up at me. "Can you feel that?"

There's a vague sense of pressure, but nothing else, so I tell her that as I prepare to pant again. I can feel it coming more clearly now that the pain isn't interfering so much.

"Alright," Fleur says, dropping the bloody scalpel back into the dish. I hadn't even felt her do it.

"On the next contraction, I want you to push, but not as hard as you have been, he's not stuck now, and I've no desire to be taken out by a flying baby," she warns me.

I giggle just as the contraction hits, and there's a shifting sensation inside me right before Fleur lunges forwards, breathing heavily and catching the baby.

"I said don't push hard," she growls at me, as she puts him on my belly and begins rubbing his limbs vigorously. The baby isn't crying.

One of the other midwives comes in, and starts chafing his legs while Fleur massages his arms and his belly. His skin is a purplish colour, much darker than the other babies, and there's a thick vernix on his skin, unlike the other three.

Fleur leans forward, covers the baby's mouth and nose with her own, and does a gentle puff with her cheeks. I can see his chest rising and then falling as the air comes back out. But then it rises and falls again, and again, before he lets out a lusty bawl that has all of us letting out laughter choked with tears.

This baby was almost united with his father!

I can't help it. It's all been too much and I start to cry. I'm not alone. Shay is hugging me, her own tears dripping on my face, while the other woman takes him away and sorts him out. Fleur bends over me, her arm rising and dipping, and a strange tugging sensation makes me want to move. I don't dare. Although I'm a shifter and it should heal quickly, I'm also a siren who doesn't, and I'm low on juice after giving birth to the four pups.

Just as a snick announces that Fleur is finished, the next contraction hits and I'm overwhelmed with that sensation of needing to push. I look down at her, and she nods, so I start pushing.

"Good, good, a few more seconds— okay, now rest. You're doing great, Catriona. I think the rest of it should come out on the next one. Ready? Here we go, push, push, push, push—. Well done. Okay, rest. Let me take a look at this and make sure it's intact."

She plops something large and purplish into the bucket and takes it over to the corner, where the other midwife joins her. The two of them paw and prod at it, while I lie there, wondering what is going on.

It's not long before she comes back, and Joe comes over with her. I hadn't even realised he'd left my side. I'm too tired to keep track of anything anymore.

"It's all there, nothing to worry about," Fleur tells me, beaming. "You're done, alpha. Now we just need to give these boys a little feed and then you can all rest."

She fusses around my nether regions a bit longer, I see several reddened towels being swept away out of sight, before she presses a large wad of something against me, and then tugs some underpants up my legs.

"I'll come and give you a bath later, but that should do you for now while your uterus shrinks again. It's done a great job of making these gorgeous wee babies."

Carefully, Joe passes me the last baby, Felix's baby, and it's not until I hold him that I realise how tiny they all are. Okay, I know people say newborns are tiny, but these boys really are. My breast is like a small pillow for them, and the boy I'm holding isn't much larger than my spread hand.

"How much do they weigh?" I ask, wondrous.

"About four pounds each for the first three," the other lady says. "Almost five pounds for this wee squirt here."

"Little squirt?" asks Toby, incredulous. "There's nothing tiny or liquid about him."

The midwife laughs. "Well, compared to a human baby, these are all extremely tiny, it's why our pregnancies are much shorter. Also, the amniotic fluid had bottled up behind his big head, I don't know if you noticed, but he basically surfed his way out, he came out on a squirt of fluid, that's why he moved so fast."

Alex snickered. "Maybe we should call him that until we can choose his name?"

"*His* name?" I look around at the three new dads who haven't relinquished their sons yet. "We have to name all four of them."

Three guilty-looking wolves peer up at me, and I'm blown away. "You've named them, without me?" I ask, plaintively, and Shayla sits up straight with a growl.

"No, we haven't," Marcus says clearly, stepping forward. "We have names that each of us prefer for our sons, but we haven't spoken to you about them yet. I thought we'd have another week. It's been so chaotic, I haven't had a moment with you to talk about it. It's something I want to share only with you, the mother of my son."

I scowl at them all. "Alright, then let's hear it," I challenge them.

Matt sits at the end of the bed, just out of reach and smiles beatifically at me. "I know this sounds like a weird name, and you might think it's hippy and out there, but I've always wanted a son called River. Of course, I'd have been just as delighted with a girl called River, but I hoped for a son."

River.

I don't hate it.

I'm not sure if I love it, though.

Matt's grin fades, but I refuse to pretend to like it to save his feelings. These boys are going to be stuck with the names we choose for the rest of their lives. It's not something you just randomly choose on a whim.

The other two hesitate, seeing I'm not gushing over what Matt wants. I can almost feel them calculating whether or not to go with their initial choice, or throw something out there for me to reject so they can work on their preferred name later.

"I don't know how I feel about it," I tell them, exasperated. "I need time to think about it. Time I would have had if you'd told me about your preferences beforehand. I'm not just going to drink the Kool-Aid because it's there. River. It's a nice enough name. I'll think about it. Now, stop fucking around and tell me what you think our sons should be labelled for the rest of their lives."

My last point makes them startle. I knew they hadn't fucking considered it.

"Dane," says Sam, bobbing up and down with his son who is really starting to complain.

"Bring him here, and I'll trade you out for Squirt."

Hesitantly, like he thinks I'm going to cheat and keep them both, Sam lowers his son to me, before scooping up Squirt.

"We're not fucking calling him Squirt," Marcus growls.

"We are until a name has been chosen," I tell him.

"Here, let me help, Alpha," Fleur says, helping me lift the loose shirt they'd put on me at some point. "I'm going to put him there, and I don't want you to help him. The sooner he works out where this is by himself, the better he'll feed."

I've read about this, but I think we've left it too long. My son roots around a bit with his nose and then lets out a genuinely distressed wail. Colostrum begins to soak through my shirt on one side, while on the side near my baby, it runs down my breast. He can obviously smell it, and it only makes him fuss more. Either way, he's not able to move any closer to it, and he's starting to really work himself up.

"Alright," Fleur concedes almost instantly, and I look up at her in surprise. "There's a difference between teaching him, and torturing him. He's too tired to try it this time, so we're just going to give him the good stuff and then try again next feed. It'll also introduce your scent to them properly. I want you doing at least one feed every day for each of them. It helps with bonding."

She helps the baby attach, and as he begins to suckle, I gasp, my uterus seems to contract in time with the pulls of his mouth.

"Yep, that's going to help too," Fleur says, waving in the general direction of my groin. "Come on, let's not waste the good stuff on the other side, you might as well feed the other ones."

With a little help from pillows and eager fathers, all four babies are attached to either my breasts or my dugs. The sensation is quite distracting. Nothing like when my mates have suckled on them that's for sure.

"Dane isn't bad either," I tell them in the following silence, as everyone watches them feed.

All eyes turn to Marcus, who is yet to put his choice out there. "Carter," he says, simply. "It was my mother's maiden name, and I'd like to remember her, whether it's his given name or middle name, I'd just like it."

I let that one roll around on my tongue a bit.

"Dane was my younger brother," Sam tells me. "He got shot by hunters when he was twelve. We managed to chase them off, and bring his body home before they could skin it."

I shuddered. Okay, I think those are actually two good names then. Three, I guess.

"River, Dane, Carter, and Squirt," I try out loud. "It has a certain ring to it."

"We're not fucking calling him Squirt," Marcus reiterates, but I ignore him.

There's a gentle tapping at the door. I try to feel who it is through the pack link, but I haven't got my head around all of them yet.

"Jordan," Matt says to me. "He's excited about something."

Everyone looks to Fleur who shrugs her shoulders. "Don't look at me, it's Catriona's call. It's her body on display."

I think about it for a moment. Nudity isn't a thing for shifters, although it's something I still struggle with, seeing them shift back and forth in front of me. It's not something I've had to face yet, but I know it will be. I might as well start as I mean to continue, and at least if it's just Jordan, then it's one more wolf I'll be semi-comfortable around.

"Let him in," I tell them.

"Wait—" Matt says, just as the door opens wide.

It's not *just* Jordan.

It's Jordan and several other wolves.

"We have a present for Alpha Catriona in celebration of the first litter of the pack, in fact the first litter of any pack for hundreds of years," one man says.

"That's Ben, he's Jordan's second in charge," Matt explains.

And his fucking interpreter, Marcus adds across the bond.

I wonder what the hell he's talking about, until Jordan opens his mouth and starts talking.

"Thir nae go'na wunt t'bee apirt," he says in a thick Scottish brogue.

I look helplessly at Marcus who looks like he's trying hard not to laugh.

Ben smiles at us. "All they know is being together. It's likely they will fuss if made to sleep apart. We've made you a cot large enough to accommodate all four of them for several months. At least until you can get them settled a bit."

My eyes water. I'd been worried about that, where they'd sleep, and here were these wolves who went out and did something without being asked.

Swiftly, the men bring in several panels and start assembling what I assume is going to be the cot. At one point, Jordan ducks outside and returns with a tiny grey mattress with yellow ducklings scattered across the fabric. It's dropped into the cot, and then a woman comes in and starts making it up with linen.

When they all step back, there's a beautiful wooden cot with wooden slats along the sides to let the air through, stained a dark colour like antique wood, and made up with pale green sheets and blankets. For now, however, once the boys have finished feeding, they're settled on top of it all, side by side like little bananas in a bunch, while I pull my shirt back down and try to look remotely presentable.

There's no way I'm getting out of bed to look, but what I can see from the bed looks stunning.

"Thank you," I tell them, with tears pouring down my face. "I was so shocked at how fast the pregnancies are, and I've felt so underprepared. You've taken a load off my mind, all of you."

The workers beam, before giving me half bows and leaving as quickly as they arrived.

"Now miss, let's get you some food, and then you need to rest," Fleur commands.

"You too, mate," Craig growls, stepping forward from the corner.

He was so out of the way, I'd forgotten he was here. Well, he's seen me pretty much naked now, so there's one more wolf in this pack who's seen me bare it all. Oddly enough, I'm not as disturbed by that as I thought I would be.

"You go eat," Shay pipes up. "I've got her."

But Fleur is stubborn, wanting to see me fed and cared for before she looks after her own wellbeing. In the end, between Shay and Craig, they have her bundled out of the room and away for a meal, while I'm left with my babies, my mates, and Ethan.

He steps forward now and bows low. "I should go now. Thank you for letting me stay, for allowing me to help a small bit."

I give him a weak smile and a nod. I don't know what to do about him, but I know I'm not going to think of it tonight.

Shay quickly returns with a plate of simple sandwiches, Fleur's orders, and my mates fuss around me, propping me up with pillows to allow me to eat.

As soon as I'm done, Marcus lowers me to the mattress and then crawls on it beside me.

"Get some rest, mate. We'll look after the babies, and you too. At least one of us will be with you at all times now."

I don't know whether to kiss him or kill him for that proclamation, but I don't get to dwell on it. Exhausted, my eyes close of their own accord.

12

Sam

G ate duty is important, but it is also boring as fuck. Still, they all took their turns rotating through it, ensuring those going out for groceries and supplies didn't bring back anything extra — under duress or not.

Now the Pasadena wolves have at least sworn by proxy to one of the council members we can be surer of their allegiance, but the witches and dragons have their own agendas. None of them are sworn to the pack, although they can hardly be expected to. Just the fact the three species are living together on the same site and cooperating is unusual enough.

There has to be a better way to do it, I'm just not sure how. As it is, we're all crammed together in buildings not meant to hold so many people, although with the help of the witches and dragons, the pressure is gradually easing.

Two days ago, Marcus approached John Davis, our neighbour to the northeast, about buying his land. He'd already mentioned selling up to Marcus a while back, but we hadn't been in a position to check it out and we certainly had no need for the extra space.

When he came to talk about it, we'd had to pose as a commune-come-cult. He'd been surprised by how many people we now had living here and their cramped conditions, and had promised to consider the offer sooner than originally planned.

I know his crop last year didn't bring in as much money as he expected, and given his age and his children's lack of interest, the small farm was going to go to waste. It's prime land and exactly what we need. The question will be timing. If the market rates give him enough to retire from this crop, the land could soon be ours. We have the money for it.

The best news is word has gotten out we're looking to expand, and now our neighbour on our southwest side has started talking about selling us the land there. The damage done to his crops by 'some drunken kids' means he's more open to the offer than he would have otherwise been. Although we could get the land for a song, it wouldn't be right to take advantage of it, when it was the attack on us that caused it in the first place.

Several of the Pasadena representatives at the pack meeting had objected to paying a fairer amount, but were overruled. Marcus is right, Lisa had been far too soft.

I stifle a yawn against the back of my hand, and a couple of the guards along with me snicker.

"Another all-night orgy?" one of them asks.

I chuckle. "I wish. More like my turn on the feed rotation. Having some of the females helping out as wet-nurses has really helped, but I still had to get up and change the boys and hand them over to be fed."

This time, the smiles are more indulgent than salacious.

"So, who's on tonight?"

I give them a grin. "Not me, that's for sure."

We all laugh together.

"Hey, Sam, heads up." One of the younger wolves is actually paying attention, something none of the rest of us are doing. I need to set a better example, Sinclair is dead, but Alistair is an unknown quantity. Who knows what kind of attacks he prefers.

A large convoy of vehicles starts coming into view from around the bend, slowly making their way up the slope towards us. We've been so busy fucking around, none of us heard them approaching.

"Are we expecting anyone?" someone asks.

"No, we're not. Alright, those of you staying in view, form up, the rest of you, out of sight," I order, and wolves scatter, only a handful staying in sight, well inside the property line.

Marcus, I send down the link.

Yes, Sam?

Have you heard from anyone? I've got a convoy of cars coming. It wasn't your father's style to be so blatant, but I don't know what Alistair might do.

That makes two of us, I'll put us all on battle alert, Dean and I are on our way, keep us posted.

Battle alert, stand-by for instructions, I send to all the wolves in my link.

As a member of the council, around thirty wolves have sworn to me rather than to Marcus, until we can work out what the pack structure will be.

Two dragons step out from amongst the trees, startling us all.

"What are you doing here?" I ask them.

"We were out jogging, Dean sent us down here. He thought it might be handy to have two guys who can torch the cars if necessary."

Huh. Why hadn't I thought of that?

"That's actually a good idea."

"Yeah, Dean's going to talk to Marcus about assigning one of our guys on gate patrol with you guys. That way we can talk through our magic to the rest of the dragons if necessary."

I nod. "I keep forgetting to include you in my plans, because I'm not used to having you on call."

The dragons give me a funny look.

"Ok, I'm guessing that look means you think I don't have the right to have you on call."

"It's not that," the dragon says. "It's the fact you're making plans. What kind of plans?"

"Oh! That! Well, I'm the pack's tactician. I'm responsible for making plans for our defence, or our attack, if we're ever strong enough."

"Does Dean know that?" the guy pushes.

"I honestly have no idea what Marcus has told him about our hierarchy. I'll mention it to him."

"I'll talk to Dean. It would make sense to include us if you're making a site-wide plan."

I nod. It really will.

The lead vehicle pulls into the drive, and all banter ceases. I stand in the centre of the road leading down to the gate, several paces back from it, while the two dragons now flank me. Two wolves are visible along the fenceline on each side, but more are hidden in the trees.

The passenger door opens, and a tall, well-built wolf steps out. I think I recognise him, but I'm not sure.

"Open the fucking gate, son," he orders.

I don't budge an inch, and neither do the wolves in my command. "To whom do I have the pleasure of speaking?" I ask.

"Are you fucking shitting me?" the man roars.

"Leon!" Marcus' voice rings out from behind me.

I remain where I am, as do those under my command as Marcus and Dean walk past us and right up to the gate, vaulting over it together.

Marcus walks right up to him, hugs him, the two of them slapping backs. They're obviously old friends, but it must be from his time in Montgomery Pack because I don't know the man, although I realise now he's an alpha. Did he try to use compulsion on me? Because I didn't feel it if he did.

"Who's the fucking pompous twat on gate duty?" Leon asks.

Marcus steps back from him, the smile disappearing from his face.

"Sam is on my pack council, Leon, and well within his right to refuse a strange wolf entry in these times."

The man's shoulders slump for a moment, before he pulls himself tall again. They're fucked, I can see that now. The convoy makes more sense. They're not an attacking force, they're another fuck-tonne of refugees.

"My apologies, Marcus." His gaze finds mine, and he lifts his chin in an age-old sign of acknowledgement. "You too, Sam."

I incline my head. I'm not giving a fucking inch. This man is up to something. If they're refugees, then why didn't we know about it until they got here? Now that I know his name, I know he's the alpha from Alphe Pack, just three hours' drive away. They're a large pack, larger than Gallus, although not as big as the Pasadena Pack, but they've got a reputation as fierce fighters. They hold a challenge event every year with considerable prize money. It's open to members of all the packs. Many of the previous winners went on to join Alphe themselves.

"This is quite the entourage you're bringing to the party," Marcus jokes.

There is an event tonight, but Leon and his wolves were not invited. Still, it's a neutral way of asking what the fuck is going on.

"My apologies for gate-crashing, but we're coming as refugees. Sinclair attacked us last night and practically burned down the place around our ears. Wolves we can defend against, mages and witches, not so much."

"I'm so sorry to hear of your losses. We have some magic users here, although nothing like the trouble that Montgomery Pack is brewing. You should know, though, my father is dead."

The shock on Leon's face is clear. "That can't be true. They attacked us last night."

Marcus' head hangs for a moment, and I just want to comfort him. I know it must be hard to see not only your father, but your only brother sucked into the darkness.

"It's true, I killed him myself several weeks ago. My half-brother Alistair now leads the pack and although he follows the same tenets, as you've seen, he's a completely different wolf."

Leon's expression is sombre. "Yes, I do believe he is. He barricaded us in our buildings and set them alight. Fortunately we have trapdoors and a tunnel system, so we all made it out without him realising, but it won't be long until he does."

"We won't turn away anyone in need, but we're already beyond our capacity when it comes to housing. We're trying to get more up as fast as we can, weather permitting."

Leon nods. "We brought tents with us, but it's cold. If you have any spare blankets, we'd appreciate it."

Marcus nods. "I'll see what we can do. We might be able to rearrange the vans so that some of them can camp inside the barn."

"Why can't the vans sit in the field?" Leon asks.

"Because they've got people living in them while they're waiting for housing."

Leon blows out a low whistle. "You weren't kidding when you said you're at capacity, are you?"

"No, unfortunately not. Tell me, do you have any tradespeople in your pack? Builders, electricians, plumbers, and the like."

"As a matter of fact, I do. Several of my men have their own construction company. So we can loan you excavators if you need them."

Dean chuckles near the gates. "I think we're pretty much covered for that, mate," he chimes in, picking at some dirt under his nails.

Leon looks from Dean to Marcus and back again. "I'm missing something here," Leon says.

"Dean, Clan Alpha of Beithir."

"Dragons," whispers Leon. "You have fucking dragons?"

"No," Dean corrects him. "I have fucking dragons. Marcus has a dragon mate and has offered asylum to my clan."

"But—"

"Not out here, Leon, too many ears. Let's get your people in the gates, I'm going to need you to vouch for each and every one of them, until all the vehicles are inside the wards."

"All of them?" Leon says faintly.

"Don't underestimate my brother, Leon. It'll be the last thing you do."

13

TOBY

I resolve the first fight before it even gains momentum, the second one, I'm barely there in time, but the third one quickly turns into a mini-riot.

We're already overcrowded, but with the arrival of the Alphe pack over an hour ago, things have gone from easing tensions, to a burgeoning civil war. It doesn't help that the new pack are fighters and look down on the rest of us for not being so.

"Stand down!" roars an alpha voice, and it's all I can do to stand on my feet. The fact I can is not lost on anyone.

Wolves all around me are on their knees or on the ground, submitting.

"What the fuck is going on here, son. Is this how you run a pack?"

Fucking bastard.

"No, but it's apparently how you run yours. Alphe wolves fight first and ask questions later. I've spent the last hour stopping arguments that could easily have been avoided if your wolves had taken even a moment to consider the other person's perspective."

"Just what are you trying to say, son?" Leon challenges.

Fuck. I hate his smug face already.

"Well, son," I snarl. "For starters, I'm on the pack council here, where you're a guest. You'll treat me with the respect my rank deserves."

Leon rolls his eyes. "Get to the point, s— councillor."

"I've been sorting out issues that could have gone another path. This latest one is about space in the barn. Your wolves entered and told the families living there they had to move their vehicles outside, because the trucks have solid walls, and your wolves are sleeping in tents."

"It seems a reasonable request," Leon says, and I want to groan.

"Alpha Leon," I growl, then pull my wolf back. "Those vehicles are shipping trucks with empty shipping containers. They might seem large and solid, but at the end of the day, they're still trucks. They're no warmer than tents. They're also occupied by the vulnerable. Children and old people live in them. The agreement was that the vehicles would be moved to circle around the edge of the inside of the barn, and the tents would be set up in the middle."

Leon doesn't reply, and I know he's mulling over my words, looking for an excuse that's plausible enough to keep the rest of us out of the barn.

It does my head in. We're facing the biggest crisis in hundreds of years, and we have the opportunity to win if we pull together, but he's still trying to work out the angle that suits him best. I guess that's how he came to be alpha, playing the long game and twisting things until the opportunity arose for him to take over.

Oh, fuck. The realisation strikes me like lightning.

He wants to take over.

It's as clear as day to me now the thought has presented itself. Leon is going to be all smiles and kissing babies, right up until the moment he pulls the rug from under our feet. I wonder if Marcus has worked this out yet.

This isn't something I can talk to him about over the pack link, I need to go and see him face-to-face. I also need to say my piece to Leon in the vain hope he gives a fuck, but I can already see he doesn't.

"Your wolves may be good fighters, but when it comes to living in a community they are undisciplined," I tell him.

Leon's jaw opens in shock. It isn't the angle he thought I'd take. I want him to know I see him coming, because I don't want him to have the opportunity to squirm away like the worm he is when his actions catch up with him.

"They are selfish, self-centred pricks, with little to no care for others unless it's with how to use them for their own ends. Your wolves might have strength, but Triune has honour, and when it comes to the crunch point, that's what's going to pull us through, nothing less."

"You don't get to talk to me like that, son," Leon says, his arrogance in full swing. "I'm the alpha of the pack that's going to save your asses, you'd do well to remember that when your crunch point comes."

I give him a scathing look. "Power and might, the way to save us all. How's that working for you so far, Leon? Because from where I'm standing, it isn't going that well. You're here on our lands seeking asylum, which tells me you weren't able to hold onto what you had. I'm going to speak plainly, because you're pissing me off no end, and you don't seem to be able to take a hint."

Leon gapes at me, but I'm on a roll.

"Come for Marcus, I dare you. Try to take this pack from him, his wolves, his allies, his land. But do it at your own risk because I'll be at the front of the line of people waiting to take your fucking throat out. The long line of people, Leon. Nobody likes a bully, and we won't tolerate one here at Triune. So, pull your people into line, or you may literally find yourselves out on your ear."

He doesn't even bother denying it.

"That will never happen, Marcus is too honourable to punish innocent wolves, and he certainly doesn't want us fighting on Alistair's side. He'll never throw us out."

I nod sagely. He's right. "True," I reply, and I see the flash of triumph on Leon's face. "He'll fucking kill you first."

I turn my back on him and walk away before I say anything else stupid. I shouldn't have tipped my hand to him. Now he knows we're watching, he'll be more subtle. We'll have to work twice as hard at catching him. Here's hoping we're not too late.

Fuck, with allies like Leon, who needs enemies?

14

Marcus

M*arcus? We've got a problem, I need some face-to-face time,* Toby sends.

I pause mid-stride. I'm on my way back to the lodge to see the pups before heading to the bunker to grab some dinner. They're growing so fast, I don't want to miss a minute. Fuck it, I can kill two birds with one stone, he can meet me in my office.

Even as the thought forms, someone else is calling me on the pack link.

Marcus? I'm near the northern boundary, we just caught a vampire, only he says he's rogue and he wants to talk to you, Matt sends.

Everyone at battle alert, I send out across the pack link. We can't afford to take any chances. So much for seeing our sons.

Toby, I'm headed towards the forest down the centre of pack lands. Find me and we'll talk on the way.

Acknowledged.

I keep my eyes peeled as I walk, looking out for him. Instead, I see tired and worried people hurrying to their designated zones. We've had to up the protection on the women's dorm, because we now have too many non-fighters for them all to fit in the bunker during an attack. It's not an ideal situation, but we're doing our best with the limited resources we have.

Leon's arrival without anything other than clothing and treasured possessions isn't helping either. Our food supplies are stretched to the limit, forcing us to head into town more frequently for groceries. It's a vulnerable point that Alistair is bound to attack, but there's little we can do about it. Becoming more self-sustainable as far as fruit and vegetables go is on the list of things to do, but the priority has to be housing and safety for now, as the plants can only grow so fast.

Toby catches me just as we pass the last of the dormitories, and we cross a laneway together before walking between the family cottages. The ones on our land are finished, except for the last three, which is a miracle in itself, and they only need water and electricity to be done. The witches and dragons have sped things up dramatically.

Work on the lodge on the Pasadena lands is moving quickly. I know it's bad politics to have two bases of power in the one pack, but I'm hoping the second one will become more like a town hall, with all of our bureaucracy there, while our one will be more like the mayor's house.

"What's troubling you Toby?" I ask him, as we walk.

My gut twists, because he's bright, and if he's picked up on something he can't talk to me about over the link, then it's not going to be a small matter.

"Look, I could be way out of line on this, it's just my interpretation," he begins, and my heart sinks.

Yep, it's going to be really bad.

"But I think Leon's out to take control of Triune. I've been dealing with his wolves all afternoon, and a pattern is emerging that has me worried. They're all about entrenching themselves at the expense of the people who were here before them. They want to kick everyone out of the barn to keep it for themselves. They're trying to control what food comes out of the kitchens and who gets to pair up with whom. Several of them have been approaching bonded females, offering themselves up as a better wolf."

While I hadn't been aware of the specifics, I'm not actually surprised. This is how Leon works. He's a great leader, but he's power hungry, and losing his land and being defeated by my brother won't be sitting well with him.

What do you do when the rug gets pulled from underneath you?

You rip it out from someone else so you're not the most vulnerable person anymore.

I've been expecting this, I just wondered when it would start.

"Great job, Toby. I've been waiting for this, I just thought he'd settle in for a day or two before he started. I guess having the event tonight to celebrate the safe arrival of the pups is too good an opportunity to miss. Leon's already sowing dissension so people are off-balance tonight. I'd say he'll try to make a speech of welcome to the pups, but he'll pepper it with enough propaganda to paint me out as a bumbling fool while he's the more logical choice for leadership."

"Fuck," mutters Toby.

"Which is why we're not doing speeches. Plus, it's boring as fuck. These people need to celebrate something, they need to be reminded of what we have, of why we're doing this. The party tonight will lift their spirits, provided it's not interrupted by an attack, and hopefully it will be one more tie that binds us together."

Toby and I just need to pass through the first part of the forest and cross the meadow where the sawmill is, and then we should quickly be able to find Matt. The stench of the vampire should lead us straight to him.

"I might have fucked things up," Toby confesses, and I watch him as his stride falters beside mine.

"I called Leon out on his shit. Basically let him know that I was watching and that I'd be first in a long line of people waiting to rip his throat out if he came at you."

My heart is filled with pride. Toby might think of himself as the stupid kid amongst us, but his grasp of politics is instinctual and more accurate than most people's.

"You did the right thing. It'll be enough for him to go to ground and be more subtle with his troublemaking. I've already got Matt working on people in key places to keep their ears open for hints of trouble. Let him think he's being subtle, we'll be more than ready when he does decide to strike, and he's going to look like an even bigger fool when he fails. He's going to be on the lookout for me to approach people as spies, not realising I've already got them in place. We've got this Toby, and I'm fucking thrilled you picked this up, it validates my own paranoia which told me he'd try something like this."

Through the bond I can feel his relief, so I let my pride leak through to him. Let him see how valued he is. That's what a pack is, that's what we do. We lift each other up, protect each other, love each other. It only makes us stronger when we stand to face those who go against us.

"Okay, do you still want me to come with you? Or do you want me to go and put out whatever spot fire he's starting up now?"

"You confronted him just now?"

"Yeah."

"Then come with. He'll be reeling a bit and double checking all his calculations before he works out what he's going to do next. Whatever he doesn't have running already, will be put on hold while he ensures it's not going to blow up in his face, because obviously whatever he was getting his wolves to do today, was already detected."

"So, what are we heading off to see?"

"A rogue vampire who wants to help. I wish I had some of Catriona's powers right now. What I really need is a living lie detector."

Toby snorts beside me, and I break into a jog. I can smell the vampire, slightly off to the west, towards where the creek runs through the bottom corner of our land. I hate that it meanders down our boundary line, because it's a source of water for us, and when it leaves our lands it becomes too vulnerable to tampering.

Matt stands with a lone vampire and no sign of the rest of his patrol. He's already sent them off to continue their rounds, which speaks to how honest he thinks the vampire is. He already half trusts the male.

They both turn to face us when we approach, Toby walking just a step behind me.

"Alpha Marcus," the vampire inclines his head. "I am Jeremiah. I represent a group of thirty vampires who wish to fight on your side. We seek the protection of your pack and your gods, for in speaking out against what is happening we've lost the protection of our own."

"Greetings, Jeremiah. Tell me, how do you know you've lost Belar's protection?"

The vampire hisses at me, and I tense, Toby and Matt joining me.

"Do not mention his name. He hears you and will cast his gaze this way."

I raise an eyebrow but nod to show my agreement.

Jeremiah squirms. "We've been hiding, fearing retaliation. I cannot return to my people now, in case I lead his wrath to their hiding place. We know we've lost his favour because we've lost our venom, every single one of us."

The vampire lowers his fangs and pauses. Not a single drop of venom is to be seen. The stuff is usually a clearish straw colour until it makes contact with blood, and then it turns black, regardless of the species they attack. To further prove himself, he bites his own arm and smears the blood across his mouth. There's still no black. They can't control the release of the venom, so he definitely doesn't have any.

"I believe you," I tell him. It's kind of pointless, the proof is there right in front of my eyes. "The problem is going to be accommodating you. We don't really have much space as it is, and we certainly don't have any rooms that are blacked out."

"Not even a basement?" he asks, hopefully.

Ok, yeah, that could work, but only for one or two of them.

"Yes, but it's not empty. We've got nowhere to put the people we have, never mind the shit we have stored in there."

Jeremiah frowns, then his expression clears. "You're building a new lodge right? Upslope? Can you get the basement done there first? We can use that until you can get everyone else sorted."

"I'm not asking you to live inside a building site," I growl at him.

"No, you're not, alpha," he agrees. "I'm begging you to allow us to stay there. It's not just a case of being thrown out, we're being hunted. At least let us help you to build a haven where all supernaturals can come."

Build a what?

I exchange a puzzled look with Matt.

"Alpha, you already have wolves from three packs, dragons, and witches. Whether you planned it or not, this place is becoming a haven for the lost and the persecuted. It's somewhere safe where we can live with integrity. I know vampires don't have the best reputation, but it's merely a case of 'the emptiest vessel making the loudest noise'," he explains. "We're not all bloodthirsty and aggressive. But the ones who are get the most attention."

"Why on earth would you hear about vampires doing the right thing? But here again we have the chance to change things, to build something special, because vampires living in harmony with wolves, dragons, and witches? It's unheard of, and word will spread quickly."

I'm already sold on the concept, the issue is the practicality.

"How hard are the daywalking charms to make?" I ask him.

Jeremiah shrugs. "I'm not a witch, I can't answer that. But I can say that we will pull our weight. Maybe you could train us to work in the mill, and we could produce lumber during the night for you to build with during the day?"

"Let's back this up a step," Matt says, looking between us both. "How did you know we're building a second lodge, and what do you know of the mill?"

Fuck. I didn't think about him being part of the attacks on us earlier. My heart sinks. This isn't going to fly with anyone.

To make it worse, the vampire looks distinctly uncomfortable.

"Okay, so, I've been coming here every night for the last few nights, hoping to find you alone. I've been looking around your lands, seeing what you're developing, how you're expanding the pack. You've all been very busy."

That's not the answer I expected. It seems Matt is in the same boat.

"So, you weren't part of the attacks against us earlier on? You're not switching sides?"

If anything, he looks horrified at the accusation. "No! Dear god, no. We refused and were imprisoned until they could decide what to do with us, but we escaped while they were out attacking somewhere. We've been in hiding since."

The sense I get from my wolf is trust. He trusts what this vampire is saying.

My wolf trusts him, I send to Matt on a very private band. *Do you know where the Pasadena lodge is up to?*

It's already weatherproof, they're starting the ground floor walls today, but it has no water or electricity yet. The pipes are installed, but not connected until the whole building is ready.

Yeah, that made sense.

"It wouldn't be much more than a cave. I'm not sure how light proof it is, and there is no electricity or running water."

"Hang on," says Matt. "How are you getting in and out of our lands so easily? The wards should keep you out."

Jeremiah shrugs. "I have little problem crossing them. I think it may be because I'm no longer tied to the vampire god."

I need instant access to a dragon, is anyone near one of them? I send to my inner council.

The pack council has expanded now to include the witches, dragons, and representatives from the Pasadena and Alphe packs.

I'm with Dean, Sam replies to all of us.

Perfect, I don't need anyone else, thanks. Then I change to a tighter band with just Sam and Matt in it.

There's a vampire who has been crossing our wards with ease. His ties to Belar are cut, would that be enough to get him access?

There's silence for a minute or two before Sam answers.

Dean says he thinks so, but he wants to meet the vampire and check. Where are you?

In the forest behind the mill. How fast can you get here?

Dean says—, oh fuck. Right, okay. Look up.

I look up but don't see anything at first. Then Dean's dragon sweeps into view, Sam clutched firmly in a paw. I want to bust up laughing, but know I shouldn't. However, it's just too funny, so I end up with a shit-eating grin instead.

"Fuck off," Sam says aloud as soon as Dean sets him down.

Dean shifts behind him and chuckles. "You should have seen your face when I picked you up!"

I can't hold it back any longer. "You should have heard his mental voice when you did. I didn't think Sam's voice could get that high a pitch!"

We all crack up at his expense, and he chuckles ruefully. There are too few opportunities to laugh right now, we need every one of them we can get.

"You can cross the wards easily?" Dean asks Jeremiah when we settle a bit.

"Yes, there's barely any resistance."

"Can I touch your skin when you do it? Would you mind showing me?"

Jeremiah looks at me, and I incline my head. "You can trust him as much as you would me, but if it makes you feel better, and if it works, then you can use the ward between our land and

Pasadena's. It's just over there. That way, you're not completely unprotected."

Jeremiah beams. "Yes, of course, that would be perfect."

The two of them stride away, leaving Matt and I alone for a second.

What do you think? I ask him and Sam on the link.

Dean and Jeremiah may be out of sight, but they have superior hearing just like us. They aren't out of earshot, not by a long way.

I think it's worth a shot. We said we'd live by the old ways. That means protecting those who are in need, regardless of race. These vampires are in need. If we're standing up for the old ways, then we can't pick and choose.

I love this man like a brother. Right now, I love him even more. This is what Matt is good at, seeing the small details and making sure nothing gets missed.

Agreed, Sam says simply. *They're also going to be a boost when the next attack comes. The difficulty will be determining which vampires are on our side. We need to come up with a method of recognising them, and then changing it every time so they don't copy us. I'd like to think there's only going to be only one more attack, but the reality is there'll be several.*

That's Sam's strength. Seeing where our strengths and weaknesses lie and coming up with strategies to deal with them.

Then let's do this. We'll announce it later tonight at the celebration. We can welcome them in at the same time. It's going to take a while for everyone to adjust to that, and I can see Leon having a field day with it, but we'll make it work. We can't afford to drop any balls right now. Toby talked to me earlier. Leon's trying to undermine me. Toby thinks he's going to make a push for leadership.

Then we need to talk to our wolf and dragon council and make sure we present a united front, Sam suggests.

Wolf and *dragon?* I ask.

Yeah, I don't think they're going to leave once this is resolved. The witches might go, and the vampires probably, but I think the dragons are here to stay. There's been a few pairing up with our females, which is causing a bit of tension, but it's only for fucking so far as I can tell. Part releasing tension, and part fresh meat and all that.

Ok, let me know if that changes. Can you gather the council together then? I ask Matt, looking at him.

Can do, Matt replies.

Fuck, I need to reassure the pack, although there's no reason for them to be entirely complacent.

Stand down, I send to the entire pack. *The matter has been dealt with.*

I can explain it to them all at the celebration for the pups, but right now they just need to get back to living. They'll be jittery for sure, but we'll deal with that later.

Marcus? It's Ken again at the gate, another voice summons me.

Seriously? What now? All I want to do is get back to my mate and my pups and celebrate that we're alive. I know this is part of being an alpha to a large pack, but it sucks that I can't even get five minutes of peace.

I'm sorry, Ken, I'm kind of in the middle of something here. Is it urgent?

Uuuh, yeah. You're really going to want to see this, and you should bring your mate and her sister too. There's a bunch of women here, they say they're sirens and that we're expecting them. My cock is as hard as a rock. I thought she was my fated mate, but my wolf is slobbering for any of them that I can get. I think they are what they say they are.

Fuck.

It's one thing to have the last siren here and everyone knows. It's another to have her sister secretly turn up. Thankfully nobody really knows about her yet, even on our own grounds.

But to have a bunch of them here with us?

The shit is about to hit the fan. Even those who were neutral will step in, if there's a chance of capturing a fabled siren for themselves.

I don't know what these women think they're doing, coming out of hiding and turning up here, but they've just put a planet-sized target on our pack.

Everyone is going to come gunning for us.

Everyone.

15

Catriona

It's one thing for Marcus to tell me there were sirens here, it's another to see them walking up the drive.

Goddess.

Taya, Sienna, Marjorie, Gwendoline, Felicity, Karen, Diana, Gina, Joelene and Indira — they're here, they're all here.

All *here*.

Together.

For me.

Shayla grips my hand so tight I fear my fingers might fall off.

They're now close enough for me to hear the gravel crunch under their feet, even over the noisy sounds of my breath getting faster and faster. My heart is racing. We haven't been together like this in hundreds of years.

It's exhilarating. My family, all together in one place. Aunts, cousins, and my other sister; Indira. Of all of us, I had only her and Shayla left. All the other beautiful women were more distantly related, great aunts and cousins, and cousins of cousins. The twelve of us are the only remaining sirens on the planet that we know of.

How can I be this happy and this terrified all at the same time? I don't know, but when my knees give out, Toby is there to catch me, and Shayla quickly takes Dane from my arms.

"Easy, baby. I've got you," Toby murmurs reassuringly.

Similarly, the women in front of me stare as Shayla holds Dane who is fussing. They won't know he's mine, not yet, but I wonder how they'll take the news. I'm not the only one who hated that we couldn't ever have a child. Maybe my baby boys will be a healing balm for them. Or maybe they'll drive a wedge between us, only time will tell.

"Kat?" Indira asks, hesitantly.

She's the last siren our mother created, my youngest sister, and she stares at me, uncertain, as her long black hair lifts in the breeze. Wolves are gathering in the periphery of my vision, the pack link buzzing wildly in the back of my skull. It won't be long before everyone knows, before they all show up to gawk, and my family will be terrified.

"Indira?" I whisper, holding my arms wide open to her.

With an inarticulate cry, she runs to me, tripping up the front steps and bowling me over as she lands, crashing us both into Toby who just laughs and catches us before we hit the ground.

Indira weeps on my neck, and I'm no better, crazy hormones, lack of sleep notwithstanding, I'm an emotional wreck. It's been nearly ten years since I've seen her, but she hasn't changed a bit. She even smells the same, patchouli and something spicy I've never been able to identify.

My wolf and dragon rise to the surface, curious about my reaction. Shay and I left her with Felicity when we all decided to split up to hide more easily. Hunting together was causing issues, and living together meant more of our scent to broadcast to other supes in the area. It's much easier to hide in pairs or alone.

I can feel my mates all growing closer, coming from whatever they were doing, responding to my emotions. Behind me at the top of the stairs, Dane starts to cry. I was about to feed him when I got the message, and I couldn't wait to see them. But if I feed him here in front of them all, it's going to give them an even bigger shock. I also can't leave them while I go off and feed him.

I look up at Shay, helplessly as she tries to settle him unsuccessfully.

"Don't hide it," she tells them. "Get up here and introduce your son."

The others have now gathered at the bottom of the stairs, giving Indira and I a moment, but several of them hear Shay and stare at us in confusion.

Rather than getting up, I reach around Indira, holding out my arms for Dane. Shay smiles and passes him down to me.

"I've been blessed by Zaya," I begin, and they gasp. It's been so long since we've heard from her directly. Some of the younger ones like Indira never have. "And Mara and V'dar. I'm not the siren you knew. I'm her and *more*. Part of this means I've been granted new powers, things we've never had before."

I can see the wonder on most of their faces, but some are already showing scepticism. I'm willing to bet they're not even sure why they're here.

"I no longer need to have sex to feed, I can draw on my mates, or even strangers, for my energy. I can heal others, and to some extent myself. I can shift into a wolf thanks to Mara, and a dragon thanks to V'dar. Both of these creatures can also generate energy to gift to me."

My family stares at me in shock and awe. I haven't even reached the good bit yet.

"The biggest change of all, is this," I tell them. Then I lift my top and start to feed Dane. I'm getting used to doing it in front of others, and I know shifters don't care about nudity, but it's still a thing for me.

"This is my son, Dane. One of a litter of four wolf shifter pups I've borne."

"That's impossible," Gwendoline says, frowning at me. Of us all, she's the oldest.

"I assure you, it isn't now," says Fleur from behind me. "I'm Mara's handmaiden, and I'm the Accoucheur to all the wolf packs. I can assure you, Catriona bore these pups herself, and went through a hell of a labour. She drained several dragons and several more wolves to the point of light-headedness, but we got them all out safely in the end."

Gwen snorts. She's always been the snotty kind. "I don't care what you call yourself, missy. I've been around for four hundred years, and I know all the stories. I'm telling you, she's tricked you somehow."

"Still refusing to see what's right in front of you, Gwen?" I chide her. She's so fixed in her ways, but she's only got a century on me, and she's younger than Fleur, despite appearances. "If he's not mine, then how am I feeding him?"

"Drugs, you can bring on milk with drugs," she says with an imperious snort.

"And how am I finding the energy to produce enough milk for him and the others without dropping dead from exhaustion?"

Her mouth opens and closes like a fish gasping for air. This time she has no quick answer and I can see the idea of what this might mean beginning to occur to her. The hope starting to gather in her heart.

"Top me up, baby?" I ask Toby.

He holds a hand in front of me, and I take it, careful not to dislodge Dane, who is sucking hungrily at my breast. I pull, drawing his energy into me. Not that I need it right now, but it's the demonstration that matters. Gwen won't believe it until she sees it and neither will the others.

"You're a siren. You can see relationships. Look at the links between my son and I, my mate and I, and my sister and I," I say, looking up at Shay to indicate which sister.

"Shay also has a dragon now, although their shift takes a lot of energy, so neither of us has done that yet."

"And as for you, *missy*," Fleur says, stepping forward. "I'm five hundred and forty-six. My goddess rewarded me for faithful service by giving me back my youth. I've waited a long time for this woman."

She puts a hand on my hair, stroking it affectionately while I continue to nurse Dane under the incredulous eyes in front of me. It's clear they all want to touch him, to hold him and see he's real, to have their hopes and dreams confirmed.

"Catriona is a miracle who has not only saved these men, but in turn has saved these packs, witches, and dragons who reside here. She's bound us together under her leadership with Marcus, improved our fertility and healing rates, and has shown us what it is to be fearless, gracious, and forgiving. We are all better off for her coming to us, and I believe she is too."

Gwen is still staring at us, her arms folded stubbornly across her chest, but the others have had enough. When Felicity approaches me, Gwen even tries to stop her, but her hand is shrugged off.

"Oh give over, Gwen," Felicity snaps, stepping forward and caressing Dane's soft head. "There's obviously more to all of this than can be deciphered in a few seconds, are you really going to spoil our reunion by refuting everything you see and hear? We're on pack lands, for goodness' sake, and nobody is rushing us, nobody is attacking. If you want a fucking miracle, there's one for starters."

There are murmurs of assent from the other sirens, and they begin to press forward, keen to see my son. I can't wait until they see the other three!

"Come," Fleur says, playing hostess in my stead. "You must all be tired and hungry. Let's see about finding you somewhere to sleep where you feel safe, and getting you a meal and something to drink. It'll just be something light for now, because we've a big celebration planned for tonight. We're celebrating the arrival of the pups. The first *litter* to be born to wolves in over a hundred years."

She sweeps all the women up with her, taking them inside, except for Indira and Shay who stay with me.

Dane has fallen asleep on my breast, milk trickling from his mouth as it pops open. It's such a miracle to me to be able to feed them, even if I can't give them every feed. The other nursing mothers have stepped up, offering expressed milk in bottles for me. I was happy to let them breastfeed, but Fleur was worried about the babies not getting enough of my scent as it was, so either I or my mates do the feeds. The guys even make sure they do the night ones so I get enough rest.

Well, they think I do, but with my wolf and dragon senses, there's no way I miss hearing the boys cry, getting changed, fed, and burped. I don't truly fall back asleep until whoever is feeding them returns to their own bed.

These are my babies, my family, and as chaotic as our lives are right now, I don't want to miss a second.

16

MARCUS

"Where the fuck are we going to put them?" Matt asks as he watches the women being swept into the lodge.

Ideally, this would be the perfect place for them, more defensible and certainly somewhere to keep them away from single males who might overstep their boundaries. The thing is, the lodge is already full of our children and elderly. We've no more room for anyone, even the living room floor is more of a campsite than anything else.

"I'm open to suggestions," I growl unhappily, looking around the chaos.

This used to be our home, the place where we played at being a pack. It used to be ridiculously spacious and even a little excessive.

Now it's not enough. Nowhere near what our rapidly growing pack needs, and I feel like a failure.

You are a failure, you've let them all down, a sinister voice says in the back of my head.

I whip around to see who's behind me, eyeing off the wolves at the door who are already salivating at the scent of so many unclaimed sirens. This is going to become a problem fast, especially when the dragons are no better.

There's no obvious sign of anyone challenging me, nobody sending something through the pack link or speaking quietly behind me. Perhaps it was just my own inner demons coming to the surface with the strain of so many wolves. There's a reason alphas don't let their packs get too big, it's too hard to hold so many bonds. It stops people like my father and now my brother becoming too strong.

It's likely a limitation set by the gods themselves to ensure balance or some shit like that, but right now, it's just giving me a headache.

"What about the Pasadena lodge?" Toby asks, also looking around as if expecting trouble.

It's obvious he's reacting to my own vibes, so I make an effort to calm the fuck down. It doesn't help that my wolf is steadily growling in the background, like he senses something I don't. It's more than a little unnerving.

"The vampires are in the basement, and there's not much more built than the shell of the ground floor. How the fuck are they going to sleep in that?" I snap, more waspish than I should be.

"And we've got more people than we know what to do with right now. So, let's start working on the lodge as well, and getting those without specific skills to outline a dorm or two on the Pasadena lands. They're part of us, which means their land is part of ours."

"We can't use another pack's land just because their alpha died!" I yell at him.

"You can if those buildings are going to fucking house Pasadena wolves!" Toby yells back.

That stops me in my tracks. Toby isn't the pissy one, that's me. He never yells back, he's too chill for that shit. Which tells me how out of line I really am.

Wiping a hand down my face I turn to him to apologise but he's holding one hand up, palm outward.

"Yeah, I'm tired too. I get it, it's not cool, but we're cool. Let's just move on."

He's a better man than I am.

My wolf grumbles in disagreement and, not for the first time, I wish I could hold him in my arms for a hug. I bet he'd be great to hug.

"Excuse me alpha," a hesitant voice asks, and I want to groan.

Both Toby and I turn to face the newcomer. I know his name, I fucking know his name! At the same time, I don't fucking know his name. At least, not this minute.

"I'm Ralph, we haven't formally met yet, but I'm Lisa's beta," he pauses awkwardly and scratches the back of his neck. "Well, I was her beta."

It's taken him this long to present himself? Where the fuck has he been while his wolves have been floundering? Hell, while I've been struggling to look after them all?

"Where the fuck were you when we needed you?" Toby growls as though he's been listening in on my thoughts.

Once again he gives me a rueful look. "I had a concussion. I've been wandering around doing things and then passing out for short periods. I kept waking up lost until someone took me to your mate a little while ago."

Catriona, did you just heal a Pasadena wolf with a concussion? I ask her.

Yeah, Ralph. Did he find you okay? He's been acting a little strange and apparently he kept falling asleep in the strangest places until someone brought him to me to get checked out. Lucky he did, he had a slow bleed on his brain. I sent him your way once we realised who he is.

Yeah, he's here, I assure her.

"It sounds like you're a lucky wolf."

Ralph nods enthusiastically. "Yeah, she said I had a brain bleed. I would have been a goner."

Has he made an oath? I ask Matt.

No, not yet.

The Pasadena beta shifts from foot to foot, which just makes me want to wait him out. If he can't even spit out a simple question then how the fuck did he become beta?

"Ok, I'm just going to put this out there. I know Lisa swore an oath to you, and we're all bound to her. I am one of her betas, but it was more of an honorary thing. I'm just really good at admin and she trusted me to help her out with the logistics. That's my thing, not dominance fights or leading by example, but getting stuff done in the background."

"Do you want to continue as a beta, or would you rather have an administrative role within the pack?"

Ralph's shoulders sag with relief. "Admin, thanks. I'm really not cut out for dominance plays and stuff, I just get shit done."

Fair enough, I could respect that.

"We could use a wolf like you, Ralph. I've got Marina, but she's more people oriented and less logistics. I think between the two of you, we could really get things rolling here. I'm sure she would be glad of the help."

"I'd love to do that, as long as you're not offended I don't want to be your beta. It's nothing personal, I'm just not good at it."

My own beta moves to stand beside him, slinging an arm around his shoulders. "How about you give your oath to me as Marcus' proxy, and I take you to the office and put you to work? We need a lot of help sorting out accommodation, food, and materials. Marina spends most of her time fielding enquiries and requirements, but if you could procure what we need, or at least prioritise stuff for us, that would be awesome."

I nod my dismissal of them both as Matt leads him away. Nothing should surprise me from Lisa's fucked up pack anymore, but this surely did. Still, we'll find a good use for him, and probably better utilise his skills than Lisa ever did.

Shouts from outside catch my attention, my wolf immediately rising to the fore. What the fuck is going on now? I get that people are stressed, but we should be working together, not tearing ourselves apart from the inside. We're fucking doing Alistair's work for him!

The sirens are all still crowded in the living room, and the smell of fear on them is almost enough to make me sneeze.

"Make a path," I call out, trying to make my way through the crowd, because it's not just Catriona's family, but Fleur and a bunch of women with small children, mostly the ones who have the upstairs rooms in the lodge. This housing crisis is getting ridiculous.

Jerking open the front door, I'm confronted by two of the Gallus pack members standing in front of it, while several agitated dragons stand on the other side. This is going to be a shit show, I can already tell.

"What the fuck is going on here?" I growl aloud, while mentally calling to the guys. *Someone get me Dean at the front of the lodge, there's trouble with the dragons.*

"We want our allocated share of the sirens," growls one of the dragons, his eyes already showing slitted pupils.

It takes everything I have not to push past my wolves and rip his throat out right there and then, my mate, however, takes things into her own hands, which only makes me crazier.

"Sure, would you like me to rip off one of their arms or maybe a leg for you to grind your pathetic cock on?" she yells from behind me.

My wolf growls, but surprisingly the dragon backs off, looking confused.

"A what?" he asks, shocked.

Catriona shoves me out of the way, and I'm surprised by the strength in her arm, until I see the dragon scales glittering silver in the sunlight. Fuck, is she going to shift? Does she have enough energy on board for that?

"Let me tell you a story," she says, angrily pushing past the wolves and shoving the dragon back a step. The scales are gone from her arm, but he allows her to do it anyway. Whether it's her dragon or her siren scent, he's already transfixed.

"Once upon a time there was a girl," she points to herself, "who loved her mother very much. Unfortunately, they were both sirens, and her mother had been caught by a wolf pack."

My gut churns, I know where she's going with this, but I don't dare stop her. Maybe it will cause all of them to settle down a bit.

"Thankfully the girl managed to escape, but she vowed to somehow get her mother free, even though the shifters forced a mate bond on her by raping her."

Several of the wolves around us growl in anger, and the dragons are right there with them. They're already protective, which is good.

"Every month she takes a horse and rides close to where their compound is, and she observes them, ensuring to always come from a different direction so she can't be caught herself. She watches as her mother grows thinner and more haggard, her hair is lank because it's unwashed, she doesn't have the strength to do it, she's skin and bone, because they're starving her of food, forcing her to produce enough pheromones so they can rut her whenever they want. Which is all the time. She's collared to a post in the centre of their village. The she-wolves hate her and teach their children to throw stones, but they don't complain when their own fertility is increased."

Several of the wolves look green, but I know this story is only going to get worse. Hopefully it will spread so we don't have to go through this again.

"Of course, the hungrier a siren is, the more pheromones she produces, until the wolves finally break and go into a rutting frenzy. The girl has to watch helplessly from a distance as they fight and claw for just a piece of her. They literally rip her to shreds, holding gobbets of flesh as they rub them against their cocks in a mindless need to rut. It takes two days for the air to clear and for them to come back to their senses. The only traces of her are some hairs stuck to the blood on the post, a few rags of her clothing, and a lot of bloodied wolves."

Someone nearby turns and retches noisily, but my mate isn't done.

"Those wolves wanted their share of a siren, and they got it. Why the fuck do you think we're nearly extinct? Why do you think we asked our goddess to make us infertile? Because none of us wanted to die like that! Entitled fucking men like you hunted us to the point where these women are the only sirens left in the world and along you come and offer to finish the job, right? What a hero. You want your fucking share of the sirens, like we're some marketable commodity? Who the fuck do you think you are, dragon, to try and reduce us to that? Who are you to try and start the siren wars all over again? Why do you think the Montgomery clan are coming after us so hard? Because I'm the one fucking thing that can stop them. We're the species who can make you all stronger, as long as you don't make us weak to start with. So take your fucking entitled ass and get out of my sight. You make me sick."

Without waiting for them to follow her orders, she stomps back inside and slams the door shut.

"Problem solved," she growls at me, and then bursts into tears.

Fuck.

I pull her shaking body into my arms, murmuring words of comfort and sorrow. I can't imagine what she went through that day, nor how much it hurt for her to lose that bond, something she didn't even tell them about. I think her mother's story was enough horror for one day anyway.

The other women come forward then, hesitating to draw too close because I'm there, but if she needs them more, then I'm willing to do whatever it takes.

"Your family wants to be here for you," I tell her gently, raising her face by her chin and making her look towards them. "Why don't you let them comfort you?"

I try to turn her from me over to them, but she grips me tightly.

"You're my family, Marcus. You, my other mates, the pups, this pack. You're my family too."

I nod and kiss her on the forehead, then her temples because I can't resist. Finally I kiss her eyes.

"The women of our family are dying to comfort you, love. Why don't you give them a chance?"

The sirens can't help but show their surprise. I'm not acting like any wolf they've ever heard of before, which makes me proud, because what these women went through is seriously fucked up, and I want no part of that. I want to show them we can be better, that we can make this a better world. I want to provide for them almost as much as I do for my mate.

"Mine," my wolf growls from my throat before I can stop him, and they all freeze. "Pack. Protect pack."

Catriona looks up at me, surprised.

"They're my family too. I protect my family."

She smiles and pulls me down for a kiss that leaves me panting and wanting, but her teary face tells me she needs those women, so I give her a gentle push towards them.

"It's time things changed," I tell the wary women. "I plan to be the beginning of that change, and all the wolves in my care will follow me or leave. You will be safe here, no matter how many people I have to kill to ensure it."

That's probably not as comforting as I wanted it to be, but it's a promise nonetheless. These women need me, and I will be here for them. Just like I'm here for my mate.

17

MATT

There's a storm rolling in. I can feel it in the air, the change in pressure, the slight increase in the breeze. I don't need a fucking app to tell me, it's coming and that's all there is to it. The trouble is, I'm not sure we're equipped to wait it out. If it brings snow, we could be fucked.

"Storm's coming," I tell Ralph and Marina. "We need to work out where everyone is staying. This could be the first snow."

Instantly she picks up her phone, opening an app and scrolling down before flipping it over to a weather radar.

"They're predicting snow, but it shouldn't hit us until about one or two in the morning. We've got a few hours to get people set up."

"I need a list of what buildings we have, what are in progress, what counts we have of people and what categories they fall into, whether it's species or ability or gender. If you're dividing people by groups, I need to understand the nuances," Ralph says. "I also need to know roughly how many per current building. I think people can sleep sitting up for a night if there's going to be snow."

Marina turns to her computer, her mouse clicking in a staccato beat as she opens file after file and orders them to print.

"Site map is on the wall," she tells Ralph, and he moves over there to familiarise himself while she gets the rest of the data for him.

"Where are the work crews up to? What assets and liabilities do we have? We can't afford to stop building, even if there is snow on the ground."

Handing him the first sheaf of paper, Marina goes back to her desk, printing even more things before joining him again at the map. The two of them are so engrossed in their conversation, they don't even notice me slipping from the room. I heard raised voices downstairs and one of them was the strident tones of my mate. I need to know what's going on.

Yet when I reach the bottom of the stairs, Catriona is surrounded by women who are cooing over her, praising her bravery, and comforting her as she sobs on her sister's shoulder. Indira, that was her name, right?

What's wrong? I ask Marcus, not wanting to disturb them. Already those on the edge of the group are giving me wary looks. I hold up my hands in innocence and skirt around them, making my way to the kitchen where Craig has Fleur pressed up against the wall in a clinch that is far from PG.

Dragon assholes wanting their share of the sirens, Marcus growls back.

Are you fucking shitting me?

I wish I was.

What brought that about?

What do you mean? Marcus' tone is confused.

If they were going to challenge for the women, surely they would have done it as soon as they scented them, but they held off for a bit. So, why cause a stink now?

I — what? They —

Something is wrong. I've never heard him sound so unsure of himself, so lost. Marcus might not have always taken his role seriously, but as soon as we found our mate, it was like his alpha gene kicked in or something. He might have done some stupid shit, but he was never hesitant about it.

Where are you?

Inspecting the Pasadena site to see what can be done about a dorm there.

We're not going to get that up today, I argue.

No, but there's a storm coming, I'd like to make as much progress as we can.

That sounds more like him, but still I want to lay eyes on my alpha, something isn't quite right. I begin to jog up the slight incline to the Pasadena lands, passing the sentries at the gate with a wave and following the drive around to the left as it meanders toward the lodge.

Marcus is standing talking to Ted, the leading hand of one of the work crews, nodding as the wolf gesticulates widely, his hands describing something that makes no sense to me without the words to accompany it.

"We need to work better with the people and tools we have," Marcus tells the foreman.

"I think Ralph is the man for that," I reply as I jog up to join them.

"Ralph Tremaine?" Ted asks.

When we give him blank looks he sighs. "From Pasadena, Lisa's beta."

I nod heartily. "Yeah, him."

"Did you get his oath?" Marcus asks me, and I flush.

"Uh, no, not yet, but I can call him up here to look at this with us and take it then."

Ted looks back and forth between us, obviously worried about our cohesion.

"As soon as he met Marina, they were printing files and talking statistics and logistics. He's got a real gift for it, and it would take a load off her plate. We're all wearing too many hats right now, and some things are slipping through the cracks," I explain. "Finding people like Ralph and slotting them into the right roles is going to make a huge difference. I bet he can ferret out a wolf or dragon for any role we need. It's just a matter of getting the data to him in the first place."

"Yeah, he's got a good head for logistics and organisation," Ted agrees. Coming from a former Gallus wolf, that's quite a compliment.

"How do you know him?" Marcus asks, eyeing Ted shrewdly.

"Our crew did some work for Lisa on one of her warehouse projects. Ralph was the project manager. He saved us a lot of trouble and both sides a lot of money."

"Well, that's good to know. Having a Pasadena wolf who already has connections with the Gallus wolves in charge of logistics should help to reduce any issues," I say.

Marcus gives me an irritated look. "They're our wolves now, Matt. They're Triune. You have to stop thinking of them as being from other packs, because they won't accept the change if their new leadership can't."

"Yeah, okay." He makes a good point, although I think it's important to remember where people came from while we're merging. It's going to help us to anticipate a lot of problems, but I'll take that up with him later.

He gives me a stern look, then turns back to Ted who's watching our interactions avidly. There's no doubt in my mind he's going to report back to the other former Gallus wolves that their new alpha has accepted them as his own. It will actually be a boost for their morale. Wolves need structure, we need leadership, and while it makes me look stupid, I'm happy to do that for the good of the pack.

"What would you need to get a dorm built up here in two days?" Marcus asks.

Ted's gaze flicks back and forth between us, like he's waiting for a punchline or something, but neither Marcus nor I waver. We need to get our vulnerable people out of that lodge, because the Sirens are more likely to be attacked than our young, their very scent will drive some of the attacking forces to frenzy, so the logical place for them is the lodge. If we can get a dorm up here, then some of the wolves from the bunker can move up, and we can put our elderly and young in the bunker instead. It saves us having to move them.

"We need it like yesterday, man," I tell him.

"It's just not possible," he protests.

"We don't need electricity or plumbing, it's going to be a pain in the ass for them, but it's better than sleeping in the snow. We just need something that's weatherproof and vaguely defensible."

The foreman sighs, looking across the site. "It depends on what resources you can get me. I've seen those dragons dig, would they be willing to flame the ground too? Warm it up and keep it warm so that concrete cures? Because we could lay those foundations and get them set in a day - enough to build on at least. While they're curing, we could have everything laid out to go for the second day, as much of it pre-assembled as possible. If I had a team of say thirty people and enough power tools for half of them, then we could potentially get the walls up and the roof on, even the windows and doors in. It would be nothing more than a shell, and still fucking cold at night."

Marcus nods, his eyes glazing for a moment.

Marina? Can you ask Ralph to come up to the Pasadena site? We've a high priority project and him need you to organise the manpower for it.

He's on his way, alpha, Marina responds immediately.

"You can take his vow when he gets here, Matt," Marcus orders. "Ted, I want a list of exactly what you need, cuts of wood, amounts of timber, how many dragons you think it will take, everything down to the last screw and nail. We can't use them to warm the ground, they set the wooden frames on fire, but maybe we can get the mages to work something to protect the wood. Let's see if we have what it takes to get this done, because the snow starts tonight."

Whatever hesitation he had before is now completely gone, and I wonder if I was just overreacting, imagining the lost sound of his voice as he spoke to me. Maybe I should ask the others if they've noticed anything, but certainly not where anyone else can hear, that's the last thing we need.

Wolf packs are limited in size by the number of wolves the alpha can control. This hasn't been a gentle build-up for Marcus, and even though he's delegating those bonds to Catriona and me, I'm still fucking concerned about his mental wellbeing. It's not just the strain of the packs riding on his shoulders, it's the war and all of the fucking details bound to it.

"Want me to talk to Dean?" I offer. It's not much, but if the alpha dragon commands it of his people, then it will probably go over a lot smoother than if it comes from us. They might be refugees here, but they still see themselves as the top dogs. Or lizards, or whatever the fuck they want to identify as.

"Yeah, that would be great. Get the numbers from Ted and Ralph and then approach Dean, better to do it with all the information at hand."

"Yes, alpha," I agree, according him a slight head bow. Let Ted take note of that and tell the others about it. The more we build up Marcus as a real alpha, the faster they'll adopt the idea themselves.

Offering a vow is one thing, following through on it is another. I intend to make sure they all fucking follow through on it, because we can't afford for these people to give anything less than their best.

Our lives depend on it.

All of them.

18

MARCUS

E very time I turn around there's someone there with some insignificant detail that would be better handled by someone else.

Why do they keep asking me?

It's not until Catriona replies that I realise I actually sent that across the bond to her.

Because you're the ultimate authority, and they're all still unsure who is in charge of what. When you don't know who to ask, then you go to the top of the food chain.

Then we need to add that to the list of things to happen tonight, I tell her. Marina? Can you get me a list of who is responsible for what, and give them a heads-up I'm going to be calling on them, please?

Yes, Alpha. What kind of duties are we talking about?

For fuck's sake, isn't it obvious?

Your pack is so disorganised, nobody knows what they're doing, or who to ask. It's your greatest weakness and it's going to allow another traitor to gain influence. You're going to kill them all.

The voice is back again. It's been popping up more and more frequently in the last couple of days. Is this what they meant by the madness of an alpha trying to bind too many wolves? I don't want to think about it, but ignoring it doesn't seem to be working for me.

Yet what else could it be? It's definitely not someone speaking over the pack link and it's certainly not aloud because nobody else is reacting. The only common denominator is me. Yet is it madness? Or just my own doubts coming to the surface more lucidly than usual.

It's pointless thinking about it, I'm just going around and around in circles, without any more information, I can only hope for the best, but I will ensure this community is safe and able to function without me. Which means delegating jobs and making sure people know where to turn is a greater priority than I'd thought. This is about more than me getting five seconds' peace, or having time to fuck my gorgeous mate. This is about protecting this community from everything — including myself.

Who's in charge of cooking, procuring food, different trades, the engineers, child minding, child birthing and fertility, assigning accommodation, taking care of non-perishable stores, foremen, warrior teams, healing, safety, fire precautions, communications, the bunker and tactics. If you can think of any other category I've missed, add it to the list and prime the people. I'll call on whoever I see fit tonight at the presentation.

Yes, Alpha, I'll get right on it, Marina replies. Her mental voice sounds a little strained, but there's nothing I can do about it, it's past time we had these details sorted out. We can't keep running from disaster to disaster and hope that our luck holds out, it will only lead to a catastrophic failure.

"Alpha?" the woman in front of me asks.

"My apologies, I was conferring with someone else. I agree, I think finger food is best for tonight rather than a sit-down meal. It gives the whole thing an air of festivity, and the goddess knows we could use a little bit of fun. The kids will certainly enjoy being able to run around, although we might need to confine them to a given area just to be safe. Hang on a second."

Lisbeth?

Yes, Alpha?

We're doing finger food tonight which means the kids will want to run around. Can you ensure there's a perimeter to keep them safe please? We don't want anyone to go missing if they hit us tonight, and snow is going to fall anyway so the boundaries will ensure no one is left out in the cold.

Yes, Alpha. I'll get right on it.

This. This is how things are supposed to work. I get given a problem and delegate the right people to fix it. I shouldn't be anything more than an overseer, rather than the person at the coalface making all the decisions. I don't want to control these people, I want to empower them so they can do things for themselves. I'm meant to be dealing with the tough shit, not the details.

Marcus? Toby calls. Leon's wolves are starting shit with the barn again.

Then put them on perimeter patrol for tonight. They don't get to celebrate with the rest of us when they're trying to pull things apart.

Yeah, they're not listening to me. I hate to do this, but if you don't get here soon, we'll be dealing with another challenge.

Seriously?

Someone find me Leon, I snarl across the pack link. *Send him to the barn pronto. That's an order.*

Marcus? Sam calls on a more private link and my gut drops.

Yeah?

I got some intel. It was wolves from Alphe who riled up the dragons, openly talking about how you had assigned them a siren to help keep up their morale until they could leave again and how you're going to do that for all the wolf packs. How they'd hate to be anyone from any of the lesser species.

How the fuck did you find that out?

Matt made a good impression on one of their fighters, Lou. He told me to go and talk to him, see if I could get any intel. Turns out, Lou was on his way to talk to Matt anyway, so I got the details instead. He'd already reported what he'd heard to Dean and the alpha sent him to us to keep us in the loop.

On the one hand, it was good we had Lou and Dean fully on board. On the other, it was just another example of Alphe fucking up a good thing. If I didn't think they'd sabotage the site, I'd send them up to the new dormitory on the Pasadena lands. The old adage of keeping your enemies closer rings in my mind.

Ralph?

Yes, Alpha?

Where can I stick a bunch of troublemaking wolves who need to learn a lesson?

How many are we talking about?

The entire Alphe pack, I growl.

How much of a 'thing' do you want this to be? he asks.

I want it very fucking clear they're about to be kicked out.

Then make them sleep in the vehicles outside of the barn. We have more than enough to make that possible, three per car, five per van and eight per truck.

Excellent, then I'll announce it tonight. Let them find their fucking way after dark when everyone else is celebrating. They won't be displacing anyone, right?

No, sir. We hadn't got as far as assigning them quarters. This will help alleviate the influx until we can get something more permanent.

If they don't stop this shit, they'll be permanently out, I snap.

Yes, Alpha, Ralph replies in a cowed tone.

Sorry, Ralph. It's not you I'm angry at.

Understood, sir. It's a tense enough situation without these people causing internal strife on top.

He's right, but it's no excuse. Still, I apologised and that'll have to be enough for now. I'll need to keep a lid on my temper.

You'll never manage this, the voice in my head insists. *It's all going to fail because you're not wolf enough.*

Yeah? Well you can go fuck yourself too, I snap.

There's no response, but there never is. I'm not sure I want there to be one either, because it would mean my madness had progressed enough where I could hold conversations with myself. Or there is someone else inside my head, which means I am a security risk to the entire community.

The group at the barn just makes my hackles rise even further. Leon has beaten me there and is already making matters worse from the expression on Sam's face.

"Enough!" I roar, startling everyone. "Make a path."

Wolves and dragons alike are standing toe to toe, a small group of sickly-sweet scented women stand behind those with Sam, while Leon folds his arms, sneering at us all.

"These creatures claim they have permission to be here. Worse, some of them are even sleeping in this barn along with innocent wolves. Your wards can't be very good if the very creatures who attack us are bedding down beside us, just waiting for the opportunity to strike," Leon claims loudly.

"Believe me," I growl, "I'm aware of exactly who I need to watch in this community, and it is not these women who have already sworn a blood oath in front of Dean. He can vouch for their intent more than you can."

"You're taking the word of a lizard over that of a wolf? And siding with creatures who attacked us over your own people?"

Mutters begin to sound around us from disgruntled wolves buying into his stupid fucking rhetoric. They should know better. Fine, if he wants to play dirty, I can do that too.

"I'm taking the word of refugees who have done nothing but try to help since they arrived earlier, as opposed to a bunch of wolves who have arrived, demanded the best share of everything and done their damndest to sow seeds of discontent, Leon. Would you like to explain why fighting-fit wolves take precedence over women and children when it comes to sleeping in a secure and warm location? Or perhaps why your wolves were overheard lying and saying I gave the dragons the largest share of the sirens like they're a fucking commodity to trade rather than people with feelings and intelligence enough to make their own choices? Perhaps you'd like to explain why you're gaslighting me right now, trying to make me out to be a poor leader when you're the refugee who lost everything and came to *me* for help?"

Leon says nothing, but his eyes glitter angrily as he takes a deep breath, desperately trying to hold back his shift. He's in the wrong and he knows it, and if he challenges me now, things will not go well for him. He has no other recourse than to stand there and take the shit I'm throwing right back at him.

"If you want to fucking challenge me for the leadership of this pack, Leon, then fucking man up and do it, otherwise stop trying to pull apart what we're building. We're under enough external pressure as it is, without your little games pulling us apart from the inside and doing Alistair's work for him. This is your final warning, shape up, or ship out, because I've had a gutful. Until

Alphe pack either swears allegiance to Triune, or until they show they can be decent allies rather than a drain on our resources, then they can sleep in the cars *outside* of the barn."

There are gasps from around me but I've had enough of this bullshit.

"If you want to follow Leon's leadership, then by all means leave, but understand that when this war is over, these lands remain mine, not those of the Triune pack. They're in my name, and Matt's, Sam's, Toby's, Joe's, and the-goddess-bless-his-soul, Felix's. If you want Leon, then you take your piddling little party somewhere else, because you won't be welcome here."

Way to destroy the morale, Alpha, the sinister voice whispers. Frankly it can just fuck the fuck off. *They no longer trust you, it's only a matter of time before Leon takes over. He's a better wolf than you'll ever be.*

I doubt it.

Mostly.

"Get these people settled, and move the fucking cars so these losers can stay on the fringes where they belong. If they want to join the heart of the community, then they better work fucking hard to be included, because they've already outstayed their welcome."

"There's no way you'd cast us out, we wouldn't survive. You'd be sending us to our deaths!" an Alphe asshole shouts from somewhere at the back, although he seems to realise his mistake, because a beat later he adds; "plus you're too desperate for fighters, you can't afford to lose us."

"I'd rather throw out traitors than waste resources better spent on wolves loyal to this community, and we've survived without you thus far, asshole, I'm sure we'll do better with more food and beds to go around."

For a moment or two, nobody moves, unsure whether the show is over or not. Leon still stands there, hatred clear in his gaze as it tries to burrow into me, but I've dealt with enough bullshit for the day.

"I gave orders!" I shout. "Get your asses in gear, we've got people to protect."

People jump, startled out of their reveries, and begin moving, hustling the new witches towards the barn and the meagre offerings in there.

"My people will freeze in those cars," Leon growls.

"Then make them sleep shifted. Three wolves to a car, five to a van, eight to a truck. They can sleep in piles and conserve heat. They'll be fucking fine and you know it. If you're all as tough as you say you are, then this will be nothing to you. Show me you want to be a part of this, or stop wasting my fucking time and resources."

"You're just like your father!" Leon shouts as I turn my back on him.

"The only difference is, I have a conscience," I call back without turning. He's lost this shit-show, and he knows it. He'd be wise to leave it alone for now and lick his wounds while he nurtures his resentment. If he pushes me again, he's out, I'm done. Let his wolves choose a leader then. I'll take any who swear allegiance, but

I'll make them do it Dean's way — a blood oath. Let it be a little more binding than a simple one. It'll make them think twice about fucking me over, and it will stop any of Leon's spies from continuing his work.

This is my pack, my people, and I will fight for them.

19

CATRIONA

"This is so fucking crazy," Shayla says, cradling Carter while I nurse River and Fleur changes 'Squirt'.

Dane has already been fed and he's having some floor time where he's happily sucking on his toes. It was hard to get my siren family to leave him alone. I know they want to hold my boys, but Dane also needs this developmental time to begin coordinating his movements, or at least Fleur has told me that. I have no idea what I'm doing.

Deftly she puts 'Squirt' down beside his brother, taking River from my breast where he's lying and licking my nipple rather than feeding. He's full, but he doesn't want to let go. Fleur ignores his wail of protest, tucking him over her shoulder with a burp cloth in place while gesturing for me to start with Carter.

Reluctantly Shay parts with my son who soon greedily attaches to one of my dugs. The other three nipples have already been thoroughly chomped on by his brothers and I'm keen for them to have a bit of a break. The boys don't have teeth yet, but a baby clamping down with their gums on breast tissue is no laughing matter. The little monsters do it regularly, Dane being the worst. He'll latch on, then turn around at the slightest distraction, trying to take my nipple with him. Unfortunately for us both, it doesn't stretch that far, so either he loses his grip in increments, or I yelp and move with him. Either way, it's unpleasant.

They've all had bottles of donated milk before feeding from me, so none of them should be hungry but there's no denying they'll always accept a little extra from me. Sure enough, under Fleur's expert patting, River lets forth a belch that could blow over a linebacker.

"Holy shit!" Shayla exclaims, half standing out of her seat. "What the hell is in that milk?"

We all laugh.

"They're just practising for when they're older and think it's funny," Fleur murmurs, rewarding River with lots of little kisses which make him giggle. It's about the only sound my sons make that you could call cute. The rest are farts, sudden bowel movements that sound wet and disgusting, and impressive amounts of wind — as well as hungry cries, tired cries, wet nappy cries and I want mummy cries. I still can't tell the difference, but Fleur assures me there is one. I think she's pulling my leg.

"We're going to have to try a different teat for him," Fleur says, musing aloud. "He shouldn't be bringing up this much wind if he has proper attachment, and he certainly does with your nipples. It has to be the bottles where he's taking in so much air. We need to get all of this up or there's going to be hell to pay later."

Ugh, I could do without another night like the last three. River has had terrible wind pains, screaming non-stop for hours on end and disturbing any shifter in a mile radius, I think.

"We could try him on some chamomile extract," one of the other nursing mothers suggests.

"Aye, that might do the trick," Fleur murmurs, wiping away the bit of curdled milk that came up with River's wind.

Smells are the other thing you can't escape as a shifter. Toby makes himself scarce as soon as one of the boys breaks wind, because he hates changing nappies if there's poo. Sam turns decidedly green, but soldiers on. The others don't seem to be bothered either way. I'm letting Toby get away with it for now, but when I have one of his pups, there will be no escape for him, even if I have to nail his foot to the floor.

It's strange to think of having more pups, I've barely begun to adapt to having these four, but I know there's no way I could deny my other men a child of their own. I might ask the goddess to slow it down to one at a time. Having children in batches is hard work.

There's a sound against the door, like fabric moving against it, and then it opens, Ethan's head poking around. His gaze latches on to my dug where Carter is equally attached, a slow smile spreading across his face.

"I was hoping I hadn't missed the feed," he murmurs happily, stepping into the room and closing the door behind him.

"You ever burped a baby?" Fleur asks, giving him a speculative look.

"Not for a long time," Ethan admits.

"Good, then practise with River," she orders, slinging a spare cloth over his shoulder and passing my son to him.

Rather than panic like some of my mates did, he simply adjusts his grip until River is happily gurgling while Ethan alternates patting and rubbing his back.

"Like falling off a bike," Fleur says, giving an approving nod before returning to the floor with my other sons. "That one gets a lot of wind, don't be tempted to put him down here until he's at least blasted your eardrums twice."

Ethan's eyebrows rise to his hairline, even as he adds a slight bounce to his movements.

"You just have to watch out for the—"

She doesn't get to finish the sentence before River brings up a torrent of milk followed by a huge belch.

"Vomit," Fleur says lamely.

Everyone tenses, waiting to see what his reaction will be, but Ethan just sighs and shrugs.

"Comes with the territory, right? Could you pass me another cloth, sweetie," he asks Indira as she stares at him in wide-eyed terror.

Confused, Ethan looks at me. "Is she okay?"

"You're a male shifter, she's a bit nervous," I tell him. "They all are."

It's true. Every single one of them stiffened when he walked in like he had every right to join us. He's not one of my mates, at least, not yet. He's not a wolf, he's a dragon, but their history with us is barely better than the wolves. No, they didn't tear us apart or starve us, but they did 'dip their wick' in us and deliberately go around creating more sirens to meet the demand amongst the dragon clans. They didn't tell their unwitting creations either.

Needless to say, they were rather unhappy when I petitioned Zaya to take away our fertility and their source of sufficient mates and extra income dried up. They might not have abused us, but they had no qualms about selling our kind to the other races who did.

"You don't have to worry about me," Ethan says blithely, stepping around her and grabbing a cloth himself, even as Indira tenses and scrambles away from him. "You might be females, you might be sirens, but I have no more interest in mating any of you than I have in mating that chair over there. You might as well be furniture as far as I'm concerned."

"You're mated?" Fatima asks him.

Ethan grins at me, a predatory look if ever I've seen one. "No," he says cheerfully. "It's better. I'm fated. The only potential mate for me is sitting there nursing her son."

So, he has accepted it all then. Good for him. Me? I'm not so sure.

"Which one is which?" Ethan asks, trying to mop River up.

Nobody moves to help him, so Fleur sighs and gets back to her feet.

"Give him here, I'll sort him, but you're on your own."

Carefully supporting River's neck, Ethan hands him back, then does the last thing I expect or need — he pulls off his shirt and uses it to mop the rest of the mess up before grabbing some baby wipes and finishing the job.

The smirk on his face tells me he expects me to look at him, and I have to admit, I can't stop myself. There's not an ounce of fat on him, broad shoulders tapering down to lean hips, his Adonis belt clearly defined and his abs so indented I want to run my fingers over them. I've never been into the bodybuilder type per se, but these taut muscles are doing something to my libido.

I want to lick him.

All of him.

I want to trace those grooves with my tongue then unfasten his pants and take that exploration further south. I want to taste him and tease him, and when we're both worked up enough, I want to ride him all the way home.

Damn, what have these deities done to me?

I don't want this. But I want him.

As if he can sense my dilemma, Ethan's smile fades and he turns his back to me like he's self conscious. For some reason it hurts, and both my wolf and dragon whimper inside me.

He's hurt and it's our fault.

"I better go get cleaned up before this starts to stink," Ethan says, heading to the door.

I don't stop him, and it makes me feel uncomfortable. I want to call him back, tell him to hell with propriety and fuck him in front of my sisters, after all, it's nothing they haven't seen or done themselves. I also don't want to share it with them. Share *him* with them.

Gah, my thoughts are so muddled and confused. I wish I knew what I wanted.

He's gone before I can make up my mind, and my family all stare at me.

"What's wrong with him?" Taya asks, and my hackles rise.

"There's nothing wrong with him, why would you say that?"

"We can see the bonds, Kat," Sienna says. "They're firm and strong on his end, he adores you, but on your side it's faint and faded. You don't feel the same. So, what's wrong with him, why are you refusing this?"

Fleur says nothing, content to listen as she sorts River out. Carter lets go of my dug with a loud pop, distracting me for a moment. I carefully balance him on my lap while I tuck a breast pad over the nipple and put the band we fashioned to hold them back in place. It's not like you can get a commercially made bra for dugs.

I grab a cloth and put it over my shoulder, standing to begin burping him as I walk back and forth, trying to pull my thoughts together.

"He's fated for me," I tell them, and they nod, expectantly. They don't get it. "It's not him that's attracted to me. He didn't see me across the room, didn't check me out, didn't decide to pursue me. Just like the wolves. They had no choice in this, it's made things hard because they feel like they're in love with me, but they don't know *me* at all. They're in lust with me, and the love is coming slowly. I don't know them either, and there's been no time to get to know them, and now I have one more male to add to my already busy dance card. I've only just got my freedom back after I needed to spend practically all day fucking them to grow the pups. It feels like I'm losing everything again."

"It's not really that different to an arranged marriage," Diana says thoughtfully. "The only difference is you're guaranteed they're attracted to you physically, and they'll never stray. There aren't many relationships, married or not, who have that surety."

The others nod, looking to me for my reaction.

It's actually a good point. I hadn't thought of it like that before. In this case, instead of an arbitrary match made by a third party, my mates have been hand-picked for me by deities. I mean, if they can't get it right, nobody can, right? So I voice my other concern.

"I guess I was just worried it wasn't real. That one day they'll wake up and realise they never signed on for this, and I'm going to be in danger again, but this time I've got four pups in tow."

"This time you've got two goddesses and a god, plus our family. I don't think it's a good idea for us to split up again. If we want the right to live how we choose, then it's time we fight for it," Gina says. She always was the most militant of us all and had been dead set against us splitting up.

I think she's wrong, I think we did far better wandering in singles and pairs, but it's been a hard and lonely life for us all. But she's right in one thing, we do need to fight.

"I agree we need to fight. Shay and I have our dragon forms now, although feeding the boys means I probably don't have the strength to shift, and I don't know that Shay will have enough time to learn how to use her dragon's body."

"We have their strength though," Shay admits. "I don't think I could stomach flaming anyone to death, but if you come at me, I'll sure as hell stab you."

Giggles sound around the room. Goddess it's good to have my family back again.

"Nobody's going to address the elephant in the room?" Gwendoline asks sourly.

The smiles fall away as we all turn to her. Trust Gwen to put a bitter twist on things.

"Nobody is going to address an alpha spreading rumours we're to be divided amongst the loyal troops, a reward for staying true to Triune."

"Oh, I'll talk about it," I snap. "About the fact he's flat out lying and just trying to stir up trouble for Marcus. Sam thinks he's trying to undermine Marcus and take over the Triune pack. That's all this is, him manoeuvring to try and gain some traction himself."

"And what if it works?" Gwen pushes, ever the pessimist.

"Then those loyal to Marcus will get us out of here. I can promise you that much."

"Those loyal, how many is that? Ten, twenty?"

"Gallus pack was larger than that. Most of them are also sworn to me. If worse comes to worst and Marcus falls, Leon will still have to get through me to get to you. He doesn't have one alpha to slay, he has two. If Marcus falls, then I'll get you out of here before Leon can come for me."

"And how are you going to get away? He'll kill you too," Gwen pushes.

"Don't you get it?" I yell at her. "I'm not the Catriona you knew. I have a wolf and dragon form. I have mates, I have a whole pack sworn to me. I don't get to run. I fight and if I die, I'd do it for all of you, every time."

The door bursts open, Ethan standing there freshly showered in a clean shirt, his chest heaving and his pupils slitted. The women scream, scrambling for the nearest exit, and not one of them steps up to save my sons. Not that they need saving.

"You, die? Over my dead body," Ethan growls, sweeping into the room and pulling me into his arms.

Oddly, he's careful not to jostle Carter who's still on my shoulder. Instead he embraces us both, and then as I look up at him in surprise, his mouth crashes down on mine in a kiss that has my toes curling.

He raises his head and looks down at me, limp and breathless in his arms and smirks. "Mine," he practically purrs.

I can feel his length hardening against my body, but Carter chooses that moment to protest. He's had enough of my shoulder and wants to be let down, his legs and arms kicking excitedly, as though some of Ethan's energy has been transferred to him.

Ethan loosens his grip and I pull back, bending over to put Carter by his brothers. It's only then I realise that when he vocally claimed me, Ethan's pupils were no longer slitted. It was the man talking, not the dragon.

20

Scott

There isn't enough room for everyone in the bunker, in fact we no longer have any space capable of housing us all at once. Our meals are taken in batches, people encouraged not to linger because the next seating is waiting for their turn to eat.

Of course our children and elderly eat first, and the Ooga Booga bird is doing a fantastic trade in humiliation for lost property. Even the newest arrivals with the witching community are giggling like mad as they watch their new peers laugh their heads off as they grovel for the return of a lost item.

Once the third seating is done, we're going to hold the presentation of the pups and have an informal meeting. It'll be short because it's fucking cold and the wind is starting to pick up. There will be a storm later tonight and we want everyone back inside and hunkered down to weather it out.

Those destined to sleep in the cars outside the barn, aka Alphe pack, have brought the vehicles in between the buildings to help with the wind chill factor. I'm not sure how much difference it will make, but if they shift, their winter coats should keep them warm enough.

"Stop it, you brute, I'm fine," snaps a familiar voice and I turn to see Fleur pushing Craig away. The huge enforcer simply grunts before laying his coat over her shoulders yet again.

He's one of the wolves I was after, so I head over to the bickering pair. Well, Fleur is arguing, Craig is simply reapplying his coat every time she shrugs it off.

"I haven't lived this long to be bothered by a simple breeze," she growls at him.

"I didn't wait this long for you to lose you to a cold because you couldn't do as you're told and wear a fucking coat. Now put it on before I put you over my knee and expose a lot more of your skin to this chill. I promise I'll heat it up again, but not in a way you'll like."

He stands there like a granite boulder, holding the coat out in front of him for her to put it on. I'm blown away when she huffs and turns around, complying with his wishes, although I'm not surprised by the satisfied smirk on her face when her back is to him. She's enjoying this far more than she should and scowls when she realises I've caught her.

I could tell him, I say quietly across the pack link. *But the pair of you are far too amusing.*

Just remember your mate listens to me, Fleur warns me.

I smother a laugh as Craig gives me a curious look.

"I was just reminding her she should be setting the example of a good mate by listening to someone who cares enough for her to go without his own warmth. The sooner she stops fussing, the sooner you'll be back inside anyway, and the sooner you'll both be warm."

The admonishment isn't lost on Fleur. While her games are amusing, she's exposing Craig to the cold too. Not that it would bother him either, but she should know better.

"What do you want?" Fleur snaps.

"Well, right now I want your mate to discuss security for tonight's event, although on second thoughts you sound in need of an orgasm or two to sweeten your disposition. As much as I need his strength, I need less of your grumbling more."

Craig's eyes light up with amusement, and it's clear to me he knows exactly what she's doing. The joke is really on Fleur now, because from the scent of her arousal, it's exactly what she's been angling for, the minx.

"You know, your own mate is looking a bit peaky. She had to take a top-up of energy from Ethan earlier while feeding the pups. Maybe you should be minding your own business instead of meddling in mine."

I know I should feel jealous, but I don't. He might not be a wolf, but it's clear from my own lack of reaction he's meant for her, just as V'dar said. While I'm not keen on even less time with my mate, I can't argue I'm missing out. With the amount of group sex we have, as opposed to one on one time, I'm not exactly suffering here. Besides, there's something powerful about watching my mate being pounded by all of us and seeing her orgasm over and over again.

"Ethan's good for her, and it's about time she did something with him. I'm sure their bond will only grow stronger every time he gives her energy. Catriona has enough mates to see to her needs, however, I'm the wolf in charge of the enforcers and the guardians and the one organising security for her and the pups tonight. If I say your cranky ass needs a good pounding, you can bet your life, my dear lady, that Craig will comply."

Fleur's mouth goes slack in shock, while surprisingly Craig lets out a deep boom of laughter. I've never heard him laugh properly before. It's a sound so full of joy that several wolves emerge from the surrounding buildings to see what the joke is. He should laugh more often.

From being in shock at my cheek, to hearing the wondrous sound of her mate's laughter, it's clear Fleur's brains are a little scrambled.

"Go on," I tell her gently. "Get him inside and reward him for taking care of you."

Fleur turns to him, a little unsure of herself, and I understand now why she's playing these games. She's trying to chase him off before he leaves her, as possibly many have done before him. The trouble is, they're mated and fated at that. He's not leaving her shy of death. He's as good for her as she is for him. It's a good match.

"Craig, find me when you're done," I tell him. "But for now, go see to your mate, she needs some TLC."

The huge wolf gives me a salute and picks Fleur up. Rather than manhandling her and throwing her over his shoulder as he's wont to do, he cradles her in his arms, carrying her bridal style back to the lodge. The entire way back, she looks up at him like he hung the moon, and I hope he catches a glimpse of her like that. She's head over heels for him and has no idea how to express it.

"Did I hear you say guardians?" Jude asks.

"Yes, you did. Do you know where Micah is?" I ask him, and the boy's face falls.

"No," he says in a surly tone. "I'm here though."

I shake my head at him. "Jude, how would you feel if I approached Micah without you? Aside from which, this is about event security for tonight. While you two may be guarding the alpha family, I need to have enforcers and security scattered throughout the crowd. It's no disparagement of you or your skill level, it's simply far too big a job for ten wolves, never mind one."

Embarrassed, he ducks his head, so I switch to a private link so he's not humiliated any further.

You need to stop looking at this as a position of prestige, a reason to strut your stuff. This is a serious responsibility, Jude. You, and me, and others are called to serve in the pack. It doesn't make us better than the person who peels potatoes or the one who cleans the porta-potties. The pack hierarchy is about governing this community, not lording it over each other. It's about caring for others. You've been called by the goddess herself to guard Catriona and now her pups too. The best way to serve others is to put yourself last. As hard as that is, it's also the fastest way to gain respect. So, if that's all you're after, a pat on the back and a bit of respect, then go about it the right way.

By now the young man's face is scarlet, but he nods.

"I will try harder, Scott."

"It's a tough role to have without a father. I know you're missing both your birth father and the father you grew up with. There are many good wolves in this pack who would be proud to take on that role of mentor and advisor. I know it's hard to go to Micah, because he's your equal, but he is your equal and he probably has as many questions and doubts as you have. Treat him like your brother and I think you'll quickly find he'll do the same. In the meantime, find yourself someone you admire and see how they do things. Try and implement some of that yourself and see if you can develop a friendship with them. Over time, it may even grow to be more. Be the person you admire in others, Jude. It's what I'm going to tell my own son when he's old enough."

Jude's eyes widen as the fact that one of Catriona's pups is mine hits home.

"You're a dad?" he whispers.

"Yeah, Jude, I'm a dad. I feel inadequate and underprepared, but I'm doing everything I can to make this a better place for him. Starting with preparing security for tonight. Want to help me out?"

"Yeah, Scott, that would be awesome." The light that shines in his eyes tells me he's taken my words to heart a little too rapidly for my liking. Apparently I'm now the person he admires the most as a role model. I can live with that, it'll be good practice for raising my own son.

"Ok, then let's go round up some reliable wolves to run interference. Tonight is an important night and I want things to go as smoothly as possible. The trouble is, not everyone is on board with that, so we need to take some precautions."

We spend the next hour touching base with former enforcers from every pack but the Alphe one. They're the ones we think are going to cause the most trouble, although some of the Pasadena wolves aren't far behind them.

"What about the dragons?" Jude asks. "Can we call on them too?"

It's a reasonable idea, I'm just not sure of our standing with the dragons.

Marcus? I call out on the pack link. *Can we use the dragon enforcers? Can I approach Dean about it?*

No! Marcus practically shouts. *The dragons can't be trusted. Nobody can be trusted, only us. Only her co-mates and her guardians.*

His voice is as abruptly silent as it was loud.

What the fuck was that about?

Stand-by, a strange voice announces across the pack link. *Vehicles approaching the front gates.*

Check all entrance points and boundaries, Sam immediately replies, *then switches to our private family link. Marcus, are we expecting anyone?*

Kill them, Marcus snarls. *Kill them all.*

Something's wrong. Something is very wrong.

Matt, do you have eyes on Marcus?

No, I think he's with the sirens.

Fuck, that can't be good. What's going on?

I turn and start running for the lodge, ignoring Jude's cries behind me. It only takes him a second to catch up, and he's already in his shifted form. Damn the boy is big. He's tall and lanky in his human form, but his wolf is enormous. He easily outpaces me when he sees we're heading for the lodge, leaping up the back verandah and pawing at the door handle. It flips open and he stands there waiting for me. He doesn't know why we're running!

Marcus, I tell him. *Find Marcus, something's wrong.*

Pounding feet sound behind me but I don't even turn to look. I don't care who it is, all I can focus on right now is finding my friend — my alpha, and Catriona. Nothing else matters.

Jude is already tearing up the stairs, people turn in alarm, voices rising asking what's going on, but I don't stop to answer. The feeling of wrongness in my gut intensifies. It's like nausea rising within me although I can't think why. The urgency to find Marcus and help him only increases with it. Time is of the essence, I can feel it.

Without hesitating, Jude pushes on the latch of a door, the one we're using as the nursery, and shoves it open with his nose. Then he pauses, the hackles rising on his back while a whimper escapes his snout.

Dread terrible and powerful encompasses me, shaking me so badly my wolf retreats deep inside. What the fuck can make my wolf back down when we're not even shifted? I don't know, but I'm sure it's not good.

The last few steps along the landing are difficult, like I'm walking through treacle, like something is physically holding me back. Inside I see Marcus backed up to the cot where the boys are beginning to stir. Blood drips from his nose and his gaze is blank and directionless, but his head follows my every single movement in an eerie approximation of attention.

"Marcus?" I say gently.

Jude enters beside me and splits off to my right where I can hear the sound of thundering hearts and rapid breathing. Every now and then a woman whimpers, but I can't smell blood, so I'm hoping it's just the terror that seems to be gripping us all.

"Kill them all," Marcus growls. "They're trying to tear us apart, make us fight over them like we did in the past. They seek to divide us. We have to protect the pack. Kill the sirens."

There's a faint hint of alpha command in his voice and Jude whines, dropping to the floor in front of the women, but he isn't there to attack them. No, his nose is pointed toward the real threat in the room, Marcus.

"Where's Catriona," I ask the women. "Where's his mate? She could probably calm him down."

"She tried," a woman sobs. "He knocked her out, said she was the worst of them all. That's her foot there."

He cut off her foot?

My eyes scan the room in a frenzy, looking for my mate, I can smell her and the scent is driving me nuts, I just want to run to where it's coming from.

At the foot of the bed, I can just see her toes, Matt says, and I realise it was he who ran right behind me. I can feel his reassuring presence steady at my side.

Sure enough, when I look at the ground I can just see the top of Catriona's toes peeking around the corner of the bed, so she must be on the floor just behind it. She's only feet away from Marcus, I don't dare go to her right now in case he hurts her again.

Mara, I pray, *we need you. Catriona is hurt, please, we need you!*

I wait but there are no answering footsteps, no sound of Fleur coming to save the day. Nobody is glowing or speaking strangely, and I realise nobody is going to. If we're going to resolve this, we're going to have to do this ourselves.

Marcus? I try sending across the link. There's nothing more intimate than the connection with your alpha, well, perhaps the exception being your mate. Hopefully it reaches him the same way it pulls at me. *We need you downstairs to help sort out the security for tonight.*

Kill them all, he reiterates. *They're only going to kill us.*

Hey? The voice from earlier calls. *What's the go with the gates? We've got people here who say they're mages and refugees. What do we do? Is anyone coming to check this out?*

Fuck.

Thankfully Sam is more on the ball.

I need someone with eyes on Dean, please? Ask him to meet me at the gate.

He's on his way, someone else responds.

Okay, I got the gate, Sam says. *You guys deal with whatever is happening at the lodge.*

What about the pups? I don't think I can kill children, can you come and do that for me? I ask Marcus.

I'm not saying any of this fucking shit aloud, if the sirens panic, he'll be on them in a flash.

What the fuck, Scott? Matt rumbles angrily.

I'll get him out of here, you sort our mate, our children, and the women. I'll take him down as soon as we're outside.

Matt's hand suddenly squeezes my arm. He knows what this is costing me. The need to rush to my mate is almost overwhelming, but I need to keep my shit together entirely for that reason.

You're too soft, Marcus growls at me. *Useless, pathetic. I should have gutted you the first day you showed up. Pussy whipped you are.*

You're right, Alpha. I'll try harder. I can be a wolf this pack can be proud of, just you watch. Come on, show me how it's done, Alpha. Let me see you tear out their throats.

Fucking useless runt, Marcus grumbles as he takes a step towards me.

I back out of the doorway and Matt moves to the side. Together we watch incredulously as Marcus stumbles drunkenly along the landing until he gets to the stairs.

Go, I tell Matt. I just need to get Marcus outside and then I can take him down. Whatever is going on, he'll be no match for me. I just have to hold him down until we can work this out.

21

SAM

Dean joins me halfway down to the gate, but I don't say anything. I can't. Part of my attention is still caught on the faint sounds from the lodge. I can hear people worrying downstairs, wondering what has our pack council running up to the nursery. I can also hear Scott's voice cajoling someone inside, but I can't make out what he's saying.

"What's wrong?" Dean asks me.

"Something's up with Marcus. He's not himself. He's talking about killing everyone but the original members of the pack and he's including the sirens in that."

Dean halts and turns to go back up the drive.

"Scott, Matt, and Catriona are with him. They'll sort it out. We need you on the gate to help us deal with these mages. If it's another attack from Alistair, we're fucked with the alpha out of action."

I'm frantic with worry for my mate. I tried calling out to her earlier across our private link but there was no response. Logically, my brain is telling me the best thing we can do is keep our lands secure while the others sort out whatever is wrong, but my heart is telling me to do a fucking about-face and go running to her.

Thankfully my head wins, even as my heart breaks a little on the inside. It feels like I'm letting her down, even though I know I'm not.

Dean puts a hand on my shoulder before we emerge from the treeline. "Let me get a feel for their magic before we reveal ourselves. I don't want to paint us as magical targets. We need to know what we're dealing with, and if they see me, they might ward even tighter."

I nod and wait, my adrenaline spiking with the need to do something; *anything*. Run toward the threat here, or back towards the one in the lodge, because I know whatever is going on there is a real threat to us all.

Before I wolf out on the spot, Dean opens his eyes and turns to me. "They're mages and have no warding on them at all. They have left themselves completely open to attack. I could kill them from here and not raise a sweat."

"Do they know you just did your magical scan thing?"

"Probably, but they're not reacting."

"Is it a trap?"

The dragon shrugs. "If it is, they're willing to die for it. There's nothing they could do to me before I stilled their hearts. They really are laying themselves open. Short of stripping naked and lying down with their hands behind their backs, you can't get any more vulnerable than they are right now."

The thing is, mages tend to work more with charms. They could have a magical throwing star just out of sight. Spelled weapons tend to be their thing, so I'm not sure revealing ourselves is the right choice, however standing here and doing nothing isn't any better, so I give a brisk nod and head out.

"Thank fuck," the wolf in charge says. "They say they're mages, refugees. Some vampires came and attacked their cadre yesterday and they've been on the run since. They moved around a bit using portals, but everywhere they went they were found."

"There's a tracing spell on us," the man at the gate says. "Aidal came to me in a dream, said to come here and we'd find sanctuary. Said it wouldn't matter about the spell because you guys were already under attack."

His gaze flickers over to the wrecked truck tangled in the fence at the front of the Pasadena lands.

"Yeah, we've had some battles," I reply. "I'm Sam, on the council of Triune pack lands. To whom am I speaking?"

"I'm Graeme Morr, leader of our cadre. I come to ask for sanctuary."

Where the fuck are we going to put them? We can't turn them away, but we simply have no space left.

"Open the gates," I tell the wolves. "They're legit."

"How the fuck do you know?" one of the wolves asks, doubting me.

I sling a thumb over my shoulder at Dean. "He vouches for them."

Graeme gives a deep bow to Dean. "We are indebted to you, sir."

Dean shakes his head. "You're indebted to Triune if anyone. I'm simply part of the pack."

"How many people do you have and are any injured? Do you have any tents?"

"There are eighteen mages of fighting strength, two elders and another twenty non-combatant spellcasters ranging from two years to ninety-four."

"Is that including yourself?"

Graeme pats the roof of the car he was standing beside and heads over to us, letting the car go on without him.

"Yes, that includes me. There are forty of us left. There were eighty-seven yesterday. We have no tents, but we have the ability to create portals. We can go shopping wherever we wish for a limited amount of time per portal. After that, they find us. It won't be difficult to get some supplies in."

That could prove very handy indeed.

"What about if you don't go through the portal?" Dean asks, obviously thinking along the same lines. "If you opened a portal to a location and some of us went through and closed it, say for a half hour period, then reopened it to let us come back, could they track that?"

"I honestly don't know. I'm not sure whether they're tracking our magic or our person, but if the portal wasn't open the entire time, I don't see how they could track either."

It's something to keep in mind for later. In the meantime, I need to get back to the lodge.

"Any good with wards to contain heat?" Dean asks companionably as we walk up the hill together.

"We could probably work something out," Graeme says. "Are you really that short of lodgings?"

I snort and look away. "We're desperately short, Graeme. We've got dragons digging foundations and heating the earth to cure the concrete so it will set fast enough for us to build on. We've got teams of wolves working in our lumber mill producing enough timber to build and someone coordinating tradespeople to try and have the buildings ready as kits so when the foundations are done they go up smoothly and quickly. We aren't even bothering with plumbing and electricity, we just want to get people out of the storm that's blowing in tonight. It's supposed to start snowing at two a.m."

"We can help cure the concrete. There's a spell for that. It'll take an hour, two tops."

I freeze in my tracks and stare. "Did you say you could get an entire set of foundations cured in two hours?"

Graeme chuckles at my plea. "No, I said I could get as many sets of foundations as you want cured in two hours. You dig them, pour them out, I don't care if it's one building or twenty, in two hours you're going to have solid foundations to work on."

Fuck. We could house the entire community in a matter of days!

My first instinct is to reach out to Marcus, until I remember he's at the centre of whatever is going on in the lodge.

"You'll have to excuse me," I tell them both. "I'm needed at the lodge."

"Go," Dean urges. "I'll start sorting people out. I'll get that Ralph fellow to see if he can get a slew of buildings outlined for us. We might as well hit this right away."

Distracted, I flap a hand in thanks and start jogging. I can hear scuffling and blows being exchanged up ahead and my pace picks up. In seconds I've rounded the last bend and the sight that greets me is not the one I expected.

Scott and Marcus are wrestling in the driveway, trading blows at a rate that makes me wince. Marcus' moves are sloppy and uncoordinated, which makes me wonder why Scott doesn't have him pinned. Right now, he's obviously the stronger wolf.

What the fuck are you playing at? I growl at him.

I'm making him forget he can shift. He can do a lot more damage as his wolf and I don't know if I can beat him. He's too busy fending me off to give in to his instinct to shift, Scott says, his tone a little frantic.

I wouldn't count on that. Any minute now he's going to snap and shift on the spot. You know how fast he can do it too.

"Wait," a voice calls out behind me, and it's all I can do not to groan.

The other cars bypassed here and went to the back end of our property, down by the mill. At least, that's where I heard Dean directing them to. The only other people here are Dean and Graeme. The mage might mean well, but his timing sucks.

Marcus growls, his eyes eerily blank, his gaze shifting to the pair of men walking towards them.

"Kill them all, kill the traitors," Marcus growls.

"He's under a spell," Graeme replies, running towards us.

Marcus tenses and I see it coming. He's going to shift and take out the mage's throat before the man has any idea of what's coming for him. I do the only thing I can think of, I force my own shift, faster than I've ever moved before, and my wolf meets his mid-leap, Marcus still only halfway through his own shift.

The pair of us land hard, Marcus yelping as a bone snaps. It'll heal in no time, but I need to use it to my advantage, so I rush him, knocking him off his feet. Before he can recover I have my teeth around his throat.

Out of the corner of my eye I can see Dean has pulled Graeme behind him, ready to defend the mage with his life. In the heat of the moment, nobody noticed, but I'm sure once this is sorted, the mage will remember.

"Hold him steady, this won't take a minute, it's not a strong spell, but it's had a hold of him for a while," Graeme tells me.

Marcus was spelled? Who the fuck would do that? Is it one of the witches? Bile rises in the back of my throat. Do we have yet another traitor in our ranks?

Kneeling beside us, Graeme pulls a handful of charms from his pocket, turning them over on the palm of his hand until he finds the one he wants. Pulling it out, he shoves the others back in, and then places his selected charm on Marcus' chest.

I have no head for magic, I don't think I can normally sense it, but whatever Graeme is doing has my hackles rising. It feels like someone is watching over my shoulder. Perhaps there is. I can't say anything to Dean, my mouth is full of my alpha's fur, so I'll just have to hang on and see what happens.

Something presses on my ear drums, making me want to swallow, but I can't. Instead, saliva pools in my mouth and drizzles slowly down onto Marcus' fur. I'm sure he won't mind if we break whatever this shit is in his head.

With a pop that sets my ears ringing, the pressure ends, as does the feeling of being watched. Instantly Marcus shifts back and I have to loosen my jaw or risk injuring him further.

"What the fuck is going on?" Marcus asks. "Who the fuck is this?"

"This is Graeme, the mage who just broke the spell over you," Dean explains as I wiggle my jaw from side to side.

Unlike my shift into my wolf form, my return to my human one is slower. I didn't know I could shift that fast. It makes me wonder if that's a learned thing. The delay, the slowness of it all, something we've adapted to, rather than what we're capable of. It's a thought for another day, though.

"Why did you have me pinned in the driveway, Sam?"

"Because you wanted to kill our mate, the other sirens, and everyone except the original members of the triune pack," Scott replies for me. "Fleur is with Catriona right now, trying to wake her up. I need to get back to our mate. Sam, you should check on your son."

Marcus blanches. "I hurt the pups?" he whispers in a pained tone.

"No," Scott tells him, "but you terrified the sirens, ordered Jude to kill them, and knocked Catriona out. You were too out of it to push a full alpha command, which meant Jude was able to resist you. We can only be thankful the spell fucked with that."

"If you'll excuse me," Graeme says, "I can trace the source of the magic now, but not forever. Already it's disappearing."

"The source is here?" Marcus asks, horrified.

"This kind of spell doesn't have a great range, and it requires constant maintenance. It's designed to plant ideas in your head. The longer it's active on the victim, the more hold it gains over their will."

"The voices," Marcus whispers.

Graeme nods. "Yes, it could sound like voices at times for sure. Telling you to do things you wouldn't ordinarily do, or burying your self-worth. The idea is to weaken you mentally until a more permanent spell can be placed upon you."

"Go with him, Sam," Marcus orders me.

"I've got him," Scott says. "Go back Graeme up. If he points to someone as a traitor, all hell is going to break loose."

"I'll come too, I don't want any of my dragons accused without me being there."

"You think it could be one of yours?" I ask him incredulously.

"No, to be honest. But I bet you don't want to think it's a wolf either."

He's not exactly right. "There's still tension between the packs, especially Alphe. I wouldn't put it past one of them to be doing something on Leon's orders."

Dean grunts his agreement as we catch up with Graeme. The mage doesn't slow down, his head swings back and forth as though he's a hound scenting the prey, and then he runs off again, the two of us jogging behind him.

"Want me to stop him, Sam?" someone asks helpfully.

"No, he's looking for something. We're just his bodyguards," I reply.

There are snickers, but nobody disturbs the mage who is now moving much faster. He rounds the corner of the barn, barely slowing as he encounters a group of wolves there, wolves who have no reason to be skulking on the far side of the building. Until I see who's standing in the middle.

It's no surprise to me when Graeme pushes his way into the centre and slaps a hand on the alpha's shoulder.

"You!" Graeme cries. "You're the source."

"Get off me, you imbecile. Do you know who I am?" Leon growls.

"A dead man," I reply, catching up to them. Then I draw my arm back and sock him as hard as I can. Leon drops like a sack of potatoes, and wolves start growling around me.

"Your alpha just used magic to attack the alpha of the pack who is hosting him. He couldn't even face Marcus in a challenge. Now he's facing a death sentence, as is anyone who we find to be in on the plot. So, make a choice, men. Either fight me now and die for your cause, or die like cowards when we catch you."

Dean steps up behind me and lets out a low growl. "Sam, get the mage out of here, I'm going to shift and flame them all."

The scent of terror coming from the wolves in front of me is so strong, it makes me sneeze. Dean is unaffected and scales begin to ripple up his arms.

"You can't, Dean," I tell him. "Graeme, can you bind them magically in some cuffs or something, until we can get this sorted?"

Graeme gives me a wicked grin. "Oh, I think I can do something suitable, move back."

The three of us step back as the Alphe wolves gather around their fallen alpha. Graeme raises his hands and several of them flinch, hunkering down, but nothing happens. Slowly they regain their composure and some of the arrogance they walked in here with. One of them even steps forward as though he's going to confront us, until he slams into an invisible wall.

He looks like a mime artist as his hands slide along a shape I quickly recognise as a dome.

"How long will that hold?" I ask gleefully.

"Until I let it go," Graeme replies.

"Clever use of a portable ward," Dean concedes, although his pupils are still slitted.

If there were any doubts about his commitment to our pack, there are none now. He really did want to kill Leon and his cronies for daring to attack Marcus. Frankly, I'm with him, and under different circumstances I wouldn't bat an eyelid, but we're trying to build a community, and that requires trust. Which means these wolves will have to be tried publicly, otherwise the rumours over what truthfully occurred will follow us around forever.

The best thing is, we're already gathering tonight for the presentation of the pups. It'll be an unpleasant interlude in what should be a community building celebration, but to rid us of the cancer growing within our ranks, I think it's going to be worth it.

Hopefully others will think twice before trying to take the pack from us again.

22

MATT

Despite the chill in the air, people are already gathering, children bundled up in extra layers or held in blankets if they're small enough to get away with it. There's a kind of festival spirit in the crowd, which bodes well for the presentation of the pups. It should be a joyous occasion, it's been far too long since any pack was able to produce a litter.

Looking around I can see various faces dotted through the crowd, Scott and Sam have done their work well. Scott getting crowd control people on board and Sam working out the best placement for them. Even now I see Jude ambling in with a group of wolves, unobtrusively finding his place. There's nothing to indicate he's anything more than another wolf keen for the celebration.

The tangy aroma of cooking meat permeates the air, adding to the cheerful mood. The mages were able to open some portals and we sent out foraging parties to malls and farms alike. It resulted in an influx of fresh meat and vegetables, including several sheep from an abattoir. They're currently being slowly cooked on a rotisserie. The smell is driving me crazy and I'm probably not the only one.

My role isn't just to stand in place and look friendly while acting as a secret guard, it's to listen to rumbles and rumours as they pass through the groups. It's a good idea to stay on top of what people are thinking and expecting.

"I heard he lost his mind and that new alpha is going to be taking over. You know, the older one who's on the council," one woman gossips to several friends. "I mean, he's a bit old for me, but at least he'd know what he was doing, right?"

The others giggle and it's all I can do not to yell at them. Where's their fucking loyalty to the pack who took them in? Fucking ingrates.

"I don't know. He's been a bit of an asshole. I've heard he's done nothing but cause trouble. He's had his wolves threatening to throw the kids and the elderly out in the cold so his fighters can stay fit. What's the point if there's nobody left to protect? I'd rather have Marcus, at least he gives a shit."

It's not the kind of endorsement I was hoping for, but at least she's for him. It's impossible to make personal connections with so many people here. I've lost count of how many we're feeding and housing but it's way more than we ever expected.

Hey, Matt? Ralph calls across the pack link.

Ralph, what can I do for you?

I just wanted to let you know we've finished a dorm. No power or plumbing, but it's weather-tight. You should be able to get twenty people in here if they stick to cots or the plain floor. Only a dozen if you're going for beds.

That's fantastic news, I'll put it on the agenda of announcements for tonight. It's nowhere near enough of course, but it's going to make a difference.

I thought it might ease tensions a bit. We should have five more dorms finished by this time tomorrow. These mages have been fantastic with their concrete-curing spells. The foundations are already laid, all we have to do is work the manpower to get the walls up, roof on and add doors and windows.

That's a hundred more wolves housed in twenty-four hours, that's outstanding! We'll also announce that. Tonight is going to be cold and hard, but if we can hold out hope to them, then they'll put up with more than they would otherwise. You've all done a magnificent job.

I can almost feel him flush with pleasure, so strong is the happiness coming down the bond to me. I ensure I send back an equal amount of pride so he knows exactly how good of a job he's done.

We've got people outlining five more dorms, and others marking out another twenty cottages. The thing is, we're going to run out of land soon, is there any way we can expand further? Otherwise we might need to look at adding multiple stories to each dorm. We can make the downstairs a general room, and upstairs into couples or family rooms.

I know Marcus is in negotiations for the farm to the east of here. I don't know where that's up to. The vampires pretty much destroyed half his crop and it's the final straw for him. I'm not sure what else is for sale around here, but long term we're going to have to look at expanding somewhere.

Okay, I'll get the engineers to look at adding second stories onto the ones we'll start tomorrow. It'll save us coming back to do it later, although it might take us another day to get them done, you should be able to house an extra dozen upstairs until we put the divider walls up later.

Thanks, Ralph. I send him another surge of approval. He's really taking the heat off us with these expansions. Okay, yes, it's because the mages are stepping up to help, but with his organisational skills we're going to be zipping through buildings at a much faster rate.

Marcus has had to spend a fortune getting all the permits sorted. Thankfully it was Sinclair's thing to interfere with shit like that. Alistair seems to be more gung ho, happy to throw lives at us until he wins. How he's holding onto their loyalty I don't know, but it's not my concern right now.

There's a bunch of Alphe wolves slowly infiltrating the crowd, moving casually just like we did when we arrived. It's exactly the kind of thing we'd expected of them, but because they didn't think we'd utilise the dragons, witches, and mages, we've got more people scattered here than they think. Graeme managed to set up those of our helpers outside the pack link with a charm that allows them to communicate with us as though they were naturally a part of the pack - of course it only works for people who've already made an oath, which makes me feel a bit better about it all.

We really are building a community here, and it makes me so fucking proud.

Heads up, I tell the others. *Alphe is making a move. My guess is they're going to swarm the stage.*

I've got a barricade spell in place, Graeme let us know. *They can rush, but they'll bounce off unless they're invited up there.*

Good, Sam says. *We've got enough people handy to arrest each and every one of them, then we'll add them to the tally of people to be expelled. We're not mucking around with these people. If they're not with us, they're against us and have no place amongst us.*

The space in front of the lodge had been cleared earlier, the cars parked off to the side or around the cabins, so it's a large enough area for us all to gather and with our shifter hearing, sound isn't an issue. Although I hadn't taken the witches and mages into consideration.

Should we move the magic users closer so they can hear? I ask Sam.

Nah, we've got a portable microphone and speaker set up, everyone should be able to hear.

The front door opens and our leadership emerges onto the verandah, a natural stage. Shit, I'm supposed to be up there, this is the presentation of my son!

Carefully I make my way forward, excusing myself and tapping people as I need to. I'm met with mutters, then warm smiles when people realise who's trying to butt in and why. It's a good feeling to know I'm so welcome amongst the pack, that we're doing things so well, people are happy to see us.

Fleur gives me 'the look' when I reach the top of the stairs and she hands over River. His face is red and there are tears clinging to his lashes, but his tiny body relaxes as soon as he scents me. There's just no getting away from *pack.* Fleur might be a part of his family, but already his tiny brain knows who his sire is. My heart grows about ten sizes. I love him so much.

Behind me, wolves snicker when they see the shit I'm in, but I don't care. My son recognises my scent and he feels safe with me.

There is nothing more important than that, and I'll deal with anything to spend more time with him.

"Hey, little man," I coo and he burbles, much to Fleur's disgust. "Daddy's here. I'm so sorry I was late, dude. I'm trying to be the best Dad I can, but sometimes that means we gotta spend time apart. I promise though, I'll make it up to you when this whole mess is over. You can sleep on my chest, because damn, I'm gonna sleep for a few days straight. We can make a man cave and hang out and chill. You can fart and shit your pants, and I'm just gonna love you more and more."

Fleur's expression softens as she listens to me babble nonsense at him. I wasn't expecting that, but I'll take the win if it gets her off my case.

"You know," I tell him, deliberately ignoring her, although I know she's listening in. "Fleur is gonna be like your granny, and Craig is gonna be like your pop. They look after your mum so well, and we're so lucky to have them. I want you to grow up loving them as much as I do."

"Alright, alright," Fleur says gruffly, but I can tell she's pleased. "You're laying it on a bit thick there, Beta."

Instead of answering, I swoop in and kiss her cheek, eliciting a growl from Craig. "Thank you for all you do for us, Fleur, but especially for my mate. We're all indebted to you for saving her and the pups."

The accoucheur loses her cool, tears welling in her eyes and her face turning pink. Craig relaxes, stepping back and giving me an approving nod, and it makes me wonder if anyone else has thanked her.

Hey, family! I send across our more private link, just as Marcus begins to call for quiet while rocking Carter in his arms. The boys are all suspiciously content and I'm willing to bet their bellies are full and their bums have been changed.

Aside from Marcus, the others are looking at me, mostly surreptitiously, although Joe has no game face, and he's just staring.

We need to make sure we thank Fleur. I don't think anyone has. She saved our mate and our pups, and not just in the delivery. Over and over again she's given to us. I don't think she gets much thanks aside from the joy of a safe delivery.

Will do, Sam says. *I'm thankful for this little chunker.*

I snicker. Dane really is solid. He's got rolls on his thighs that Catriona swoons over, she likes to pretend to chew on them and Dane loves it, he giggles his heart out. I tell you, there is nothing more guaranteed to bring a smile to your face than the sound of a baby's giggle.

Marcus gives me a quelling look before he begins to address the crowd.

"Wolves, witches, dragons, mages, vampires, and anyone else I've forgotten—"

Catriona elbows him hard and he grunts, although his hold on Carter doesn't falter in the slightest, I can hear his slow inhale as he breathes past the pain. Damn she's gotten stronger since V'dar gave her a dragon!

"Sirens," Marcus gasps, hamming it up. "Of course, how could I forget the sirens?"

The crowd chuckles, won over by his goofing off. Some of the tension already beginning to dissipate.

"We have a lot to get through tonight, some of it pleasant, some of it not so much, but all of it important for this community we're building."

"Get on with it, it's fucking cold!" a heckler calls from the back.

There's a slight eddy in the crowd around him and I know one of our enforcers has moved to stand near him. If he plans on causing trouble he won't get far. Marcus notices too, because he gives a nod, as if agreeing, but I know he's tipping his chin at whoever has moved into place.

"You're right, it is a little chilly, and we need to get you all and these little men back inside where it's warm, but it doesn't mean we're not going to celebrate! So, here is the first piece of good news, although I think most of you have already smelled it by now."

Again, the crowd chuckles good-naturedly. I don't think there's a person standing in front of us who hasn't been by the kitchens to check out the sources of the smells, nor have the fire pits with the spit roasts gone unnoticed.

"We have fresh meat! Our new allies, Graeme's cadre of mages, have opened portals to allow us to shop in safety some distance from here. We've been able to procure more blankets, cots, pillows, and food. Lots and lots of food."

A cheer sounds from the crowd. You can put up with a lot if you have a belly full of hot food. It was a good idea to lead with that.

Carter startles and begins to whine, so Marcus adjusts him until he's facing backwards, his chin on his father's shoulder as Marcus deftly pats his rump in a steady rhythm. I can see parents in the crowd nodding in approval as he settles his son without even thinking about it. He looks like a truly experienced father, and that will give even more confidence to the pack, no matter how ridiculous the reason.

"I know you're doing it tough, we all are, and we're all pulling together in amazing ways. I cannot thank you enough for your forbearance as we scramble to deal with situations we couldn't even dream of when we started building this place. I mean, we have over four hundred wolves here, mages, witches, vampires, sirens and dragons. In my wildest dreams I'd never thought of housing even half that amount of people. Thank you for being as courageous and kind as you have been."

There's a smatter of applause which swells until they're all cheering. Marcus lets them go for a bit, letting them get it out of their system. He really is a master at this, manipulating them to follow his lead.

He raises his hand again in a sign for quiet, and they all obediently settle.

"I would like to introduce my son and his siblings to you. This fine fellow is Carter, born of me and my mate Catriona, the first wolf to bear a litter of pups in generations. My thanks to you my love for this blessing in my life."

He leans over and kisses her cheek to the whistles and catcalls from the men in the audience. Catriona smiles shyly, completely unlike her, and kisses Carter's downy head instead. The three of them look like a picture from a textbook on family values or something. If we took a photo, it would earn a fortune on a stock site, that's how perfect they look together.

Marcus looks at me, his gaze soft and proud. I take it as my cue and step forward.

"This is my son, River, born of me and my mate Catriona. I give thanks to the goddesses for their aid in his delivery, and for his safe arrival."

I look over at Sam and wink, and he steps forward with a grin.

"This chunker is Dane, the light of my life and born of me and my mate Catriona. I'm so fucking grateful to be a dad," Sam says with a broad grin, and there are a few hearty laughs and a few gasps as mothers slap their hands over the ears of some of our younger wolves. As if the little shits haven't heard it from someone at this camp already.

Catriona looks down at 'Squirt'. She really struggled to find a name for him, and I'm hoping she has one now, otherwise the kid is going to be haunted by it forever.

"This is my son, Wyatt, born of me and my mate Felix. His father's name was Wyatt, and Felix's middle name was the same. I see it as a fitting tradition to use it."

This time, her announcement is met with a roar of approval as the pack greets the boys for the first time. Oh, they've seen them here and there, but for most, this is probably the first time they've seen them altogether.

Instead of getting upset, the boys perk up, burbling and drooling as if greeting the pack in return. River blows bubbles and then farts loudly. The sudden stench that hits my nose tells me there was follow-through as well. Despite the noise of the crowd, very few missed hearing that, and they laugh at me.

"On that note," I tell them all with a chuckle, "I think I'm needed elsewhere."

I pretend to hold my son at arm's length, but I'm sure to carefully support his neck. They might be growing faster than human babies, but it doesn't mean I'm going to risk him.

"Here, beta," one of the sirens says as she pops out of the door behind me, "let me take him."

The women aren't comfortable coming out into the crowd like this, and I can't say I blame them, especially with Alphe being poised to cause trouble. One by one, sirens come forth to take our sons back inside and get them ready for bed. They sleep a lot more than I'd realised at this age, but in a way it's good, because I'm far too busy trying to save this community to devote the time to my son I'd like to. At least he's sleeping through my absence.

With the boys gone, however, Marcus' face takes on a more serious mien. It's time for the shitty part, and frankly I can't wait to get it over with.

23

CATRIONA

*K*at, *you should go inside with the others,* Marcus warns
me. *Alphe is going to try something.*

He seems to forget that one, I'm also an alpha, and two, I
have a wolf and a dragon form to shift into if needed.

*I'm good, you focus on what you need to do, my wolf is with me and
I topped up on energy before we came out. I can shift if I need to.*

I'd prefer not to need to, I'd rather get to know my wolf in more
peaceable circumstances. She hums in agreement while my dragon
hovers protectively around us both, as if she can spare us from
harm while still inside me.

"You've all worked hard to get to this point, and your council is
proud of you. However, not everyone has pulled their weight,"
Marcus says aloud, even as he sends irritation through the bond to
me. "One group which has actively tried to undermine everything

we've achieved here. This has culminated in a magical attack on me, something wolves don't do, and yet the magic was traced back to a wolf amongst our community. All the magic users present have been cleared, which means this wolf arrived on our lands with the intention of causing disruption, harm, and confusion, all so he could take over this pack."

There are cries of outrage from the crowd, many of the eyes looking up at us have turned golden as wolves rise to the surface. I'm sure some are Alphe members, getting ready to attack, but the vast majority are wolves from Pasadena, and Gallus. They've already been through enough, they don't want their sanctuary here threatened any more than we do.

Ethan surreptitiously moves closer to our impromptu stage, yet my initial thought he's trying to be near me to protect me is dispelled when I see him focus on two wolves who are standing oddly. Their hands are clamped to one side of them and they look off balance.

Sam? I say across the pack bond, but when I look at him, his gaze is already fixed on the wolves who have their heads tucked down as if listening hard.

They've got knives, almost short swords tucked against their sides. When this erupts, and it will, I want you back out of the way. I know your wolf can protect you, but she hasn't been taught how to fight yet. I don't want to risk the three of you.

My dragon preens at being included although she would simply char them before they could get near us. How she could do that without hurting our own people I don't know, but I'm not going to push the issue right now. Meanwhile my wolf sulks. She might not know how to fight yet, but she's sure she could be deadly.

Against prey or a human, I have no doubt of your ability, but against highly trained fighters, ready to cheat? If they killed you, they'd instantly cripple our pack and they know it. None of your mates or your guardians would be able to control their beast's grief. It would be an instant coup with a power vacuum like that. Only Dean would be strong enough to stand up to them, and as the vast majority of people here are wolves, they wouldn't listen to him. So, for all our sakes, please, keep your skin intact, my loves?

Both of them relent at his sweet-talking, and I find myself equally charmed. He'll teach us to fight, I won't even ask. If we're the thing that makes this pack vulnerable, then I know Sam will have factored in a way to make us stronger. That's why he's our tactician.

"Bring out the traitor," Marcus says, and Graeme leads the way, coming around from the right-hand end of the verandah, Leon behind him, and two more mages follow behind the alpha.

There are shocked murmurs and protests, several people boo, but whether that's for Leon or for us holding him prisoner I don't know.

"Leon Tresch," Marcus says loudly, "you are charged with treason against the Triune pack, using magic to unduly influence the alpha, and sowing discord and strife wherever you could in order to weaken the pack structure and allow you to take over. How do you plead?"

"I have done everything I could to protect you fools!" Leon yells in response. The microphone is near Marcus, but nowhere near close enough for Leon to use intentionally. "Marcus is a pup, not fit to lead you all through this war. You need an experienced warrior, someone who understands tactics and politics, someone who could negotiate a way forward and find the best outcome for us all. Instead he's going at this gung-ho, the same as he's always done, because it's all his father, Sinclair did. This pup is from the same man who first started this war, and now his brother is leading the next round of attacks. Do you really trust him to take care of you when the shit hits the fan?"

"Silence him," Marcus snaps, and not only is Leon's voice silenced, but the crowd. Well, I think they are until a child begins to cry at the rising tension.

"Had I known you would use this opportunity to gaslight me even further, I would not have given it to you. I have proof that Leon used a charm to attack my mind, making me think I was going mad from holding the vows of so many wolves. He eroded my self-esteem and my thought processes until this afternoon he was temporarily able to overtake my personality and work me like a puppet."

There are gasps of fear from the crowd.

"He wouldn't have been able to do it if your mind wasn't so weak in the first place," one of the Alphe wolves calls out.

Immediately two of the enforcers are on him, and magical cuffs are slapped around his wrists. As soon as they click closed, he becomes docile and pliable, and the enforcers lead him off to the side where two more are waiting to receive him. He's quietly led to a clear patch of ground and made to sit on the wet grass.

I think I'm one of the few people who even noticed.

The mage, Graeme, steps forward. "My name is Graeme Morr and I am the head mage of our cadre. I wish to give evidence in this charge."

It's not how we usually do things, but Marcus graciously inclines his head and pulls me back to stand beside him, figuratively giving Graeme the stage so to speak.

"I am eight hundred years old," Graeme begins, and there's a shocked murmur from the crowd. Most didn't know of the mages' prolonged lifespan. I guess it is a need to know thing.

"With such a long lifespan, I have become rather adept at working magic, especially understanding how magic works and how it is used, how to trace it, and how to destroy detrimental spells." He pauses, looking over his audience to see if he has their attention, but he needn't have bothered. They're enraptured.

"The spell used on Alpha Marcus was by no means a simple one. The magical source is from outside of this territory, I have not only ascertained this, but had it verified by three of my cadre. The application is simple, a handshake would have been enough, as long as the caster, or in this case the owner of the charm, had access to the magic. A simple cut and a drop of blood on the gem would have activated the spell, and the first person the owner touches would become the target."

That's despicable, using touch, something almost sacred to shifters, to deliver a curse is beyond disrespectful. I can see people becoming angry. I'm sure they feel as violated as I do, and I'm only a new wolf.

"The spell is slow moving, insidious and persistent. It gradually wears down the victim's natural defences and begins to implant negative ideas. Sometimes in their own voice, and sometimes it gives the delusion of speaking with the voices of the known dead. Anyone Marcus has ever loved and respected would have been utilised in such a manner. The spell turns his own memories against him. Eventually the spell erodes the target's will until they become a puppet of the caster."

"He lies!" shouts a wolf, one of the Alphe fighters. "He's been paid by Triune to cover up the madness of the alpha so they can keep control!"

Once again enforcers move in, although this time the man struggles harder, but he still loses and joins his companion on the grass.

The two wolves with knives begin to press forward, discreetly making their way to the front. One of them keeps glancing at me, and I have no doubt I'm his target. The other merely keeps his gaze on our feet. I'm sure he'll be noting who is standing where and will plan his moves accordingly. They've both forgotten one thing, we can talk on the pack link without them hearing, because they're not part of our pack.

Micah, Jude, there are two wolves in front of me with knives, they're slowly pressing forward. Sam has told me to keep to the back or risk crippling the council with my loss. I'm counting on you to protect me.

Good call, Sam says, coming to stand behind Graeme. *I've got the mage in case they go for him instead.*

"This man is beyond reproach," Dean says, stepping forward. "While he had his cadre investigate, I conducted my own search and came up with the same conclusions. Two independent magic users are telling you the truth. Leon Tresch came to Triune lands with this charm upon him. The intention is clear, to undermine the alpha and take over the community for himself. I would add one more piece of evidence."

The dragon alpha turns and levels an angry look at Leon who doesn't flinch. "He incited Marcus to kill everyone who wasn't part of the original Triune group living here. He planned for the alpha to commit a crime so heinous, there would be no salvaging his reputation. He even mentioned slaughtering children."

There's an outcry from the crowd. Nobody, but nobody fucks with the kids.

As if the tumult was a signal, the two knife wielding wolves surge forward, and suddenly there are screams and cries from the crowd. It's not just them launching an attack, but the other Alphe members who were identified. Well, at least I think they were.

Catriona, inside, Marcus says, slamming me with an alpha command. I can resist, but I don't want to. Not because I'm afraid of them, but I'm afraid of distracting my family.

Deftly I slip between the fighting wolves and head for the door, but a body slams into me. I'm seconds away from attacking when I recognised the surprised face of Graeme.

"He just lifted me! Threw me like I was a toy!" He's looking over his shoulder at Dean who hasn't hesitated to dive into the fray, attacking Alphe wolves from behind as they battle with enforcers and holding them still for arrest.

Single-handedly Dean is turning the tide, and his own enforcers are now closing in on the troublemakers. Those not involved directly in the fighting are scrambling to get out of the way, but I see a child go down when her mother is cut at the tail end of a slash by a knife-wielding Alphe wolf, and everything in me screams to go to her aid.

"I've got her," Graeme murmurs, holding me back.

Someone trips and falls towards the young girl, and a primal scream surges up my throat, but all that emerges is a strangled sound as I see the wolf bounce off a small dome over the child's head, sliding in surprise down to one side. I can't make out who it is through the press of bodies, but the widened eyes were enough to tell me the dome isn't visible any closer than it is from here.

"I need to maintain line of sight," Graeme says, but the girl is already scrambling to her feet, the protection likely enlarging with her.

Her mother reaches out a hand and the two connect, and the child is pulled out of danger, other wolves forming a physical barrier and some even escorting them towards the bunker where the mother can get first aid.

"We're targets, and we're drawing them here," Graeme says gently as he opens the door and drags me inside. "Let's take ourselves out of the formula and we can work together to defend those inside if necessary."

Wearily I nod and lock the door, then barricade it just in case. We can't close the shutters, it would mean opening the windows and exposing ourselves to attack. Instead we close the curtains so they can't see where we are, and then we sit and wait.

"The other doors?" I ask the others.

"Closed and sealed like that one," Gwen answers while she strokes a soothing hand down Felicity's back.

They're all shaken, but none of them will admit it, at least not right now. When there's a lull, an opportunity for them to flee, they will. I just don't know how to convince them to stay.

It feels like hours, but it is probably only ten minutes later when a loud banging at the door makes us all jump.

Catriona, it's Marcus. I need to see you're okay, please? he begs.

"It's just Marcus," I tell the others and most of them sag in relief.

"How do you know?" Gwen asks sceptically.

I smirk and tap my temple, not bothering to answer as I remove the barricade and unlock the door.

"Thank fuck," Marcus grumbles, pulling me into his arms.

"How many dead?" I ask him.

"Seven, none of them are ours."

"How many arrested?"

He smirks. "Thirty, and the other seventy have surrendered. They were not involved in the fighting and have offered to give their oaths."

"Injured?"

"None worth treating. Shifting and a good night's sleep will see to the worst of it, so there will be no demands on you."

"How?" It's the only question I can think of. Seven dead Alphe wolves, no serious injuries, and seventy wolves willing to switch packs? No, that was too easy.

As if to underscore my disbelief, the faint rumble of thunder sounds in the distance. We might have weathered one storm, but we've yet to face another.

"Come on, Alpha," Marcus encourages me. "We have damage control to do."

My family cries out as he leads me outside. They still don't trust him, they can't believe that a wolf lives for his siren mate. They don't understand the bonds between us. Even knowing I have a wolf of my own doesn't change how they see it. I'm a siren to them, I have been for hundreds of years and I cannot become something else. Well, at least not so far. I think if I shifted they might see me differently.

"Triune prevails!" Marcus roars, thrusting our joined hands into the air.

"Triune prevails!" comes the answering cry of those who stayed to fight.

Slowly, others emerge from around the side of the lodge. The sounds of triumph encouraging them to come and see the outcome. Singly, in pairs, and in small family groups, they return. It's clear Marcus has been fighting. It is just as clear that I have not. I'm not sure how they will take that. I'm supposed to be one of their alphas.

As if reading my mind, Joe sidles up to me. *You only risk one alpha at a time. It's why Lisa ran her pack. She lost her mate, and stayed on to lead. You would have the option of doing the same, or taking another alpha mate, although Matt could likely step up, saving you from that. Or you could step down when a suitable alpha contender was found. No putting all the eggs in one basket, especially alpha eggs.*

He slips in behind me and nuzzles into my neck as his arms wrap around me. There's blood on his hands and he's getting it on my clothes, but I just can't bring myself to care. They're safe, and we won, that's all that matters to me.

24

JOE

Breathing in the scent of my mate does a lot to calm my wolf. I'd hovered nearby when she paused at the door with Graeme, but once she was out of sight I let all my inhibitions go.

Who the fuck did Leon think he was, trying to start a coup when he was there on his knees. He had to have known Marcus would do the honourable thing and try him at some point, I guess he just hadn't counted on his fucking twisted spell being broken. Instead of being faced with a weak and faltering alpha he could control, he encountered Marcus in his full fucking glory. I've never been so proud of my brother as I was tonight.

And these fuckers? They deserve to die.

I ripped the throat out of the first one to come at me, half shifting in my frenzy to end the threat to our pack. My clothes were shredded as I completed the shift in record time, and then it was game on. My wolf and I integrated seamlessly and we worked together to take down as many of the fuckers as we could. The others were arresting them, but I needed blood.

Nobody but nobody threatens our pack. In my eyes, they were no better than Alistair and the fuckers who were threatening the world. If they weakened us to the point where Alistair won, their victory would be short-lived, but not a single one of them would have thought that way. No, all they could see was what they thought they were entitled to — control of our pack and lands.

There is no doubt in my mind the first thing they would have done was expel the other races, even the dragons. It's just Leon's style. Make it all pure, build them into the strongest pack, and then work to take on the next challenge. In a way, he's no better than Sinclair or Alistair, he just goes about it differently.

Leon is sly and underhanded, and undeserving of the beast that resides inside him.

If it were possible, I'd fucking strip them all of their wolves and send them out to live as humans. See how they fared then. Death is too quick of a punishment for them. In fact, I might suggest that to Marcus. We pray to Mara to take away their wolves, leave them helpless and crying — exactly as they would have done to the weaker souls we've fucking fought so hard to protect here.

You alright, man? Sam asks, eyeing me as I inhale my mate's scent and grind my hard cock against the cleft of her ass. Damn but pregnancy has done wondrous things to her body, adding curves and soft parts I just want to explore for the rest of my life.

Yeah, I'm fine, why?

Joe, Sam says carefully, *you went feral. Completely berserk. The only deaths here today were caused by your wolf. I need to know you're really okay.*

I lift my head from Catriona's neck, giving up the comfort her scent brings for a few seconds so I can comfort and reassure my pack-mate in turn.

He didn't kill them, I reply.

Sam opens his mouth to protest aloud, but I hold up a hand.

We killed them, Sam. My wolf and I were one, and we took out the threat to our pack. They didn't deserve to share the air we breathe, nobody threatens our alphas and lives. It was no accident, Sam. Not in the slightest.

"Fuck," he whispers aloud.

Berserkers don't run in my family tree, Sam. I'm here and I'm sane. I'm just really, really pissed.

Alright. I have to let Marcus know.

Do it, I encourage him. *Or I will. He needs to know where I stand. I won't let these fuckers take her from me. Or him. Or you. Any of us. This is my pack, and I will fight until the light leaves my eyes.*

Instead of walking away, Sam comes over and slings an arm around my shoulders, his other one encompassing our mate.

"I fucking love you, Joe," he says softly.

"I love you too, brother."

He gives us one last squeeze and walks off, heading to the other side of Marcus. He must use their private link because Marcus gives me a quick look and a nod of approval, before returning his attention to the crowd before him.

"A storm is coming, people," Marcus calls out, and instantly everyone hushes. "Not just the clouds gathering overhead, but a torrent of evil. They will take everything from us, and then they will move onto the next target, gathering strength with every blow they make."

He turns his head to the cuffed and silent wolves sitting off to the side, staring into space.

"We each have a choice to make. There are two sides to this conflict, but there are also two paths to take. You can pick a side, or you can run and hide and hope you survive the aftermath. Those wolves on the ground chose to make a third side. Their own, where only their self-interest was considered. They're parasites, scavengers and traitors. They are no longer welcome on Triune lands. The question I ask now is whether you join them as they leave, or stay with us and fight?"

"Fight!" yell a couple of wolves, One from Gallus and another from Pasadena.

It's not them we're interested in. Well, not with this question. They've already proven their loyalty. No, even without being told, I know to look for the Alphe members. I'm not alone. People draw back until those from the disgraced pack are left standing in the middle, vulnerable and frightened.

The few women there try to stand tall, but you can almost see their shoulders curve in. The lack of children in their pack is noticeable. If I had to guess, I'd say there hasn't been a child born to Leon's pack for some time, a warning sign itself he was on the wrong path.

One Alphe member falls to his knees, and like a set of dominoes, the rest fall with him. Seventy wolves, all humbled and kneeling. Seventy strong fighters who could make a difference for our community in the upcoming battles.

"I wish to make my vows to the alphas," the first wolf calls out, and instantly the others copy him.

"Then make them," Marcus says, stepping forward. "Make your oath to me and be welcome in this pack."

There are gasps from the crowd at his declaration, but it's not until people start to point and whisper that I turn to look at him.

Marcus' eyes glow blue, and his hands burn a bright white. Signs of blessings from both the goddesses.

"I have been strengthened to carry this extra burden. You need never fear again that you will be stuck with a mad alpha. I am enough for you all."

The wolves on their knees practically yell over the top of one another to give voice to their vows. If there were any doubts amongst them, there are none now.

Marcus, the prisoners, don't kill them.

Neon-blue eyes turn to regard me coldly.

And what would you have me do with those who defy my will, my son? Mara asks.

Take back the gift you gave them. Take the wolves from them and let them live the rest of their lives as humans, yet don't leave them without hope. Let them live their lives in the hope of regaining your favour, that you might one day return what you take.

You seek revenge.

And you do not? I challenge her, stepping away from Catriona.

A cool sensation runs down my legs, and when I look down, crisp white cotton slacks hang from my hips.

V'dar would not approve of your arousal and your lack of attire.

There is only one mate for me, I promise her.

This I know, but the call of a goddess is another thing altogether. I do not wish to inadvertently start something I have no interest in continuing.

Ouch. She made that pretty fucking clear. Still, my erection was for my mate, not her, and I think she knows it. If this saves her pride, so be it.

A smile flickers across Marcus' face and is gone. *You are not the submissive wolf you play at. Your thoughts are amusing.*

I shake my head. *I submit to* her, *every single fucking time. I'm not a dominant wolf, but I have my own strengths and talents. Loyalty is one. A need to protect my family is another. These people are my family, and I would lay down my life for them.*

These people? she asks, using Marcus to gesture to my family around us. *Or these people?*

This time her gesture encompasses the crowd before us.

Both, I tell her. All of them. The ones up here are my mates and close family. The ones down there are my pack. Witch, dragon, mage, siren, or wolf; no matter what they identify as, they are mine, ours, and we will die for them if need be.

Don't be so hasty to throw your life away, my son.

I'm in no rush, Goddess. Believe me, I have a lot of plans I'm dying to put into action.

A cool breeze caresses my face, and then Mara laughs, Marcus throwing back his head and erupting in peals of high-pitched laughter. Damn, I'm going to have a field day teasing him about that.

You are a very refreshing wolf, Joe, Mara says. *I think perhaps V'dar should come visit you for some tips. The apple — I would never have thought to use it like that.*

I shrug my shoulders. *I've watched a lot of porn.*

Again she laughs and reaches up with Marcus' hand to stroke my face. *I find you worthy, Joe.*

If she means for me to become her mate, she's misunderstood me entirely.

No, Joe, she chides. *I give you my name. Call it three times and I will come, no matter what.*

A searing pain blazes across my head, and when it recedes, I know her name. Not the one we wolves call her, but her *true* name.

The blue fades from her eyes, and instead I'm faced with my alpha's glare.

"Did you hear all of that?" I ask him, unsure what to say.

"Every fucking word," he growls, and then turns away from me.

Well, that isn't ominous at all.

"The goddess in her wisdom has sought to intervene," Marcus tells the waiting crowd. Despite the stiff breeze that is blowing harder and harder, you could hear a pin drop.

People look to me then back to Marcus, as if I know whatever the fuck he's going to say next.

"The traitors have defied her will," Marcus says. "They are to be stripped of their wolves and spend the rest of their lives trying to earn them back."

When he finishes speaking, a blue glow surrounds the prisoners and gradually they blink back to alertness. Without their wolves, they're entirely human, and the spells on the cuffs no longer affect them.

"What the fuck are you playing at now, Marcus?" Leon snaps, proving the goddess also gave him back the power of speech.

"Why don't you ask your wolf?" Marcus taunts.

Leon's eyes glaze over, and then he looks back up to glare at us. "Well, it's not fucking possible while these cuffs are on us. Whatever spell you've put on them, I can't feel my wolf."

Marcus smirks. "By all means, release the prisoners."

Instead of walking over there, Graeme simply raises a hand and all the cuffs drop to the ground in a jangle of metal.

"I can't shift!" one man cries out, proving he intended to attack.

"Fuck shifting, I can't feel my wolf!" cries another.

"What the hell have you done?" Leon shouts, furious. "Give them back right now."

"It was your own goddess who took them, you fool," Dean growls at him. "We all watched her do it. You all glowed blue, and then you woke up because there's no magic left in you to react to the cuffs."

One of the men leans over and pukes, while the others stare at Marcus ashen-faced.

"She did give you one last chance," Marcus offers them.

Immediately he has their undivided attention.

"Live as you should have. Become men worthy of the gift of a wolf, and in time, she may forgive your betrayal. You have defied her will, and she's sorely pissed with you all. She's not the only one, but you can thank my brother here that you're not dead, because that is the sentence you faced."

"You're lying. You've simply given us some drug that masks our beasts," Leon insists. "If my wolf was gone, the rest of my pack would be frantically searching for a new alpha."

"We already found one, you fool!" snaps one of his former packmates. "We all gave our vows to the alpha worthy of them, while you were spaced out and drooling on your clothes."

"You ungrateful mutts!" Leon roars. "This was for you, all of this was for you. I was making us stronger, invincible, and you run the first chance you get."

The wolf shifter sneers at his former alpha, going as far as to stride up to Leon and stand chest to chest with him. Only the witches and mages might struggle to hear what they say next, because the rest of us have excellent hearing.

"No, Leon. This was all about you. I warned you, hell, your entire council warned you not to take this path, but you had to go ahead and do it anyway. You lost, Leon. Our lands were overrun, the majority of our pack killed, and you came running here with your tail between your legs. Rather than being grateful at finding safety, you turned this into a campaign to regain all you lost. You're a fool, and you've gotten exactly what you deserve."

Leon swings an arm up to punch the guy, but he's quicker and there's a clear crack of bone when his hand hits Leon's ribs. The former alpha crumples to the ground with a pained cry. Yeah, that's gotta suck. He can't even shift to heal it, and his wolf is no longer there to help with the pain. He's experiencing his first broken bone as a human, and it's not a pretty sight.

"Lock them all in one of the trucks in the barn," Marcus orders. "They're going to feel the cold more as humans now, but I'm not turfing out our people to make them more comfortable."

"What about the people who were sleeping in the truck?" someone asks angrily.

Marcus smirks. "I have some good news," he replies as the traitors are dragged away. "And some bad news."

Mutters sound from the crowd. They're not happy, but hopefully Marcus can turn this around before he loses them.

"Tonight, and tonight only, those who slept in that truck will sleep here in the lodge. We'll all have to squish up, and it's likely many of you will sleep upright, or probably won't sleep much at all. Maybe you can do it in shifts."

The grumbling grows as those who sympathise with the people unhoused voice their opinions to their neighbours.

"The good news," Marcus says loudly, and the crowd hushes, but the tension is thick in the air. "Tomorrow night, you will sleep in your own completed dormitory. It will have room for twenty people to sleep on cots, which we will procure with the help of the mages."

Gasps sound from those affected, and the tone and spirits rise a little.

"Thanks to the mages and their amazing concrete setting spells, and the dragons and their magnificent trench digging, we've managed to speed up the laying of foundations. With the arrival of Ralph," Marcus says, craning his neck to search the crowd. "Where are you, man? Get your ass up here!"

There are good-natured chuckles and eventually Ralph makes his way to the front of the crowd. Marcus gestures madly for him to come up on the verandah, but the wolf refuses, at best he stands on the bottom step, so Marcus walks down a couple to stand over him, resting his hands on Ralph's shoulders.

"This man has a gift," Marcus explains. "He is a genius at logistics and has organised our work crews, timber production, procurement, and more. Because of his skill, we've seen a thousand percent increase in our efficiency. We should have five more dorms finished in two days' time, two storey dorms that should house approximately thirty-two people each. That's a hundred and sixty more people housed in a matter of days. And while those are going up, the foundations will be laid for more cottages, so smaller groups can find their own places to stay."

A loud cheer goes up from the crowd echoed by a roll of thunder that is much, much closer than the last one. That storm blew in fast, and they said it wouldn't arrive for hours yet.

My wolf whimpers inside me, restless. He fears something is wrong, but it's only a storm. Alright, it might have some lightning, but the majority of us sleep inside, we should be fine.

The wind is really picking up now, and the first drop of rain hits me on the cheek, despite being under the overhang of the verandah. It's so cold, it doesn't just sting, it burns. Fuck, it hurts!

When I hold a hand up to my face, it comes away wet with blood, and still the pain continues. What the fuck is going on? Was I hit with a projectile instead?

Someone in the crowd cries out in pain, and then another. The wet splatter of raindrops punctuates the cries, almost like one is an echo of the other. Splat, cry, splat, scream, splat, yell.

When the second drop hits my arm and the burning happens again, my shocked brain begins to register what is happening.

"Get under cover!" I yell. "The rain is burning, get out of the open and under cover. Inside, inside everyone. The wind will blow it into you if you stay out here. Keep clear of the cars unless you're in the barn, find shelter in a building."

People are screaming and the smell of blood is thick in the air. Children are scooped up and carried as adults run towards the lodge, the bunker or the barn. Everywhere else is just too far away.

Despite the pain, I step out into the downpour, helping those too shocked or hurt to get into shelter. The screaming gets louder, and some people are on the ground, too injured to help themselves. They're probably not shifters. I can feel my wolf healing me as fast as I'm injured. I don't know how much longer we can keep this up, but as long as there are injured people in need of help, I'm going to keep helping.

I reach for the first body, dragging them up onto my shoulders in a fireman's carry, and start running for the lodge. Unfortunately it means they're sheltering me rather than the other way around, but I can move faster this way and we'll both be out of it sooner.

As soon as I reach the stairs, the body is yanked from me and lifted inside. Instead of following, I turn and head back out into the rain. All the able-bodied people have left and only the dazed and confused ones remain.

Each body means something in this community. I can't fail them.

I grab another and turn back to the lodge. Shadows move around me as others get the same idea, and together the five of us start rescuing people even as our own bodies are gradually shredded.

If I thought the pain of a raindrop burned, it's nothing compared to the agony of when a second one hits where the skin is broken. It's like salt on a wound, or acid on a cut.

Actually, that's far too apt. It's acidic. Acidic rain! This isn't natural, it's magical, I'm sure of it, which means we're under attack.

Marcus! I yell at him.

Little busy carrying bodies, Joe, he replies.

Ah, so he's one of the shadows out here.

Yeah, me too. I was the first.

I fucking know, you nutjob. But if you're going to kill yourself doing this, the least I can do is shoulder some of the burden.

Literally, I say, adding a mental snort.

He doesn't reply.

Marcus, this isn't natural, it's magical, I tell him.

Yeah, I gathered that, Joe.

No, Marcus, listen to me. This will stop and they'll follow through. We're supposedly weakened and demoralised. It's the perfect time to attack. We need to be ready for a direct hit.

Fuck!

He's silent then, but I can feel the buzz in my head that tells me he's blistering the pack link with orders to various people.

I can feel myself start to flag, my wolf running out of strength to heal me when we're constantly getting drenched in this fucking stuff.

There's a tremendous roar, and then the rain stops, although the sound doesn't. It takes me a moment to realise something is sheltering me, holding the rain off my skin. I look up expecting to see a dome of some sort by the mages, but it's not see-through, in fact it couldn't be more fucking solid if it tried.

It's a fucking dragon. Wings spread wide, it's sheltering us even as it roars in pain. It's an advantage I won't waste. I try to pick up my pace, but my body isn't having it. Another body is gathered in, and now that the way is protected by the giant beast above us, more people make the foray out into the mud, the grassy area now distinctly brown, and smells of burnt vegetation, clothing and skin alike are now free to assault my nose. As bad as it was, the rain was clearing the air, but now I'm left gagging on the stench left behind.

The next body I grab is a child and my heart breaks. She's screaming in agony, a stuffed toy of some sort is sheltered under her body, like she threw herself over it to protect it.

"Mama," she cries, and I notice the witch close by. The woman is breathing, but she's not conscious.

"She's coming, little one," I tell her soothingly as I jog back to the lodge. She's so light I can barely feel her.

The girl sobs and cries for her mother, and I hand her up the stairs to the waiting people before heading back to get her mother. There aren't many bodies left, and I think by the time I get this one back to shelter, there will be none left to come back out for.

I'm almost at the mother's body when a sharp sting on my arm reminds me of the pain my own body is in. Fuck, that felt like a fresh drop. I look up and regret it instantly. My time is up, and judging by the massive holes in the wings of this dragon, so is his.

Gathering every ounce of energy I have, I sprint to the woman, more and more droplets hitting my body as I run. There isn't much left of his wings, and I fear soon his dragon will force his shift back.

The mother of the child groans when I pick her up. I kind of want to do the same, but I don't have enough breath in my lungs to voice it. Instead I begin the trek back to the verandah, my body protesting every step. Halfway there, I'm met with two people, one takes the woman from me and jogs easily away, the other slings me over his own shoulder and carries me up and into the shelter.

With a pained roar, the dragon shifts, and there are cries for someone to go and save him. I hope he's okay, because he just saved a fucking lot of lives.

It's my last thought before the pain of my injuries forces my mind to shut down.

25

CATRIONA

"Do something!" I scream as everyone stares at Joe in shock.

His face is covered in blood and I can hear the hiss as each droplet hits him. I'm trying to get out there myself and help, but Micah has me wrapped in his arms and he won't let go. I don't want to hurt him, but if someone doesn't go and help my poor, sweet Joe, I'll rip his arms off.

Before I can shout again, Matt is flying past me with a rain slicker on. It won't last under the rain, but hopefully it will protect him for a little longer.

Shayla runs past me and shoves at Graeme. "Can't you do something? Make one of your barriers?" she snaps.

Instead of getting aggressive back, Graeme gives her a tired look. "I'm trying. Believe me, I'm fucking trying, but there's more than one spell involved in that and I can't fight them all. My cadre isn't here with me, otherwise we could combine strengths. If you have a way of getting to the bunker and bringing them back safely here, then we can put some real force into it, but alone? I'm no match for the people causing this. There has to be at least a dozen of them."

My loyal sister then turns to the dragons in the room. "What about you? Can you all combine magic? Or can you lend your strength to Graeme?"

"Our magic is very different to that of a mage or a witch. You're asking to combine fire and ice and make light. It just doesn't work that way."

"But what about the wards around our lands? They're made of multiple types of magic," Shayla protests.

While she argues, people are leaping off the verandah, joining Matt and Joe. If they can't protect them, they're going to help reduce their exposure time. My heart swells in love for everyone who is putting their lives on the line to help those too hurt to move.

"Again, it's not that simple. Our wards are actually done in layers. Think of a layer of straw, another of wool and a third that is a tarpaulin. Each layer gives more protection as a whole, but none of them interact with each other. The tarp keeps things dry, and prevents air from escaping, the wool traps a layer of air and holds the heat, and the straw makes a solid bedding and good insulation. They benefit each other, and combined they are greater than they are individually, but if you destroy the tarp, the wool and straw will be relatively unaffected."

"We have to be able to do something!" Shayla cries, articulating the angst in my heart. "Those are my sister's mates out there. They're going to die if we can't help them."

"Then allow me," Connor says, stepping forward. "Maybe this will convince you of my sincerity. I would die for you, Shayla, you're my mate!"

Before she can protest, he pulls her into his arms, slanting his mouth on her own and kissing her soundly. When he raises his head again, she stares at him in a daze.

"I thought you said your magic wouldn't work?" she protests weakly.

"It won't," Dean confirms, looking at Connor with a frown.

"But my strength will," Connor replies. He passes Shay to his alpha, then strips down until he's naked.

"Your hide won't last long, Connor," Dean warns him. "And you can't exactly fly them back, what are you doing?"

"Proving myself," Connor replies, giving Shay a significant look. Then he runs out the door, launching himself from the verandah with a roar that is quickly converted to his dragon's voice as he shifts.

Connor spreads his wings, turning until the entire area is covered, well, at least the part where people are lying. I can't see his back from here, but on his tail, the golden sheen of his scales slowly starts to fade. The scales turn brown, then they begin to look lacey, before blood starts to pour down his hide. Yet he doesn't move, doesn't even flinch, holding his wings above him as he patiently waits for the vulnerable to be rescued.

With the area safer, more people leap down into the mud, grabbing survivors and bringing them inside to be triaged. The sirens come into their own then, each leaping forward and helping, assessing wounds, dealing first aid and most importantly singing. Not all of our songs are for luring people to us. Some are to pacify, to lull, or to bring ease and comfort. Those writhing on the floor in acidic agony need that comfort right now.

The burn wounds are horrific, the redness and blistering are bad enough, but the full dermis burns are horrific, and it angers me when I see children amongst those hurt. What kind of monster does this?

This time, when I push against Micah's hold, he releases me and I surge forth to give my own aid.

"I need people with strength to be my battery," I call out. Instantly I'm surrounded by dragons.

"I have a dragon, can I do this too?" Shayla asks.

"I don't know. I can close my eyes and send my awareness inside their bodies when I'm touching their skin. I don't want to overwhelm you, but if you can help, that's awesome. If it works, maybe stick to first and second degree burns for now. Ease the heat and the pain, encourage the skin to heal, make the inflammation settle. I can deal with the deeper injuries because I know what normal looks like, if that makes sense?"

Shay swallows hard. She hates sickness. Her birth mother died of a plague and although she caught it, she somehow survived. This is pushing her to her limits, but if she can heal people, it might help alleviate the trauma of watching her mother die.

Hesitantly she reaches out and touches a clear patch of skin on the man we're kneeling beside.

"Take the hand of a dragon," I tell her softly, not wanting to startle her. "Feel his dragon, feel his strength and energy."

Shay's small hand is engulfed by the giant mitt of Isaac. He watches her curiously, his slitted pupils telling me his dragon is just as aware.

"That's it," Isaac coos. "Feel the big brute, he's reaching out to you, sending you what you need."

I watch the pair a moment longer, seeing the beginning of a bond growing between them. At this point, it's the beginning of a friendship, but I'm willing to bet Isaac will push for more. Good luck to him. Connor hasn't made any headway, and he's her fated mate!

I'm not sure exactly how that happened either. One minute he was drooling over me, the next it felt like, his attention had shifted to Shay. Not that I'm complaining, I'm already considering a dragon mate of my own. Connor isn't my type anyway, but he seems completely smitten with her. If she's not careful, she's going to end up with her own harem.

The wolf beneath my hand shakes with the pain of his burns, and my heart breaks for him. I wait just a little longer to see if Shay is coping okay, but I can clearly see the red patches fading and the blistering reducing. It's not until I dive into his body myself that I see she isn't soothing the nerve endings, so although the physical injuries are going, the pain isn't.

"Shay," I tell her gently. "You need to calm the nerves too. He's going to have phantom pain if you don't. You're doing a great job with his skin though."

She gives a grunt of acknowledgement and this time I leave her to it. I'm still not entirely sure how this works, but I know I'm always drawn to the worst injuries first, so I allow my consciousness to float for a moment before it's pulled to his back. I'm hoping it isn't true, because the poor man is lying on it, which would only exacerbate his discomfort.

The true horror of his injuries isn't immediately apparent. He's in so much pain I can't work out where to attack first, but if anything, the levels are only increasing. Even as I address an open wound, I feel the edges of it fraying under my touch, coming apart all over again. Disturbed, I open my eyes and stop drawing on the dragon beside me.

"Alpha Catriona?" the woman asks hesitantly. "Is something wrong?"

"Roll him on his side, I need to see his back," I tell her.

Immediately two more dragons step forward, carefully rolling him over yet not disturbing Shay where she's still healing the wounds on his arm.

There's a hiss and a sizzle and the stench of burning flesh hits me anew. It takes me a moment to realise what's going on, but when I do, I want to vomit.

"Get their clothes off!" I yell to the room. "The acid is still in their clothes, they're still being burned. Get their clothes off and wipe the skin down where you can. We need blankets, because with burns like these the first thing they're going to have difficulty with is regulating their temperature. Strip them down, wipe them over and cover them up. Do it, quickly."

Moments ago bandages were being applied where appropriate and hands were held, tears wiped and comfort given, but with my cry the room explodes into action. People scatter everywhere, fetching blankets, cloths, basins of water, scissors, and knives.

Frantically we work on our own patient. He's been lying on a puddle of acid, and it was continuing to burn into the skin on his back and legs.

As soon as he's stripped, I delve in again, leaving the others to wipe him down. I grab hold of my dragon and pull, the woman giving a short grunt and dropping to her knees beside me. I can't afford to be gentle, the wolf I'm caring for is in shock and if we don't stop this now, we could lose him. I push my hand onto the raw surface in front of me. There is no intact skin left for me to reach, and I shove my power into him. I'm not going to be able to heal the first-degree burns, not if I want to give him a dermis back. I think he'd rather feel sunburned than cooked alive.

It's the beginning of several long hours, the rain doesn't let up and those not involved directly in helping the patients are busy in the kitchen preparing food to sustain us all, or working out a better bedding system.

"The tyres are melting!" a voice calls out, and there's a surge of people to the windows. I'm too involved with my latest patient, a little girl who is skimming along the edge of survival. Any time she rouses, she cries weakly for her mother. There's no answer from the semi-healed people around me, so I can only assume the woman is one of the unconscious.

Her delicate, heart shaped face is marred with angry red lines that I may be able to fix later. Right now I have her on her belly while I try to heal the large scores on her back. This shouldn't happen, the children shouldn't be suffering like this. This is beyond wrong, this is evil, pure evil.

Mara, I pray, *your people are suffering. Even the children are hurt. Please, we need your help. There are too many who are injured.*

I close my eyes to the child's suffering, and I push every ounce of my strength into her. There's a thud behind me and I know I've worn through yet another dragon, but I can't let her die. Not a child. She did nothing to deserve this. Nobody here did, but the innocence of a child is undeniable.

"Catriona," Shay calls me, and my heart stutters. She only uses my full name when she's upset. "Kitty-Kat, stop."

No!

She can't be dead. Not a child. *Please, please, please, Mara, don't let her be dead.*

"She is not dead, daughter, but if you would kindly step out of the way, then my sister can heal her."

I open my eyes to see Mara, Zaya and V'dar beside us. Mara's eyes are wet with tears and her lovers rub her back soothingly. Quickly I move out of the way, and the goddess takes my place, resting a hand on the little girl's forehead and lower back.

In the blink of an eye her wounds are gone. I blink again, just to be sure, because I can still see the outlines of the angry red wounds, until I realise it's not a retinal imprint. It's scars. They look old, faded and silver, but this little girl will carry the evidence of this attack for the rest of her life. Long may the goddess let her live.

With a startled wail, she wakes and sits up, looking around the room, her eyes glazed as they pass over us. "Mama!" she cries, dismissing us as not the person she needs.

"Come on, little one," Mara says, taking her hand and pulling her to her feet. "Let's go and see if we can find her. I think she might be having a nap over here."

Blearily I stand, wiping the sweat from my brow.

"Why didn't you call us sooner?" Zaya chides, reaching out and pulling me into a hug.

Around us, everyone stands in awe. The deities are here, completely manifested and standing in the living room of the lodge.

"I wasn't thinking," I admit ruefully. "We haven't always been able to get a hold of you, and I guess I just got into the habit of doing stuff myself."

Gently she bops me on the forehead. A literal goddess bops me!

"You always reach us. We cannot always come, but we always hear your calls. As soon as we are able, we respond, but often you have already dealt with the situation yourself. Do not be afraid to ask. We will come whenever we can, if we don't, then go ahead and do things, but remember you are not alone in this war."

"Yes, mother," I say, and she beams at me, pulling me into her embrace.

In a macabre parody, a voice calls out in the background. "Mama! No!"

Together we turn where the girl is weeping over the body of a woman. Mara draws the blanket back up over her face and pulls the girl into her embrace, comforting her. The girl will not lack for people willing to raise her, but it's small comfort right then. All she wants is the one woman who will never hold her in her arms again.

The child's keening cries cast a pall over the room. If the others feel anything like me, then they'll feel like we let her down. Like we failed. Because surely we could have saved them both, right?

Wearily I turn to find the next patient, but V'dar is already there. As I approach, he rises to his feet, his hands bloody where they must have rested on the wounds.

"Rest, little one. You have done enough," V'dar says. "This is work for the gods."

Rendered useless, I stand there wringing my hands. If I'm not healing, then what do I do?

"Kat," Shayla says quietly, plucking at my arm. "He's not the worst injured here, but he's still in pain."

Turning, I see her gaze shyly darting towards Connor and skirting away again, like a timid creature not sure of their welcome.

"He's hurt," Shay whispers, her voice sounding pained.

V'dar gives us a coy smile, moving on to another badly burned wolf, so I grab her hand and we head toward the dragon together.

Connor makes no sound as we approach, but he inhales deeply, a shudder rippling across his skin. "I'm fine," he rasps, but given the state of him, he really isn't.

I reach a hand out to touch him and he doesn't even react, although again he breathes in deeply and then sighs, turning his head away.

"Connor," I say gently. "I know your dragon is strong. What he did out there, it was amazing. My mates and I will forever be in your debt."

"You're welcome," he says quietly, still looking off to the side.

"Connor, look at me," I order, and it's only when he turns his face back to me that I finally see what has him so quiet.

He's blind.

Dark red rivulets, burn marks, run down his forehead, leaving blank patches in his brow and eyelashes and turn his pupils milky white, great sections of colour bleached in his iris. His left cheek is so pock marked with burns, I can actually see some of his teeth through the hole.

He hasn't just been burned, he's been devoured.

Shay lets out an inarticulate cry and rushes to him, but I hold her back, looking at his wet clothes. "Shay, we need to get him naked," I tell her, and she gives me a funny look.

"What the fuck, Kat?" she protests.

"His clothes are covered in acid. He's still burning, we need to undress him."

"No!" Connor growls, defiant. "Colin, I need your help."

Isaac, formerly known as Colin, makes his way across the room to us. "What do you need, dude?" he asks cheerfully, surreptitiously casting glances at Shay.

"I need a shower to wash this shit off me. My eyes are damaged, can you help me up there and out of my clothes?"

The other dragon looks from Connor to us and back again. "Looks like you already got yourself a couple of pretty little helpers here. If I had two sirens standing there trying to get me naked, you can bet your ass I wouldn't be complaining about it!"

"No," Connor snarls again. "I will not be the subject of her pity."

Of all the stupid pig-headed things to say, that was the wrong one. He can't see me reach for him, so he has no hope of dodging me as my hand snakes out and grabs his own. Connor tries to pull back, but Shay is there just as fast, a pair of scissors in her hand as she starts cutting away his shirt.

Isaac has a hold of his other hand, so he's helpless against her, which only makes him struggle harder against me.

"Stand still," I growl at him, both my wolf and dragon lending their voices to me.

Both Shayla and Isaac freeze, but so does Connor so I ignore them and send my awareness inside him. The mess I find on his back is nauseating.

I don't understand the mechanics of shifting, especially not for a dragon shifter who develops two extra limbs, but I can see the wing bone structure inside his back. How does it not show on his human form? He, and all dragon shifters, should be hunchbacks if they did. I guess that includes me too.

My dragon snorts, amused by my thoughts. I get the clear sense she would never allow us to look so deformed. My wolf swishes her tail, reminding me she also gains an extra appendage, thus dragons are not the only impressive creatures.

Regardless of their responses, the bones are there in Connor's back, some of them pitted and damaged from the acid. I can even sense the membranes of his wings. There're so many holes it looks like fine lace, and several of the joints have melted and fused together into place.

Even if he grows the hide back, he'll never fly again with joints that are frozen solid.

The rest of his back is like badly ground beef. Bone, sinew and muscle are all exposed to the fabric of his clothes which hold enough acidic rain to keep burning through yet another layer of tissue. If he doesn't shift soon, he's going to bleed out. His legs are only marginally better, it seems they were protected by his dragon's bulk, but the clothing clinging to them is beginning to take a toll.

"Clothes, now," I snap, and there's a rustle of fabric as Shay begins to move again. Oddly, Connor doesn't, and when I open my eyes to check on him I find him frozen in place, the same with Isaac on the other side. I might have released Shay, or at least given her another alpha command, but I haven't released the two men.

"Alpha," a voice calls out. "Alpha Catriona, we need you over here."

"I'm a little busy," I call back.

Catriona, Joe calls me. *The gods have just healed a few vampires, but now they need to feed. We need to decide who's going to donate before they go feral and start killing people.*

Well, fuck. Can't Marcus deal with it?

He's holding one of them in a headlock, I've got the other and Toby has a third. Two more are just regaining consciousness, but we're out of strong wolves and you need the dragons as batteries.

Use the worn out ones. Get them to sit on the vamps.

"V'dar!" I call out, looking around for help. I can't heal Connor on my own.

"I can save his eyes or his wings, but not both, I have used too much power today," V'dar says from right behind me, making me jump."

"Eyes," Connor says without hesitation. "I want to see her just one more time."

"So fucking melodramatic," Shayla says with an eyeroll, but tears are pouring down her face. I'm grateful Connor can't see them, it's obvious he's too proud to allow her to grieve for what he's lost, or rather what he's going to lose.

I nudge her with my elbow and pass her a clean cloth, pantomiming wiping my face. She gives me a confused look and reaches forward to clean Connor's face.

"He's going to see you in a second," I tell her, then I take the cloth and start wiping away at her tears. Catching on, she takes it from me and finishes the job.

"Catriona," Joe calls again.

"In a second," I snap. I need to be here for this. I don't know why, but I need to see it with my own eyes. He was flirting with me less than twenty-four hours ago, and now he claims Shay is his mate. I need to know.

V'dar's hands glow green as he pushes his power into Connor, and rapidly his face clears of all injury. The eyebrows still have bald patches and his eyelashes look a little freaky, but his gaze is clear, the golden tones of his dragon and the slitted pupils of his beast show the two of them aren't looking at me. No, only one person has their intense focus.

Shay.

"The wounds are healed, my child, but the damage is done," V'dar says sadly.

Connor nods, his gaze fixed on Shay.

"Stubborn fool," she says hoarsely, tears thick in her voice.

"Yep," he agrees.

"Why did you do it?"

"It was needed," he says with a shrug. "You needed me to save them, so I did."

Shay launches herself at him, and he catches her, almost as if he anticipated her movement. Their mouths fuse together and the pair of them are lost to the rest of us.

Isaac takes the scissors from Shay's hand, how she didn't stab him with them I don't know, and he begins to work on Connor's jeans while I unlace his boots. It's an awkward mess, but we manage to undress him while he continues to hold his mate in his arms and devours her mouth thoroughly.

"You can use my room," I tell them. "First on the left at the top of the stairs. It stinks of sex, you can't miss it."

Connor flips me the bird even as he moves in that direction.

Alpha! Sam calls across the pack link, and it's only then I realise he's not in here with us.

Where are you? I almost scream.

In the bunker. Catriona, we need you. We have a lot of injured people here and several are going into shock, but that's not the worst thing.

My heart thuds in my chest.

Ten of the pups are missing along with two teenage carers. The kids were restless, so some of the teens took them down to the orchard to play hide and seek while we held the meeting. We can't reach any of them.

Ten pups and two teens. If ever there was a time we needed the goddess, it's now.

26

Catriona

Mara! I call in my head, forgetting she's still in the room with me.

"Yes, daughter?"

I spin on the spot towards her. "We have missing pups, we have injured people in the bunker we can't get to, and we can't stop this rain. Can you help us?"

"We cannot, daughter," V'dar says. "This dark magic has Belar's stench all over it. Were this the work of an ordinary mage, any one of us could overcome it, but it is many mages working together in conjunction with Belar. His magic is holding the spells together. I would need Aidal or Yna, possibly both, to overcome it."

"Mara, can you at least tell me the pups are alright? That they're hiding under a cabin or something?"

Her eyes glaze for a moment then turn sad. "They will not last much longer. They're sheltering under a tree, but the rain has stripped almost all of the leaves and the branches are beginning to fall. If they do not kill the pups, the rain will."

I want to scream. How could Yna and Aidal stay neutral in a battle like this? Are they really so self centred that they would ignore the atrocities being enacted here?

"Call them," I order, fed up with the attitude of the absent gods.

"What?" Zaya says.

"Fucking call them, make them come here, manifest like you are. Let them see what their chosen children are doing. Let *them* feel the responsibility of their actions."

V'dar looks at me in shock, then he takes the hands of his two lovers and the three of them disappear.

"Fuuuuuuuuuck!" I scream. Have I just chased away our strongest allies?

Moments later they are back, this time with two struggling people between them.

"The siren is right," V'dar says, holding onto a burly man with a pointy goatee and dark, angry eyes. "You should be held accountable for your actions. Your unwillingness to call your people back into line, to offer help, to prevent the horrors your children have perpetuated has consequences. This is one of them. You need to witness the death of ten pups and two teens as they lie unconscious in an acid rain that reeks of Belar's magic."

Mara and Zaya hold a struggling woman between them, but after V'dar's speech, she stills, her head canted to the side.

"Belar?" she asks.

Zaya rolls her eyes. "Go open the door, take a deep breath and tell me you can't smell the stench of his magic all over that rain."

The woman, who I presume is the goddess Yna, does just that, while the man, I'm guessing Aidal here, stills and waits for her response.

Yna grabs the door handle and swings it open, the wind immediately gusts inside and there's a wet splat as a raindrop is blown inside to land on her. As quickly as she opens the door, she slams it shut, slapping a hand across her own shocked face. When she pulls it away, her face turns lax in shock at the blood there.

"No mortal's magic could hurt me so," she says on a groan.

"That's because it is Belar's," V'dar growls. "There are innocent pups dying out there, because he brings our war to the human realm."

"That's still not grounds for me to interfere," Yna says stubbornly.

"Then what about the damage to the environment?" Zaya counters. "Not only is this acid affecting the land it's falling on, this storm has been called from elsewhere. Some place is losing this rainfall. Then you have the wind factor and the change in atmospheric charge with the lightning. This storm is throwing off the equilibrium, never mind the long-term damage it's doing to vegetation, soil pH, and aquatic wildlife."

Yna looks conflicted, but I've had enough.

"What about your witches who were hurt tonight? It isn't just the wolves. We have mages, vampires, and witches here too. Children were hurt. I thought they were supposed to be sacred to everyone?

There are ten young pups and two teens dying out there right now. Are you telling me you don't give a shit? You're fucking disgraceful."

"Show me," Aidal demands, and Mara holds out her hand to him. His expression tightens as he witnesses whatever is going on in the orchard.

I don't even want to imagine it. Those children lying terrified, bleeding, dying with every drop that hits them. My heart is pounding, and adrenalin floods my body. Maybe I can shift into my dragon and bring them back. Even one would be worth the damage to my shifted form.

Inside, my dragon hums in agreement, while my wolf paces, restless with the inaction when there are pups in danger.

In the background I can still hear the young girl's sobs as she cries for her mother. It only fuels what I'm feeling, making me wonder if those poor pups are doing the same thing. Whimpering and crying for their parents.

"I cannot defeat him," Aidal says. "He has corrupted his magic and combined it with those who are working with him."

My shoulders slump, this was our last hope for saving those kids and getting aid to those trapped in the bunker.

"I can, however, provide a shield for those who would go to rescue the children. We can bring them back here and heal them."

"I'll go!" Joe says, already walking to the door.

"Joe," Matt says, "you're barely healed from the last time you ran out into the rain to save someone. I'll go. Who's coming with me? We've got twelve young people who need to be brought back."

"I'll go," Micah says, giving Jude a significant look. "You watch Catriona, I'll go play ambulance."

"On it," Jude replies, walking over to stand beside me. The look he gives me tells me in a flash I won't be going out this time either.

"The bunker," I cry. "We have injured there in need of healing too."

Several of the dragons step forward followed by more wolves. Witches offer to go to the bunker to help with the healing there. In all, we end up with a dozen volunteers to bring back the children, just in case some of them are heavy. Aidal accompanies them outside while the rest of us prepare to wait.

"Let's get everyone here comfortable and out of the way. I imagine these little ones will be in bad shape when they come back. We're going to need space to work on them."

"That won't be necessary," Yna counters. "I will heal them as they return. They will sleep a lot for a day or two afterwards, but that is probably for the best. They are going to fear the rain for a long time. We will try to end the storm before then."

"I can call on the Seelie and Unseelie courts to come and help restore the shift in the weather systems," V'dar offers. "It won't be perfect, and they'll probably cause their own fuss, but it will help with the equilibrium. The balance of this planet is precarious enough as it is."

Shay and I look at each other. It's been a long time since either of us dealt with the fae courts. V'dar has no reason to fear them, they're his creations, but the fae were some of the worst when it came to abuse of sirens. Their whole mentality regarding pain and suffering is very different to any other race living on this plane of existence. I'm not so sure it's a good idea to make them aware of a fatima of sirens.

From the grimace on her face, Shay agrees with me.

Of all the sirens left, I think the two of us have had more to do with the fae courts than any of the others. We were caught right in the middle of one of their conflicts for years. I'm pretty sure we managed to hide the existence of others, so it would be a shame to undo all our efforts now. Because once they find us again, they'll never rest until they control us all.

In the meantime, we busy ourselves getting those who are recovering from their healing into a more comfortable setting, making room for the young ones about to arrive. I get so lost in my tasks that it feels like only seconds before the first of the dragons returns with one of the teenagers. Her back is a mess, the clothing already gone along with most of her flesh. Her bones show white against the pallid tissue beneath them. I don't know how she's still alive, but there's a steady moan coming from her as the dragon reaches the top of the stairs and leaps through the front door.

Instantly Yna is there, resting a hand on the girl's face where the least amount of damage has occurred. I watch in wonder as the flesh returns, along with the colour in her tissue, before a thin and fragile dermis begins to form. In seconds she's completely healed, although I've never seen skin so pearly white, clear of freckle, mole or blemish.

It makes me wonder whether it was like that beforehand, or whether some of the things that made her, her, are gone forever.

This time it is indeed only seconds before two wolves race through the door, the bundles in their arms relatively unharmed compared to the teenager.

"She was lying on top of them, curled around them as much as she could. Only their legs were really hurt, she managed to cover their heads and torsos," a wolf says, and I recognise him. It's Sebastian. He and Cara were expecting twins. I've had my pups, I wonder if she's had hers.

Yna's face softens as she takes in the damage to the limbs of the youngsters. They can't be more than five years old, if they're even that big.

"This is not right," she says softly.

No, it fucking isn't, but I get the feeling if I push her on this now, she'll only resist me harder.

The goddess heals them both, and the little boy raises his head, looking blearily around the room. "Mama? Tina?" He's not a shifter pup, he's a witch!

Across the room the grieving girl raises her head. "Luca?" She rises rapidly to her feet and runs across the room. "Luca!" she screeches, grabbing hold of him and pulling him tightly to her.

If he's five, she's no more than eight or nine. She clings fiercely to her brother, weeping as they hold each other tight.

"I want Mama!" Luca cries. "Tina, I want Mama!"

Oh goddess. His mother is the dead woman.

The older girl, Tina, looks at me helplessly.

"Yna, make him sleep now," I order, and she bristles at my tone. "His mother is over there, asleep." I point to the part of the room where the dead have been laid out, and understanding crosses Yna's face.

With a sadness in her eyes that reflects the trauma this boy will face when he wakes, she rests a hand on his head and he sags in his sister's arms.

I quickly scoop him up, holding his cold little body to my own, and Joe comes over with a bath towel to wrap him in. He'd drown in a blanket he's so tiny. It occurs to me then, he's not that much bigger than my own boys really. Okay, double their length, but it makes me see him in a different light. He's a lost little boy, so close in age to my own.

"What will happen to us, Alpha?" Tina asks me.

"Where's your father?"

"He died in the fighting when we were trying to leave our house to come here," she replies.

I hadn't realised there was a widow with children amongst the witches. I'll have to talk to Ralph to make sure there aren't any more of them. Jude is at least old enough to cope without his father, but young ones like these need a second caregiver, at the very least to give their mothers some respite. It's also an opportunity to help those who are unable to have children.

"Then we'll find a new family for you both to live with. You won't be separated. Alice will probably look after you for a little while until we find just the right people to house you with."

"I want to stay with you," Tina says, throwing her arms around me. "You saved us. You gave us a home when we lost ours. I want to stay with the alphas."

I look helplessly to Marcus, but he looks like he's considering it.

It would help strengthen the bond between the witches and us. It's normal for the alphas to take in orphaned pups, even if it's only for a while. Alice is older and probably wants to retire, but she could help with babysitting, Marcus muses.

Marcus! I growl at him. *We've got four children of our own to care for, and I'm struggling with that enough as it is. Besides, maybe the witches have their own traditions or help for them. They could have other family amongst the refugees.*

Yna chooses that moment to interfere. *The children are alone in this world. They have no other family,* she says sadly. *I would be honoured if you took over their care.*

The Marcus gives me is all wolf, and I know what he's thinking. The goddess promised I'd have pups to all of my mates. I suppose even to Ethan if I accept him. Marcus is already dreaming of getting me pregnant again. Too bad for him, because he's had his turn fathering a pup already.

If we take on these children, then we'll have to delay the second litter, I warn him, thinking it will change his mind.

I don't think so, we'll simply get more of the childless mothers to help us out. It will be good for these young ones and a great community building exercise. Plus, if the presence of sirens really does create an upswing in our fertility, it will be great practice for some of these women to discover first-hand what's involved with raising a child.

I hope you're going to include young men in the rotation then, because there's no way we're turning our females into baby-making factories. The fathers need to be on hand to do their share too!

Marcus grins at me and moves closer to caress Tina's head. He's won already and he knows it. "Of course you can stay with us. You can help with the babies. Four more little brothers to play with, won't that be fun?"

"Ew, no thanks," Tina says, screwing up her nose. "They poop their pants and it stinks. My dad used to turn on the fan in his face so he wouldn't have to smell Luca's smelly nappies while he changed them."

My mate roars with laughter, a sight which lightens my heart. It seems like forever since he smiled. Was it really only a few hours ago we were preparing to present the pups to the pack? A sudden thought occurs to me. Where are the traitorous wolves?

"Marcus, where are Leon and his buddies?"

"In the back of a truck in the barn. We already had them moved before the rain hit."

Well, that was one less thing to worry about. Now all we had to do was stop this rain so we could get to the people who needed us in the bunker. At least the rain meant it was too warm for snow.

"So, how do we stop the rain?" I ask the room in general. I'm not looking at Yna as I stroke my hand down Luca's hair while Tina clings to me again.

Joe saves the day by swooping in and carefully scooping Luca's limp little body from my arms. "Come on, Tina," he cajoles her. "Let's go find a bed for you two upstairs. I think there are some really soft air mattresses in Marcus' office. You two look like you could use a good sleep."

By now, the others have returned with their charges, two of them carrying in a teenage male, the last of those to be rescued. He's still awake, and looks around for his charges before he allows Yna to get anywhere near him for healing.

"You're the last," she reassures him.

"They're safe?" he asks, even as his own body leaks blood all over the floor.

"Don't tell me," I murmur to one of the dragons. "He was covering kids too?"

The male nods.

We'll need to reward the teens somehow, because a simple 'well done' doesn't seem adequate. I'll add it to the list of things we need to do. Which triggers a thought at the back of my mind. Someone was asking me something and I told them I was too busy with Connor. What was it?

My heart just about explodes out of my chest when I remember.

The vampires!

Terrified, I turn to look for them. Joe and Marcus were holding them captive, but if Joe is with the kids upstairs, then who's holding his vampire now?

Nobody.

Not a single person is in a chokehold and nobody is struggling with confinement. What's going on?

"What are you looking for?" Dean asks me.

"Ravenous vampires."

V'dar chuckles. "I took care of them, daughter. They should not experience hunger for at least a week now."

He took care of them? Like gave his blood to them took care of them? How fucking strong are they going to be now if they've drunk the blood of a god?

"They didn't feed from me, daughter," V'dar says, grinning broadly. "I simply met their nutritional needs with some magic."

Ok, so that's another problem off my list. "Thank you," I tell him, sincerely grateful we didn't have to find food for freshly healed vampires.

"Did someone say nutritional needs?" Fleur asks, leading a bunch of people forward all laden down with platters. They lay them around the dining table buffet style, and someone brings out a stack of plates. "Don't be shy. The majority of you were either healed, did the healing, or are simply in shock. Come and get something to eat while we work out how to end this shitshow."

"They're probably expecting us to end it," Matt warns the group as he settles on the foot of the stairs with a plate balanced in his lap.

Scott brings one to me, always looking out for my wellbeing.

"If we end the rain, we need to be ready with a plan to defend ourselves, because they're going to breach our boundaries straight away while we're demoralised and confused. Alistair is probably expecting to take us out in one fell swoop.

"Not as long as we are here," Yna promises.

My heart gives a painful thump. Does this mean she's siding with us?

"They will not pass my wards," Aidal says, agreeing with her. "This is no longer your battle alone. If Belar wants to bring this battle to the Earthly plane, then we will join him here. Let us see how he fares against five of us, instead of three."

"He won't stand a chance," Yna states boldly.

For a witch goddess who was determined to remain neutral, she's changing her tune pretty quickly. What's to prevent her from changing her mind again? Is it simply the fact these two little witches lost their mother and were also hurt in the process? Or maybe the fact that Marcus and I are adopting them?

Yna frowns at me, reminding me they can all hear my thoughts.

"The word of a goddess has meaning, little siren," she says solemnly. "I give my word to protect you all from the ravages of Belar. He takes his desire for power too far. This world is already imbalanced, I will not allow him to push humanity to annihilation for his own titillation."

I'm not going to question her any further, lest I piss her off enough to precipitate a change of heart. Or, you know, make her smite me or something.

"Get some rest, everyone," V'dar advises. "We will address this imbalance in the morning, and we will be ready when they come."

My mates look to me eagerly, at least the ones who are here do. As much as they want to take me to bed and feed me, I just want to curl up and sleep a thousand years.

Strong arms scoop me up off the floor before I can even see who it is.

"You healed a lot of people today, you need to rest," Ethan says. "You too, alpha. You housed a goddess, fought a battle, and were healed after running in that rain. Come and care for our mate, as you sleep together."

Our mate.

Our.

Does he even realise what he's saying? Am I a foregone conclusion?

I'm not given a chance to protest as Ethan hurries me up the stairs. The more time I spend around dragon shifters, the more I get a feel for their scent. Well, the scent of their beasts. It's like warm leather, even though there's nothing leathery at all about their hides. Their scales are hard, harder than I thought, and there's always a faint whisper of sound as they move sinuously. How I heard that over the rain earlier, I don't know, but I did.

When Ethan opens our bedroom door, we're confronted by the site of Connor's pale ass as he thrusts his hips towards Shay. She cries out in pleasure as he roars and bites her neck. From the smell in the room, it's not the first time either.

"Time's up," Ethan calls cheerfully, ignoring Shay's gasp and Connor's growl. "Your alphas are exhausted from everything they've been through. They need the bed back. You can stay here with them, but Catriona and Marcus have reached their limit. The rain will be lifted in the morning, and we'll all need our strength for what's to follow."

Without pausing, Ethan sets me on my feet and has my pants unbuttoned and at my feet before I even realise what he's doing. My shirt comes off next, and then he's lifting me onto the mattress, even as Shay and Connor are hastily abandoning it.

"Go see Fleur," Ethan says, shucking off his own clothes and climbing on the bed beside me. "She'll find you somewhere to finish what you're doing."

He flips me onto my side and pulls me back against him, where his hard cock presses against my ass. For a second he stills, taking a deep breath in my hair, drawing my scent into him, and then his whole body relaxes. I can feel his arousal levels lower as he settles in to sleep.

"What the fuck?" Marcus protests.

"If I don't stay, you'll fuck her all night, and she needs to sleep. As do you. Think of me as the ultimate cock-block," Ethan says softly, his breath already evening out.

"If he thinks his presence will stop me from fucking the living daylights out of you, he's sorely mistaken," Marcus says with a grin, but then he yawns loudly. "He does, however, raise a good point."

Climbing in beside us, he lays on his back, pulling my head forward to rest on his chest. Nestled between the two of them, I feel safe and warm, and despite my discomfort having a naked Ethan pressed against me while he's still hard, sleep gradually begins to overtake me.

Joe and Scott join us soon after. Scott spooning up against Marcus, while Joe shifts and curls up at our feet.

I can stay awake no longer, and sink with a groan into the blissfulness of sleep, where the nightmares wait to devour me.

27

ETHAN

The sense of urgency that grips me is alarming. Something is wrong. Something is very wrong. We have to run, now, we have to go. We've lost. Time is up.

Run.

Run.

RUN!

Yet no matter how my heart pounds, my feet don't move more than a snail's pace. I'm surrounded by mist, but it's not so thick I can't see where I'm going. Slowly I drift towards the lodge, my steps making no sound, while the mist eddies around me like swirls through paint.

I don't so much climb the stairs as rise. One moment I'm at the bottom, the next I'm at the top. Why couldn't I move that fast before?

The door opens before I can touch it, the sense of wrongness coming from the other side makes me want to go in the opposite direction, but I have to enter. I have to see.

I have to know.

The pale timbers of the interior walls are streaked with blood. Arterial sprays, slashes, and drag marks. Even the vaulted ceiling doesn't escape. Bodies lie strewn everywhere, pieces scattered around like pick-up-sticks. Throats are ripped open, gazes are glazed or whitened in death. Everyone is pale. No matter their original skin colour. Gums and lips are bloodless, every drop sucked out of their owners.

All I can smell is death.

Marcus, Matt, Jude, everyone. Even Fleur and the pups. Nobody is spared. Most startling of all is my own body, lying stretched out, the head tilted back and twisted at a disturbing angle, the bone clearly crushed. It's the fastest way to take out a dragon shifter, and few are strong enough to do so. Even Alistair's vamps would be pushed to achieve it.

A scream sounds from upstairs. A high, terrified sound pierces the air, unending in its torment. The person obviously runs out of air, but the faint wheezing sounds that reach me says they're still trying. The voice is one I know, I'm sure of it. As much as I want to flee, I have to help them.

My body rises, not even bothering with the stairs, and I float along the landing to where wet squelching sounds come from. The door to the alpha's office is slightly ajar, and as before, it opens without me even touching it.

Inside, Shay is spread across the desk, four monstrous creatures hold her limbs while a fifth stands between her legs, his arm rising and falling in a movement that is undeniably obscene. The threat is there. He's not raping her, but he's going to.

That's not the worst thing I see though.

The wet sound— It's them— They're—

They're eating her.

Alive.

Even as I watch in horror, one of the great beasts leans forward and takes another bite out of her calf, while another delicately plucks off another finger with his very front teeth.

Trolls.

I don't know how I know, I just do. I've never seen anything like them before. Tall with overlong arms and short legs like an ape, their elongated torsos are covered in loose, wrinkled skin. Baggy and greeny-greyish, it looks more like some bizarre elephant hide than any actual skin. Even my dragon is repulsed.

Potbellies interfere with their access to their victims, but large, lantern jaws make short work of anything, including Shay's thigh bone as one chomps through a leg then carries it off to the side to eat in peace.

A prominent brow ridge shadows their eyes, thick hair above it cascading down like a strange second set of eyelashes. It makes it almost impossible to see where they are looking. Which is how they catch me off guard.

"Ssssssiren," one growls in a sibilant lisp, face turned towards me.

"Mmmmeat," murmurs another.

Despite their short legs, they move fast, galloping towards me on their hands and feet. A hand is around my throat before I can even register they've moved and everything turns black as the air cuts off.

"Mmmmeat," is the last thing I hear.

My heart pounds as I sit up in bed, frantically looking around me. Beside me, Catriona tosses and turns, her voice crying, begging, pleading for someone or something to take her and let Shay go.

"Catriona!" I find myself reaching for her even as my muddled brain tries to make sense of the nightmare.

Pulling her into my arms, I give her a gentle shake, before smoothing her hair back from her sweat-slicked brow. Tears pour down her cheeks as another desolate moan escapes her.

"Not the pups," she whispers. "No, Marcus!"

Her anguished cries are ripping my heart to shreds, and my dragon rages inside me, furious at being unable to protect his mate.

Movement at the end of the bed has me tensing until I see Joe, freshly emerged from his shift.

"It's on repeat," he says, fear rolling off him in waves. "She's dreaming that on repeat. You need to wake her."

I don't even stop to work out how the fuck he knows that. I shake her again and call her, but she seems trapped in her torment.

"She's a fucking siren," Joe snarls. "Give her what she needs, man. Kiss her like you mean it, and let it feel good."

"Are you fucking insane?" I snap. "You want me to get hot and heavy right now when she's caught in a nightmare? In *that* nightmare?"

Not bothering to answer, Joe surges up the bed, pulling her face to his as he kisses her desperately. Catriona moans again, but I don't think it's in pleasure. It can't be. She's still shaking and crying, but damn it looks good. Despite my intentions, my cock stirs.

Joe must be thinking along the same lines, because he groans against her lips, grinding his hips against her as he devours her mouth. That's sick, I need to get him off her, until I look at her eyes to find them open, her arm curls around his head and she pulls him to her harder. It's only when her skin begins to luminesce that I realise what she's doing. She's feeding from his arousal. The damn crazy wolf had the right idea all along.

So, now I have a front row seat to her making out with Joe as his movements become faster, his hands roving over her body as I hold her up for him. I might be the third wheel here, but it's fucking hot.

"Get that fucking nipple in your mouth," Marcus orders, and I look up to find him glaring at me. "Our mate needs us, and when she needs us, we never say no."

His arm curls possessively around her body, slipping down between her thighs where he begins to stroke her, eliciting a low moan from Catriona. The scent of her arousal hits the air and my cock jerks upright in record time. Now I'm the one kissing down her neck as I grind my erection against her thigh.

"Joe," she moans. "Joe, I need—"

"You need his cock inside you, filling you with his seed. You need to feel him breeding you, filling you with another litter of pups, just like he was promised."

Joe moans, his hips pumping faster. Okay, so apparently he has a breeding fetish.

"Then you're going to take that big dragon dick like a good girl, you're going to spread those pearly thighs open for him, and he's going to knot you, Catriona. Did you know that dragons knot? He's going to fill you so full of sperm, you're gonna look like you're pregnant already, and he's going to put a baby in your belly too."

Fuck.

Fuck!

Apparently I have a breeding fetish too, because the idea of her belly swollen first with my seed, then with my offspring makes me want to pull Joe out of the way and get things going. The sooner I pump into her, the sooner she starts having my young.

My dragon is going nuts, his arousal so potent I nearly come on the bed then and there.

I suck my way down her neck, moving on to her breasts which I lavish with my tongue. Scott moves in to claim the other one, which makes me wonder where Marcus went to. I don't wonder long, because Joe thrusts hard into our mate, and then the alpha thrusts hard into Joe, pushing him even deeper into Catriona.

Fuck that's hot. A surge of something, passion? Lust? Desire? Arousal? Something strong hits me, and I feel like I'm going to come, but then a strong hand wraps around the base of my cock, squeezing it to the point of pain and bringing me back from the edge.

I look up in surprise, following the arm back to Marcus who gives me a feral grin. "You're welcome," he grunts, as his hips stutter and he gives one more hard thrust into Joe as the three of them cry out in unison.

They remain frozen for a moment, an erotic portrayal of lust and love, a sight so beautiful my heart yearns for it.

Marcus withdraws first, pulling Joe back with him, and the two of them cuddle for a moment before he gives a rude gesture to the space between Catriona's legs.

"If you think she's done, you're wrong. If she's this hungry, let's feed her, yeah?"

His hand slides up and down my cock a couple of times, the sensation is mind-blowing. I've never had a man touch my cock before, and it's not repulsive like I expected it to be. I mean, it's a fucking hand on my cock, right now, I don't give a shit who's on the other end of the arm. That shit feels good.

I can't deny the pull towards Catriona, but I'm not like these wolves. I won't take what's not offered. Yet when I look down at her, the sheer need on her face blows me away.

"Ethan!" she whispers, her hands reaching up for me, and I'm lost.

If this is her siren's call, then I'm fine with that. She wants me. *Me!* Her mate. She wants me.

And I'm hers. All hers.

I'm sliding inside her wet heat before I even realise I've moved. Gods above, how can anything feel this good and still be legal?

She's calling out my name, mewling her need, yet my movement is slow. I'm not small in girth, and I can feel her stretching around me. I don't want to hurt her, so I'm taking it slow, as torturous as it is.

Catriona writhes, she fucking squirms, her legs wrap around my hips and she tries to pull me deeper, but I've got more control than that, and I've got my own grip on her hips. She can pull all she wants, but we're going at my pace, and that's one I'm sure won't hurt her.

Every inch, every little bit feels even better than the last, and it takes my dragon's strength to hold us back from falling over the precipice. I'm not going to blow while in the middle of my first thrust.

"Ethan!" she wails, but I'm still not all the way seated, and nothing else is going to happen until I'm all the way home and she's all the way around me. Then it's game on.

"Fuck man, it's hurting her, stop holding back," Joe cries out.

What? Exchange one kind of pain for another? Besides, this isn't hurting her. She's not starving. This woman has too much leeway over these wolves in the bedroom. It's time she learned to take as well as give. And I plan to give everything I have to her, if only she'll be a good girl and wait for it.

"Ethan!" she growls, and it isn't her wolf. Her pupils are slitted and I can sense her dragon just below the surface, just as eager for me to sink all the way in as I am. She knows the game I'm playing, even if Catriona doesn't.

In a movement that catches me off-guard, Catriona lets go with one leg and then thrusts her hips, rolling us over until she's on top, and then she slams down the remainder of my length, making us both cry out. My sound is genuine pleasure, but it's not until I see her head thrown back and her hands plucking at her nipples that I know for sure hers is too.

"Mine," she growls, lunging forward and initiating our mating with her own bite. Her teeth have lengthened, her dragon coming to the fore and my own rises up to meet her.

"Ours," I growl back, holding her hips and making sure she's all the way down my cock. If she wants to be pounded by me, who am I to object?

I lift her hips and then pull her down hard as I thrust up with my hips, my heels digging into the mattress. My hips meet the backs of her thighs with a loud slap that resonates throughout the room. The wolves present watch avidly as I fuck their mate from beneath. She's not mine yet, but she's started the bond, so she will be soon. My dragon rumbles at the prospect.

I hold her there against me for a beat, before lifting her again, only to thrust hard and fast inside her. Catriona's breasts bounce with the wild movement, an almost hypnotic sight, and I want to feast on them as I impale her with my hardened length.

With my strength and my greater size, I don't need to use a trick to flip us over, I simply do it, pinning her to the mattress as my hips slowly withdraw. My arms cage her, pinning her own to her sides as I fuck her hard, my back arching so I can grasp a peaked nipple in my mouth. My mate mewls her pleasure, and someone's head comes in on the other side to suck the other one, as her arms come up to hold both of us in place.

Something sweet and slightly salty hits my tongue and I realise it's her milk. Her nipples are leaking, so I suck down hard, drawing the sustenance from her. It tastes of her, of Catriona, and it's like a drug. I'll never get enough. Even when she's finished feeding the pups, I'm going to keep stimulating these babies and drinking from her forever, because I can't get enough of her, whatever part of her I'm devouring.

"Stop drinking, you dope," Catriona says with a giggle. "The boys will need that for their breakfast."

Now, there are many sounds I want to hear from my mate right now, but giggling isn't one of them, so I oblige her, but only because it suits me, and not her. My dragon is greedy, he wants all of her, now and forever. If these wolves want to be a part of this thing we have, then they're going to have to fight to make their own place, because my dragon plans to dominate every second, of every minute, of every hour of her time, for the rest of her life.

Instead of obsessing over her breasts, I lower my gaze to her pussy, where my dick slides easily back and forth through her slippery folds.

"Look at that pretty pussy stretched wide to take you," Marcus murmurs. "All wet and juicy, I bet she feels fucking amazing."

She does, she really does, and despite my desire to fuck her for hours, because I'm capable of that, I find my pace picking up.

Slap, slap, slap. Our bodies meet and part, our pleasure rising, twining together, joining our souls until we're one entity seeking oblivion together.

Fuck he feels so good, I hear her think. *I need to come, why won't he come? Why can't I make him come?*

All in good time, little mate, I send back to her, and she blinks, her eyes widening.

You can hear me?

It's a dragon thing, Catriona. I can hear any dragon I choose to, as can you.

They can hear us right now? She asks, eyes wide with fear.

I chuckle and pound into her harder. *No, my love. You have to choose who to send your thoughts to. I can hear you, because you want me to, and I do too. It's a choice to connect between us each time. Don't ask me how we know when someone is talking to us, we just do.*

I need to come, she says desperately.

I know.

No, Ethan, please, it's starting to hurt. I need this. I need to feed.

What my mate asks for, she gets.

I pick up the pace, letting myself go, pushing her deep into the mattress with each thrust. Wolves hold up her legs on either side for me, so I lean forward on my hands and kiss her. I need to hear her breath hitch when we fall over the edge together.

Closer.

Sweet gods above. Closer.

One.

More.

Thrust.

My gums throb as my teeth elongate, and my head snakes down to sink them into the flesh of her shoulder as I fuck her like I'm never going to stop. My groan is stifled by the flesh in my mouth, but her scream of pleasure is not. Damn, I've never felt anything so good in my life. My vision goes hazy, my dragon roars in triumph, and black spots appear before my eyes, until I realise I've stopped breathing and draw in a desperate, gasping breath.

She's mine. Catriona is mine, and nothing will ever part us again.

Nothing.

Ever.

28

Marcus

"Tell me what you saw," I growl at Joe while Catriona and Ethan cement their new bond again. My cock is aching to go in and join them, but I can't relax, not when there are so many threats hanging over us. As tempting as it is to lose myself in her body over and over again, I think she needs this time with Ethan more.

"She's out the front of the yard, there's fog, but not thick. More like a heavy mist."

This puts an immediacy to things that has my hackles rising.

"She kind of drifts, the way you do in dreams. Up the stairs, in the door, even though you know something bad is on the other side. It's a slaughterhouse, blood everywhere, we're all dead. There's screaming upstairs. She floats up the wall and onto the landing, and when she gets into your office, five monsters have Shay on the table, and they're eating her limbs while one is about to—" Joe swallows hard. He can't even say it.

"Force her?" I ask gently. His father raped his mother regularly. Nothing else distresses him like a woman being harmed.

He nods. "Hurt her," he whispers.

"Ok, what happens then?"

"They see her, they know what she is. One of them says siren, another says meat. Marcus, Shay is alive. She's frozen, and one grabs her by the throat and chokes her, and then the dream starts over again."

"Monsters?" I ask, doubtfully.

"Ugly, saggy skin, grey green. I've never seen or heard of anything like them, but the word 'trolls' keeps going through my head."

I've never seen one, but I've heard of them. They're assassins from the unseelie court. Is it a coincidence Catriona dreams of this the day after V'dar spoke of contacting the courts? Somehow, I don't think so. I need to talk to her when she surfaces.

It's the morning after the rain began, the children are already up and playing in the way that kids do, ignoring the obvious and only processing what's right in front of them, but I notice they all flinch when the wind gusts and the rain hits the windows with a little more force. They might seem fine, but they're going to have issues for a long time to come.

"Marcus?" Joe prompts. "Have you heard of them?"

"Yeah, I've never seen one, but I've heard of them."

"They're real then? They're not just figments of her imagination?"

"Wrinkled grey-green skin, a jaw that can cut through a car door, bad smell?"

"There were no smells, but yeah, the rest fits."

"And they killed everyone in the lodge?"

Joe cants his head to the side while he thinks. It reminds me of a confused puppy, but I'd never tell him.

"I don't know. There were limbs ripped off and piled up, but Ethan had his neck broken, and some of the others had been drained of blood. I mean, aside from the blood all over the walls, there wasn't a lot of blood on the floor."

Vampires then. Which means this is Belar's work.

I'm surprised when I get to the bottom of the stairs to see all the deities there talking quietly. Did they stay the night?

"It's easier to stay than dematerialise and manifest again and again," Mara says, answering my thoughts.

"Do you know anything about Catriona's dream?" I ask them. "It was oddly specific."

Mara, Zaya, and V'dar turn pointed looks at the other two gods who squirm under their glares.

"It seems Aidal and Yna decided to follow our example and bestow gifts upon Catriona without warning her," Zaya grumbles.

V'dar's expression softens and he puts an arm around her shoulder. "What Zaya means is they didn't warn *her*."

"She is my daughter. I know the sirens were yours first, but she was born under my care. Catriona is mine! Of course they should have warned me!"

"And they honour her, and thus you, with their gifts," V'dar tells her gently.

Zaya huffs, but I can tell she's not truly angry. Irritated maybe, but V'dar is right, their gifts are an honour for Catriona. Even if they do terrify me.

"So, weird nightmares are a gift?" I prompt, playing stupid.

Yna snorts at me. "You presume to manipulate us when we can hear every thought that crosses your mind?"

She has a point.

"In that case, what the fuck is going on with my mate, and why did she dream about us all dying?"

V'dar snorts. "That's a bigger question than you think."

I gesture to the acid rain still falling outside. "I'm not going anywhere."

"Did Catriona tell you she saw the plethora of possibilities that we can see as gods?"

She had. I still can't picture it, but I understand what she was talking about.

"Keep that in the back of your mind when Yna and Aidal explain the gifts they've bestowed on her."

Aidal glares at him, but steps forward. "Also keep in mind that V'dar has not explained the gift he bestowed on top of that of his dragon."

My gaze snaps to the dragon god who simply shrugs. "Mara and Zaya know."

"Care to share?" I ask sarcastically.

"Telepathy," Dean says from where he sits on the bottom stairs. "It is a dragon gift. If you and the others are sharing her dreams, then she has the gift of telepathy. It's like a pack link, but it means she can send or receive thoughts from anyone she chooses, not just members of her pack. Even the dead, the vampires, aren't immune to her reach. She doesn't just hear them, she can scan them too. At least, if she has a gift strong enough."

The god bows his thanks to Dean and turns back to me. "That," he says simply.

Alright, so that explains how first Joe and now Ethan have shared her nightmares. It doesn't explain why we only see nightmares rather than other more pleasant dreams too.

"Because all of her dreams are nightmares," Zaya says sadly. "We shelter her from the vast majority of them, but sometimes she needs to see them.

"Why are her dreams not happy?" I ask, concerned. Is she not happier with us than she was when she was single?

"Because of the amount of trauma she has faced in her life," Mara explains. "Think of your mate like a soldier. She might not talk about her life much, and frankly I don't blame her, but she has lost a lot of family, spent centuries in hiding, and experienced more pain than any of you can imagine."

"But this wasn't something from her past, Shay is alive, so watching her die isn't something she's experienced."

"Witches have the gift of precognition," Yna says abruptly. "This is the gift I gave your mate. She's able to get glimpses of the future. The more powerful the vision, the more likely it is to occur."

I look at Joe who shrugs. "It was pretty fucking clear, but I don't have anything to compare it to except one of her memories. It was as clear as that."

Yna nods. "It wasn't a dream, it was a vision, a warning. Each and every choice she makes has the potential to lead her closer to this version of the future, but it is not set in concrete."

"So," Joe muses, "if she dreams this again and it's more blurry, then that possibility is reduced?"

"Yes, although some factors carry more weight than others, and some consequences have knock-on effects that are unseen. Maybe you all have to die for everyone else to live, for example."

No, I cannot accept that future as our reality, as an inevitable progression of horrors, even if it does save everyone else. I've barely begun to know my son, I can't sacrifice him to save the world, I just don't have it in me.

"Nobody is asking that of you, Marcus," Mara says soothingly, rubbing a hand up and down my arm. "V'dar was merely making the point that no future is certain. Even if you feel you are navigating away from this potential horror, you might be working towards an even greater one."

"So, how is this a gift?"

"There are precautions you can take to alter certain situations. For example, if you see Dean having a heart attack in this room over and over, you could install a defibrillator and increase his chances of surviving. He might not be able to avoid the heart attack, but it does not mean he has to die of it."

I have my doubts about the usefulness of this. We could chase our tails the whole time, taking precautions for disasters that will never actually happen. The real issue will be the things we never see coming. It'll be too easy to become complacent, to think we have all our bases covered and to relax our guard.

To be honest, this 'gift' seems more like a curse. Priming us for entirely the wrong things.

Yna nods at me as if I've spoken aloud. I guess to her, I have.

"You see a part of the challenge of being a god," she says. "Catriona will see glimpses of potential futures, while we see all of them, without always understanding which decision will change the path onto another future line."

"So, you're working as blind as we are?" I ask her.

She smiles indulgently at me, like I'm a child who hasn't quite grasped the concept. I suppose I haven't really. Until I can experience it, I probably never will, but I think I understand what Catriona was telling me a little better.

"I agree, you have a small understanding, a tiny fragment of the puzzle. I hope it helps you to think less harshly of us. We are divine, yes, but we are not fate."

She speaks about it as though it's a living entity. Frankly, if it is, I don't want to know.

"What about Aidal's gift?" Dean asks from across the room.

My head is spinning so much from Yna's revelation, I had completely forgotten we're about to be blindsided by something else.

"Shouldn't Catriona be here for this discussion?" Scott asks, before anyone could answer.

"She listens," Zaya replies with a small smile. "It is good you care for her so. Understand that we do too, even if it's not in the same way you do. She is aware and has been listening."

Catriona? I call.

I am listening.

Three words, and yet I feel her censure. She's right, we plunged ahead into this discussion, far more focussed on the information than we were on the person it affects the most. I'm going to have to work this out with her later.

"Catriona is now able to see auras. It will take a little practice for her to be able to do so, and a few months to get the basic tenets of her ability. It takes years to master it, but it's a powerful gift in the hands of someone who knows what they are doing."

I sigh. Sure, in the future this could be great, but right now it brings nothing to the table. Nothing that will help us win this war.

"Don't be sure about that," Aidal scolds me. "Just because she is new to it, does not make it a powerless gift. Some things, the most basic of emotions, are easily read. It is when the person lies to themselves, or is under the influence of other things that it becomes more complicated. Anger, lust, hate, love, envy — these base emotions are clear, and the stronger they are, the easier they are to read."

"There's an added bonus too," Mara says with a sly smile. "We all can read auras and so those addressing us have learned to mask their emotions. However, it is not as simple as a ward. They have to direct the energy towards each one of us. Catriona, as an unknown threat, will be able to read people who we can't."

Okay, that could come in handy, just as soon as she learns how to tap into this gift.

"Combine it with my telepathy gift, and you have a woman who can read the intent behind the words," V'dar offers. "Manipulation becomes clear to her, the difference between hearing what you want to hear, and hearing what is truly being said is a massive advantage when trying to discern who is friend and who is foe."

"You think we will have the opportunity to test that?" I ask him.

"I know you will. I have summoned the seelie and unseelie courts. While I love all of my children equally, I find they are most slippery when it comes to negotiation. Even now they push at my barrier across the portals, seeking entry. As soon as I allow it, they will be here."

"Can't they wait until after we've won the war and help restore the balance then?"

V'dar wags his head from side to side. "I have summoned them, if I make them wait, they will make us pay for it in one way or another. They might refuse, or they might make the price higher."

"And if they come now?" I push, because my plate is already full. I don't want the drama he's hinting they will bring.

"They might be more amenable to negotiation, but it also gives them more time to cause mischief in other ways."

"So, they might help, but either way it's going to cause trouble?" I surmise. Fucking fantastic.

V'dar winces. "To be clear, they will help, it will be invaluable."

"But the cost is high."

He nods.

Everyone looks to me for a decision.

The lodge is a shambles, we've got those recovering from healing resting wherever they can find somewhere comfortable, there's clear evidence of trouble with blood all over the floor, and signs of people sleeping rough with cots and blankets everywhere. If we're going to do this, then we'd best not look quite so desperate.

"We need to clean this shit up, and find these people some space upstairs. Let's look more confident than we are for starters. If we look like we're begging, they're going to make us beg."

Fleur sets a group of people to work scrubbing away the blood, it needed doing anyway. The sirens start helping people upstairs. I think I can kiss my office goodbye, and the library. It's not like we're using them at all anyway. The cots and blankets are cleared away, most taken down to the basement, and the children are spread around Catriona's bedroom, the younger ones at least. The teens are given space amongst the adults.

The two witch children we're adopting follow Catriona around like lost pups, and I guess they are for the moment. We're the only authority figures in their lives. Some of the witches try to coax them away, but they only cling to her tighter. There will be no hiding them, because I know my mate, she will be here for this whether I want her to be or not.

Surprisingly, Shay stays beside her too, Connor hovering closely behind the pair, Ethan equally protective. We're going to be ready, at least physically, very soon, so it's time to confront my mate. The growing nausea in my gut is not mine, and I know she's not pregnant. At least not yet. The thought of her round again with pups makes me smirk. As soon as this war is sorted, we're fucking her into the mattress.

The four of them watch me warily as I approach. "What do I need to know?" My gaze is on Catriona, but the question is equally for the four of them.

"The unseelie like to eat us," Catriona says, turning pale. "Just like the vamps get stronger with our blood, the unseelie get stronger with our flesh."

My wolf surges forward, augmenting my voice. "They are not setting foot in my home," I growl, turning back to V'dar.

"They will not harm her while I'm here," V'dar reassures me.

"And when you're not?" Catriona challenges him. "Because we both know that once they've opened a portal somewhere, they can return to that place whenever they want."

V'dar's face flushes. The fucker! He wasn't going to tell us that. Is he fucking on our side or what?

"Or the fact that while the unseelie like to eat us, the seelie use us as sex slaves?" Shay adds.

My vision turns red. He would leave us open to predators who would try to steal my mate and her family?

"They don't do that anymore," V'dar says placatingly.

"Only because there are no sirens left on the fae lands," Zaya practically spits. "Or have you forgotten that little fact too, my love?"

Damn. To be honest I'd kind of forgotten she was the goddess of the sirens.

"Zaya," he coos to her, trying to calm her down.

It's the wrong fucking move, even I know it. It's like adding water to an oil fire, rather than calming things down, she explodes.

"They are not coming here, Vee," she screeches at him. "I barely saved this many of my daughters, I will not lose any more to those monsters."

The change in him is instantaneous, and I'm reminded we're dealing with gods when the room darkens and V'dar seems to increase in size. No, not seems. His head is literally brushing the ceiling.

"You forget who you talk to, mother of sirens. I gave you that title, and I can just as easily take it away."

Fuck!

"And the rest of us?" Yna says, stepping forward. "Is this the freedom of will you promised us when you created us? We can do what we want until it's not what you want?"

Aidal and Mara move forward to join them, the four deities standing against the one who began it all.

"They are my children!" V'dar roars.

"And so are we!" Yna yells back. "And so are they! You say you don't favour one over another, yet here you stand favouring the seelie and unseelie over the sirens and the shifters."

I'm fucking thankful she's on our side, because anyone willing to stand up to V'dar when he's pissed has brass balls. Even my wolf cowers inside me.

Her lips twitch and I realise she's heard me, but I don't dare respond aloud. The room is a powder-keg waiting for a spark.

V'dar finally begins shrinking and I swear he ages as he does so. "Very well. I will put limitations on the ones who come here, they will not be able to return without an invitation. Will that satisfy you?"

Catriona makes a strangled sound that has us all turning to face her. "So, they can create a portal here, but not pass through it. But those who didn't come the first time can pop in if they like?"

I didn't even realise that was possible, but from the flush on V'dar's cheeks, he knew. The fucker knew there was a loophole. No wonder the fae are so wiley, they get it directly from him.

"If I make the portals rather than them, will that make a difference?" Yna offers.

V'dar looks relieved. "Yes, they will not be able to return to this site as they will have no inkling of where it is. Would that satisfy you?"

I look towards Catriona who looks like she's sucked on a lemon, her lips are so tightly pursed together. She gives a stiff nod. Shay puts an arm around her shoulders and also nods.

"Then can we please begin this meeting?" V'dar moans.

Rather than let him push his agenda, because I'm no longer sure he's on our side, I turn again to my mate. "What else do I need to know?"

"Everything," she says. "Fucking everything, but there isn't time."

29

CATRIONA

Marcus and the others need to know my history with the seelie court, but I don't even know where to begin. Should I start with my exile to the human plane? Or perhaps before that when the seelie caught my mother and I and used us as breeding slaves?

To the side of the room, Zaya gives a slight shake of her head.

Don't tell him I was a slave? Yeah, he won't see reason after that, but he's going to want to know why the rest of the sirens were sent to the human plane with Zaya, and how she came to be our goddess in the first place.

"You know some of the history of the siren wars," Zaya says, taking over before I can even find a place to begin. "How the vampires used siren blood to increase their speed, wolves used them for fertility and pleasure, mages and witches used their saliva, blood, hair, and nails for spell ingredients, even their bones ground up were powerful."

A steady rumble comes from Marcus' chest, his wolf obviously hating it all, but he nods, still in control.

"You know what happened to Catriona's siren mother," Zaya continues. "Well, the treatment of sirens in the fae realm was little better. Powerful groups kept them as pleasure slaves and created more and more, whether the women were willing or not. Troublesome wife? Fuck a siren and convert her afterwards. Then you had your own pleasure slave and she no longer had any power. Best of all, it acted like a divorce, freeing you to take another wife or mate."

"That's fucked up," Matt growls.

Zaya nods. "I was V'dar's chosen vessel amongst the sirens back then, and I prayed to him all day every day for a change in our circumstances. Did he not love us? Did he not care that we were treated little better than animals?"

"She was persistent," V'dar agrees. "It wasn't that I didn't care, but I couldn't change their fate without changing who they were. In order to save them, I had to destroy them, and I didn't want to do that."

"Eventually he caved and agreed to have us exiled to the human plane, and he made me a goddess to look after them all."

"Let me guess," Marcus says snidely. "It removed the problem, but not the reason?"

Zaya nods. "The fae have continued to hunt us in the human realm. They didn't care that we turned to ash as soon as we crossed over, every hunting season they developed new wards to try to bring us back against our will. For the first thousand years, they didn't work, but eventually they found something that did."

"It was horrible," I say, interrupting her narrative. "By then our fertility had been reversed by Zaya, we could no longer create new sirens, but they never gave up trying. I was the pet of the seelie queen, and she would allow the members of her court to use me as they saw fit, until one of them was brave enough to set my mother and I free next to a portal. He told us to run and never return. I heard later that his death took two years."

The seelie are savage in their revenge. If I'm recognised when they arrive, it will become a point of contention.

Mara shudders. "They'll want you back."

It isn't a question, but I nod anyway. "Even though they shouldn't have had me in the first place, they will see me as their property. They're spiteful enough to deny whatever we ask because of it. Frankly, the destruction of the human world would amuse them, and give them greater opportunities to hunt for more toys. They're not above stealing humans or any other species found here."

"Humans wouldn't last long in the fae realm," Mara cries.

I agree. "A month, maybe two. They see humans as little better than animals. A smart horse, perhaps. The death of this realm would mean nothing to them."

"They aren't that bad," V'dar dares to chide me.

"Would you care to visit my memories? Or perhaps your lover's? See how we both suffered under their *care*."

Wisely, V'dar says nothing.

"Then you can't be here for the negotiations," Marcus says, folding his arms across his chest like the decision is made.

I open my mouth to protest, but surprisingly Matt is the one to step forward, holding up a hand.

"Aidal, can you disguise them?"

The god looks at Matt thoughtfully. "I can," he says hesitantly. "The fae are master tricksters though, I don't know whether they would see through it or not. If they came armed with truth charms or something to cast aside concealment, then the point is moot."

"Marcus," I argue. "I have to be here. V'dar refuses to see the flaws in his children, and nobody else here has enough experience in dealing with them."

"Zaya does," Matt replies.

The answer again takes me by surprise. She actually does. It's like a weight has been lifted from my shoulders. Zaya is the answer. She's stronger than any fae now V'dar has made her a goddess. They can't simply take her back. If she's willing, then I would be only too happy for her to take my place.

"Zaya?" I ask her gently. "Is this something you want to do?"

The goddess gives me a warm smile. "Yes, daughter. I think I'm now in a position where I can hold my own, and I have a few choice words to say to those who kept me as a slave."

"Perhaps I should do the talking," V'dar interrupts.

"Or perhaps you shouldn't," Yna counters. "You're already biassed towards them. How about someone with a vested interest in the wellbeing of this planet gets a say. Hmm?"

The god at least has the grace to flush. No wonder they're at war. Even those on the same side have difficulty seeing eye to eye. It must be exhausting.

"Come on, Kat," Shay says, linking her arm through mine. "Let's go check on your boys, they must be about due for a feed and I know Ethan likes watching that."

My newest mate flushes pink but doesn't deny it. We haven't even spoken about my claiming him and him returning the favour. The deed is done, so to speak, but what that means for our relationship, or even the future, I don't know.

Reluctantly I allow myself to be dragged from the room, kissing each of my mates quickly as I pass them. Well, those who are here. Aidal has assured us that everyone in the bunker is healed, but my mates didn't return with him. I understand why — the people there need leadership in these desperate times. Especially the wolves.

Thankfully, despite running the longer distance, nobody died. Then again, they were all shifters and able to partially heal themselves anyway. The vampires mostly went to the barn, their speed getting them there in time. The witches were caught in here with us or out in the rain and we rescued them. The majority of the dozen deaths were witches, with one mage elder dying of shock before we could get to him. I think he had a heart attack.

When we get to the top of the stairs, I take one last look at the tableau before me. Matt is directing the arrangement of furniture, Fleur is dealing with refreshments under Aidal's instructions, and Zaya and Marcus are quietly talking, possibly planning discussion points. There really is nothing for me to do, but it doesn't stop me from wanting to do it.

It takes Dane's hungry wail to bring me back to reality. They've gone far longer than normal between feeds, and by the time I get into the room, all four of them are bawling lustily, their tiny faces red with distress.

"None of them will take the bottle," Gwen says, teasing River's lips. "There's only one person they want."

As usual, Dane is the loudest, so the sooner I get him settled, the sooner we can soothe the others. I don't hesitate to undo my top and bare one of my dugs, gesturing to Gwen to bring him to me.

"If we can get him settled with cushions, you might be able to feed two at once," she says.

I shrug. I'm willing to try it. I feel so bad for making them all wait, I'm willing to try anything.

It takes a few minutes — he's too hungry to latch properly and too impatient to wait for my milk to let down, but eventually he's latched on, his tiny hands patting at my side as the women settle him sideways with his body curled around towards my back.

River is brought to me next, his eyelashes clumping with the tears he's shedding. He too takes a few minutes, but after the fourth time he pops off the dug, I know I need to calm him down more, or he'll never settle to feed. I cradle him in my arms, holding him to me and humming softly while I kiss away his tears. His fingers tangle in a lock of my hair and he pulls, but after a moment he relaxes his grip and then clenches and opens his hands repeatedly, finding comfort in the movement.

When he takes a deep shuddering breath, I move him back into position and try again. This time he latches on with no problem. The relief of two of them feeding at once is indescribable. I hadn't realised I was getting so full of milk, and hearing them all cry at once has only made me produce more. There's a sour smell as I uncover one of my breasts, ready to take on a third baby.

"Are you sure?" Indira asks.

"I might as well try, Carter isn't getting any calmer."

Wyatt, however, is only grumbling gently as Sienna dances around the room with him, bobbing up and down and singing a nonsense song about catching fish alive. As if you'd catch them dead!

It's only when the wailing stops as Carter chomps down on my nipple in his impatience, that I realise everything outside of the room is silent. Did they ward us against the sound? I'll bloody skin Marcus alive if he allowed that.

"Something's happening," Indira says, her voice shaking slightly.

"What do you mean?" I ask, more sharply than I intended.

"Can't you feel it? The magic? It's building up. What is that?" she cries.

Picking up on her distress, Wyatt begins to cry, which makes his three brothers let go before they join him.

Gwen swoops in and picks up Dane, while Indira takes River and I'm left trying to reattach Carter. Yet he's not having a bar of it, so I give him to Diana and hold my arms out for Wyatt. If I can feed him something, he may settle which will allow the others to enjoy their full bellies, even if they haven't had a full feed.

Now that Indira has mentioned it, I can feel the magic, like a buzzing against my skin. How did I not notice it before? Or is it simply the fact I'm so used to it that I ignored the danger.

V'dar must be opening the portals, because that's what I can sense.

"Calm down, Indira," I tell her. "It's V'dar opening portals to the fae realm to allow the representatives of the seelie and unseelie courts to arrive."

Wyatt greedily attaches on to the last untapped nipple and begins to feed in earnest. Hopefully at least one of my boys will get a full feed. Gwen tries to tempt Dane with a bottle of expressed milk and has some success, at the very least he stops crying, and soon River and Carter settle too. Well, mostly. Carter won't take the bottle, but my arms are already full with Wyatt, so Diana holds him in place.

Once the boys are feeding again, I feel that peaceful lassitude slipping over me. Fleur says it's happy hormones from producing milk. I'm not sure I feel happy, but I do feel relaxed and sleepy. How I can do that in the presence of fae, I'm not sure, I'm just grateful the boys are able to distract me a little.

There's a startled sound from downstairs, and then the murmur of rich voices. The fae are here.

"Shhh," I say to the others, trying to listen in on the conversation, but even with my improved senses, I can't quite make everything out.

My dragon huffs in annoyance, *she* could hear everything if I wanted.

It never even occurred to me to ask, because she's too big to shift into here.

The thought earns me a snort, and suddenly I can hear the conversation downstairs as if I were in the room. Duly noted, my dragon can boost my hearing. Why don't the others tell me these things?

"Your abode is ... quaint," a familiar voice says, and my heart sinks. It's the fae queen herself. I suppose if a god summoned you, you would come in person rather than sending a representative.

"I'm glad you like it," Marcus says stiffly, trying to ignore the insult. It never ends well to take affront with the fae, they're rather practised at riling up their opponents. It makes them easier to swindle.

"Entirely unsuitable accommodation for the sirens you're hiding here," she says with a pointed sniff. "They cannot stay in a hovel like this, I will bring them back to the palace with me."

"If they wished to go, I would let them, however they very clearly stated they have no desire to enter the fae realm again."

"Well, of course they did. They're not exactly smart enough to know what's best for them."

I want to slap the smug expression from her face. I don't even have to see her to know how she looks right now. I've seen the fae queen in action more often than I care to admit.

"Only the wisest of fools would believe that," Marcus replies, calmer than he was before. Well, at least outwardly so.

"V'dar, you begged an audience with me only to allow this beast to insult me?" the queen asks archly. "I thought you had better manners than that."

"Naida," V'dar says in a chiding tone, one you use with a child, or someone not too bright. "I thought you had grown up. I can see that is not the case. Do I need to appoint a new sovereign for your realm?"

"And now you lower yourself to their level? Perhaps we need a new god."

The whole lodge trembles, and I can only imagine V'dar has grown to his full height again.

"You forget yourself, faeling. I could end your long reign with a blink of an eye and not lose an ounce of sleep over it."

"Temper, temper," Naida says, but her voice is a little shaky. Kudos to her for trying to fake it, even if she fails.

Still, what has come over V'dar? Why has he changed his stance?

I must have asked this over the pack bond, because Matt replies to me.

Zaya insisted on showing some of her memories to him. She said it was time he took the blinders off. It seems to have worked, he was already pissy before they arrived.

They're both there?

Yes, and Joe says the creatures that come with the unseelie king are the same kind as in your dream.

Trolls. There are trolls literally in my house. I want to vomit. Whatever protections V'dar thinks he has laid around this meeting, they're sneaky enough to find a loophole, I'm sure of it.

"Stop there, where do you think you're going," Marcus snaps.

"Mmmmmeat," comes the rumbling reply.

"Mine," Marcus growls back.

There's a tense silence before a word barked in a language I don't understand precedes a heavy footstep, claws clicking on the floor. The troll has been called back to his master's side, I presume.

"I believe the creature is mine, actually," Naida says imperiously, over her fright. "If you return her to me unharmed, I promise to consider whatever you wish to ask of me."

"She belongs to me first and foremost," Zaya snaps. "If anyone were to lay claim to a siren, it would be me."

"You've gained a little backbone since we parted, Zaya. Don't worry, I'll have no trouble breaking you again. I rather enjoyed it the first time."

"Enough!" V'dar growls. "You will not threaten my mate, foolish child. This is your last warning."

"Is she hungry? Is that why you cannot control yourself, V'dar?"

"Do you have a death wish? Or are you just stupid?" Mara retorts. "Keep prodding him, I think the fae realm could do with a makeover. Perhaps I could send my wolves as guards until such time as stability returns. I imagine wiping out the imperial family could leave quite the power vacuum behind."

Naida snorts. "You could both try."

"As you wish," V'dar purrs.

There's a gasp and a thump, and then Naida shrieks in fury.

"That was my daughter, you buffoon!" she shouts.

Another gasp and another thump. "Yes, and that was your son. See? I can do this all day, and I haven't even raised a sweat. How many progeny did you create with that vile womb of yours, Naida?

Believe me, if I use my power at its full force, I can find every last one of them and end them in a heartbeat."

There's silence for a few moments before the heavy, clawed footstep sounds again.

"No," Naida shrieks. "You cannot eat them!"

"Why not, dear cousin? You know no matter where or how you bury them, my people will find them. There is not a tree in the realm who can withstand our power. We take what we want when we want it, and you can do nothing about it."

The gasp this time is deeper, and the thump louder. What the fuck was that?

"You killed my guard? For what reason? He has done no harm."

"Neither did the prince and princess," V'dar says casually.

"And I did not threaten you," the king protests.

"You say this, and yet when you spoke about taking what you want, Istal, your gaze was on the door of the room where the sirens sit listening. Your threat was more subtle, but present nonetheless. The sirens and their goddess are under my protection, should a single hair be harmed on their bodies, you will answer to me."

"As you wish, my god," Istal says, but I don't trust him for a minute. He's definitely lying. If I could see him, I'd have proof.

If I weren't feeding my sons, I'd already be on the landing looking.

"Whatever you wished to ask of us, I am no longer able to provide," Naida says, her voice shaken but cold. "You insult me, kill my children, and steal my property. I am now forced to return home to bury my dead. Perhaps I will be free in a few months' time."

"Oh dear, please, allow me to help you," V'dar says angrily.

There's a soft hiss, and Naida cries out again.

What just happened? I ask Matt.

He turned the bodies to ash, then produced two urns and put the ashes in them.

Matt was wrong earlier. V'dar isn't pissy. He's *pissed.*

"You can hold a memorial when I've finished with you. Which means you're free to offer your assistance now."

There is no response, and the tension is killing me. When Carter and Wyatt finish their feed, I allow the others to take them away and burp them while I busy my hands covering myself up again with fresh breast pads inside my bra and bindings so I don't rip that door open to see what is happening.

I pull my clothing into place, but when I stand, Shay is in my face. "No," she says firmly. "V'dar is winning, do not interrupt now."

Either she has her dragon helping her, or Connor is. It's clear she's been following the conversation as well as I have.

"I will not help a barbarian such as yourself," Naida says foolishly in her grief.

I know the instant V'dar has had enough. This time, instead of a gasp and thump, there's a thump and then an outcry from several of her retinue, which is quickly silenced by a succession of thuds. The silence following this is ominous.

"Not the queen," V'dar says. "You may feast on the others, but not in this realm."

Fuck! I'd forgotten that. Trolls can find their way back to anywhere they've fed before. If they take even a nibble while they're here, it would be like setting a pin on a map.

"The wolves will throw the carcasses through the portal when I open it again, I have no desire to witness their consumption, and I do not trust them enough not to snack as they work."

"As you wish, my god," Istal says, his voice is now shaken too. Perhaps we will be safe after all.

"The rain outside has acid in it, the storm is unnatural. I called on you, my children, to help restore the balance. It seems I have left the seelie court to themselves for far too long. I think it is time I redress the imbalance there."

"I can take the acid, my god," Istal says quietly.

"And the destroyed rubber?" V'dar pushes.

"Yes, my god. I did not dare ask for that, but my people would make good use of it."

"You are humble, this pleases me, Istal," V'dar purrs.

I can hear footsteps, several people moving around, and then the faint squeak of the front door.

A low drone starts outside, an ominous, rumbling sound. It rises and falls in pitch, setting all my hairs on end. The magic that washes over me feels oily and heavy, but it doesn't linger, passing through the room and beyond in moments.

It feels like an hour has passed, but it's probably only half of that before the door closes again.

"Would they feel that?" V'dar asks.

"No, my god. The acid is an ingredient, not part of the actual spell. The fresh water will soon wash away any lingering after effects, although I cannot restore the pH of the soil or the life to the plants and animals harmed."

Magic, V'dar's magic, sweeps over my skin, and I can only presume he has opened the portal again.

"You have pleased me well this day, Istal," he says. "I wish you safe travels back to your home, and a good feast."

More shuffling ensues and I can hear faint thumps. I assume that's the bodies being thrown through the other side. Soon after, the magic stops and silence reigns. I didn't even hear the king and his trolls leave.

I find out why a moment later when the door crashes open, a huge troll blocking the doorway.

"Don't let it draw blood!" I scream, but before the thing can take another step, it collapses into a pile of ash.

This time, when the magic comes, it rips across my skin like sandpaper, and I can see V'dar's head from where I'm sitting. His hair brushes the timbers of the ceiling. I don't know why he always grows when he's mad, but it's an impressive sight to say the least.

Shay isn't fast enough to prevent me from jumping over the ash to the bannister, where I can see the portal to the unseelie kingdom open again. The king and his trolls turn surprised and bloodied faces towards us. They had already begun feasting.

"Did you forget something when you left, Istal?" V'dar asks, dangerously quiet."

The guilty look that flashes across the king's face is his undoing. The limb in his hands falls to the ground as he falls away in ash, as do the trolls with him, and then the bodies they had begun to feast on. The ash from behind me swirls through the air, slipping into the portal before it closes.

"Now I need to replace two royal families," V'dar grumbles.

"Will that be enough to stop any trolls from returning?" I ask fearfully.

V'dar shrinks down again before he answers tiredly. "Yes, chosen one. You are safe from your vision. I can no longer see any variation of that threat in your future."

I sink to my knees in relief. Seeing that thing right in front of me was as frightening in reality as it had been in my dreams.

"We will find some members of the seelie court to help restore the balance after the war has been won," V'dar says wearily. "For now, we need to plan, because together we can take out the storm, and when that happens, our foes will be ready to attack."

Bring it. I'm tired of living in fear, and I think everyone here feels the same. It's time to take the battle to them, rather than waiting for it to come to us.

30

MARCUS

Alistair might have Belar on his side, but us? We've got five gods. I think we've got this. Or at least I'm telling myself that.

The pack is delighted to learn the rain is no longer lethal, but it still takes a bit of convincing to get people moving around in it.

Aidal is able to confirm the rain only extends a few metres past our boundary fences, and I wonder how Alistair is going to explain that to the humans. Then I realise he isn't. They aren't going to hide our presence from the humans anymore, not if they plan on taking over the planet, which means they no longer care what they do and who they expose themselves to.

I try calling our neighbours to tell them some trouble is in town and to go hide in the basement, but the phone lines are dead.

Either they've been destroyed by the acid, or pulled down to isolate us. It doesn't matter, with the might we have on our side, there's more than one way to skin a cat.

The mages oblige us by opening portals to the neighbouring properties.

John Davis, our neighbour to the northeast gapes at us as we exit out of a hole in the air.

"This got somethin' to do with my wrecked crops?" he snaps.

"Yep. Came here to see if you're still thinking about selling. Thought I'd offer above the market price, and a bit more to keep your mouth shut on top."

"Define market price," he says, not giving an inch.

I smile. "What the bank has it valued at, plus whatever the going rate is for your crops, undamaged, plus a nice little retirement fund. Call it an apology for the trouble we brought to your doorstep."

John looks away from me and spits on the ground, Graeme tenses beside me, but I know what that means. We've won.

"Can't say I'll be sorry to leave," John says, sticking out a hand. "I will miss having good neighbours though."

I take the offered palm in mine and give him a strong shake. He won't respect anything less. I'm not sure if he's referring to us, though. "Good neighbours are hard to find," I say, lamely.

"Yes, you are," he replies, then turns and walks to the house. He doesn't even name a price. John's old-school, and I respect that. I suspect he knows it too.

"John," I call out as he hits the porch. "I'm gonna wire you a bonus right now. How about you take Martha on a little holiday. Throw some clothes in a bag and leave within the hour. Go somewhere nice for a couple of weeks."

He pauses, his foot still on the last step, but he doesn't turn. "That bad, huh?" he asks.

"Worse," I reply.

"Martha, get your fat arse in the car, we're going." He doesn't look back as he goes inside.

Martha can be heard calling him all the names under the sun, but the truck backs out of the garage only minutes later and rumbles off down the long drive that's in much better condition than our own.

"Just like that?" Graeme says, surprised.

"Just like that," I reply. "We bought the original Triune lands off him years ago. I know he's noticed we haven't aged all that much. He's just not the type to pry. I've got enough set by to thank him for the rest of his life."

"You're good people," Graeme says.

I shrug, not comfortable with the compliment. I wasn't always 'good people', but I've learned to be. "I try."

The neighbours on the other side are a little trickier, but when I name a figure more than twice what their land is worth, they jump at it. Fully furnished is my demand, we don't have time for them to fuck around with moving it all out, plus it's more space for us to put people once we get this threat sorted. They agree, and within the hour they're gone too. There's nobody else to protect in this little valley, and I have to hope it's enough.

"Where are the defences up to?" I ask Sam when we get back. He's been locked up in the office all morning with the betas and leaders of the other communities.

"I think we have a plan," he says with a grin. "We know they have superior numbers, so we need to go at this the way any smaller army does — guerilla warfare style."

Now that's a term I'm not expecting to hear, but it makes sense. Ambush style combat would definitely suit us because we know the terrain so much better than Alistair's brutes.

Eagerly, Sam pulls me over to the map on the wall. It isn't showing our new purchases, but we're not defending them. As far as Alistair is concerned, they're neutral territory, just space to pass through. If he catches on we now own them, he'll destroy all the infrastructure there. So it's better to just leave them alone for now.

"See these orange markers?" Sam asks excitedly.

I can't miss them, they're all over the fucking place and they make no sense. "Yeah, what are they for?"

"Booby traps," Sam replies with a grin. "The dragons are going to dig a hole, we'll cover them with tarp, and the magic users are going to make them into nice little nests for us. We can hide a couple of people in there at a time, the top will be like a one way mirror. We'll see out, but they can't see in, and they can't scent us either."

"So, we lie in wait until we can pick off a few of their troops at a time?" I ask, and he nods.

"We're getting loaded up with charms too, like small grenades. The witches are down in the bunker at the moment practising aim. Shifters, or those with a strong arm, are going to lob them and the witches will use magic to guide them. They're strong enough to stun vampires so our fighters can move in and take them out quickly, but not enough to cause damage to our buildings."

That's a handy little trick.

"We won't have a lot of them," Graeme says, butting in, but Sam doesn't seem to mind in the least. "Only one per pair, I'm afraid, but if we have enough pairs close by, they can use one or two to hit a large group, and then all the fighters can move through them and take out the vampires first, as they're the more deadly fighters."

"Probably because we're already dead," Jeremiah quips and everyone chuckles.

"Mara has been doing some scouting for us," Sam adds, pointing at the clusters of blue pins on the periphery of our boundaries.

The gods haven't left our sides since they manifested, and it's been a huge morale boost for everyone. I'm so fucking grateful they're still here.

V'dar looks across the room at me and winks. The god fucking winks!

"How the fuck are you doing that?" I ask Mara.

She gives a coy smile. "Wolves are hunters," she says enigmatically. "I'm the goddess of the wolves. I'm the ultimate predator. I can give approximate numbers of heartbeats for the shifters, mages and witches. Vampires are a little harder, but I can sense them as a patch of coldness. The larger the cold area, the more bodies present."

According to the map, we're surrounded. Not every inch, but there are forces gathered on all four sides. The corners seem to be the best points in terms of numbers as they have the least amount of blue around them. I point them out to Sam, who shakes his head.

"Witches," he says. "We don't know what they're up to, but I think we can be sure it won't benefit us."

I look back at the map again. This is the largest force sent against us yet. My brother is getting desperate. Add in the acid rain to soften us up, and it points to only one thing.

"It's do or die time, people," I tell them. "They're sending everything they have against us. They're also confident they're going to win, so we need to be smarter than they are when we deploy our people. Every single person is going to count."

"What about the children and elderly?" My brother will go for them first, because it will draw the rest of us out.

"Evacuated," Sam says proudly, grinning over at Graeme who inclines his head.

"What? To where? I know it's going to be tough to guard them, but we don't have the manpower to guard them somewhere else." I snap. Fuck, this isn't going to work.

"Hear me out!" Sam begs, and I give a brusque nod of my chin. This had better be fucking good if he's going to divide our forces.

"Alistair has brought everything here, right?" Sam asks.

"I presume so, but we can't be sure."

"Okay, but we know until he takes us out, he's not going to waste time going after them, even if he does find them."

Begrudgingly I agree.

"So, we also have the Alphe assholes who are looking for a way to gain credit with Mara. They're useless here as fighters and we don't have the manpower to guard them anyway. So, we're sending them as nominal guards, and they're all going back to the Pasadena properties that remain undamaged."

Hiding them where my brother has already swept the people away, and he has no inkling we're using mages to create portals, and even if he did, he'd have no way to trace them. Alright, it's not as stupid an idea as I originally thought.

"They'd still be vulnerable," I grumble.

Sam grimaces. "I know, but less so than they are here, and let's face it, if we lose, they're dead anyway. At least they'll have a chance to regroup where they are."

It galls me that he's right, but it is the best option.

"Actually," Dean says, joining in. "I might be able to improve on that a little."

"How so?" Sam asks, his face alight with interest, rather than dismissing the dragon or being angry someone thinks they can do better. This is another reason he's such an amazing tactician. He considers everything. I'm fucking proud to call him my brother.

"I've heard from two clans we thought were lost. I sent out messages when we were under attack, but we never heard back from them, at least, not in time. They're willing to take our dragon elders, even my mother, and they're sending fighting dragons to help us out. It's almost a hundred shifters, Marcus. We could probably hit those troops outside right now and decimate their numbers."

Sam staggers back. "A hundred?"

"Close to it," Dean says with a grin.

"And with your own clan's fighters?"

"Yeah, over a hundred."

"This is a fucking game changer," Sam whispers, spinning to look at the map.

"They can make their own portals and be here within the hour," Dean clarifies.

Sam, however, is no longer listening, his gaze sweeping back and forth over the map as he takes in the new data. I can feel his excitement through the bond.

"How well do you see through clouds?" Sam asks distractedly.

"In our shifted form, we've got a heat sensing option in our vision, much like snakes. I see what you're getting at. We could hide above the cloud cover and then swoop down to launch the first strike on your signal. It would decimate their troops before they could scatter."

"Yes," Sam says, pumping a fist in the air. "Alistair is so fucked," he growls, making us all laugh.

"Jeremiah," says Suzanne, one of the witch elders. She holds out a drawstring pouch to him. "Daywalking charms in case the fight lasts past dawn. Even if it doesn't, I'm sure we could use your help in the cleanup. There's one for each of you."

Jeremiah looks down at the bag in his hands like he's holding the world's greatest treasure. For him, they probably are.

"Thank you, we will take great care of them and return them to you when we're all safe," Jeremiah says with a bow.

Suzanne snorts. "Don't think I didn't notice you using your speed to bring in witches out of that rain," she says tartly. "Consider these a gift, a token of our appreciation."

Yna beams, pleased with the exchange, and everyone can see the gratitude on Jeremiah's face. It's just one more connection between our peoples, one more step in rebuilding the old ways where supes mingled rather than staying isolated and self-involved in our own communities.

"Jeremiah," V'dar says in his rumbling voice. "You defied your own god to come here, and not only have you sought refuge, but you've proven yourselves time and again with your generosity. I know Belar has cut you off and I wish to offer you my blessing. Once upon a time the vampires were my children too, and I would welcome you back under my care."

The ancient vampire looks like all his fucking Christmases have come at once as he sinks to his knees in front of V'dar.

"Whatever vow you ask for, whatever you need or wish, if it is ours to offer, we do so gladly," he says fervently.

For the first time, I see a gentleness in V'dar that shows how much he loves his children. He's often so removed from everything, and at times more than a little sly, but I can see how much he cares.

"My son, your nestlings please me greatly. Be blessed with increased strength and a reduced need to feed. To you alone do I give the ability to reach my chosen vessel with your mind. Should you need any aid, call her and she will find it for you."

He gives a significant look to Catriona who nods eagerly, her eyes shining with tears.

I'm not so keen on that part, but if it's only the ability to communicate I can live with it. If the sneaky god thinks to add another mate to her already full dance card, we'll be having words, god or not.

Be easy, little wolf, he says in my mind, startling me. *It is not her his fate is tied to.* The god's gaze certainly looks in her direction, but there are two other sirens in the room besides Catriona. Shayla and Gwendoline flank her on either side, both of them looking at Jeremiah with the kind of suspicion I felt when I thought the god was playing matchmaker again.

"Is that everything?" I ask Sam, as if nothing else just happened. "Where are the sirens going? I don't want them near those Alphe fuckers. Dean, would your dragons take them with the elderly?"

"Or you could ask us what we want," Catriona interrupts defiantly. I know in an instant whatever comes out of her mouth next is going to piss me off as much as I just pissed her off.

"We're staying," Gwendoline says decisively. "We're tired of running and hiding. You've offered us sanctuary here, and frankly I'd rather die fighting than be caught later on."

Before anyone can protest, Zaya steps forward, beaming. "I will numb the bonds between you, daughter. So any losses will not incapacitate the others in their own struggles."

The argument I was going to make is defeated before I even get a sound out.

"I could use your help, if you're willing. There's a slight risk to it, but I'm hoping it will give us a secret advantage," Sam says, refusing to acknowledge my growl of protest when I'm fucking standing right beside him.

"What do you need, bossman?" Shayla asks cheekily.

Connor growls and moves to stand closer beside her, but she simply swats him with the back of her hand when he tries to pull her back behind the others. Shayla is no shrinking violet, and the dragon is a fool if he thinks he can control her.

Just the dragon? Zaya asks in my mind, smirking at me.

I ignore her comment and focus on what Sam is saying.

"With guards, of course, if we could get you all running from building to building in small groups or pairs, we could lay down enough scent trails to make it impossible to tell where you're hiding."

"I could go one better," Susanne says. "We can make some charms to hide your scent that only work when you put them on. So you could run from one building to another, put the charm on and your scent disappears while you move somewhere else and repeat the process. They're going to come up with dead end after dead end. It will drive them a little crazy if any of them actively decide to hunt you."

"Well," Graeme says, drawing our attention. "If you can do that, I can layer those scent trails so we can turn them off and on like neon lights. One minute the scent is here, the next it's over there. Think of it like a railway map but with only certain lines being open at certain times. We could do it with everyone, or at least people from every species. Which means they won't be able to tell a fresh trail from an old one. It will help hide our people as we manoeuvre around the site from one hidey-hole to another."

Sam's face lights up. "How long will the charms take to make?" he asks Susanne.

"Give me enough pendants already made, and we can have it done in three to four hours," she replies.

"We can make some portals to go buy some cheap ones at a market stall somewhere," Graeme says, making me realise it's the weekend.

We've been stuck inside our own borders for so long that the passage of time completely escapes me.

"Then aside from these few tasks, we're as ready as we can be," Sam announces.

V'dar nods solemnly. "Then we stop the rainfall tonight."

"Wait," Matt says, and we all look at him. "In the heat of battle, how will we know if someone is ours? I mean, I know a lot of the faces around here, but say I meet one of Dean's new dragons. I won't recognise him, and he won't know any of us either."

"That's an easy fix," Zaya says, drawing a finger down through her blonde hair. In its wake, a light teal colour appears. "Look for that."

"In the dark?" I ask, confused.

She sighs and the room dims, her hair lighting up like a beacon.

"As much as we appreciate it, goddess, that glowing light is going to lead the enemy right to us," Sam says as respectfully as he can.

Zaya gives a tinkling laugh. "Only if they can see it, silly. Only those wearing the mark can see the mark on the others, but in case one of us ends up in a well-lit area—"

A large pile of black beanies materialises on the table in front of us.

"Hand those out to everyone."

There's nothing else to do. We're set, at least as much as we can be. Everyone has their orders, their locations, and their missions. As soon as darkness falls, the rain will stop, and the fun will begin.

I can't fucking wait!

Fleur has all the kitchen staff make us food that will not only last, but can be eaten on the run. Pies, sausage rolls, sandwiches, and pasties. Things that can be held in one hand and don't need a plate. They are stored in the three kitchens we have and put under protective spells so they won't spoil and can't be touched by the enemy.

Of course, not everyone feels the same. Catriona feeds the boys again, tucks them into their cots with their nurses, and expresses more milk just in case. We don't know how long this battle will take, or whether we'll even see them again. That bit is hard. Saying goodbye to the son I've barely begun to know. We also can't let them pick up on our tension, so we keep it light for all our sakes, but as soon as we leave and the gods set the wards in place, Catriona falls apart in my arms.

"Baby, you have to stop or your milk will curdle," I tell her seriously. It has the desired effect. She laughs and swipes at me as I brush the tears from her face. "We'll never get date night again if you put up this kind of fuss when leaving for a couple of hours."

"Ha!" she says. "Ha! As if we'd even get out of the front door before you had your cock inside me."

She's not wrong. I shrug and smirk at her.

"I'll take you on a date," Ethan says, smoothly sliding into the conversation.

She's been avoiding him, unsure of our reaction, and not knowing how to handle the change in their relationship status. Truly, the only person she was fooling was herself. Yes, she had the right to say no, but we all knew she wouldn't.

Well, except the dragon. I'm pretty sure he was sweating bullets over it all until she claimed him.

She's been avoiding him all day as we prepared, and he hasn't pushed it, but I know every time she turned around, there he was. Waiting. Watching. He'd give a little half smile and take a step towards her, and she'd spin away and find something else to do. It was kind of funny to watch, and he'd chuckle softly every time. He was enjoying it. The thrill of stalking her. Pursuing her. Hunting her.

Even now she tries to turn away from him, but she's in my arms and I hold her still. I think it's time he caught her and she faces up to what's going on in her life. We could all die tonight, and it would be a shame for this to be unresolved.

Ethan's grin grows wider as he realises her predicament. He stands there, watching, that half smile on his face, as she wriggles and squirms, trying to get out of my grip. All she achieves though, is giving me a hard-on as her butt keeps grinding against me, and when I've had enough, I grind back against her, and instinctively she stills. The perfume of her arousal is heady and my reward.

Ethan takes a deep breath, his pupils widening with lust and elongating slightly as his dragon takes interest. Slowly, he prowls toward her, and other than a slight twitch, she doesn't move. She's the prey caught in the gaze of a predator, only I think she wants to be caught as much as he wants to catch her.

When Ethan reaches us and aligns his body to hers, she sighs and becomes pliant, trapped between our hard bodies. I wish we had time to take this further, I'd like nothing more to see where it goes, but the house is getting dark and the rain will stop soon.

"When this is over," I promise the pair of them. "We're going to pick this up right where we left off."

I grind against her ass again to make my point, pushing her harder against Ethan in the process. He stills, taking a deep breath. It's probably to try and get himself under control, but if he's scenting what I'm scenting, it's only making things worse. Or harder. Take your pick. For me, it's definitely harder.

"You three have the worst fucking timing," Matt groans from somewhere behind me.

"But after the battle we're going to have the best fucking time," I quip.

Ethan snorts, but the mood is broken now, and we pull apart.

"Just remember," I tell him as we head towards the stairs. "I prefer her ass."

Catriona slaps me across the chest, but Ethan chuckles. "I can work with that."

He gets a slap too.

We're all smiling as we reach the bottom of the stairs where everyone stands bathed in the dim light of the fireplace. We've banked the fire, the doors and windows will probably be smashed at some point, but why waste the fuel creating heat that's only going to be lost later. We can warm ourselves in more creative ways anyway.

"Ready?" Graeme asks as we join them.

"As we'll ever be," I reply.

"Go, find your stations," V'dar orders. "You have three minutes, starting now."

31

Marcus

Catriona and I move silently to the back door. The lack of light outside doesn't bother us as our wolves help us to see in the darkness. Stealthily, we make our way around the side of the lodge towards the porta-potties. Jude and Quentin had the right idea during the last battle. No matter what else is going on, this place reeks and it's going to allow us even more protection. Our scents will simply disappear.

Catriona isn't shifting. She's got a blade in each hand. We haven't had time to teach her how to fight properly as a wolf, so she'll only shift if she's got the time to do so before being struck, and as the last possible resort.

I remember the nightmare I had long ago, where a dragon stood behind her and breathed flame, devouring her in an instant. I think I actually had it wrong, It was the image of her dragon overlaid, because she never actually fell or burned. I'm hoping that's what it meant, and I'm hoping like hell she doesn't need to shift into something that big.

The dragons are currently flying above the clouds. Their heat-seeking sight should come in handy as soon as the signal is given. Once the fighting devolves into a grand melee, they'll land and shift, using their strength in other ways. It's too risky for them to continue using flame when they're just as likely to hurt our own people.

I'm just waiting for the signal from Sam to say everything is ready and they're working on the spell. The anticipation has my wolf restless, and I can feel him pacing inside me. It's time for us to take cover, so I peel back the tarp over our hidey-hole and Catriona jumps in.

"Is this not the best date you've ever had?" I ask her, and she giggles.

"Well, it beats the night the best friend of that stage five clinger brought him back onto my radar," she replies, and I pretend to wince.

"Woman, you wound me!"

She giggles again.

"If I remember correctly, you had several rounds of epic sex that night. First with Toby, then with me and finally Matt."

Catriona laughs outright. "No, it was more like, First with Toby, second with Toby, almost third with Toby — although he enjoyed that one. Then it was a hate fuck with you, and a don't you dare fuck with Matt."

Our light banter has suddenly turned awkward, and I kick myself for killing the mood when things are tense enough.

"No regrets?" I ask.

"None," she whispers and kisses me briefly, before pointing upwards. "Listen."

I listen but I don't hear anything.

"It's stopped raining."

She's right. I can't hear a sound at all. Anywhere. Other than the slow drips from buildings still shedding the last of the downpour.

Sam? I call through the bond.

Yeah?

The rain has stopped.

Yeah, I told Catriona, didn't she pass it on?

I grind my teeth together. *No, she didn't.*

Want me to report to both of you? he asks, and I can hear the teasing note in his voice. Hardy har, har. I know he's pushing my buttons, but tonight really isn't the time to give me shit about my alpha tendencies.

Although we're underground, we're dry, and we're relatively warm. The stench from the porta-potties doesn't even permeate, although I know it's pungent enough outside our hiding spot. The tarp, to us, is like a window, and Catriona and I face each other, scanning the area around us, waiting for the enemy to come to us.

As quickly as possible, I shed my clothes and shift. I don't want to be vulnerable above ground while I do so. It'll be a little awkward leaping up out of the hole, but I should be able to do that and cover Catriona's exit while she climbs out.

There.

Just behind her left side, a shadow moves in the darkness. I give her left cheek a lick and lift my snout in that direction. She nods and points behind me, raising three fingers. I can still only see one, so I wait a little longer. Sure enough, two more shadows join it. I give her two more licks on that side and she nods, holding up three fingers on each hand and pointing them in the right directions. We wait a little longer, but no more arrive.

As quickly as they came, the three I saw slip away again, and I use a paw to bat down the fingers pointed in their direction. Six was too much for us, but three? We should be able to handle three.

We wait a little longer to see if the first three return, but when they don't, I give her a clear nod. It's time.

Catriona stands and flips the tarp back in a smooth movement that exposes us both. The porta-potties are directly behind us, so there's no chance of anyone sneaking up on us from that direction, unless they were sitting on the roofs. I leap out and attack the closest figure, the stench of vampire clogging up my nose as I rip his hand off.

The vampire screams, clutching his stump to his chest. It will distract him for a moment or two while I attack the second one, because the third one has gone for Catriona. I don't have time to see whether she made it out of the hole or not — I'm too busy avoiding the attacks of the second vampire. In the distance the sounds of battle ring out, and the vampire in front of me must hear them too, because unlike me, he doesn't ignore them. For half a second, he pauses, his head turned slightly, and it's all the break I need.

I leap up and rip out his throat — nearly taking his entire head off in the process. It's not a killing blow, he's capable of healing, but only over several hours. For this instant, though, he's as good as dead. I'll finish him off once the others are taken care of.

The handless vampire is still screaming over his stump, so I attack quickly, this time getting the head off with a deft twist of my body. The head goes flying in one direction, the rest of the corpse collapsing in the other. I take a second to check on Catriona, but she's wiping her blades on the body of the vamp she's decapitated.

Good girl, I send to her, and she grins at me.

Want me to finish that one off for you? I can't imagine they taste good.

If you wouldn't mind, they taste like the porta-potties smell.

Catriona wrinkles her nose in disgust. *Remind me not to shift then.*

I send amusement back to her as she casually slices off the vampire's head and casts it away. Then she covers our hole back up again, and we move to our next location. The idea is to keep our forces mobile, ambushing smaller groups so we can whittle down the larger force in guerrilla warfare. It's the only way we stand a chance. Well, at least without the dragons. Speaking of which, where are they?

Dean? I ask Catriona.

On the count of three, drop to the ground, she replies.

One.

Two.

Three.

I hit the ground hard, just as a searing heat erupts above me, and Dean takes out the three vampires who have circled back upon hearing their companions' cries.

As if his attack was a signal, dozens of dragons swoop down, searing flame in a multitude of locations. From the looks of things, the large forces we had initially scouted have divided up into smaller groups. Our entire perimeter is being attacked.

Are the wards down? I ask her, and she nods.

Damn. We'd hoped they'd last longer than that, but the gods had pulled their own barricades down earlier, to hide their presence. Instead they redirected the magic into warding our little ambush places, a much better use, in my opinion.

Keep moving, I tell Catriona.

She scrambles to her feet and we move into the forest as planned, making our way slowly down to the front gate. She's pretty quiet for a human, well, in human form at least.

Ask your wolf to help you with stealth, I tell her. *I can still hear you.*

She nods and then her footsteps disappear. Damn, she's going to be amazing when she shifts.

Dean says there's another group of three just off to our right. He can take them out, but there's a risk it will start a fire in the forest.

Tell him we've got it.

I made a deal with the alpha earlier. I would allow his dragons to mingle with the sirens a little more, and he would be our personal scout for the battle. Of course we both know it's Catriona who's managing to keep the two groups apart, but I might have offered to keep her distracted at appropriate times. Ethan is also in on the plan. We won't let the women be forced or coerced. It's more a case of preventing Catriona from being a cock-block over and over again.

In fact, I think all her mates might be grateful enough to Dean, to help. We just need to get through this shit-show first.

The waft of something sickly-sweet hits my nose, and I want to cough, but my wolf and I hold back, not willing to give ourselves away. This is a little different. With vampires we can use brute strength, but with witches we need to either divide them further or take them down fast, because they have magic they can use to hurt us.

Witches, I tell Catriona. *I'm going to go over to the right a bit more and make a little noise, see if I can't spook them into separating. Squat down and wait for me.*

Alright, be careful.

She's got a charm with a stun spell in it, but we want to save that for when there's a big group, too big to fight or flee from. It would be wasted on a trio of witches, especially as it can only be used once.

Carefully I slink across the wet ground, avoiding anything that could give my presence away. It takes me a bit longer, but eventually I'm far enough away that the witches are almost between Catriona and I.

Finally, I find what I'm looking for. Many of the branches have been reduced to flimsy messes like soggy cardboard by the acid, but this one was thick enough that it still retains some shape. Hopefully it's kept enough structure that it will snap loudly when I stand on it.

Just to be sure, I practically pounce on the thing and I want to yip in delight when it gives a resounding crunch.

"What was that?" a voice whispers.

"I don't know, let's check it out," says another.

"We're not meant to leave the area, guys," argues a third. "We're supposed to stay here and be ready for our part in the spell."

"I'm not waiting for something to sneak up on us," the first one says, heading towards where I snapped the twig.

Two are going for the distraction, I think the third is staying in place. Ask Dean for confirmation, and if that's the case, get him to guide you in. I'll keep watch on the other two.

On it.

I don't hear her moving, at all, then again, it's hard to hear anything over the noises of the two witches bumbling through the forest.

What I do hear, however, is the distinctive sound of a blade slicing through flesh, and a low gurgling sound as she completes her kill. There's no thud, which means she's lowering the body to the ground.

What does Dean recommend?

He says to move to your left, I'm going to come from the other side, and we can take one each. They've found your stick and are looking down at it.

Then we'll do that.

Slowly, I retrace my steps towards the night-blind witches. The fools are using the torches on their phones to light their steps now. As long as they're pointed towards the ground, they won't see us coming.

I can see Catriona moving into place, but the two witches are so busy arguing over whether the twig was freshly broken or damaged in the storm, they don't even notice.

Just then, however, Catriona missteps and she breaks her own twig. She's put on a beanie to cover her lock of hair, and rather than looking menacing, she looks a little lost.

Play harmless, I order her, as the two witches turn, raising their hands in front of them.

"Oh thank god," Catriona says, stumbling towards them. "One of those mutts took out my group. I barely got away and I've been looking for everyone since."

She's got a hand on her chest over her heart as though she's relieved, and I notice the witches relaxing a little as she stumbles closer.

"Why didn't you announce yourself?" the first witch asks.

"Oh yeah, good one. Just wander around blind and say, hey there, which side are you on? Do I look like a complete idiot? What if you were one of *them?*"

The witches lower their hands and that's when we strike.

Now! I send to her, and she lunges forward with the knife, cutting the woman across the face as I tackle the man and rip his throat out.

Catriona stabs the woman in the heart, but she still raises her hands, so she cuts the woman's throat.

"Yeah," she growls as the woman's arms drop. "What if you were one of the assholes determined to kill me and my pups and enslave the entire planet? As if the vamps would let you live once they'd won."

"Ooh, I don't know," says a voice to the right. "We might let some of you live, after all, we've got to feed off something, and you smell pretty juicy."

Dean says he's alone, Catriona warns me, just as the vamp strikes — towards her and not me. I don't understand why, I'm the greater danger, but then he grabs her right hand and squeezes it until she drops the knife, while his teeth are poised at her throat.

"Shift back now and I won't kill her," the vampire says, licking her neck.

"You'd have to be alive to do that," Catriona replies and stabs him with the knife in her other hand.

The vampire growls and darts away. He's injured, but he's not dead, and I'm willing to bet he's hoping to feed off one of us to regain his strength.

There's a loud crash off to one side, and then Jeremiah appears holding the vamp's head in his fist by the hair. "Heard you needed some backup," the rogue leader says.

"You have our thanks," Catriona replies, clearly unsure how to take this.

Jeremiah's eyes are red, although judging from the blood on him, he's already fed well.

"I'm no danger to you," he says, reading her hesitance correctly. He pats his belly. "I'm full. I'm just a little excited, this is a lot more fun than being hunted."

He absently throws the head away and scratches his cheek where the blood has dried, flaking away with his ministrations.

"Damn stuff always itches," he grumbles, then looks around. "You've already had some fun then."

I lower my head and raise it in a slow nod, then shift back, careful to move slowly so I don't startle him.

"My, my," Jeremiah says, eyeing me up and down. "What a juicy cock. Lucky girl."

Catriona giggles.

Me? I stare. "Are you alright?"

Jeremiah raises a hand and wavers it from side to side. "Mostly. I got hit with a potion and I feel a little bit drunk." He holds up his index finger and thumb an inch apart. "But it's fucking fangtastic."

V'dar, I pray. *We have an injured vampire and I'm not sure what to do with him. We can't leave him like this, he's vulnerable.*

"Jeremiah," V'dar says, appearing right beside me and startling the three of us. "Marcus says you're hurt?"

"Hurt, drunk, whatever — I feel good!" Jeremiah replies, and V'dar looks curiously at me.

"He got hit with a potion," I explain.

V'dar reaches out slowly, and Jeremiah stands still until the god's hand rests on his forehead. "Aah, I see. It's a toxin. You feel great now, but you won't if this spreads. If you'll allow me to heal you, I can set things right. You might want to sit down."

Bemusedly, Jeremiah falls to his knees. "I knew it was too good to be true. I haven't been drunk since I was reborn. It's not fair you know," he protests, and Catriona giggles.

"Well, I'll see what can be done afterwards, okay?" V'dar promises.

"Okay," the drunken vampire agrees.

"I'd appreciate if the two of you could watch my back while I do this," V'dar says, and then closes his eyes.

I cast my senses out as far as my wolf and I can reach, but I don't catch anything. Catriona however, turns pale.

Dean says there's a group of ten heading this way. They seem to be looking for something. Probably the witches we took out.

Tell him to let Sam know there are groups of witches waiting for a signal to cast a spell. We've taken out the corner lot here, but there are probably others in the other corners too, maybe some along the sides.

Why not just tell Sam?

Because I'm listening for the group approaching us.

"V'dar," I say gently. "We've got incoming."

"Almost done," he grunts.

I just catch the sound of movement, right before V'dar steps back and Jeremiah leans to the side and retches noisily. Well, if they didn't know where we were before, they know now.

"Everyone touch me," V'dar orders, stepping back to Jeremiah and putting his hand back on the vampire's skin.

I move in and touch the back of his neck, while Catriona takes his other hand.

Seconds later the first vampire slinks into view. I don't know what V'dar is doing, but the stranger looks right through us as he reads the scene.

Two more vampires join him and they hiss, looking around them in all directions.

"Whoever took them out is long gone," the first one says. "None of these tracks are recent."

"That's Silas," another one says.

"His nestlings are fucked then, how many did he bring with him?"

"All of them," the first one snarls. "Over a hundred progeny just dropped dead."

"I told them we shouldn't bring the sires," the third one says.

The other seven vampires join them.

"Is that Silas?" someone asks.

"Yeah," the first one confirms.

"Fuck. The masters. We need to protect the masters."

The group quickly zap away, presumably to find their masters.

I'm still listening when V'dar lets his hands fall, so I remove mine from his neck. When I'm sure all is clear, I reach for Sam.

Sam? There are vampire masters here and it sounds like they have large groups of progeny. We just took one out by accident, so over a hundred vamps should have just dropped.

"What's he doing?" Jeremiah asks.

"Updating the bunker," V'dar replies.

Yeah, we got reports of vampires dropping and screaming. They didn't die, but they were easy to take out, Sam replies.

"The masters have lied to their creations, probably to keep control," I tell the others. "They think if the master is killed, they die. They don't, but they do drop to the ground and are vulnerable."

"So, any vampire who suddenly drops, we take out before they get back up?" Catriona asks.

"Sounds like it," Jeremiah replies.

"You didn't know this?" I ask in surprise.

"I've never sired any progeny. It's never been something I needed to know."

"And someone would have told you if you had?"

Jeremiah chuckles. "I can't sire anyone until my master gives his permission. He'd then teach me how to do it. It's how they keep control, the less we know, the more they can control us."

That makes sense.

Sam, I call. *Get people to let it slip we're going after the masters. We're not, but it will make the vamps panic and go looking for their own to protect them. It should add to the confusion for a bit. If the dragons see a big cluster of vamps, tell them to flame them immediately. We can guarantee there's a master amongst them.*

Good call, Sam replies. *On it.*

I grin widely and explain to the others what I just did.

"Well, that's going to cause some chaos," Jeremiah says with a grin.

"And make it easier to pick them off," V'dar adds, nodding in approval. "I like the way you think, Marcus. Now, if you'll excuse me, I think I need to go answer a prayer or two." He taps his temple for emphasis and disappears.

"Whatever works," I tell Jeremiah.

Catriona just smiles and walks over to me, which is why I see the change in her expression. From proud and amused her visage turns to terror, her gaze fixed over my shoulder.

"Trolls," she whispers, and my guts turn to lead.

Who the fuck let *them* back in and how the fuck are they getting past Dean?

32

CATRIONA

Trolls!

Maybe I say that aloud because Marcus grimaces before he turns around.

There are three of them, more than the three of us can handle. We'd be pushed to kill one.

V'dar promised. He said we were safe. So how did they get here?

There's a fourth figure, I can't quite make him out, but he's smaller and he's coming up behind them, Dean says.

Possible fae or shifter coming up behind them, I warn Marcus.

They're not attacking, which is unusual. What's holding them back? Are there more coming up behind us? No, that doesn't make sense. Why wait? They're more than capable of taking us out.

"Hello, brother," says a human voice, and a growl rips from Marcus' throat.

"What are you doing with this filth, Alistair? Haven't you sunk low enough?"

His brother merely grins. "You're the one mated to a siren with a vampire beside him, Marcus. I had to do something to defend myself."

"Defend yourself?" I screech and the trolls growl at me. "From what? Us living our own lives on our own land? You're insane."

"Probably," Alistair says with a manic grin. "It's hard work hosting a god, you know."

The smile falls from his face, and then his eyes turn pitch black. Not just the iris and the sclera, the whole socket. I don't know what's looking out of his skull right now, but I know it's nothing good.

Mara! I scream-pray. *Zaya, V'dal! Help us, Belar is here!*

"Uh, uh, uh," Alistair says in a sing-song voice that's not quite his own anymore. It's a little deeper, a little raspier. "No speaking to other gods when your attention belongs to me, little snack."

Dean? I try again.

"Control her," Alistair snaps, only it's no longer remotely his voice. The god is fully in charge. "Or I'll let my pets eat her first."

One of the trolls takes a lumbering step forward and then halts, as though it was a puppet being jerked forward.

"Your little pet can no longer hear you, nor can he see us. Handy that," Belar drawls.

Jeremiah darts away, and Belar sighs. "Go, fetch him back. Eat him if you like, but bring me evidence. His head will do."

Two of the trolls plod away, their pace inexorable, yet not slow. The noises they make as they crash through what's left of the undergrowth rapidly fades. I can only hope Jeremiah keeps running, because once they have his scent, they won't stop hunting him until either he's dead, or their master, in this case Belar, calls them back.

I'm terrified for Jeremiah, but at the same time, I'm glad he ran, because now we only have one troll left to deal with. Plus an insane god.

"He's smarter than I thought," Belar rumbles unhappily, looking up at Dean.

The dragon roars, and then his wings snap to his sides and he begins to fall, faster and faster until he lands with a jarring impact that makes me fall over.

"Go, eat him, but bring me his head," Belar orders, and the last troll wanders off in the direction of Dean's impact.

I can just hear his dragon's wheezing breath and soft groans. This can't be good.

"He summoned the others, but it doesn't matter. You'll both be dead by the time they break through my wards. It will undermine everything, I know you two are the key. Once I've cut off the head of this little pocket of resistance, the packs will fall. You were too greedy, Marcus, taking so many wolves for yourself. You're probably just as mad as I am."

"You can think that if it makes you feel better, Alistair," Marcus says, ignoring the god. "The truth is, though, I'm the better wolf, the more able leader. I always was. It's why our father tried so hard to get me back, because he knew you'd never measure up. He was right, of course. You've cocked this all up, and now you need the god to inhabit you just to get a little revenge? You're pathetic."

The black recedes from Alistair's eyes as his personality pushes forward. "You're a liar!" he screams, frothing a little at the mouth. "You were his biggest disappointment. He said that all the time."

"Only because of the two of us, I had the greatest potential," Marcus says, goading him further. "I bet if you challenged me, you couldn't even win in a fair fight. You'd need your god to step in and save your sorry fucking hide. I'm holding four hundred wolves, Al, even father never got that many under his sway, and I'm doing it without breaking a sweat. You were never any threat to me on your own, and you know it."

"I challenge you!" Alistair screams.

"It's not an official challenge if you're hosting a god. If you get a proxy, then I should as well. Let me call one of the gods to reside in me and see how we go. Or man up and make yours step aside for a minute."

Alistair's eyes turn black again as he laughs, the sound turning deeper and deeper as Belar takes control again.

"Nice try, wolf, but it will take more than that to remove me from my host. Besides, who said I was interested in fair or honourable? I just want you dead, I don't care how it's achieved."

Marcus gasps, or he tries to, his hands clawing at his throat as his chest stops moving. His face turns pink, then red, then puce, before the purplish colour starts turning blue. Belar is choking him.

Every fibre of my being screams out in protest. No! This cannot be happening. Not here, not now, not to us! We have the pups to get back to. The hot sex he promised me later tonight.

This.

Is.

Not.

Happening.

Fury seizes my insides and something blooms. Something dark and dangerous. Something I haven't had to deal with in a long time.

My siren form.

Kept weak and underfed, sirens never had any chance at our oppressors, but if we were healthy we were a force to be reckoned with.

I still am.

I allow her to grow within me, my dragon and wolf both push power into her as she grows in her anger. This is our mate, our chosen one, and this thing, this godling thinks it can take him from us?

No. We will not let this happen.

"Belar?" I croon. "Belar? Come to me. I need you, Belar."

The blackness in Alistair's sockets turns to grey, just as Marcus sinks to his knees. I can hear his gasp for air, but I don't dare divert my attention from the monster in front of me to tend to my mate. He's going to have to take care of himself.

"Belar? Come, be my lover. I'm hungry, Belar. I need you. Tell me you won't neglect me?"

"No, no neglect," he mumbles, drool spilling from his mouth.

"That's it, come to me," I croon some more, turning it up a notch. Blood leaks from his nostril and more from Alistair's ear, but I don't let up my power in the slightest. His hands reach for me and I hold my own up in response, careful to keep the knife in my offhand hidden. I will only get one chance at this.

"Come, come, come," Belar chants, unable to articulate anything else under my power.

He steps into my embrace a little faster than I anticipated, wrapping strong arms around me. There's no way I can stab him from the front, so I'll have to take a risk and do it from the back. The chances of me succeeding are greatly reduced, but perhaps I can shock him enough to allow me to get a second chance.

Keeping the blade tucked tight against my arm as Belar dazedly tries to kiss me, I run my hands up and down his spine, feeling the vertebrae and then sliding across at what feels like the right height, noting where his ribs lie so I don't get the blade stuck.

Before I can strike, however, Belar gives a grunt, the black bleeding into his eyes again as he pulls away from me, the tip of a knife sticking out of his chest. The trouble is, it's too high to be his heart. I won't have the same problem.

As Marcus pulls his blade out of Belar's shoulder to try again, I plunge mine in, this time in the right spot. Blood spurts out of his mouth and onto my face as he roars in anger.

"Belar," I croon again. "My Belar. Why do you forsake me?"

He stumbles, trying to right himself, the dual attacks obviously leaving him dazed and confused. It's enough that he lets his wards down, because all five deities are suddenly with us. Without pause, V'dar steps forward and rips Alistair's head off.

Yna chants, holding the god to Alistair's body as it dies, and Aidal places his hands over mine on the blade, his magic pouring into them and through my body before passing into that of the wolf-cum-god.

There is an explosion of light that throws me back through the air, and then my body hits a tree and everything goes dark.

33

Marcus

Light bursts from my brother's body, ripping it to shreds, and Catriona is thrown backwards, slamming into a tree before slumping to the ground.

Hundreds of voices scream out in agony as not only the alpha wolf of the attackers, but the god of the vampires die in the same instant. The attacking forces are decimated in one fell swoop, and it isn't even something we planned.

We won, but by a fluke. The cost, however, may be just too great.

"Catriona!" I scream, both internally and externally, but her limp body doesn't move. It doesn't matter, I'm coming for her.

"No, wait," Aidal says, stepping into my path, and I nearly kill him on the spot. "She's full of magic right now, if you touch her, you'll likely die."

"I don't care!" I growl.

"The pups, Marcus," Mara cries, and I stop pushing. "The pups will need one of you."

One of us. Only one of us?

"Then let it be her," I growl, resuming my efforts to reach her.

There's the crashing sound of trees being smashed nearby, and then three angry trolls lumber into the scene.

V'dar ashes one instantly, but another hits him in the head, knocking him to the ground. In the confusion, Aidal lets me go, but Zaya is there in his stead.

"Marcus, stop. This needs to happen," she pleads.

"She needs to die? Like this? After everything she's been through, you're telling me this needs to happen?"

Instead of answering, she grips my head, and my vision turns white even while the sound of fighting occurs around me.

There's a bright horizon, but darkness between me and it, like the sun is rising just out of sight. Bright white lines shoot out from my feet, racing towards the edge of the world, and then the sun rises. Only it's not the sun. It's pictures. Each light connects to a picture and each picture shows something different. Catriona dying. Catriona living. Belar living, Belar taking her by force, Alistair mating to her, the Earth dying, humans screaming, bleeding, hiding in fear. Each scene playing over and over again on a loop.

Every disastrous picture is preceded by an image of Catriona living. The only one where the Earth has a chance of surviving is the one where she dies. Just one. The only place where she dies, but it's the only place where the rest of the world lives.

NO!

I can't.

I don't want to live in a world without her in it.

My sight returns to me, just in time to see her chest fall as she sighs. Only it doesn't rise again.

"Noooooooooooooooooo!" I scream, my entire world crashing down around me. In the distance I can hear the others crying out in their grief as they feel the bonds between us snap. Nothing matters. Nothing, Nobody. Nothing.

"The pups," a voice is screaming at me. "Marcus, the pups. The pups need you!"

The pups? Fuck the pups.

"No, Marcus, your son. Carter. He needs you. He's lost his mother, don't let him lose his father too."

Carter.

Son.

Pups.

My existence is just three words. Carter. Son. Pup.

"That's it, Marcus," a female coos to me. "Look, here he is, your son. Carter."

Something is screaming, a woeful terrified sound. It's only when a hand claps over my mouth that I realise it's me.

"Marcus, here, your son is here."

Something warm is pressed against my face. Soft and downy, it squirms and moves, lips sucking at my cheek, seeking something I can never give him.

Carter.

My son.

Instinctively my hands come up to grasp him, holding him tight to me while I slowly sink to my knees.

My son.

The only part of her I have left.

My son.

My reason for existence.

"Have you got him?" someone asks.

"Yeah, I got him, he's going to be ok. Go, do your thing. Make this work."

It doesn't make sense. None of this makes sense.

There is me.

My pain.

And my son.

34

CATRIONA

*C*ome back.

A voice is calling me, waking me up but I don't want to listen. I'm tired and it's restful here.

"Five minutes more, Shay," I grumble.

"She'll be fine," someone else says. "I vote yes."

"Aye from me."

"Yes!" shouts someone, and I grumble about them being too loud.

There's laughter, lots of laughter.

"I too vote yes."

"It seems fitting. She killed him."

"Then it's unanimous," a voice says. It's familiar, I can't quite place it, but I know it.

"Mum?"

"In a way, yes, daughter. Open your eyes, it's time to wake up."

Opening my eyes is quite possibly the hardest thing I've ever done. It feels like someone welded them shut and then buried them in cement.

Grit clings to them and I raise my hand, trying to wipe it away. I think I'm going to need some help, because they really are stuck closed with gunk.

"Do I have conjunctivitis?" I ask.

"Ooh, I forgot about that part," says the familiar voice. "Quick, get her some water. I nearly scratched my lids off trying to get them open the first time."

"What is that?" another voice asks, sounding disgusted.

"I have no idea," a man says. "I like to think of it as a kind of vernix."

"Eww, V'dar, that's gross," says another familiar voice. "Just because she's reborn, doesn't mean she's literally reborn."

"Why not? I mean, I'm not examining it too closely, if you want to disagree, then you get in there and study it, otherwise I think my term is quite apt."

"Okay, honey," the first familiar voice says. "I'm going to pour some water on your eyes to melt some of this crud off it."

"Okay." It's not like I'm in a position to argue.

No, you're really not, the voice says, but this time in my head.

"Who are you?" I ask, surprised.

"I'm Zaya, daughter. Although I suppose I can't call you that anymore."

"Then who am I?"

I'm distracted then by the cool water flowing down my face. It's going to get all over my clothes and whatever I'm lying on. It feels like a bed. I hope it doesn't get onto the mattress, that's going to ruin it.

The woman, Zaya, laughs as she gently cleans my eyes with a cloth and more water. Gradually I can feel my lashes being freed, and finally I'm able to open one eye.

Not that I can see anything other than her elbow as she works on the other side.

"Almost done," she murmurs.

"Who am I?" I ask again.

"I'm hoping that as soon as you can see, everything will come back to you. I don't want to jinx it by telling you first."

Okay, because that wasn't cryptic at all.

She laughs again.

"Alright," she says with a determined note in her voice. "Here's a towel, take it and dry your face and see if you can open them both."

Blindly I hold out my hands and she deposits something soft in them. That's a towel? It's the softest fucking towel I've ever felt. It feels like it's made from clouds.

"It kind of is," she says.

"What kind of is?"

"The towel, it's kind of made of clouds."

Was she just listening to my thoughts? Or did I say that all aloud?

"A bit of both, sweetie," she says.

As much as I don't want to stop rubbing this stuff against my face, I know I have to if I want to get some fucking answers around here. This mystery stuff is bullshit.

With a final swipe, I lower the towel and open my eyes only to see a face right in front of me.

I gasp and lean back, falling onto the bed.

Zaya laughs, and holds out a hand to help me back up. "That was just mean," I tell her.

She laughs harder. "True, but very funny. You should see the look on your face!"

Unless it's telling her to fuck the fuck off, I don't care what I look like.

Zaya laughs even harder.

A beautiful brunette walks over to stand beside her. "Does she remember yet?" the woman asks.

"She knows who I am, not so much you."

The brunette frowns and a name tickles the back of my head. "Mia? Mina? Mika?"

"Mara," the woman snaps, and I grin.

Sucks to be on the receiving end, doesn't it? I ask, as my memories come flooding back.

"Marcus?" I ask. "Is he alright?"

The two women exchange a sombre look.

"What? I'm sick of this twenty guesses, I'm in the godly realm, I can see that. What's wrong with my mate? Is he—?"

I can't even say it. Losing Felix was hard enough, and I'd only just begun to know him. Losing Marcus, hell, losing any of them would kill me.

"He's not coping well with your absence," Mara says gently. "None of them are, although the pups are helping centre them. Those with their own sons are doing slightly better, Marcus, however, is the exception."

So, she's saying they're falling apart while I'm in a dream state, and Matt and Sam are doing slightly better than anyone else and Marcus has lost his shit.

"Yes, pretty much that," V'dar says, strolling over to join us.

"How long have I been unconscious?" I ask.

If they're losing their shit, it's been a while.

"You're not unconscious, Catriona. You're dead," V'dar says bluntly, and the two women give him identical glowers.

"You can't just blurt it out like that," Mara says, smacking him with the back of her hand.

"Why not? Pussyfooting around wasn't helping."

"She's just been through a massive trauma, give the woman a chance to recover before you tell her she's dead and we made her a goddess," Zaya says, then slaps a hand over her mouth as she turns wide eyes to me.

I'm not quite sure that was an accident.

In fact, by the twinkle in her eye, I'm bloody sure it wasn't.

"I'm a goddess?" I ask, stunned.

"Yes," Zaya says, clapping her hands together giddily. "Isn't it wonderful?"

I'm not so sure about that. "Goddess of what? Please don't say the seelie court. I'll kill them all before I help them."

Mara snorts and Zaya slaps a hand over her mouth again, but I can already hear the giggles behind it. V'dar gives me a sour look.

"No, not the fae courts. That mess is still mine to deal with."

"Then what?"

"The sirens," Zaya says, jumping up and down in excitement.

"But you're the goddess of the sirens." This is all so confusing. I remember hitting a tree. Did I knock myself into next week, and this is all some bad dream?

"Not anymore," Zaya sing-songs. "You killed Belar, so the vampires didn't have a god anymore. I felt so bad for them, not all of them were like him, in fact very few wanted to go along with this war, but he's their god and he compelled them to fight."

"He *was* their god," Mara corrects.

"Right," Zaya agrees. "But now it's me and I'm going to make things so much better for them. You showed me how to care for my people. Now vampires have different needs, I'm coming to understand that as I change to be more like them, but I'm sure there are some things I can do to help make it a little easier."

"You're changing?" I parrot, only able to take in small chunks of information. This is so overwhelming. "And I didn't kill Belar, Aidal did. He pushed his magic through me."

"We'll call it a joint effort then," Aidal says, coming forward with Yna to join us. "You'd already established a direct connection to him with your siren's call. I just utilised what was in place and pushed my magic through you. It was a combination of that along with the explosion and then the abrupt stop on the tree that killed you. Sorry about that."

I can't even unpack that statement to process it. Maybe another time.

"Okay."

But if I'm here and my mates are back on the human realm, will I ever see them again? Will I see my sons? How am I going to fulfil the prophecy where I gave them all sons? That doesn't make sense.

"Oh, you're not stuck here forever, silly," Zaya says, still giddy as a loon. "You're just like me, transitioning into a new form. As soon as everything is settled within you, you can go back and see them."

What is wrong with her? I wonder.

It's the transition, Mara says with a fond smile in the other woman's direction. *She was like this just after she ascended and joined us here. You'll probably be like that in a few days too.*

A few days? So, my mates have to wait a bit longer?

"Hang on," I say, my thoughts catching up with me. "You said they were losing their shit. I assume it's because they think I'm dead. Did anyone think of telling them I'm coming back?"

"Oh, we couldn't," Zaya says, as Mara and V'dal try to hush her. "We weren't sure the transition was going to work until today. You were so badly damaged after being Aidal's conduit, we didn't know if your spiritual body would recover."

They didn't know — I can't even process it. They didn't know if it would work?

Who the fuck are these people?

"We're still us, silly," Zaya chirps happily. "Come, let's explore your garden while we wait. I want to see how you're going to decorate it."

Before I can protest, she pulls me to my feet and links her arm through mine.

"It'll be so much fun!"

I half turn back to face the others. "Can someone tell my mates I'm coming?"

V'dar gives a short bow and disappears.

I'd love to be a fly on the wall for that conversation. In the meantime, I guess I need to transition, decorate my garden, and turn into a raving fucking lunatic like Zaya. I suppose there were worse things in the afterlife.

The fucking afterlife.

Because I'm dead.

And a goddess!

35

CATRIONA

It's here, the final day. The day I get to see my mates and my sons again.

I don't know what V'dar said the day he returned to Earth to tell them I was coming back, but I do know he returned with a black eye and a busted lip. He won't tell any of us about it, but he can be sure I'm going to pump my mates for the story. Even if I have to read their memories.

I'm going to be stuck with V'dar for centuries. I need a little leverage here.

My garden looks amazing, even if I do say so myself. It takes a little while to manifest it, but every time I do it, the details become clearer and things happen faster. Of course, it would be ready by now if I'd stopped adding stuff to it when Mara and Zaya suggested.

It just doesn't feel finished though. Maybe it never will. I'm okay with that, it's *my* garden.

Goddess, please, make him leave me alone!

That's taken a lot of getting used to as well. Hearing the prayers of the women who were once my sisters. I mean, they still are, but it's weird, you know? Hearing the innermost thoughts of their hearts when they talk to me.

Of course, half the time they do it, they have no idea. I even get the random prayers of some humans who insist on worshipping a female deity. We're not sure why I'm getting those yet. Nothing has appeared in any of our visions of the future. Mara seems to think I've touched on their lives in some way, but I'm not so sure about that. Now, if they were men, sure, I've fucked a lot of them in my lifetime, I could understand some class-five clingers lingering in the ether, but women? Sorry, not my cup of tea.

This time, however, it's Gwendoline, and I just want to laugh. Two dragons and a wolf have taken to pursuing her in earnest, and she's not having any of it. If they were genuinely bothering her, I'd do something about it, but she's getting quite a kick out of the attention, and she's feeding from all three of them on a regular basis — of course they're going to think it means something a little more.

The thing is, they're the only ones she can get near, because the three of them have chased off everyone else. They're all as bad as each other, and I'm including Gwen in that. It'll do her some good to get tangled up with a few males on a more permanent basis.

Catriona, please? Gwen begs. *I'm not into vampires.*

A vampire? Ok, that's something new.

I can't actually go down there and help her, in fact I'm pretty limited with what I can do so far, but I can protect her if she needs it.

Moving through the small trees to my favourite place to meditate, I set myself up quickly and then close my eyes. This is the tricky part, but every time I do it, it's becoming easier. In fact, everything with my new life takes some getting used to. Hopefully soon this transition period will be done, and I can get down there to see my mates and my children. I've no idea how the boys are coping without me. Feeding them must be a nightmare.

And there I go again, losing track of my thoughts and more importantly, the thread of Gwen's prayer. What if she's in danger?

Gwendoline, Gwendoline, Gwendoline.

I'm chanting her name to myself as I focus on roughly where she'll be, casting my consciousness down to the lodge, searching until I find her in the kitchen of all places. Gwen might be many things, but a decent cook is not one of them.

Sure enough, there's a vampire nearby, but it's his identity that surprises me. Jeremiah stands in the doorway, watching as Gwen peels potatoes, nearly skinning her fingers in the process as she shakes with nerves.

I'm relieved to see him looking so well, especially considering the last time I saw him, he was running away through the forest with two trolls at his heels. Gwen, however, is terrified.

When I was alive — okay, that's the strangest thought I've ever had. Yet, when I was alive, as a siren, I could see the connections between people. Their relationship strength, the potential and I guess, the status. As a siren goddess, however, I can see something else.

Fate.

I've never heard of a vampire having a fated mate before. Sure, they take on lovers and can form intense relationships, but I've never heard of one being magically bound to another, nevermind to another species.

Yet Jeremiah is clearly meant for Gwen, and she's equally made for him. They're the oddest pairing I've ever seen, but the connection is undeniable.

He's holding himself as still as only a vampire can, in order not to startle her, not realising the unnatural stillness is what's making her so nervous.

Move! I yell at him, but it's futile. He can no more hear me than see me. Nobody can. I've only barely mastered the ability to find the people I'm looking for, hell, even making my way back to this plane was a challenge at first. But I've been working hard, so fucking hard. V'dar says I'm picking things up faster than any of his other creations, but I have more motivation than most. I have my mates and my children to come back to.

It's agonising watching the boys grow up, even if it is only a matter of days, perhaps weeks. Time is still a little wobbly for me. Every day I see changes in the boys, and every day it breaks my heart all over again that I can't even touch them.

Today is the day. V'dar promised.

Catriona, please?

Gwen's desperate prayer reaches me as the cup slips from her hands and onto the floor, Gwen disappears before it even hits the floor, smashing spectacularly. It takes me a moment to realise she's on the other side of the kitchen in Jeremiah's arms, trembling in shock.

"What are you doing?" she screeches at him.

Slowly he releases her, setting her back on her feet.

"I didn't want you to get hurt," he says quietly, pointing to where the shards of china are scattered everywhere. "I was worried one of them might cut you."

Gwen's face blanches, but then she pulls on her old armour, the sour disposition she's used to protect herself for centuries. She reminds me a little of Fleur come to think of it.

"It's just a little bit of glass, seriously, talk about overreaction."

Like she hadn't almost fainted at the thought of him touching her.

Brushing past him like he didn't terrify her, she starts picking up the pieces, cutting herself of course. Immediately Jeremiah is by her side, taking the fragments from her and tossing them away while he uses a tea-towel to apply pressure.

Instead of being grateful, however, the silly woman screams, snatching her hand back, and scrambling across the floor to escape him. Everyone in the kitchen stops to watch the show and Jeremiah sighs.

"Gwen, I have far more control than to be tempted by a spot of blood. Were you to be unfortunate enough to lose a limb, I would still be in control of my reaction. I am not a fledgling vampire. Besides, the thing I wish to devour the most is not your blood."

The colour returns to her face as her siren senses kick in and she detects his arousal. How he could be interested in sex at a time like this, I don't know, but she's not immune to it either.

"But sirens and vampires have never—"

I laugh. The foolish woman is so flustered, she can't even bring herself to say 'fuck'. It's the funniest thing I've witnessed in a while. Thank goodness she can't see me.

"I can promise you, lovely Gwendoline," Jeremiah purrs, "they most assuredly have. You would not be the first siren to sample the pleasures a vampire can bring to his partner."

"But don't you—?" she flounders again.

"Blood play can be a part of what we do, Gwendoline, but it is by no means the limit of my talents."

Discreetly, movement begins in the kitchen, people trying to give them as much privacy as possible in a community where the majority of its members have supernaturally good hearing.

Taking the hint, I leave. Gwen doesn't need me, as bumbling as she is right now, she's going to be fine. Besides, I need to talk to Zaya. As the new goddess of the vampires, and a former siren herself, she might have some insight into this unusual pairing.

Before I leave, I take a moment to check in on the boys. It's nap time, and I find them all sleeping contentedly. Surprisingly, Marcus is there with them, sitting on the floor by their shared cot and watching them sleep. Carter stirs and my mate tenses, but as soon as the boy relaxes, so does he.

Marcus looks terrible. Not as bad the first time I returned, but still not well. The dark circles under his eyes tells me he's still not sleeping well, and the stretch of his skin across the bones of his face shows where he continues to lose weight. I'm going to have to scold him. He's not the only one to lose a mate in this war. There are plenty of devastated souls in the community, and it's awe inspiring to see the others gathering around them to offer comfort and support.

I know he's hurting, and I won't diminish that. Our bonds have broken, although V'dar says we should be able to forge new ones. They just won't be quite the same. They can't be, because I'm no longer the woman who died in the forest.

That thought makes me giggle, remembering the first time I came here, worried some axe murderer was going to jump out from behind the trees while I lived my own version of a b-grade movie death. In hindsight, it wasn't such a silly thought. Only I wasn't murdered, per se. I just died while killing a god.

"What did I tell you about coming here alone?" V'dar asks, making Marcus jump as he materialises in the nursery.

"Sssh, you'll wake the pups," I scold. Unlike Marcus, V'dar can see and hear me perfectly. "Besides, I didn't come here, I came to answer a prayer and I found something unusual enough that we need to talk about it."

Marcus is of a similar mind to me, taking V'dar by the elbow and escorting him from the room. "I don't believe you gave me any instructions regarding the care of my sons," Marcus says caustically. It's clear he still hasn't forgiven V'dar for his part in my death, or rather, for not healing me when I was dying.

"You're still barely strong enough to come here, Catriona," V'dar continues, ignoring Marcus. "And now you won't have enough energy to materialise safely. You're going to have to wait another day, perhaps two now."

"She's here?" Marcus asks desperately, grabbing V'dar's shirt and shaking him. "My mate is here? Where is she? Why can't I see her?"

"She's here in spirit," V'dar says, gently disengaging my mate.

Marcus must have called the others, because Matt stumbles out of the office, Sam hot on his heels. The front and back doors slam simultaneously, and the roar of a dragon announces Ethan's arrival too. Within minutes, all eight of my mates are here, staring at V'dar and looking around for me.

"Where is she?" Ethan growls, his pupils thin slits. "Marcus, where is she?"

"Here in spirit," Marcus snaps, his anger with V'dar clear. "V'dar was just explaining why we now have to wait another two days."

The angry growls coming from my mates startles me. Worse if they keep that up, they're going to wake the boys.

"Sssh, you'll wake the pups," I whisper-shout. Which is ridiculous, nobody other than V'dar can hear me.

"She says you'll wake the boys and to calm down," V'dar interprets for me. "She's right, so how about we take this conversation to your office, Marcus."

Grumbling, my men move down the hall to the office, while V'dar rounds on me. "You, young lady, will return home. The longer you stay here, the longer you will have to wait to manifest."

It's so unfair. They've been encouraging me to answer prayers as often as I can, it's a good stamina building exercise apparently. Yet now it's a reason to make us wait longer.

36

CATRIONA

Unable to take the disappointment, I return to my garden, but in my distress I can't even make it materialise, which upsets me even further.

Mara and Zaya find me weeping there in a blank space not long after. Rubbing salt into my wounds, the area quickly transforms into the joint garden they made now they are living together with V'dar.

"What's wrong, sister?" Mara asks.

"Gwen needed help, she was afraid. I tried to answer her prayer, but it wasn't anything she couldn't handle, and then I went to check on the boys and V'dar turned up and said, now I have to wait for two more days!" I wail.

"Oh that man!" Zaya says in a sigh.

"He's worried about you," Mara adds. "You went through so much before you ascended, he's never had such a damaged soul before. He's afraid to push you too far in case he loses you again."

Zaya nods. "The visions we've had of the future have shifted significantly, and we're unsure which paths are most likely yet, but they show dire consequences if you are lost, which is still a possibility."

Instead of comforting me, I only weep harder. I could still lose them all, and in doing so, put them at risk. How much more of a price do I have to pay to have love in my life?

"Why don't you bring them here?" Yna asks, joining us. She and Aidal have paired up since the battle, something unheard of before.

There are lesser gods and demi-gods who look after specific areas of the different planes of existence, but only the six of us live here full time. It's not exactly a bustling community, and I wonder why none of them had paired up before.

"Belar," Mara answers my unspoken question. "It's only now he's gone that we realise what a divisive presence he was. He stopped any of us from forming attachments, or alliances as he saw them, I guess. He never wanted any of us to get stronger than he was, despite the fact V'dar is stronger than all of us combined."

"Then how is it he wasn't able to break Belar's magic when they attacked?"

"The short answer is limitations. You're only starting to learn what they are for your new form, but even V'dar has them. He's stronger here in the godly realm, but on Earth there are limitations to stop us from causing inadvertent harm. Belar worked out a way to get around them by combining his magic with the witches and mages on Earth. I could go into a longer explanation involving planetary alignment and the physics of magic, but I have to admit even I get a little lost when V'dar explains it."

So, that's why we needed him bound in Alistair's body, because then he was confined by the limitations of the body he inhabited. If he'd manifested himself, something I was learning takes a lot of power, then he would have been stronger and likely unaffected by my siren magic.

"Yes, basically that," Zaya agreed.

"So, why didn't he manifest if riding Alistair left him so vulnerable?"

"Because doing so used up too much of his magic which would be better spent attacking."

Okay, that made more sense now. How had I not thought to ask all of this before?

"Catriona, you've been through several intense months, and that's without dying. You've had a lot to process in that time. I'm sure you'll have questions for us for a few hundred years yet," Mara soothed me. "Don't be so hard on yourself."

"I'm still asking questions, especially now I've changed form," Zaya said with a grimace.

"Which still doesn't answer the question, why don't you bring them here?" Yna said with a huff.

"Because she wants to see the babies too," Mara replies.

"I can manage the babies," Yna offers. "If the rest of you can help bring the others, four small souls is childsplay. No pun intended."

"It's actually a sound idea," Zaya says. "In fact, we could make quite the *reunion* of it."

Her emphasis on the word throws me. What does she mean by that? However, the others all share a secretive smile, and Aidal bows before disappearing. Zaya jumps up and down, clapping her hands, and I look at them all unimpressed.

"What the hell is going on?" I demand.

"A surprise," Zaya says, giggling.

Damn, I thought we were past the drunk Zaya stage, but she only laughs at me and wraps me up in a hug.

"You'll love it, Catriona," she promises.

"You will," Yna agrees, rubbing a hand up and down my arm. "You've been so patient through all of this and you've worked so hard to get things right. Let us help you out a little. You don't have to do it all on your own, you know. You've got us now."

"Why don't you get your garden ready, we'll tell V'dar and bring your mates and children. This is going to be such a wonderful day, Catriona," Mara says, before disappearing.

The other two follow her, leaving me alone in their joint garden which is already fading without their presence.

Not wanting to destroy their work, I move a little distance away and then begin constructing my own. I've always loved Japanese gardens, and coming here has not changed that, so I have twisting pathways, each corner giving the viewer a different aspect of the garden to admire. Large bonsai, called omono, litter the landscape, while Japanese maples add a rainbow of colour. It's the godly realm, who says they all have to be displaying foliage in the same season?

A large koi pond with small red bridges materialises, and off to the side is my favourite part, a large open area covered in white stones beside a small stone pavilion. I like to walk through there and rake patterns on the ground, the movement bringing me a sense of peace I've found nowhere else before now. It's my own little zen garden.

To prevent the place disappearing into the white mist, I add a small wall around it, giving the whole thing a completed look. In the far corner is a larger pavilion, big enough for all of us to sit on the thin silk covered mattress, surrounded by throw cushions. It's the perfect space for the babies to roll around on the ground while we can sit and relax.

I feel V'dar materialise before I see him. It's something they've been teaching me to do, project my presence before showing up. It stops us popping in and scaring the pants off each other but, as I've discovered, it also works as a polite knock too. I've seen more of V'dar's pale ass as he fucks one or the other of his mates than I care to. It's no wonder they emphasised that early on in my training.

"Come in," I call, although it's not necessary. I could easily ward the area off if I didn't want him to.

"Catriona?" Matt's voice is hesitant as he looks around my piece of paradise. "Kat, are you here?"

It's only then I realise I'm not fully materialised. I was so focussed on setting up my garden, I let my appearance go. Yep, I have to focus on that too.

"Where the fuck is she?" Marcus growls. "I thought you said we would see her?"

Aah, there's my alpha. Just as big of an asshole as when I met him.

"I'm here, love," I say, materialising right in front of him.

"Kat!" his cry is hoarse and then his lips are on mine, his hands digging into my flesh as he grips me tightly.

It's like we were never parted, as my mouth opens to his questing tongue, and he moulds our bodies together. There's a heated presence at my back, a feverish mouth on my neck, while someone else takes one of my hands and sobs over it, another person places a kiss on the other one.

It's wonderful, comforting and completely overwhelming at once. Marcus and whoever is behind me are already hard, their hips thrusting against me as they seek to relieve our tension. The lust that floods me from all sides is enough to have me panting, but the cry of a baby is like a bucket of cold water over me.

"My babies!" I cry, as I pull myself free of Marcus' mouth.

Reluctantly my lovers part, and I'm able to see it's Ethan who's crying over my hand. My first priority is to comfort him. I can only imagine how hard this has been on them all, but for Ethan to barely claim me and then lose me must have been devastating to say the least.

Dropping to my knees, I pull him into my arms. "I'm here, Ethan, I'm here."

"I know," he sobs. "I don't even know who to thank. I want to say thank you to someone, but where the fuck do I even start, Catriona? You're a goddess!"

"You can thank us all," Yna replies, holding Carter who giggles as he pulls at her hair, stuffing it in his mouth. "We voted and agreed her place was with us, rather than the afterlife, so we combined our magic to tether her soul here. Catriona is the first of us to be created by everyone, rather than just V'dar alone."

"I was kind of tapped out," V'dar admits ruefully, rubbing the back of his neck in embarrassment. "It was either them helping me, or you wouldn't be able to stay."

"And you needed me to stay," I add. He simply nods in reply.

"Stay for what?" Marcus asks suspiciously.

"Who the fuck cares, Marcus," Matt snaps. "We have her back!"

"Come," Yna says, leading the way. "Let's all sit and have tea, then we can talk."

"Talk," Joe mutters. "Yeah, let's do that. Drink tea and talk."

Mara laughs, playing with River as she follows Yna. "If you're nice, we might take the boys for a walk and give you all time to reconnect."

"You're the best goddess ever," Toby says. "I think we should make you a shrine or something, you know, burn candles and shit. People should take you more seriously. We could convince some wolves to be priests and priestesses and they could do ceremonies and stuff, sing your praises day and night."

I shudder. That sounds like a lot of prayers coming all the time. Nobody needs that level of noise in their life.

"Unnecessary," Mara says, laughing over her shoulder, "but I like the way you think, Toby."

"Are you alright here, Catriona?" Scott asks, moving to walk beside me. Marcus is on the other side with a firm grip on my hand he's unwilling to relinquish.

"Still looking out for me, Scott?" I ask him gently.

"Even a goddess needs someone to take care of her."

He's still so sweet. I lean over and give him a brief kiss.

"Believe me," Marcus growls from the other side. "I plan to fucking take care of her."

"No," Joe jokes. "You plan to take your time fucking her."

The others laugh but Marcus just grunts. Joe isn't wrong, and the thought of them all with me and in me stirs something inside me I haven't felt since I came here. Lust.

"I can't feel your wolf," Sam says from somewhere behind me.

Damn. I thought we could hold off on that discussion for next time, but I guess it's happening now.

"I can't feel her dragon either," Ethan says, stepping in front of me and making me stop. "What's going on?"

"They died when I did," I tell them gently, and I can see the grief reflected in my mates' faces. I grieved their loss too when V'dar first told me. "Eventually I will be able to manifest as a wolf or a dragon on earth, but they will simply be me in a different body, not my alternative souls coming to the fore."

"How can you be so calm about this?" Ethan asks, the devastation clear on his face.

"Because time moves differently here," I tell him. "I have been gone from Earth for a short time. One month, correct?"

"Almost two," Alex says.

Damn. I've lost count again. "As much as time can be examined here, I've been here almost three years." I reply, and I watch that filter through their thought processes. "I found out about their deaths a couple of years ago. For you, it's much more immediate, this is still fresh in your mind, but I've had quite a long time to process this already."

"But you haven't aged," Alex protests.

"Come," I tell them. "Let's go and sit."

This is another discussion we'll need to have, but hopefully not today.

37

CATRIONA

T he boys are all settled on the mat, Carter is on his belly and trying to lift his head. Wyatt, surprisingly, can do it for a second or two, while River and Dane prefer to be on their backs. River with his toes in his mouth, and Dane waving his limbs happily like a drunken frog swimming.

"They're growing so fast," I murmur, as I kneel on the mat beside them. "How is the feeding going?"

"They're getting used to it, but they're not exactly thrilled," Alex says, dangling his fingers above River, trying to get him to grasp them instead of his feet.

"I can't feed them any more. My dugs were lost in the transformation, and my milk has long since dried up."

Yna makes small tables appear laden with tea and nibbles, each within easy distance of the men, but none of them bother even looking. I feel bad for her, so I pour myself some tea and pick up a tiny cake, popping it in my mouth.

"Is that even real?" Alex asks, watching me eat.

My mouth is full, so Mara answers. "Yes and no. It contains energy for us, but for you it would act as regular food."

"So, do you like, you know, poop?" Toby asks, and I laugh, covering my mouth to stop from spraying crumbs everywhere.

The other gods laugh with me, while Matt looks at him in disgust.

"Man!" Scott protests. "What is wrong with you? We're here in the godly realm, finally reunited with our mate and you want to know if she poops?"

Toby shrugs, unrepentant. "It's a legitimate question, right, Marcus?"

I know what he's getting at then. Marcus' preference for my ass is well known, although I don't think it's going to be his priority today, not if the hungry gleam in his eyes is any indication.

I open my mouth to suggest tabling the topic for another time, but Aidal answers for me.

"No, we don't, and if you need to go while you're here, I ask you hold it in. I really don't want to deal with it."

Nobody responds, however, because we're all looking at the person behind him.

"Felix!" I cry, the first person to react. Marcus is on his feet instantly, a hoarse cry torn from his lips, but before he can envelop his old friend in a hug, I move to stand in his way, my back to Felix as I protect him from the onslaught.

"Wait, just wait a second. We need to check he's here."

"We're all fucking looking at him," Marcus snaps. "He's fucking here, Kat!"

Stupid stubborn alpha fool.

I turn my back on them, looking up at the second man to ever break my heart. The first one wasn't worthy of it, but this one is.

"Are you alright?" I ask him.

"You're not pregnant anymore," he says, his gaze travelling up and down my body. "Did you lose them?"

"It's been a while, Felix. The war is over, we won, mostly. I didn't lose them, Felix, they're here. Would you like to meet your son?"

Tears well in his eyes. "I get to meet him?" he husks.

Instead of answering, I turn and scoop Wyatt from the floor, supporting his neck and bringing him to his father.

"This is Wyatt," I tell him. "I'm sorry I didn't get a chance to ask for your input, but the guys said you were close to your father, and it's your middle name too. I thought it was the right choice."

"Wyatt," Felix whispers, tears pouring down his face. He leans down, inhaling deeply, drawing his son's scent into his soul. Even if he no longer has a wolf to help him remember it, I'm pretty sure he'll remember it on his own.

The others stand and crowd around us, each wanting to greet their lost brother, all except Ethan, who hovers to the side looking worried.

"Hey, man!" Marcus says, wrapping Felix and Wyatt in a gentle hug.

"Marcus, it's so good to see you."

"Brother," Toby says, clapping him on the back, while Matt also gives him a hug. Joe grabs him by the ears and pulls their foreheads together, saying something quietly that makes Felix chuckle. Sam waits his turn, then also gives him a hug.

"I don't remember your names," Felix says to the others, and I can see the reactions around the group. Scott and Alex are trying not to appear hurt, and Ethan is unsurprised, but it's his initial brothers who are confused.

"Kat?" Sam asks. "What's going on?"

Fuck, this isn't going to be easy.

"Souls in the afterlife don't retain their memories. They can regain them while here in the godly realm, but when Felix returns later, he won't remember this."

"So, it's like 50 fucking *First Dates*?" Matt growls. "*Groundhog Day* for him as he resets every time?"

"Not quite," I tell them, trying to help. "Every time he comes here, he'll remember the other visits. He doesn't lose anything overall, he just doesn't remember while he's in the afterlife."

"It takes a lot of energy to contain the souls in the afterlife," V'dar explains. "We can't keep a hold of all their memories, however we can restore them when they come here. Don't ask me to go into the physics of it, even Aidal's eyes glaze."

I want to laugh, but I can see nobody else is amused. V'dar gives me a tight smile and a wink. He knows I get it, but the others aren't in the headspace.

"Think of it like a pause button," I tell them. "His memories are paused while he's in the afterlife. Yet he still has the opportunity to gain more while he's here. He's able to meet his son! How many people can you say get that opportunity?"

The sense of oppression lifts as they realise exactly how large a gift they've been given. They have the chance to reunite with Felix, something that should be impossible.

"So, why doesn't he remember us?" Alex asks.

"Scott likes to feed her," Felix says in response. "I don't know how I know that, I just do."

"It takes a while for all the memories to load. The more memories, the longer the lag," Aidal explains. "He doesn't remember you quite yet, but he will in the next ten minutes or so."

"How long will we be gone?" Sam asks, ever the tactician.

"Only a few minutes at the most," Yna answers him. "In your case, it's simply a matter of reinserting you into the right time frame. You won't be missed, but you will be extra tired."

"This is really a whole other world for you, isn't it?" Matt asks me, and I nod.

The silence is awkward until Joe speaks. "Why are we in a Japanese garden? Are we like, above Japan or something?"

I laugh. "No, this garden, the pagoda, even the cushions you're sitting on. They're all here because I willed them into existence. Even my body is a manifestation of my thoughts."

"So, you just float around in a blank canvas without a body?" Alex asks, confused.

"We are made of pure will, and a whole smack of magic," Zaya replies.

"What are you the goddess of?" Toby asks.

"The sirens," I reply.

Marcus looks sharply at Zaya. "I thought you were the goddess of the sirens?"

"I was," she replies cheerfully. "But with Belar's death, we needed someone to care for the vampires. V'dar has his hands full with the fae mess, so we decided since Catriona was going to be here anyway, she could have my job, and I'd take over from Belar. We've both been going through transition together. It's been so much fun, hasn't it?"

"How about we take the boys for a walk and let them all catch up?" Mara interrupts, before I can tell Zaya where to stick her drunken squirrel act.

I'm relatively sure it's an act now, because she couldn't be that dense and a goddess at the same time, right?

Zaya gives me a wink, scooping up a giggling Dane and wandering off out of the pavilion. "Don't worry about a noise ward, I'm sure Aidal will take care of that. He's very good at them."

Aidal turns bright pink, fleeing before we can laugh at him.

Yna shrugs. "I'm a screamer, I'm not apologising for that."

She picks up Carter and follows a laughing Zaya. Mara shrugs and grabs River, which leaves V'dal to carefully take Wyatt from his father's arms.

Felix watches wistfully as the gods leave with the children.

"You can go with them," I tell him gently, not wanting him to feel obligated.

"No," he says with a soft smile, stepping over to where I'm sitting and pulling me to my feet. "I just want to have my cake and eat you."

"Dude," Joe laughs. "You totally fucked that up."

38

CATRIONA

My clothes disappear with a thought, the lust coming at me from my men making me impatient. "No, I think he got that perfectly right."

Felix pulls me into his arms, so I make his clothes disappear too. All around me I can hear the others undressing, and with a smile I do the job for them.

"None of you are actually here, although you're all right here. Just take it as given that I have a few new tricks," I tell them.

"I have the same old tricks," Felix says, "but I don't think you're complaining."

He lifts me up and I wrap my legs around him, reaching down with one hand to position his cock while I grip tightly to the back of his neck with the other.

"You're sure?" he asks, poised at my entrance.

I jerk my hips forward and down, pulling him inside me. "Very," I purr, before I kiss him.

It's hard to concentrate on things when you're having sex. Having a vagina for one thing, keeping your body corporeal for another. It's even harder when you can feel the lust of your mates beating at your skin like a thousand fingers tapping you on the shoulder.

The koi pond is the first sacrifice. The wall is the second, but I don't think any of them notice, they're all focussed on my pleasure, and working out how they're going to join in on it,

"On your knees, Felix. You need to share her," Marcus orders.

Felix drops to his knees, and the surprise of it shakes my attention further. The zen garden goes, quickly followed by the pavilion beside it. These men are wrecking my garden in the best way, and I don't care. I want them to wreck a hell of a lot more than that.

Marcus slides a hand between us, his fingers dancing across my clit, making me gasp. The pavilion we're sitting in disappears, which is when the others notice the changes.

"What the fuck is happening?" Matt asks in alarm.

"I think we're taking good care of our mate," Sam replies, his gaze hot and heavy as he watches me ride Felix slowly. "Having trouble concentrating, Catriona?"

Yeah, he totally gets it.

"Can you kick your legs out, Felix?" Marcus asks.

In response, Felix groans, holding my hips tightly as he tries to make me move faster, but I'm enjoying this pace.

"I'll take that as a no," Marcus says. "Matt, lift her up off him for a second."

What? No!

Before I can protest, Matt hooks his arms under my thighs and lifts me, Marcus still strumming my clit like he never plans to stop.

"Straighten out, Felix, on your back," Marcus orders.

Bossy fucking alpha.

I must have said that aloud, because Marcus' fingers stop moving, and he pinches my clit instead.

"You might be the goddess here, Catriona, but you always were our goddess. I'm still your alpha, and we're doing this my way."

I'm impatient. If he's going to do this, he needs to fucking do it faster.

With that thought, Felix is on his back and I'm impaled on him again in the blink of an eye. Toby chuckles, while Marcus and Matt try to work out what the fuck just happened.

"I think you just need to tell her what you want and she'll make it happen, Marcus," Toby tells him.

"Is that what just happened, Catriona?" Marcus asks in a dark tone that has my juices gushing. "Did you just speed things up?"

"Not deliberately," I reply. "I wanted it and it happened."

"We're going to have to work on that impatience of yours, love," he says.

"I've waited three years, Marcus. I think I'm entitled to be a little impatient, don't you?"

I half expect him to protest further, but he gives me a gentle kiss on the shoulder as I start riding Felix in earnest. His eyes are closed and his hands are on my breasts, tweaking and teasing my nipples. I'm not the only one desperate here, and I can feel him rapidly approaching his climax. I don't want this to be over so quickly, so I take some of his arousal and feed it to the others.

"Fuck," Toby growls, moving forward to stand beside me, his cock throbbing in his hand. "If you're going to tease me like that, honey, you better be ready to follow through."

"Not yet," Marcus growls, pushing me slightly forward in direct contradiction of his words. He only shoves my mouth closer to Toby's waiting cock. "Let me prep her first."

His fingers slide into my channel beside Felix's cock, making us both groan. If Marcus wants me ready, I can be ready. My muscles instantly relax, stretching as he scissors his fingers, proving to him I'm ready for what he's going to do next.

He doesn't do what I expect.

Rather than using my juices to lube up my ass, Marcus presses his cock into me, sliding along Felix's shaft and making me feel so full. Oh man, I have missed this.

Felix groans and I can feel his climax approaching again, but Marcus isn't anywhere near close enough. HIs fingers are now preparing my ass though, so I know his arousal is about to skyrocket. Once again I use my new powers to accommodate his need. Being instantly ready without any pain or discomfort is a great party trick and it's going to make our time together so much more fun, but it's something we can explore later.

"Are you so eager for me to fill that tight ass, mate," Marcus rumbles behind me.

"Yes, alpha," I moan, leaning forward onto Felix's chest to give him more room.

"Good girl," Marcus says, as he slaps my ass. "Good, fucking girl."

His cock is now covered with my juices and he eases it slowly past the first ring of muscle, but I really have rearranged myself inside to take him in.

"Fuuuck," he moans, once he's seated inside me, his lust ratcheting up and feeding my own.

I need more, however, more mates, more cock, just more. I take Felix's edge off again, feeding it to Scott who moans and drops down beside us.

"Tell me what you want, Catriona," he pleads.

"With Felix," I reply and he doesn't waste time complying.

Yes. So full.

"There's still one hole left, sweet girl," Toby says, as Marcus sets the pace, fucking into me and pulling Scott out when his hips drag backwards.

"Give it to me," I order, and Toby doesn't hesitate.

Marcus slaps my thigh, unable to reach any other part of my flesh for the press of bodies, as Joe, Sam, Matt, and Alex crowd closer.

"Fuck I'm not going to last," Felix groans beneath me. This time I don't hold him back, and his eyes widen as he feels his climax approaching.

"Come for me, Felix," I purr, and he does. Just like that.

Despite neither of us having wolves, I can feel the urge to bite him, so I do, and he grunts and fucks me harder as he falls over the edge, taking me with him.

"Mine," he growls, sinking his own teeth into my shoulder, and I scream around his flesh in my mouth as a bond snaps into place. It's not the same kind of bond I had with his wolf, it's more, stronger, deeper and it has a feeling I can only describe as indestructible. Only my own death as a goddess can break this thing.

I feed our pleasure back into the others and Marcus is the next to join us, his snarl feral sounding as his teeth sink into my opposite shoulder. Scott and Toby come at the same time, Scott biting down hard on my upper arm, while Toby sinks his teeth into my wrist.

Four complete and powerful bonds snap into place, tying us all together even closer than we were before. It's not just separate bonds with each of my mates, it's a web of our souls wound together.

My pussy is pulsing, milking the men inside me as my heart fills with joy. I have my mates again, I've regained what I lost and it's even better than before. I can feel their love pouring through the new bonds to me, and I start weeping with joy. This is better than I could ever have imagined.

There is no time to rest, though, as the rest of my mates clamour to be next. The lust coming off them has my head spinning, and I barely know what's going on when Toby withdraws from my mouth rather quickly and a new cock replaces him. Before I can even tell who it is, he's climaxing down my throat, chanting my name over and over again, causing me to clench around the men who haven't had a chance to withdraw yet.

"Fucking shit, I'll never get tired of feeling that," Felix groans. He's not quite ready to go again, but he will be soon. "Come up here, pretty girl, and ride my face while my brothers fill you up with more pups."

Is that even possible? It's something I've not even dared to ask V'dar.

My arm stings as yet another bite is applied and it's only then I realise who it is. Joe. My sweet, sweet, submissive Joe. Of course he got off on watching me being pleasured.

"Holy fucking shit," he sighs, staggering backward and collapsing on the cushions. Those and the mat are the only things surviving from my garden. I don't give a fuck, my mates are the only decorations I need.

"What?" Alex asks, concerned. "Guys, get off her. Something's wrong."

They don't move, better able to sense the lack of my concern than those of my mates who I've yet to bond with.

"The bond," Joe says into the silence, when none of us moves. "It's fucking amazing. It's like my soul is glued to hers, but not just hers, I can feel Marcus and Toby, all of them."

"We're a pack," I tell them. It doesn't matter that I don't have a wolf to share this with them. They're mine, and now they will be forever.

Scott pulls back followed by Marcus, and I flop forward onto Felix's chest.

"Have we worn you out already, Catriona?" Felix asks with a chuckle.

I nod. "Just give me a second. I'm juggling a lot more than I do on Earth."

"What's that supposed to mean?" Alex asks.

"When I manifest down there, I'm there. It's like the old times. I'm Catriona, a siren, and we can fuck however we wish. Here, I'm holding onto the mat and the cushions—"

"Fuck them, let them go," Marcus orders.

"Unless we're going to fall through the clouds or something," Joe adds worriedly.

I laugh tiredly against Felix's chest.

"No, nothing like that," I assure them, releasing the illusion.

"Is that all?" Scott asks, stroking a hand across my hair.

"Ooohh, that feels so nice," I murmur.

"No falling asleep, Catriona," Marcus says, giving me a sharp slap across the ass.

"No chance of that with your bossy ass around," I grumble, and the men laugh.

"It's not just that. I still manage your arousal, taking from one and feeding to another to synchronise our pleasure."

"You could do that before, though," Matt says, sounding confused. His arousal is dissipating, so I take some from Marcus and feed it to his beta. Marcus is always horny around me.

"At the same time," I tell them. "I'm trying to stop my vagina from disappearing. I'm pretty fucking sure you'd all notice that."

"What?" Toby cries.

"She told us about it before if you remember," Alex explains, "She said she had to hold onto the manifestation of this body. They're all thought and magic, right? Well, I guess she has to hold onto her shape. I can see how that would be a little difficult when said shape is also being thoroughly distracted."

"That," I murmur, flapping a hand in the direction of his voice.

"Can we feed you? I thought you fed when we fucked you?" Scott asks, his voice full of concern.

"I forgot to feed," I lie. The truth is, I'm terrified in case I take too much.

"Yeah, that was a lie," Marcus says, and I curse the new bond between us, because I didn't expect that.

"I was scared to take too much," I confess, and the others murmur words of comfort.

"Feed from me," Joe says, offering his hand.

"Not without V'dar being present," I tell them. "If I take too much here, you go back with Felix to the afterlife."

It's a sobering thought, and I feel the enthusiasm of the other unmated men wane. Well, I feel their lust wane. It's the same thing.

"Then we wait until next time," Marcus says, taking control again,

Before he can talk himself into this, I take the last of the lust surging around his body and renew the passion in the others. They are not leaving until we're bonded.

"Catriona," Matt says warningly, but I crawl off Felix and reach up to take his semi-erect cock in my hand. "Catriona, wait."

I suck him in, taking him deep down my throat as he groans, his lust instantly rising. None of my mates can resist me, even if they think it's for my own good, and it's quite a balm to my ego after being without them for so long. It was one thing I'd fretted over. Would they still want me now I'm changed.

The answer is a clear yes, and I'm not letting them get away from me again. Life is too unstable, too unpredictable to let opportunities like this pass by.

"Fuck," groans Marcus. "Look at her suck down that monster cock."

His arousal is already growing, but once again I steal it to feed it to the others.

Ethan is the most reluctant to participate. I know he didn't get to see how we operated on Earth, but this needs to become part of his norm. I have nine mates. I can't give them all the one on one time they want. Especially at the moment.

In my peripheral vision I can see Marcus stroking his cock as he watches me, even as I keep stealing his pleasure and feeding it to the others. He makes no sound of protest though, and I think he understands what I'm doing. The more aroused my mates are, the faster we'll climax together.

It's kind of pathetic when you remember I'm the goddess of the sirens, but it's been a busy day. That's my excuse and I'm sticking to it.

Ethan bears the brunt of my torture, I'm pushing more and more pleasure into him until he comes to me, picking me up from where I kneel and holding me in his arms. I wrap my legs around his hips and don't even wait for his consent before I'm sliding down his cock.

Behind me Matt groans in disappointment, but doesn't interfere.

When I hit the base of Ethan's shaft, he holds me there as if unaware of how it happened.

"Ethan?" I whisper.

"There aren't any fucking walls," he groans, making me laugh.

"I think I can help," Matt replies, coming to stand behind me.

His finger rubs my ass and I know what he's asking without words. I simply steal more of Marcus' pleasure and feed it to him. If I say something aloud, I'm worried I'll scare Ethan off. He's not used to sharing me with the others.

Before the dragon can even register the intrusion, Matt's cock is seated firmly inside me, a thin membrane separating the two of them. They're about the same girth, so I'm feeling quite full, and now I have the advantage of leaning back against Matt to push against Ethan.

I'm swirling the arousal between the three of us, pumping us all higher and we're not even moving yet.

"Fuck!" Ethan shouts, caving and snapping his hips forward, fucking me hard.

In response, Matt moves closer, squashing me between them as his hand circles my body and finds my clit with unerring precision. There's so much fluid down there already, he doesn't even have to find some, circling the hardening nub with his fingers as he sets a counter rhythm to Ethan, the two of them slamming into me with gusto.

The orgasm hits us faster than I expected, but I've been so caught up in trying to hold my body together, I stopped paying attention to the lust I was spiralling between us. Taking from Ethan and feeding to Matt, which only increases my pleasure, so I feed both my and Matt's increases to Ethan.

All I know is that it feels so good I think my head might explode. The two of them come with twin roars, each biting into my flesh which must be starting to look a little mangled by now. The bonds snap into place and Ethan stares at me in surprise.

"Mate," he says softly, in awe.

Through the bond I can understand his hesitance. He didn't think it would work without a second dragon to ground us. He was afraid his own dragon would reject it or prevent it somehow, but I can feel his beast's clear approval as he fills us with his seed, and the desire to breed us as soon as possible.

I wonder if I'm in charge of my own fertility, because as much as we needed the first litter of pups, I'd rather take it a bit slower the second time around. Maybe two or three, rather than four at the same time.

I'm shoved forward and then Matt is gone, another eager mate holding me from behind, his cock pressing against the groove of my cheeks.

"I'm sorry, Catriona," Alex says. "I can't wait anymore. I need this bond, my wolf is going crazy. Please say you'll bond with us again."

I lean back against him, cupping a hand around the back of his neck as I slowly stir the lust inside him. "Of course I want you back."

"And me?" Sam asks hesitantly from beside us.

"Yes, Sam. All of you."

I add him into the feedback loop of pleasure.

"Lie down, Alex," Sam says, an eager look on his face. Does he want my ass instead?

Instead of complying, Alex holds me up so Ethan can withdraw carefully, before the two of them lower me to the ground again. As soon as I'm standing, albeit a bit wobbly, Alex lies down on the soft floor, his cock standing proudly in the air and bobbing with his pulse.

I step over his legs, getting ready to kneel down over him, when Sam puts a hand on my arm.

"I want to see you when I fuck you, Catriona," he says, and my core pulses. "Can you ride him reverse and let him take that sweet ass?"

Oh my stars. When did he get such a dirty mouth?

He knows you like it, Marcus sends to me, and I almost weep at the sound of his voice in my head again. I really missed that, although I probably shouldn't tell him. From the smirk on his face, though, I'm guessing he already knows.

Toby and Scott move forward, helping me lower my tired body until I'm poised just above Alex's cock as he eagerly lines it up with my ass. Together they lower me further, and Alex moans, his hips rocking slightly in his desire to be fully seated sooner.

"You're going to have to work for this, Alex," Sam says as he watches us, fisting his cock slowly. "I'm going to fuck her up off your cock, but if you want back in you're going to have to make it happen."

The desire is already growing in the men around me, their bodies keen for another round, even as mine is on the edge of dissipating from fatigue. I need this though. We all do.

When I'm fully seated on Alex, he pulls me back to lie on his chest, and Toby lifts my legs to lie outside of Alex's, exposing me to them all.

"Now isn't that a pretty fucking sight for sore eyes," Marcus says, taking over when Sam seems to freeze. "I think that pussy needs filling though, brother. You up for the job?"

Sam doesn't say anything but he drops to his knees and begins to kiss a path up the inside of my thighs, switching from one side to the other and driving the anticipation higher. His journey culminates in a lick from my core to my clit, a long, dirty groan erupting from my mouth as he circles the hardened bud with the tip of his tongue, then flattens it for another long lick.

"You still taste amazing," Sam says, as he crawls up my body.

"I bet she tastes even better with all that cum seeping out of that pretty pussy. You should taste it, Catriona."

Sam moans, his mouth crashing into mine even as he lines his cock up with my entrance. He pauses once, lifting up, a question in his gaze and I nod. Then his tongue plunders my mouth, mimicking the action of his cock as it fills me up.

I can taste the saltiness of our combined juices as he fucks me with abandon, and Alex doesn't slack from underneath, his hands on my hips gripping so tightly I'm sure there would be bruises if that were possible.

He pulls me back down in a counter thrust until Sam's hips slam into me again, pushing me back up, forcing me to ride both cocks with little to no input from me.

"Are you going to make us both come and fill you up?" Alex asks in my ear, and Sam fucks into me harder.

I don't need to spiral the pleasure between these two, they're already racing towards the precipice, but I do anyway, the unspoken request enough to send my pulse racing. They want me. All of them, and I'll give them everything I have.

The pleasure is building so rapidly, I include all my mates in it, feeding lust from one to another to another until we're all groaning. The others stand above us, jerking on their cocks, watching as my last two mates hurtle towards our joint climaxes. The feeling of connectedness is like nothing I've ever experienced, so when we all orgasm together it's all I can do to hold onto my body, even as I weave our souls together in a brilliant pattern of love.

Alex's bite is high on my neck, just under my ear, while Sam bites down just above the swell of my breast, the pleasure-pain combination sending us all into a second orgasm which I feed into the mates standing around us as they jerk out their pleasure, spilling over the top of all of us and marking us all in their scents.

It's us, all of us, bound together for eternity, and I wouldn't have it any other way.

THE END

MORE FROM JADE THORN

I hope you enjoyed this book enough to leave a review. If you want to find out more about my books, you can click on any of the links below, or turn the page for my other titles.

Jade
xoxo

Check me out on **Patreon**:
https://www.patreon.com/JadeThorn

Join me on **Discord**:
https://discord.gg/zDaGpKY8Qw

Discover me on **Faceboo**k:
https://www.facebook.com/groups/thejadelibrary/

Sign up for my **monthly newsletter**:
https://www.subscribepage.com/a7z5v5

Watch me on **TikTok**:
https://www.tiktok.com/@jadethornauthor

For **more books** from Jade, please turn the page!

THE SIREN SAGA

Completed Series

Catriona is a siren. They're supposed to be extinct, but they've been hiding for a very long time. Now, a chance encounter in a bar has led to her being claimed by a pack of wolf shifters, and it's the flashpoint of a war between those who want a chance to live, and those who want everything. Catriona and her fated mates must find a way to stop the horrors that will arise, while finding their own way forward in their strange new relationship.

This is a 'why choose' romance with fated mates and dark themes including but not limited to past trauma, difficult childbirth, and discussion of torture. There is dubious consent in the first book. Not suitable for readers under the age of 18 years.

Book 1: Siren - mybook.to/_Siren

Book 2: Sovereign - mybook.to/_Sovereign

Book 3: Saviour - mybook.to/_Saviour

CLUB FRENZY

Erotic Novella Series

Club Frenzy is a vampire run club that is a registered feeding place. Humans flock there for the thrill of it, and vampires linger for a meal. Explore three short stories of love and lust and plunge headfirst into the Frenzy.

Double Frenzy - mybook.to/Double_Frenzy

Lust Frenzy - mybook.to/Lust_Frenzy

Lycan Frenzy - mybook.to/Lycan_Frenzy

Fighting Frenzy - TBA

Or get the original 3 novellas here:

Club Frenzy Boxed Set - mybook.to/Club_Frenzy_Boxed_Set

THE MAGIC AND CONTEMPT UNIVERSE

Of Magic and Contempt - Completed Series

A slave to her coven, Melody is being sent to Adolphus Academy with a mission: she must defeat and bond The Apex — five incredibly powerful shifters who will make the perfect breeding stock for the army her aunt is building. If Melody fails, she dies — if she succeeds, The Apex will.

This is a dark 'why choose' romance with a slow burn. It contains content that some readers may find distressing. Recommended for readers 18+.

Book 1 - Beneath Contempt - mybook.to/Beneath_Contempt

Book 2 - Held in Contempt - mybook.to/Held_In_Contempt

Book 3 - Civil Contempt - mybook.to/Civil_Contempt

Book 4 - Breeding Contempt - mybook.to/Breeding_Contempt

Book 5 - Surviving Contempt - http://mybook.to/Surviving_Contempt

For Magic and Contempt

Claremont College isn't your average witching academy. Witches here specialise in healing magic which sounds rather benign, but when your familiars are ghosts, it makes you rather unpopular at social gatherings. Aside from death magic and beast magic, it's one of the least popular branches of arcane study.

For Leigha, it's as exciting a world as that famous wizard, although at times just as dark and macabre. Join her and her familiars as they discover that magic isn't all there is to life and love can't save everything.

This is a 'why choose' romance with dark themes and a slow burn. It contains content that some readers may find distressing. Recommended

for readers 18+.

Book 1 - Criminal Contempt - https://mybook.to/CriminalContempt - coming 2023

Book 2 - Self Contempt

Book 3 - Day of Contempt

With Magic and Contempt

Nobody wants to have death magic and the stigma that comes with it, but Heather is so desperate to escape her well-meaning but controlling mother, she wouldn't exactly turn it down. So, when the most unusual magic revelation ceremony in history identifies her with death magic before all her other strengths are revealed, she's not sure whether to be pleased or not.

If only one of her other strengths had been revealed first, her destiny would be very different. Very, very different.

Book 1 - Inherent Contempt

Book 2 - Simmering Contempt

Book 3 - Beyond Contempt

Standalone

Finding out you're a witch in a modern world that doesn't believe in magic can be enough of a shock, but discovering the cat in your apartment isn't a cat at all?

Join Becky on a hilarious journey as she discovers the perks and the pitfalls of being a witch with beast magic.

Contempt of Court - a comedic standalone - TBA

THE BROTHERHOOD

Grace isn't your ordinary witch and neither are the members of the Elite Squad in the Brotherhood. Seven cities across the USA have come under attack by demons. It's up to The Brotherhood to find who or what is behind it all, and push them back to the demonic plane.

At the same time, they also need to navigate their own issues and find the delicate balance between seven men who want the same woman.

Please note, this series has content that some readers may find disturbing. Recommended for readers 18+.

THE PORTAL CONNECTION SERIES

Being revealed as a Portal is like finding out you have the plague. Nobody wants to be anywhere near you, especially if you're as strong as Jacinta is proving to be. As if she didn't have enough things on her plate already - like her new lecherous boss, now she has to contend with her Events increasing in frequency and strength.

Then there's the Pure Human movement who see all Portals as mutants who should be destroyed. At least her protective detail is on her side. They're not friends, but they seem to like her.

Don't they?

A 'why choose' series, recommended for readers 18+.

Book 1 - Stellar - mybook.to/Stellar

Book 2 - Supernova - mybook.to/Supernova_

Book 3 - Quasar - http://mybook.to/Quasar - coming 2023

Book 4 - Black Sun - http://mybook.to/Black_Sun - coming 2023

THE SINNER'S FAIRYTALES SERIES

Book 1 - Gluttony by Kira Roman, a Red Riding Hood retelling - https://mybook.to/_Gluttony

Book 2 - Sloth by AJ Blackburn, a Cinderella retelling - https://mybook.to/_Sloth

Book 3 - Wrath by Jay Leigh Brown, a Sleeping Beauty retelling - https://mybook.to/_Wrath

Book 4 - Greed by J. Kearston, a Rumpelstiltskin retelling - https://mybook.to/_Greed

Book 5 - Pride by Kris Butler, a Rapunzel retelling - https://mybook.to/_Pride

Book 6 - Lust by Alexandra K. Martin, a Golden Bird retelling - https://mybook.to/_Lust

Book 7 - Envy by Jade Thorn, a Snow White retelling - coming 2023

www.ingramcontent.com/pod-product-compliance
Lightning Source LLC
Chambersburg PA
CBHW020243120726
47904CB00001B/78